KERI ARTHUR

Hunter Hunted

A LIZZIE GRACE NOVEL

ISBN: 978-0-6483246-1-4

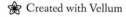 Created with Vellum

With thanks to:

The Lulus
Robyn E
Indigo Chick Designs
The lovely ladies at Hot Tree Editing
The ladies from Central Vic Writers
Damonza for the amazing cover.

CHAPTER ONE

The woman sitting opposite me was plump, with merry blue eyes and purple-tinted gray hair. She was one of the café's regular customers, and came in at least three times a week. If Belle—the café's co-owner and my best friend—wasn't helping her to communicate with the daughter she'd lost five years ago, I was using my psychometry skills to find whatever item she'd misplaced that particular week.

I crossed my arms on the table and leaned forward. The candles flickered at the small movement, sending a warm glow across the older woman's pretty features.

"What can I do for you this week, Mrs. Potts?"

"I need you to find my husband."

Amusement twitched my lips. "You've misplaced him?"

Her expression became cross. "No, of course I haven't. I'm not *that* forgetful."

The growing number of visits stated otherwise, but I kept my mouth shut. We'd only just reopened after the bomb—which had been an act of revenge for the rat infestation I'd left two fellow witches after they'd run us out of "their" town—had destroyed part of the first floor's roof. While that area was still being renovated, we'd finally been given clearance to open the café. The last thing we needed three days out from Christmas was me losing us a very good customer.

"Then why do you want me to find him?"

"Because the bastard's run off with that floozy of his again, and I've had enough."

I blinked. Mrs. Potts was eighty-three, and her husband five years older.

Meaning he probably didn't exactly run, came Belle's amused comment, *but I'm seriously impressed he has the time or energy for a floozy at his age.*

Although I wasn't telepathic, the ability to share thoughts so clearly was one of the many benefits that came with Belle not only being a witch, but also my familiar. If witch records were to be believed, it was something that had never happened before, and had caused much consternation to my high-profile, blueblood parents. Not only did I have the audacity to be severely "underpowered," but I'd gone and gotten myself an even lower-powered witch as a familiar rather than the more acceptable spirit or cat.

I'd like to have that sort of energy now, I replied, *let alone when I get to their age.*

She snorted. The sound rattled loudly through my brain, making me wince. *Your problem is more a lack of opportunity than energy.*

True. Between my natural wariness of relationships, Aiden's initial distrust of all things witch, and the more recent complication of concussion—which he'd gotten saving my life—opportunities to do anything more than kiss had been few and far between. It didn't help that fate

herself seemed determined to interrupt my pursuit of satisfaction.

But at least Aiden had a doctor's appointment later
today, and should finally get the all clear to resume normal
activities.

*Is "normal activities" the new code word for hot monkey
sex?* Belle mused.

Hardly. He's a werewolf, not a monkey. I did my best to
ignore the images that nevertheless rose at her comment,
and said, "Perhaps you should be consulting a lawyer, Mrs.
—"

"I have," she said curtly. "But I need you to find Henry
so I can serve the papers in person."

"I don't think that would be a—"

"Maybe not," she cut in again, "but I want to see the
bastard's face. He never thought I'd have the guts, you see.
Not after putting up with his behavior for so long."

"If he usually *does* come home, why not just wait?"

"Because I've had all his stuff thrown onto the lawn. If
he doesn't collect it before the storm hits, it's going to get
ruined."

"You could always throw a tarp over—"

"Why? He deserves ruination after all these years of
legging it with other women."

I do like her style, Belle commented, *even if she's taken
entirely too long to do something about the situation.*

*She's eighty-three, Belle. I wouldn't want to be starting
over again at her age.*

You didn't want to start over again at twenty-five, she
said. *I'm just thanking the stars and the spirits that we
decided to come to a town where there's a hot ranger to tempt
your recalcitrant hormones. I couldn't have stood another
three years of bitching about a self-induced lack of sex.*

3

I didn't bitch. I paused, thinking about it. *Not much, anyway.*

I think our definitions of "not much" are vastly different.

Amusement bubbled through me. I cleared my throat and tried to concentrate on Mrs. Potts's problem. "Have you told your lawyer you intend to personally serve the divorce papers?"

"Of course." She opened the purse sitting on her lap and carefully pulled out a gold watch in a plastic bag. "He was wearing this until a few days ago. I presume he took it off because he didn't want the floozy seeing it."

I plucked the bagged watch from her fingertips. Even though the plastic was quite thick, I could feel the pulse of life. That my psychometry skills were picking it up so strongly without direct touch was a good sign.

"Why wouldn't he want his girlfriend seeing it?"

"I gave it to him for our fiftieth wedding anniversary, and it's inscribed," she said. "Besides, given the amount of money he's been taking from our account on a regular basis, she'd probably have it off his wrist and spent inside two seconds."

Meaning the floozy is also a gold digger? Belle said. *This just gets better and better.*

I undid the bag and slid the watch into my palm. While the reading room—a small, dedicated space at the back of the café—was packed with a multitude of artifacts and spells specifically designed to counter arcane forces seeking to enter or attack, they didn't interfere with our psychic talents. The metal warmed my skin, and the beat of life grew stronger. It was pretty clear I'd be able to find the errant Henry without much problem.

"Well," Mrs. Potts said. "Are you getting anything?"

I nodded and met her gaze. "You know how this works,

though. I may not be able to give you something as specific as an address."

She frowned. "But you were the one who found Marjorie's daughter in the forest, weren't you?"

"Yes." And too damn late to save her life. I thrust away the images of alabaster skin and bloody neck wounds and added, "But I used a different level of psychometry to track her down."

One that involved me using a personal item to form a much closer connection to the mind of my target. Doing so generally made tracking them easier, but it was not without its dangers. While such connections were generally only light, there were some occasions where I'd been drawn so deeply into the mind of the other person I experienced whatever they were feeling or doing. Which was fine if they were doing something innocuous, but far less so if they happened to be in a life-or-death situation. It was not unknown for psychics to be so caught up in such events that they lost their mind or even their life.

Which wasn't likely to happen in *this* situation, but I still had no desire to risk a deeper connection with Henry, especially if he and the floozy were getting intimate.

Considering your lack of late, maybe it'd ease some tension.

Will you shut up and let me concentrate.

Her laughter ran across my thoughts as Mrs. Potts said, "Yes, but if you can find Karen in the middle of a forest with just a locket, you can surely repeat the results here. I know this situation is nowhere near as urgent, but he's betraying me—betraying the memory of our daughter—and I just need this done."

Now, while I still have the courage. She didn't actually add that bit, but it was nevertheless evident in her expression and her eyes. The annoyance that had briefly flared disappeared. For Mrs. Potts, it really *was* just as urgent; her whole life was about to change even if her life—and Henry's —wasn't physically on the line.

Besides, given the steady pulse coming from the watch, it was likely I wouldn't have to go deep. I could simply use that pulsing as a psychic GPS signal to locate him.

I took a deep breath and then nodded. "Okay. But it means you'll have to drive—I'll need to concentrate on the vibes rolling off the watch."

Her eyebrows rose. "I don't drive. You know that."

I knew a silver-haired man generally chauffeured her to the café, but I hadn't realized she didn't have a license.

"Freddie always drives me," she continued blithely. "You've said hello to him often enough. Lovely chap, he is— can't do enough for me."

Suggesting Mrs. Potts might also have a bit on the side, Belle said.

I don't even want to think about it. To the older woman, I said, "It mightn't be best to serve your husband divorce papers in the company of another man, Mrs. Potts."

"I guess it *might* give rise to unnecessary presumptions. I'll call Gina. She'll help." She dug her phone out and then paused, frowning, "You will be able to do it this afternoon, won't you?"

"Yes." I pushed upright. "You call Gina and I'll go tell Belle what's happening."

She nodded and started calling as I headed out the door. The stairs to the left of the reading room were blocked by heavy plastic, which stopped most of the dust if not the noise coming down from the renovations. The main café area—a warm and inviting space filled with mismatched tables and colorfully painted chairs—was half-full, which wasn't bad considering we'd only announced our reopening two days ago. The Christmas lights strung across the ceiling spun color throughout the room, and there was a small but pretty Christmas tree in the corner close to the kitchen. We'd also hung a bunch of mistletoe over the doorway for a bit of fun, but so far only one young couple had stopped to kiss underneath it.

The main serving area—where we made the coffee and plated up the cakes—lay to the right, opposite the kitchen. Belle flashed me a smile as I headed behind the counter. She was a typical Sarr witch in coloring—ebony skin, long, silky black hair, and eyes that were a gray so pale they shone silver in even the dullest of light. She was also six foot one with an Amazon's physique; to say she was stunning would be an understatement. I, on the other hand, had the crimson-colored hair of the blueblood Marlowe line, emerald green eyes that were now ringed with silver—the only fallout from my desperate and dangerous merger with the wild magic that inhabited this reservation—and freckles across my nose. I was also five inches shorter with a body that would *never* be described as athletic.

"Will you be okay here if I disappear for an hour?" I grabbed three takeaway cups and began making coffee. Gina was another regular customer and a founding member of the local gossip brigade. If made a coffee for myself and *not* the two older women, half of Castle Rock would know about my "selfishness" within minutes. While the brigade generally used their communication powers for good, I had no intention of ever getting on their wrong side.

"It's nearly two, and I doubt there'll be a last-minute rush before we close." Belle finished decorating a piece of salted caramel cake then slid the plate next to the coffee mug already waiting on the counter. As Penny—our middle-aged waitress—swooped in to whisk both away, she added, "But don't forget Zak and I are going down to Melbourne to see *Les Mis* this evening, so you'll have to do the prep for tomorrow."

"I should be back, but if for any reason I'm not, just lock up and I'll get to it when I can."

She raised an eyebrow. "Are you expecting trouble?"

I hesitated. "Not with Mrs. Potts, no."

"Meaning you *are* expecting something."

"No, not really. It's just that every time I've used my psychometry talents to track someone of late, I've ended up finding a body." I shrugged. "But Ashworth is the acting reservation witch now, so he can take care of any damn problem that arises."

Ira Ashworth had initially only come here to take care of a soul eater and the witch who'd called it into being. He'd offered to stay not only because the Faelan Reservation was without a government-approved witch to protect it, but also because he was apparently fascinated with the "conundrum" Belle and I presented. One that had nothing to do with the fact we were witch and familiar—something he wasn't yet aware of—but rather his conviction that while we might separately be under-powered, together we were as strong as any witch outside Canberra. According to him, our magical abilities combined in a way no one had ever thought possible. We'd long been able to draw on each other's strength, but neither of us had—until that moment—been aware the merging was much deeper than that.

"Don't be surprised if Aiden and his rangers still come to us for help," Belle said, amusement evident. "I don't think they really like dealing with Ashworth's forthright cantan-kerousness."

A smile twitched my lips. I actually liked that in the

man, if only because he very much reminded me of my grandfather—one of the few relatives I'd gotten along with. Of course, he was also one of the few who didn't see the need to constantly bemoan my lack—maybe because he, too, hadn't come up to expectations, be they his own or that of others.

"I think you'll find it's more a case of them liking the free chocolate brownies we give them whenever they're here." Even Aiden had readily admitted his lust for those brownies was almost as fierce as his desire for me. I glanced around as Mrs. Potts came out of the reading room. "All set?"

The older woman nodded. "She'll be out the front in five minutes. Come along."

Her imperial tone had my smile growing. I slipped lids on the three takeout cups, grabbed my handbag from out of the open safe, and dutifully followed.

"Good luck," Belle called after us. *And just in case the unease you're feeling is something wicked this way coming, be careful.*

Let's hope it's not, because I'd really like to spend our first Christmas here in peace and quiet—and maybe even in the arms of a good man.

Amen to that, sister.

The wind swirled as I stepped outside, flipping my hair across my face and tugging at the ends of my dress. There was nothing untoward to be felt in that breeze, and the day was bright and warm, holding a promise of the heat supposedly coming over the next couple of days.

And yet....

And yet that vague sense of unease was getting stronger. I studied the street but there was seemingly nothing out of place or wrong. Nothing that twinged the radar of my "other" senses, anyway.

But energy—dark energy—was nevertheless gathering beyond the confines of Castle Rock.

"I hate this weather," Mrs. Potts said, with an abruptness that made me jump. "I much prefer the colder months. Ah, here's Gina now."

A silver Mercedes came to a halt in the no parking zone outside the café. Once we'd all climbed inside, I handed the ladies their coffee, then wound down the window.

"Is that really necessary?" Gina said, somewhat crossly. "The air conditioning—"

"I know and I'm sorry, but the open window allows me to track locations better."

"It won't be for long," Mrs. Potts said. "You know Henry won't be too far away—his eyesight isn't all that good these days."

Gina sniffed then glanced at me through the rearview mirror. "Where to, then?"

"Straight ahead for the moment."

"You'll tell me when to turn?"

"Yes."

Gina nodded and pulled out into the traffic, seemingly oblivious to the screech of tires that immediately followed. Which made me wonder if the unease was nothing more than the fact I was placing my life in the hands of a woman who didn't appear to take much notice of other road users.

I hid my amusement and tried to concentrate on the steady pulse coming from the watch. Despite Mrs. Potts's conviction that Henry wouldn't be far, we were soon heading out onto the Pyrenees Highway.

But the farther we moved from Castle Rock, the sharper my unease became. Whatever I was sensing, it was very dark and very powerful. No good would come from it, of that I was sure.

At least it wasn't coming from the watch, and didn't seem to involve Henry even if it *did* appear to be in the same general area.

I shivered and fought the desire to call Ashworth. If I was sensing it, surely he would. He was, after all, the more powerful witch. Besides, Mrs. Potts was paying me to find her husband, and the task deserved my full attention.

As the pulsing directed us past Muckleford South, Mrs. Potts sniffed, a sound that somehow managed to be both unimpressed and haughty all at the same time. "The bastard's gotten gamer in his old age. Normally he struggles just driving me to the supermarket."

Gina snorted. "Even near blindness hasn't got a hope when the dick is involved, my dear."

I just about choked on my coffee. Mrs. Potts turned around and raised an eyebrow. "You okay?"

I nodded and somehow kept a straight face as I added, "We need to slow down—the vibes from the watch are getting stronger."

"Newstead," Gina mused. "Karla comes from here, you know, and she's been missing a lot of our gatherings of late."

Karla wasn't someone I knew, but then, the entire brigade seldom came out in force. They were twenty-seven strong when in full cry, and we rarely had enough vacant tables to cater to them en masse.

"Can't be Karla," Mrs. Potts said. "She's smarter than that."

Gina snorted again. "She also has a liking for fine things, and you did say he was spending money like it was water."

Though I couldn't see the older woman's expression, the

glow of her aura jumped into focus. It ran with a mix of muddy red and orange, indicators of both anger and stress.

"She wouldn't do that—we've been friends for ages." But there was doubt in her voice.

I wanted to reach forward and squeeze her arm in comfort, but knew enough about Mrs. Potts to know she wouldn't appreciate it.

The watch's pulsing shifted as we entered Newstead. "Turn left at that hotel and then slow down. We're close."

Closer to Henry. Closer to the source of darkness. Trepidation stirred, along with the feeling that whatever was happening out there in the wilder emptiness beyond Newstead, it was slowly coming to a peak. I tightened my fingers around the watch and tried to concentrate. But between the tension radiating off the two women and that gathering tide of dark energy, it was damn difficult.

We turned and crawled down the road. The vibes coming from the watch were now so fierce it burned my palm. I undid the belt and scooted forward to look through the front windshield. "He's on the left—in that red brick house."

Gina had barely stopped the car when Mrs. Potts was out and striding toward the door, her entire body vibrating with indignation, anger, and perhaps a little fear. I shoved my empty coffee cup in the holder then scrambled after her. While I doubted her eighty-eight-year-old husband was going to be much of a threat, I wasn't about to let her face him without backup, just in case.

She flung open the screen door and then pounded loudly on the wooden one. For several seconds there was no response, then footsteps echoed.

"Who is it?" a surprisingly young-sounding voice said.

"That ain't Karla," Gina commented. "Karla has a voice rougher than a bullfrog."

"It's the mail," Mrs. Potts said. "I've got a registered letter you need to sign for."

A smile touched my lips. Mrs. Potts might well be eighty-three but she wasn't a fool.

After a pause, the footsteps continued and the door opened. The woman on the other side was probably in her thirties, with dark brown hair and bright blue eyes. Her gaze swept Mrs. Potts then moved to Gina and me.

"So, not the mail service then," she said. "What can I do for you all?"

"You can tell me where that lying, cheating husband of mine is," Mrs. Potts all but spat, "because I have indeed got a registered letter he needs to see and sign."

The woman frowned. "I'm afraid I don't—"

"Millie," a male voice said from the rear of the house, "what are you doing, girl? The kids—"

"Kids!" Mrs. Potts all but screeched. "You bastard! How dare you do this to me—to *us*."

She pushed past the rather startled Millie and stormed down the hallway toward the end of the house. I swore under my breath then apologized to Millie and scrambled after the incensed Mrs. Potts. I managed to grab her arm and stall her charge if not her anger just as she entered the rear living area. Two men—one around the same age as Millie, the other undoubtedly the cheating Henry—were sitting on the floor playing with a boy and a girl who looked to be about one year old.

Mr. Potts, I began to suspect, wasn't cheating. At least, he wasn't doing so right now. It was a suspicion that firmed when Millie came into the room, and the similarities between her facial features and his became evident.

"Mrs. Potts," I murmured, "I think you'd better calm—"

"You," she said, shaking her finger at the errant Henry, "have gone too far. Your carousing was bad enough, but kiddies—"

Millie cleared her throat. "I'm not sure who you are, but I think you're under the wrong impression here—"

"I'm this man's *wife*," Mrs. Potts said. "And you—"

"Millie is my daughter," Henry cut in heavily. "From the one and only affair I had some thirty-five years ago. I didn't know about her until after we'd lost our own daughter; it certainly wasn't the right time to mention her, and the longer I left it, the harder it seemed."

Which didn't explain why Millie didn't seem to know about Mrs. Potts, but I let that ride. This was *not* my family or my fight.

"Oh." Mrs. Potts's voice was faint. She groped for the nearby chair and sat down. "Oh. Dear."

For several seconds, no one said anything. I cleared my throat and then squatted beside Mrs. Potts. "Maybe we should leave—"

"No." She took a deep breath and then patted my hand. "This needs sorting, here and now. But thank you, dear. I appreciate your help."

Which was a dismissal if I'd ever heard one, but I nevertheless hesitated. She squeezed my fingers and added, "I'll be fine. Truly."

After another slight pause, I gave her the watch, then rose and left.

Gina trailed after me. "Do you need a lift back to town?"

I shook my head. "You'd better stay here and make sure she's okay. She'll be in shock."

Gina nodded. I grabbed my handbag from the car, but

didn't go much farther than the road. The dark force was now so fierce it felt like a thousand gnats were biting me.

I studied the area, all senses on alert, trying to find the source of the dark energy. There was absolutely nothing nearby. Whatever it was, it remained some distance away... but that thought had barely crossed my mind when it surged, hitting with the power and fury of a gigantic wave and sending me staggering back. I caught my balance and swung around. Laughter drifted from the old pub, a bright sound that clashed with the dark force in the air. Whatever it was—whoever it was—it was coming from the other side of Newstead.

The wave hit again. Stronger—darker—than before. My skin crawled and my throat went dry.

It wasn't just energy, but magic.

Black magic.

Blood magic.

I closed my eyes and took a deep breath. It didn't do a whole lot to calm my racing pulse or the deep surge of fear.

Only a very powerful dark practitioner could perform that sort of magic in the middle of the day. Usually it was done at midnight, when the moon was at her highest point in the sky and the full force of her power could be drawn on rather than the practitioner's own.

Don't chase after it, came Belle's thought. *Call Ashworth.*

I will. I am. I dug out my phone and immediately did so.

A third wave hit. It felt like I was drowning in evil. Whatever the dark witch was doing, it was reaching a peak.

"This is an unexpected honor," Ashworth all but drawled. "Have you two finally decided to come clean about your past?"

"We've nothing to come clean about," I bit back. "And I think we've got a dark practitioner on the reservation."

"What? Why?" Ashworth's tone was suddenly no-nonsense and sharp. "What's happened?"

Meaning he *hadn't* sensed it. "Three waves of dark energy just rolled over me."

He swore. "Where are you?"

"Panmure Street in Newstead. I'll meet you at the pub on the corner."

"I'm ten minutes away."

If he was *that* close, how in the hell could he have missed it? "Hurry."

He hung up. I slung my handbag over my shoulder and hurried toward the main street.

So much for not chasing after the source. Belle's voice was tart.

If Ashworth can't sense the waves of power when he was only ten minutes away then he sure as hell isn't going to be able to track the source down.

He's a verified witch. I daresay there are all sorts of finding spells for this sort of thing that we don't know about.

Maybe, but I'd rather not take the chance.

Belle grunted. It wasn't a happy noise. *You want me over there?*

No. I'm just the bloodhound. He can take care of the actual problem.

You keep saying things like that and yet you always end up right in the middle of all the bad shit.

Exasperation filled her mental tones but before I could say anything, a fourth wave hit. This time it was strong enough to knock me onto my ass and leave me breathless.

Holy fuck, Belle said. *That's—*

Scary. I picked myself up, dusted the dirt and stones

from my hands and butt, and sprinted for the pub. Though the main road was empty of traffic, I could hear the roar of an approaching engine. Ashworth, I hoped.

Yeah, Belle said, *and if he isn't sensing it, then it has to be running along psychic lines rather than magic.*

Ashworth's Ford Ranger appeared in the distance. I moved across to the curb to wait. *Except it is magic—and blacker than black.*

This is what the damn council gets for not protecting the spring sooner.

Wellsprings were the main source of wild magic, which was said to develop close to the heart of the earth's outer core. No one was really sure why it became a collective force in the first place, let alone how or why it then found its way to the surface, but there was no argument about the danger such springs represented if they were left unprotected. While wild magic was neither good nor bad, without a witch to protect and channel it, the darker forces of the world would sense its presence and be drawn to it. And once it was stained by evil, it could very much make a place unlivable for all but those who followed darkness.

The Faelan Reservation had two such wellsprings. While the newest one was now protected by both the ghost of the reservation's previous witch *and* the soul of his werewolf wife—who also happened to be Aiden's sister—the much larger one had been left for far too long. And though it was now protected—by both Ashworth's magic and mine —Belle and I suspected it was altogether too late.

And the surge of dark magic coming from somewhere up ahead all but confirmed it.

I stepped back slightly as Ashworth's truck came to a rubber-burning stop, then opened the passenger door and climbed in.

"Where to?" His voice was curt, but it wasn't anger; it was frustration.

"It's coming from up ahead somewhere." I buckled up then wound down the window. Metal tended to blunt magic's force somewhat, and I needed to feel the air—and magic—to track it.

"And you're sure it's magic?"

"As sure as the sky is blue." I glanced at him. He was bald, with a well-tanned face full of wrinkles and eyes that were muddy silver in color. The power that rolled off him was fierce, but nevertheless spoke to the reason why he was working with the Regional Witch Association rather than up in Canberra serving the needs of the council and the government. He might be powerful, but his magic was little more than a flickering candle compared to the output of the high-ranking members of the royal lines. "There's been four waves of increasing intensity. And it's black."

He swore, threw the truck into gear, and hit the accelerator. The tires spun for a second, then the truck shot forward. "I'd love to know why you're sensing it and I'm not."

"Me too, especially given you're the stronger witch."

"Which seems to have no meaning in this reservation." He glanced at me again. "Perhaps the reason you're sensing it rather than me is the connection you appear to have with the wild magic."

I hesitated. "Maybe, but I haven't felt the wild magic's presence."

"I guess that's something to be thankful for." He flicked on the blinker and overtook a slow-moving car. "Can you still feel the waves?"

I hung a hand out the window and let the air run through my fingers. The dark energy within felt like soup.

"No waves, but the magic is still there, and its viscosity is increasing."

He swore again and the truck's speed increased, the engine so loud it was pointless trying to talk. We raced out of Newstead and followed the highway around a sweeping right curve. There was nothing out here. Nothing except golden fields, livestock, and clumps of trees. While there were rolling hills in the distance, the nearby area remained boringly flat and open. Not an area that would have been my first choice to raise a powerful spell.

A fifth wave hit. It swirled in through the open window, a dark, bloody-feeling heat so fierce I started sweating.

Ashworth sucked in a breath, and I glanced at him sharply. "You felt that?"

"Yeah. Whatever it is, it's close."

"But there's nothing around here!"

"Whoever it is might be using a concealment spell."

I frowned. "But if they're doing that, why wouldn't they also add a containment restriction?"

"Maybe they think they're far enough away to avoid detection. Which," he added grimly, "was almost the case."

"It was only luck that I was in Newstead. Up until then, all I'd felt was a vague unease."

"Which is still more than I got."

The road swept left as we roared toward what was marked on the car's GPS map as part of the Cairn Curran Reservoir even though right now it was little more than scrubby ground and dead trees.

The foul feel of the magic air playing through my fingers sharpened abruptly. "Turn right just ahead."

The tires squealed again as he did so, and dust flew as we briefly skidded onto the gravel shoulder. The road began to narrow and the trees closed in. But he hadn't gone very far when he slowed and turned into what was little more than a goat track. Another kilometer in, we stopped.

The dark force was so strong it hurt to breathe it in.

Ashworth scrambled out and ran to the back of his truck. I jumped down and rubbed my arms as the twin charms around my neck—one designed to ward off evil and the other ill-intent—flared to life, a bright heat that did very little against the soup surrounding us.

Ashworth tossed me a small white pouch as he strode past. "Wear this. It'll help."

I quickly slung it around my neck; almost immediately the dark force retreated and breathing became easier. I hurried after him, my heart beating so hard it felt like it was going to tear out of my chest. My magic was no counter for whatever—whoever—lay up ahead, but that didn't stop the desire to wrap a repelling spell around my fingers. But this close, *any* sort of spell might just alert the witch to our presence and turn the darkness in the air against us.

Presuming, of course, he or she wasn't already aware of our presence. It was totally possible that the thick force we were feeling now was a nice little trap about to be sprung.

And yet you continue to follow Ashworth into the heart of that darkness instead of staying behind like any normal sane underpowered witch would.

I think in this case, two witches are better than one.

Three would be better. I'm on my way.

Belle, don't—

La la la la la, she cut in. *Not hearing you.*

Damn it, it's too dangerous! It's better you remain safe so that, if the worst happens, I can draw on your strength.

If the worst happens, I need to be close enough to ensure your soul moves on rather than linger. Besides, I'm already in Newstead.

Then pull over once you near the road that runs along-side the reservoir—it's close enough to help, but far enough away that you won't get caught in any magical backwash.

A compromise I can live with. Be careful.

Ashworth swung left and dove into a thick clump of trees. I followed, raising an arm to protect my face from the backlash of low-hanging branches. But we weren't exactly quiet, and the sound of us crashing through the scrub echoed across the otherwise silent day.

The dark flow of magic stopped with a suddenness that sent me stumbling.

Ashworth swore and plowed on. I had no choice but to follow. He might be the stronger witch, but he couldn't face this threat alone. Not when the dark witch up ahead appeared to be far stronger than even he.

The trees drew closer together, the scrub thicker, tearing at my dress and leaving bloody scratches across my arms and legs. It didn't matter; nothing did except reaching the dark magic's ignition point before the witch disappeared.

We scrambled on. Up ahead, beyond the tree cover, came the sound of an engine firing up—and it very much sounded like a motorbike rather than a car or truck.

Then, above all that noise, came another.

A short, sharp crack.

One that I was all too familiar with thanks to a very recent encounter.

It was a gunshot.

Ashworth swore and—with surprising dexterity for a man in his fifties—spun and launched at me, hitting so hard we crashed to the ground in a tangle of arms and legs. My breath left in a gigantic whoosh, my head cracked against something solid, and stars danced briefly.

Neither of us moved. I could barely even breathe, my body tense and my heart pounding somewhere in my throat as I waited for either a second shot or someone approaching.

Neither happened.

The motorbike was revved and then left, the sharp drone of its engine quickly disappearing.

Ashworth swore, untangled himself, and then pushed up.

Belle, I said, as I scrambled after him, *any sign of a motorbike coming your way?*

No. I'll go back onto the main road and see if it makes an appearance.

Be careful.

As someone else has been known to say, careful is my middle name.

I snorted but didn't reply, trying to catch Ashworth while avoiding as many of the slashing tree branches as was feasibly possible.

Five minutes later, we hit a clearing.

In the middle of it lay a man.

A man whose brain matter was spread all around his head like a bloody halo.

CHAPTER TWO

B ile surged up my throat and I swallowed heavily. In truth, this actually *wasn't* the worst thing I'd seen in recent months—that honor went to the teenager who'd been made a zombie by a vampire intent on revenge, and whose disintegrating body Aiden had been forced to destroy.

I slid to a halt well short of the dead man's thin and somewhat wrinkled body. A multitude of hurts instantly raised their ugly heads, but I did my best to ignore them and scanned the nearby ground. There was no sign of additional blood, no sign of any sort of animal sacrifice, and no immediate source for the foul magic that still pulsed around me.

Just the almost faceless remains of an elderly man. Whether he was even our practitioner or not, I couldn't say. "Can you see—?"

"There's a protection circle on the other side of the body," Ashworth said, obviously guessing what I'd been about to ask. "The spell stones are damn massive, too."

My gaze jumped beyond the dead man, and my eyes widened. Spell stones were usually quite small—they generally tended to be little more than an inch or so in diameter.

These things were huge chunks of black quartz that glittered like diamonds in the fading afternoon light.

"Why on earth would anyone want to use stones that large?" I asked. "What sort of spell was he even creating?"

"I have no idea."

I narrowed my gaze and studied the stones. After a moment, I saw the shimmer of magic. "There appear to be multiple layers placed onto those stones."

"And they're not all protection, I'd wager. Stay here."

A somewhat unnecessary order given I had no intention of going any closer to either the body or the circle than I absolutely had to. "Is there any sign of a sacrifice or blood within the protected area?"

"Not all blood magic requires a sacrifice."

"But it *does* require at least some blood, otherwise it wouldn't be called blood magic."

His smile flashed briefly as he knelt beside the stranger and placed two fingers against his neck. Why he was looking for a pulse, I had no idea, given it was very obvious the man was dead.

"Some dark witches do take apprentices," he said, "and a part of their duty is providing a source of blood for their master's minor magics."

"This doesn't feel minor."

"No." He thrust back to his feet. "This man's soul has already risen, so it must have been his time."

I raised my eyebrows. "You're a spirit talker?"

"Not as such. I can sense souls, but I'm not at all proficient when it comes to talking to them." He walked on toward the circle. "Whatever he was doing, it was a nasty piece of work."

That was evident from the force of his spell. I shivered

and rubbed my arms. "Is there evidence of blood usage within the circle?"

He hesitated, his gaze scanning the ground ahead. "There's a large area of staining near the middle of the circle, but I'd need to get inside to know what it is. And I can't get inside until it's deactivated."

"*What?*"

He glanced at me. "The circle's still active, and there are live threads moving within it."

My stomach twisted. A protective circle in which dark magic had been performed was bad enough, but one with a still active spell was akin to a ticking time bomb. Especially when we had no idea *why* it was still alive or what the spell was.

I forced myself closer, though I took a somewhat large detour around the witch's body. I stopped on the opposite side of the circle to Ashworth and crossed my arms. After a moment, I saw what he meant. The spell threads were barely visible wisps of pale green smoke, and moved around the confines of the circle in a manner that suggested they were guarding it. I had no idea what sort of spell it was, as I'd never seen threads like it—not entirely surprising given we'd left Canberra well before we could get into the study of darker spells and how to deactivate them.

"You've really no idea what sort of spell it is?" I asked.

"No, but if our dead man was responsible for it then it should have died when he did."

"Could it be a counter against whoever was here with him—a means of retribution if they betrayed him?"

"If he mistrusted his partners, he wouldn't have left the safety of his circle." Ashworth grimaced. "You'd better call the rangers. I'll see if I can uncover a bit more about the threads inside this thing."

I nodded and dug out my phone. *Belle, any luck with the motorbike?*

Nope. It hasn't come out roadside as far as I can tell.

I swore softly, even though it had always been a vague hope at best given this area contained a whole lot of nothing into which evil could easily disappear. *You might as well head back home, then. You've a date to get ready for, remember.*

Indeed I do. Catch you later.

I hit the number for the ranger station. Normally I'd ring Aiden direct, but I knew he was at the doc's right now.

After several rings, a familiar voice said, "Ranger station, Jaz Marin speaking. How can I help you?"

Jaz was a brown-haired, brown-skinned wolf who'd come here from a New South Wales pack and had subsequently married into the Marins. She and I had become friends thanks to a mutual love of good hot chocolate, cream cakes, and British baking shows. "Jaz, it's Lizzie—"

"Oh dear," she said, trepidation evident in her tone. "There can be only one reason for you to be ringing when you know Aiden isn't on duty."

"And I'm afraid you'd be right."

She blew out a breath. "You want to give me the details? I'll pass them on to Tala."

Tala was Aiden's second, and a straight-talking, no-nonsense wolf. We weren't exactly friends, but she'd at least come to accept that psychic talents did indeed exist and that they could also be quite useful.

I told her what we'd found and provided directions, but didn't bother mentioning the magical elements within the clearing, as they may or may not be relevant.

"Tala's in Rayburn Springs," she said, "so it shouldn't

take her more than twenty minutes to get there. You hanging around?"

"I daresay she'll want me to."

"Probably."

"Then I will. Thanks, Jaz."

I hung up and shoved the phone away. Ashworth didn't look happy.

"Is there a problem?"

He rose. "Yeah. The magic inside this thing *is* active but I've never seen anything like it."

If Ashworth had no idea what it was, we were in deep shit. "Do you think he was an unvetted witch?"

Unvetted witches were generally half-breeds who'd somehow avoided the accreditation process that both uncovered their power levels and aligned them to one of the major or minor houses. Belle and I—despite the fact we were full-blood witches—were technically unvetted, as we'd never gone through either the accreditation or registration ceremony that happened when a full-blood witchling reached eighteen years of age.

"No, if only because there's too much power and control involved." Ashworth swept a hand over his bald head, frustration evident. "I think it more likely he's an extremely well-trained full-blood witch gone bad."

My gaze swept briefly across to the other witch's body. Again bile rose, and again I swallowed it down. The short crimson-red tufts that topped the remains of the stranger's head certainly indicated he was from one of the blueblood families. The remnants of his features weren't Asian, which cut out the Kang line but not the Marlowe or Ashworth lines.

"Does that happen often?" I'd certainly never heard of any such event in my years up there, though that sort of thing was probably only spoken about in hushed voices behind closed doors.

"More often than people think," Ashworth said. "Not everyone is happy with the hierarchy situation in Canberra."

And much of that discontent, I suspected, came from within the inner circles. While the three royal families were supposedly of equal standing, in reality the Marlowes held more powerful positions in the capital than either the Kangs or the Ashworths. My parents were considered to be amongst a mere handful of the most powerful witches Canberra had ever produced—a fact that went a long way to explain their utter disappointment in producing such an underpowered witch as me.

"They keep a log of heretics though, don't they? Which means you should be able to find his identity through his prints easily enough."

"Heretics are treated no different to any other criminal —their prints are only taken *after* they're caught and charged." He grimaced. "And it's been my—admittedly limited—experience that heretics on the run tend to get rid of as many identifying marks as possible. And what they can't erase, they conceal."

Concealment had certainly worked for Belle and me, but it wasn't like anyone other than my parents had any reason to bring me home. Heretics were another matter entirely—and had been responsible for many an atrocity committed against witches over the centuries. There'd been more than a few stake burnings that were the end result of heretic interaction with humanity, even if it was something as simple as a spell going bad.

"It's easy enough to change your hair, grow a beard, or even use contacts to change your eye color," I said, "but how on earth do you get rid of something like fingerprints?"

"They can be surgically removed, burned away, or otherwise mutilated."

"All of which sounds damn painful to me." And from what I could see, the stranger's fingertips appeared intact—although I wasn't about to get any closer to check. "Doing any of those things would raise red flags if they were ever stopped by cops, or tried to head overseas, though. I wouldn't have thought the pain worth it."

"That's because you and I are normal, sane people. Besides, any witch capable of producing a glamor can get past most security checks. They haven't invented machines that can detect spells as yet."

No, they hadn't, but most major airports these days did at least have witches on staff for that very reason.

"You know," I said, "I think that's the nicest thing you've actually said to me."

Confusion ran across his features. "What?"

I grinned. "You called me a normal, sane person."

He snorted. "A normal, sane person with a past she doesn't want revealed."

It took every ounce of control I had to curtail my instinctive response—a response that went along the lines of "mind your own goddamn business." "And what the hell do you think I'm concealing?"

"You tell me. All I know is there's a story behind you and Belle, and it's one that has me intrigued."

"Ever think that what we're concealing might be nothing to do with who we are, but what was *done* to us?" Or, at least, to me.

Surprise crossed his expression. "Abuse?"

I smiled, even though my insides were churning and the

little voice in my head was screaming for me to just shut up. But I had to go on—had to at least give Ashworth some sort of believable explanation. If he kept digging, my parents would come.

Or my father and Clayton would.

The shudder that ran through me was horror. Pure, utter horror and fear. I swallowed heavily and said, "Yes, and I have no intention of ever being found by said abusers. So if you can just drop the damn subject, I'd be obliged."

He studied me through narrowed eyes for a few seconds, and then grunted. Whether that was agreement or not, I couldn't say. I took a deep breath and then waved a hand to our dead witch. "He's got the coloring of the royal witch."

"So have you, my dear." Ashworth's tone was wry.

I couldn't help smiling. "Yeah, but I'm an underpowered half-breed and I don't think he is."

"I'll agree with your latter point, but the jury is still out on the former." He raised his hands before I could say anything. "I saw no lie in your words when you spoke of abuse—quite the opposite, in fact—so I won't continue my investigations in Canberra. But you should be warned I *will* continue to haunt your steps, even if only to satisfy my own curiosity."

Which I guess was at least something of a compromise, and one I could live with. "You think I'm somehow concealing the strength of my magic?"

"Definitely not, but there *is* something else going on with you, and it's *not* the connection you have with Belle."

But *did* have a whole lot to do with my connection to the wild magic, if I was reading him right. There wasn't a whole lot I could do about that, though—nothing I could do to even *hide* that connection, given most of the time I didn't initiate contact. And it wasn't just the wild magic coming from Katie's wellspring, but rather the larger, older one. It had helped me long before Katie had ever come to my rescue.

"There really *is* nothing more going on than what you've already seen."

"Perhaps, and perhaps not." He shrugged and motioned to our dead witch. "To get back to our friend here, he's not someone I recognize, if that's where you were going with that question."

It wasn't, because I was well aware that it was rare for RWA witches to return to Canberra once they'd left. "I was simply noting that—given the fact he's obviously from one of the royal lines—it's likely someone up there will recognize him."

"If luck is on our side, yes." He glanced at me. "But even if he *didn't* hold royal witch coloring, I'd have to call this in. As I said, I've never seen a spell like this, and I've been with the RWA for more than thirty years. Someone more up-to-date with spellcraft is going to have to deal with this thing, and I'm afraid that means Canberra."

I half smiled. "The likelihood of that person being the person I'm running from is remote."

"I hope so, for your sake." His voice and expression were grave. "Because that brief glimpse of honesty I got was dark indeed."

Suggesting he, like many RWA witches, held some truth-seeking abilities. They might not be able to drag the truth out of people—there were spells designed for that sort of thing—but they could generally tell fact from fiction.

I hesitated, and then said, "While it is doubtful I'll know whoever they send, if you could send me a text with his name before he gets anywhere near us, I'd appreciate it."

It was, after all, always better to be prepared. But sooner or later the one thing I feared *would* happen, especially if we remained on this reservation. The wild magic had been left unprotected for too long, and its siren call would still be echoing through the deeper, darker places of the world.

A sensible person intent on remaining unfound would leave—would get as far away from this place as possible. But we'd been on the run for twelve years now, and I wasn't the only one getting really sick of it. I wanted to put down roots. Wanted to belong somewhere.

Castle Rock, more than any other place we'd been to, felt like home.

Ashworth studied me for too many uncomfortable seconds, and then nodded. "I can do that."

"And you'll not tell Aiden what I've said?"

Surprise flitted across his features. "Aren't you two involved?"

"Yes, but I want to find the right time to tell him, and that time isn't now."

He frowned but nevertheless agreed. The relief that swept me was so strong my knees threatened to buckle.

I swallowed heavily and said, "How safe will it be to leave the circle as it is until the Canberra witch gets here? I know we're basically in the middle of nowhere, but I wouldn't want anyone accidently tripping the damn thing."

"I'll put a repelling spell around it to stop anyone investigating too closely. Are the rangers on the way?"

"Tala's already in Rayburn Springs, so she shouldn't be too long."

"Good. You want to head up to the road to ensure she doesn't miss us? I'll get working on the barrier around this thing."

It was a dismissal, but one I was more than happy to

obey. In all honesty, the more distance I put between me and the brutal, bloody death and lingering threads of dark energy that lay in the protection circle, the better.

By the time I found my way back to Ashworth's truck, my head was thumping and my arms and legs had gained a new array of bloody scratches. I found a medical kit in a back storage unit and quickly cleaned them all up, then took a couple of painkillers. The blow I'd taken to my head had left a lump, but it wasn't that large and there was no accompanying cut. And, hopefully, no concussion.

It'd be the mother of ironies if Aiden got the all clear only for me to be similarly incapacitated.

It was fifteen minutes before I heard the sound of an approaching truck. I pushed away from Ashworth's truck and walked into the middle of the dirt road so that I'd be easier to spot. After a moment, a green-striped white SUV— the standard-issue vehicle for reservation rangers—came into view.

Tala halted beside Ashworth's truck and climbed out. She was a Sinclair, and had the traditional dark skin and black hair of that pack, though her hair was shot with silver that gleamed brightly in the late afternoon sunshine. She was only half an inch or so above my own height, but had an air of authority that made her seem so much taller.

"The boss isn't going to be happy about this." Her expression suggested she wasn't all that happy, either. "Not this close to Christmas."

"I'm not exactly doing a dance of joy over here, you know," I bit back. "Nor am I giddy with excitement over the fact we have another magic-related death on the reservation."

She glanced at me sharply. "I thought the victim had been shot?"

"He was."

She hauled her kit out of her SUV and then said, "Mac and Ciara are on their way—can you wait here for them? Mac will take your statement when he arrives."

Mac was another of the seven rangers who worked in this reservation, and Ciara the coroner. She also happened to be one of Aiden's sisters. He had eight siblings all told, including Katie, who might not be flesh but was still very much a part of this place.

"Do you need me to guide—"

Tala snorted. "No—the trail you two left is very evident."

I left her to it and retreated to the truck's cabin to wait for the other two. Ciara arrived first; she looked no more impressed than Tala.

"Seriously, we need to stop meeting like this." She hauled her kit out of her truck. "Couldn't we do coffee and cake like normal people?"

"I love to, but given your council left the wellspring unprotected for too damn long, I'm afraid events like this are going to keep happening."

Her gaze shot to mine, surprise evident. Which made me wonder just how much Aiden had told her about the wild magic and the reason for the recent influx of supernatural creatures.

"So we're not dealing with a shooting?"

"We are. But the dead guy is a seriously strong dark witch."

"Oh, great." She glanced around as another green-and-white SUV appeared. "That'll be Mac. I'll head in."

Mac had the typical rangy build of a werewolf, with brown skin and hair that suggested he hadn't originated from the three packs within this reservation. He greeted me cheerfully and got down to work, quickly taking my statement. Ashworth appeared just as I'd finished. Once his statement was taken, we were cleared to leave.

I climbed into the truck and buckled up as Ashworth reversed out. "I gather the circle is now secure?"

"Yeah. I warded against both human and animal interference, so it should be safe until a higher-up arrives." He glanced at me. "Which should be tomorrow afternoon. I'm picking them up at Melbourne airport."

My stomach began churning again even though the likelihood of it being someone we knew *was* pretty low. Lots of witches lived and worked in Canberra, and surely fate wouldn't be cruel enough to toss someone who actually knew Belle and me our way.

The way our luck is running of late, Belle said, *it'll probably be your goddamn brother.*

Don't even think that! Besides, can you imagine Julius daring to step beyond the sanitized halls of the High Witch Council?

Not without a truckload of smelling salts and hand sanitizer, Belle commented. *A man's man Juli is not.*

Which was something of a huge understatement. But he *was* a powerful witch—maybe not as strong as Cat, the sister I'd failed to save, but still way up there on the power scale. In my parents' eyes—especially with Cat gone—he could do little wrong.

There is a little bit of me that hopes Ashworth is right, that the two of us combined are as goddamn powerful as he thinks, and that we could make your parents, our former teachers, and everyone else who ever put shit on us eat their words.

There was definitely a part of me that wanted the very same thing. I might now be an adult, but that long-rejected child remained deep inside, still hungry for the approval of her parents.

Them finding out would only worsen our problems, Belle. After all, it wasn't *just* because I'd been underpowered that we'd run, but rather what they were forcing on me.

Her sigh was wistful. *I know, but it's still a nice dream to have.*

Could you imagine Juli's face if we fronted up as equals?

It would be the sulk of the century, Belle said. *Maybe even the millennium.*

The understatement of the decade. I glanced at Ashworth. "Did they give you a name?"

"No," Ashworth said, "as they weren't entirely sure who the Heretic Investigations Center had free. They'll send me a text later."

I nodded. "Then let's hope he or she will be able to track down the bastard who shot our dark witch *before* he or she releases whatever spell he was creating for them."

"There was no trace of magic outside the pentagram," Ashworth said, "so it's possible whatever he was doing has been masked. We may not be able to find anything until the shooter *does* unleash the spell."

"I hope like hell you're wrong."

He snorted. "So do I."

We continued on in silence. Ashworth dropped me off at the café and I quickly went inside. Dust danced through the late-afternoon sunshine streaming through the side windows, but nothing else moved. Belle had already left for Melbourne, and the builders had obviously packed up for the evening. I ducked under the plastic and headed upstairs to shower. We might have retreated to a hotel room to sleep, but most of our clothes and personal items remained here. The explosion had taken out both the roof near the top of the stairs and the nearby kitchenette, but the bathroom, our two bedrooms, and the compact living area had all escaped major damage. The fire that had followed the explosion had been contained—and then extinguished—by spells from both Belle and Ashworth, so while we'd had to wash every item of clothing and linen we owned, we'd avoided major water and smoke damage to the rest of the building *and* its contents. We did have insurance, of course, but there were many things—like the books Belle had inherited from her now dead grandmother—that simply couldn't have been replaced.

I had a long hot shower that did little to ease the accumulation of aches, then smeared antiseptic over the deeper wounds. My headache had lessened though the bump was still sore, and I didn't appear to have any of the other signs of concussion. Which hopefully meant it wasn't going to be a problem.

I shoved on a pair of shorts, a tank top, and my runners, and then clattered downstairs to do the prep work for the next day. It was around eight by the time I finished, and my stomach rumbled a noisy reminder that I hadn't yet fed it. As I grabbed a frying pan to cook up a steak, my phone rang.

Aiden.

A grin split my lips. I hit the answer button and then said, "So, what's the verdict?"

"I've got the all clear to resume all normal activities."

"An event I've been looking forward to."

"You're not the only one." The low, hungry note in his warm tone had anticipation skittering. "Would you like to go out for dinner?"

"Love to. I was just about to start cooking myself something, so you've timed your call perfectly." I hesitated. "Has Tala contacted you?"

"Yeah. I was talking to Ashworth before I called you. He said a more knowledgeable witch from Canberra would arrive tomorrow."

"The magic our dead witch evoked was very powerful, Aiden, and Ashworth didn't feel it until we were close. We do need someone stronger."

"So he said. Odd that you felt it and he didn't."

"I have no idea why, if that's what you're asking. Where are we going for dinner? Are we doing fancy or casual?"

"Nice change of subject there, Liz," he said, amusement evident. "There's a new restaurant in Argyle—only been open a week but getting good reports. Thought we might try that."

Argyle also happened to be where his apartment was. While all three packs had their own home territory within the reservation, most wolves also owned—or rented—separate accommodation where they could take non-wolf lovers. Outsiders weren't welcome onto pack grounds except under exceptional circumstances, and being a wolf's lover or girlfriend would never be classified as such. Wolves might play outside their own species but they very rarely stayed. Katie had been the rare exception, and her marriage to Gabe had only been approved because she'd been dying.

"That sounds like a plan," I replied lightly. "What time?"

"How much time do you need to get ready?"

I laughed. "I can be ready in ten."

"I'll meet you out the front, then."

"Done."

I hung up then flew upstairs, hurriedly changing into a pretty summer dress before putting on some makeup and slipping on a pair of sandals. I then grabbed a larger handbag out of my closet, transferred my purse and phone, and shoved in underclothes, shorts, and a tank top, as well as my toothbrush. To say I had hopeful expectations of staying the night at Aiden's would be another of those understatements.

And if fate intervened with said pursuit of happiness *this* time, I was going to be right royally pissed.

I took two more painkillers to take care of the fading remnants of the headache then clattered down the stairs, swept my keys off the bench, and went outside. The last rays of the day gave the darkening skies a golden glow, and the air was warm and filled with the scent of eucalyptus. There was no hint of magic or evil entwined in that scent. I hoped it stayed that way.

A blue Ford Ranger swept around the corner, its headlights briefly blinding me. Aiden pulled to a halt in front of our café and then leaned across the seat and opened the door.

"Evening, gorgeous," he said. "Loving that dress you're almost wearing."

I grinned. Though the shoestring sheath dress wasn't close-fitting, it sat well above the knee and was low cut at both the front and the back, which meant wearing a bra wasn't an option. But given I wasn't exactly well-endowed, the fall-out factor wasn't much of a problem. Not that I'd thought Aiden would mind if it had been.

"You did say not long ago you'd love to see me getting my pins out more often." I tossed my bag onto the back seat and then climbed in. "I thought that since this is really our first 'official' dinner date, I'd treat you."

"I appreciate the effort." His gaze swept me again and became concerned. "Why are you so scratched up?"

"Tree branch backlash. Nothing too bad." I shrugged.

"Did Ashworth tell you anything about the witch that's arriving?"

He raised an eyebrow. "Why? Are you worried?"

"No." I hesitated. "Well, maybe. I've already told you I don't want to be found by my parents."

"But your parents are in Darwin, not Canberra."

"No, they were assigned to Darwin, and that's where I was born. They didn't remain there." The lie tasted bitter on my tongue—more so because he was so obviously aware that they *were* lies.

But all he said was, "How likely is it whoever the council sends will know you?"

"Very unlikely, but I can't help being afraid, Aiden."

He frowned. "What do you have to be afraid of? However much your parents mightn't like your witch powers, they surely wouldn't physically hurt you —would they?"

"Perhaps not," I said, even as foreboding stirred. "But there's all sorts of abuse, Aiden, and some of them take a long time to recover from."

Especially when the emotional scars ran as deep as mine.

His frown deepened, even as understanding stirred. "You're an adult—they have no legal control over you. And they *can't* hurt you unless you allow them."

"Which is utterly correct in theory, but difficult in practice."

And I rather suspected that if I ever *did* meet them again, I'd once again be that frightened sixteen-year-old faced with an untenable situation.

It was only thanks to Belle that I'd escaped. She'd been my strength—my rock—during those last few bitter weeks in

Canberra. In fact, she was the only reason I was even alive today.

I flexed my fingers, trying to ease the inner tension. Trying to push away the hurtful memories. "Witch legalities tend to be a little different than human or wolf."

"Your parents aren't witches. They're human."

I cursed inwardly. It was getting harder and harder to keep the lies straight and yet no matter how much I hated doing so, I also couldn't stop. I might like Aiden, but he was never going to be anything more than a good time. Never going to be the person I settled down with. Until I found that man, my secrets would remain mine.

"My grandmother was half witch, my mother quarter. That brings us all into the legal sphere of the council."

And while I hoped—with every ounce of my being—that the documents I'd been forced to sign at sixteen wouldn't stand in a court of law, I had absolutely no desire to ever find out if they did or not.

Aiden didn't say anything, though his skepticism spun around me, sharpening the weight of guilt.

We headed out of Castle Rock and cruised down the highway toward Argyle. I wound down the window, stuck my hand out, and let the cooling air play through my fingers. It remained empty of any threat, and I couldn't help but wonder if the unease I felt was more anxiety over the unknown witch's arrival than any real sense of danger.

We found parking in one of the side streets just off Vincent Street and the highly decorated main shopping strip. Aiden placed a warm hand against my spine, causing my breath to hitch a little as he lightly guided me to the restaurant, which went by the rather amusing name of The Blue Roo. The main room wasn't very large—there was perhaps a dozen tables, all of which were full, which was a positive sign considering it hadn't been open long. The brick walls were painted a dark blue that contrasted nicely against the white furniture and bright pots of flowers scattered in corners and hanging from hooks on the walls. An unlit fireplace dominated one wall and to one side of it was a small but beautifully decorated Christmas tree. At the far end of the room lay the open kitchen, a corridor to the lavatories, and an ornate, cast-iron set of stairs that led up to the next floor.

A young woman in jeans and a black shirt with a small blue roo stitched onto the left side approached and said, "Evening. Have you got a booking?"

"Aiden O'Connor."

She looked it up, then grabbed some menus and said, "Follow me, please."

We were led up the stairs then across to a corner table that was only lit by a small candle and the light streaming in from the nearby window. Aiden seated me and then sat opposite. The table was small enough that our knees touched, and it caused all sorts of havoc to my already giddy pulse rate.

"This is all very romantic," I said, smiling at the waitress as she handed me a wine list.

"Thought it was needed after all the near misses we've had of late. What would you like to drink?"

There were several of my favorite wines on the list, but given I'd taken painkillers not too long ago, I erred on the side of caution. "I'll just have a lemon, lime, and bitters, thanks."

Aiden ordered one of the many local craft beers, and then raised his eyebrows. "That's a rather staid choice, isn't it?"

"You're closeness has me giddy enough. I don't need alcohol."

He laughed. The warm sound caressed my skin as softly as any touch. "I'm supposed to be the one with the smooth lines, not you."

"I believe in equal opportunity when it comes to that sort of thing." I grinned. "What time do you have to start work tomorrow?"

"I'm on the early shift, unfortunately."

"Which sadly means there'll be no long, lingering wake up. Such a shame."

He smiled. In the flickering candlelight, his eyes were a very vivid blue and his dark blond hair ran with silver. Like most wolves, he was rangy, but his shoulders were a good width and his arms well muscled. He was, by anyone's account, a very good-looking man, despite the somewhat sharp planes of his face.

"There can be," he said. "We just have to wake up earlier."

"I wouldn't advise waking me too early. Not without a coffee in hand. It could get ugly."

Amusement played about his lips. "How ugly are we talking about? Because with so many younger brothers and sisters, I'm a dab hand at dealing with ugly."

"I'm talking 'even Belle fears to tread' type ugly."

"Ah. Well, let's forget the whole waking early without coffee feature of our relationship."

"If you want to have *any* sort of relationship, I'd certainly advise it."

"It's good to get these things sorted beforehand—fewer missteps to be made. To that end, be aware that you can wake me any damn time you please, with coffee or without."

His eyes took on a devilish glint. "But preferably without coffee. Or clothes."

The waitress arrived with our drinks. Once we'd both placed our food order, he leaned across the table and caught my hands in the warmth of his. The seriousness in his expression had my pulse racing again, but this time for all the *wrong* reasons.

"Before we go any further," he said softly. "There's something you need to know."

I briefly closed my eyes and knew without him saying another word that that this was it. That the next few seconds would be make or break for Belle's and my hopes of having a long and happy life within this reservation

The council had finally come to a decision about us.

CHAPTER THREE

F ear surged but just as quickly died when I caught the spark of happiness in his expression. It wasn't bad news. It was *good*.

Even so, I wasn't about to celebrate until I actually heard the words.

"I was called into a council meeting this evening," he continued solemnly, but with the happiness spreading.

"About Belle and me?"

"Yes." He paused, and I had to fight the urge to rip my hands from his, slap his arm, and tell him to just get on with it. "They've bent to pressure and have decided to allow you to stay despite the fact you weren't honest about being witches."

Even though I'd already guessed the result, the wave of relief that hit was so damn fierce tears stung my eyes. I blinked them away rapidly then gave in to that urge, ripping one hand free and then slapping his arm. "Damn it, you had me petrified for a few seconds there."

"I didn't mean to. I'd thought you'd guess the result given I couldn't contain my joy."

"I did, but that doesn't negate the fact that for a second there, I panicked." I sent Belle a quick message and, as her mental whoop of joy echoed through my thoughts, added, "Who beside you was pressuring them?"

"Anyone who has ever eaten in your café, the ladies of the gossip brigade, my pack, a good portion of the Marin pack, Ashworth—"

"Ashworth?" I cut in, surprised. "Why on *earth* would they listen to him considering he's only temporary and they don't like him anyway?"

"Because he told them in no uncertain terms that it's only thanks to your intervention that the wild magic isn't more problematic than it is."

I frowned. "Why would he say that when it's not true? I've used the wild magic but I'm certainly not able to properly protect it."

I *had* helped Ashworth out when he'd gone up there to protect the place, layering a final line of defense around the main wellspring that was unlikely to stop anyone of true power.

Besides, it was only thanks to Katie's presence within at least a portion of the reservation's wild magic that I was even sitting here tonight. If not for her intervention, the bullets that had smashed into the café door and through my car's headrest would have instead done to my brains what had been done to our dark sorcerer's.

"He said you've an unusual affinity with the magic here, and that they'd be the biggest damn fools ever if they let such a rare connection go." He smiled. "Of course, Ashworth being Ashworth, he then went on a ten-minute rant about how their inaction with the wellspring would affect the entire reservation for years to come, and that the darkness we'd witnessed in the last month or so was only just the beginning."

"Gabe said the same thing."

Aiden nodded. "I'm not sure the council actually believe the whole Katie and Gabe thing, but I think Ashworth finally got through to them. It's why they finally contacted Canberra for a permanent replacement."

"I'm surprised Ashworth didn't put himself forward for the position." Especially considering his intention of finding out what was going on with Belle and me.

"The council did offer it to him, though I think it was a case of better the devil you know. He turned them down—said they needed a much younger witch who was more up-to-date with the latest in spellcraft."

"I guess today's event proved that. Neither of us have any idea what sort of spell had been created."

"Something that was mentioned when Tala was called upon to give them an update on the murder." Aiden released my hands and then picked up his beer. "To your continuing presence here on the reservation."

I lightly tapped my glass against his. "To not having the best damn brownies you've ever tasted leave the reservation."

He grinned. "Definitely."

Our meals arrived—rare steak for him, and a decently cooked one for me—and the conversation moved on. We talked for hours about his family and my travels—where Belle and I had been, and why we'd left—until the candle had burned down low and the staff were making polite "please leave" motions.

Once we'd split the bill—he wanted to fully pay but I was having none of that—we left. The night was much cooler and goose bumps skittered across my skin. Aiden wrapped an arm around my shoulders and tucked me close.

"So," he said casually, but with an underlying tension I could feel through every movement, "would you like to come back to my place? Or would you prefer to go back to your hotel?"

I raised an eyebrow. "Do you really have to ask?"

He gave me an endearing, lopsided smile. "I learned long ago never to take things for granted, no matter how well things might appear to be going."

"So you've said before." I studied him for a second, catching the briefest glimmer of pain in his eyes. "But this time I'm sensing there's a story behind it."

"Indeed there is, but it's one I'd rather share on a cooling night."

"So it's a tale full of woe and misplaced expectations?"

"And heartbreak. Don't forget the heartbreak."

"Never." I couldn't imagine anyone actually *wanting* to break this man's heart, but someone obviously had. "Are you in need of a comfort cuddle?"

"Comfort cuddles never go astray," he said evenly. "But right now, I'm thinking sex would be better. Hot, sweaty sex."

My pulse leapt into overdrive again. "I could certainly get behind an aim like that."

"Good, because I really wasn't planning on going solo."

I laughed. "Neither was I, trust me on that."

"More than happy to hear that." He opened the car door for me then ran around to the driver side and climbed in.

It didn't take us long to get to his home, which was situated within a six-unit complex built close to the sandy shoreline of the vast Argyle Lake. His apartment sat at the far end of the complex, close to curving shoreline and surrounded by trees. It was a two-story, cedar-clad building complete with a long first-floor balcony and a wall of glass that overlooked the water. Belle and I had stayed here the night the café roof had been blown off, but this was the first time he and I had been here alone.

It was a thought that had butterflies stirring. I suspected their origin wasn't only expectation, but also nervousness. After all, not only had it been a rather long time since my last sexual encounter, it was also my first with *this* man. And many of my previous "first times" had been plain awkward at best, and damn unsatisfying at worst.

Aiden opened the front door and ushered me inside. The lower floor was basically one long room divided by an open wooden staircase. At the far end was a modern kitchen diner, complete with a bench long enough for six people to sit around. On this side of the room, there was an open fire-place, around which was a C-shaped, hugely comfortable leather sofa. The TV—a monster of a thing—dominated the corner between the fireplace and the outside glass wall. The stairs led up to two bedrooms, each with its own en suite. Aiden's was at the front of the building and had balcony access and long views over the lake. There was only one acknowledgement of the festive season in the room, and that was the rather sad-looking tree that sat on the other side of the fireplace.

"Not even a real tree, let alone a decorated one." I shook my head, my expression one of mock sadness. "I expected more, Ranger."

"I'm not about to cut down a real tree, and there are decorations—it has tiny lights at the end of each branch."

"Which don't work if you don't plug it in."

"I'm not here enough to worry about it." He closed the

front door but didn't turn on either the overhead or tree lights. They weren't needed—the moonlight now streaming in through the glass provided more than enough light.

"Coffee?" He brushed past, sending a shiver of delight rolling across my skin. "Or perhaps something stronger to settle the nerves?"

I smiled and followed him down to the kitchen. "A wolf's nose is keener than I thought if you can smell my nerves."

His grin flashed, bright and warm. "Who was talking about *your* nerves?"

I smiled, hooked my purse over the back of the nearest bar chair, and then sat down. "I'm glad I'm not the only one having an attack of 'it's been so long, what ifs?'"

His grin grew. "In my case, it's more a case of wanting so badly I'm afraid it'll be over in a heartbeat."

I accepted the glass of whiskey and raised an eyebrow. "So that much-vaunted control you were boasting about—"

"It was lies. All lies. I apologize in advance for any inadvertent hastiness."

I laughed. "Then I shall apologize in advance if it takes me a little longer to get fired up, despite the raging desire."

He sat down on the next seat then spun me around and positioned his knees either side of mine. He raised his glass and said, "To hastiness, nervousness, and an end result that will blow both our socks off. If we were wearing them, that is."

I touched my glass against his and took a drink. It was a really lovely whiskey, but it also really *wasn't* what I wanted to taste right now.

He tossed his drink down in one gulp then grabbed the edge of my chair and pulled me even closer. He slid one finger under the left shoulder of my dress and gently guided it down my arm. I shifted the glass from one hand to the other and let the sleeve fall to my waist. As I took another drink, he repeated the process on the other side, leaving me half-naked and trembling with expectation.

I followed his lead and downed my drink. The alcohol burned all the way down and swamped the butterflies in an instant. I put the glass on the counter and then said, "I hardly think it fair that I'm partially naked and you're not." I began undoing his shirt buttons. "I expect full equality in this relationship, you know."

"More than happy to oblige." His breath hitched as my fingers played with the top button of his pants. "But you're playing with fire if you go there right now."

I laughed then leaned forward and brushed my lips across his. Tasted the hints of clove, nutmeg, and toffee that were the lingering remnants of the whiskey, and the trembling heat that lay underneath them. He groaned softly then wrapped a hand around the back of my neck, holding me still as he deepened the kiss. All too soon it became so fierce and urgent that I could barely even think, let alone breathe.

He broke off with another groan and began to touch me, using both hands and mouth to explore and tease. I arched my back, thrusting my breasts forward, silently pleading with him to do more. He caught one nipple in his mouth, gently teasing it with his teeth before using his tongue to amplify the delicious sensations shuddering through me. Then he swapped to the other nipple, repeating the process, time and again, until my whole body was trembling and awash with desire. Then, finally, his fingers slid past my belly button, past the pooled layers of my dress, past the elastic of my panties, and into the warm wetness waiting there. He caressed and teased and brought me right to brink of satisfaction, only to pull away. I groaned and cursed him.

He chuckled softly, a sweetly evil sound that hung on the air as he began the whole process again. And then again. But just as I ready to scream in frustration, he caught my face between his hands and gently kissed me.

Then he pressed his forehead against mine, his breath short, sharp pants that burned my lips. "You have no idea how badly I want you right now, but I wanted our first time—"

"Aiden, if you don't stop worrying and get naked—right here and now—I *am* going to take matters into my own hands."

His laugh skittered across my sweat-dotted skin. "I do love a woman who's not afraid to state her needs."

"*This* woman's needs are great, so get moving."

To say we got naked in record time would be another of those understatements. He pulled a foiled condom out of his jeans pocket and then wrapped his arms around me and kissed me again. It was no less urgent than before, and the trembling need in my body grew.

"Here or upstairs?"

"If you dare move anywhere, Ranger," I muttered, "I will scream."

He laughed again and put the condom on. I pushed him back onto the bar chair and then climbed onto his lap, straddling his legs and then lowering myself onto him.

He slipped inside slowly—easily—and oh lord, it felt so good, so *right*, that a shudder ran through me and a groan of utter pleasure escaped. It was a sound he echoed, but for several seconds, neither of us moved. His breath washed across my lips, and the heat pooling deep within was gathering strength and demanding release. He slid one hand around my waist and the other up to my left breast, cupping it, teasing it with fingers and thumb as I began to rock against him. Slowly at first, and then with increasing urgency. The exquisite pressure built and built, curling through my body, shaking me with its power, until it became a tidal wave that would not be denied.

"Oh... God." My voice was little more than a fractured whisper. "Please...."

Our urgency increased. I gripped his shoulders, thrusting down harder—quicker—onto him, pushing *him* deeper. All too soon the shuddering took hold as my orgasm hit and pleasure ripped through my body. I groaned, a sound that seemed to tip Aiden over the edge. He came, fast and hard and with a deep roar of utter pleasure.

For several minutes, neither of us moved. I couldn't move—satisfaction seemed to have sapped my strength and if I hadn't already been sitting I think my knees would have given way and had me falling.

Eventually he kissed me again, with a passion that spoke of need barely quenched.

"That was amazing."

"Indeed." I loosely locked my arms around his shoulders. "But I'm told werewolves have extraordinary stamina, and I'm feeling the need to examine whether this rumor is true or not. How many condoms have you got on hand?"

"More than enough, let me assure you." He placed his hands under my butt and rose. As I wrapped my legs around his waist, he added, "Shall we go fulfill this desire of yours?"

"Please do."

He laughed and carried me up the stairs to his bedroom. Over the long course of the night, he did indeed prove werewolves had amazing stamina.

But then, so did some witches when they were in the arms of the right man.

"Well, well," Belle said, as I wandered into the café the next morning. "Don't you look like the cat who got all the cream?"

I sighed and leaned against the cake counter. "And very good cream it was, too."

"I'm very happy to hear that." Belle pushed a cappuccino toward me. "I'm guessing you'll be absent from the hotel room for the next couple of nights, then?"

"The next couple of *weeks*, if I have any say. I've three years of abstinence to make up for, remember."

"If you can make *that* up in mere weeks, I'll be seriously concerned about the state of your libido."

I laughed. "How was the show?"

"Good, but then, you can't really go wrong with *Les Mis*."

There was something in her voice that had instinct stirring. "But there nevertheless was a problem?"

"Could be." She pursed her lips. "I think the wolf grows restless."

"That was always going to happen." Although it was a truth I wasn't willing to confront just yet given my relationship with Aiden had barely gotten off the ground. Or, more specifically, into bed.

"I know, but I did think my fabulousness would hold his interest a wee bit longer."

"It certainly should have."

She smiled. "Luckily, there are plenty of other canines in this particular den."

"I think they'd all be rather offended to hear you refer to them as mere canines." I took a drink. "Has he said anything?"

"No. And it's not like he'll take on other lovers without talking to me first. He is, above all else, honorable that way."

"So it could be nothing more than an off night?"

"Could be. I doubt it though." She shrugged. "It doesn't really fuss me, to be honest. I'm having a thoroughly good time with him, but I've always known it would be a short fling rather than anything deeper."

Because werewolves didn't do deeper—not with the likes of us. It was something I needed to keep reminding myself about given my past habit of falling for entirely the wrong man.

Belle leaned her hip against the counter and took a sip of her coffee. "What are we going to do about the witch that's coming in?"

I shrugged. "Avoid him seeing us standing side by side at all costs, but other than that, there's nothing we *can* do."

"True." She sighed. "I guess the real worry will come once they contract a reservation witch."

"Yeah, but let's not stress about it until it happens."

She raised her eyebrows, amusement evident. "This from the woman who was all doom, gloom, and 'my parents are going to find us and drag us back to Canberra' only a day ago?"

I grinned. "It's amazing just how much good sex can brighten one's outlook."

"Obviously." Her amusement faded. "What did the threads within that protection circle look like? I might do a run through Gran's books, just to see if she mentions anything along those lines."

I gave her a description and then said, "Weren't you the one berating me for sticking my nose into dark events when there was no need?"

She sniffed. It was an amusingly haughty sound.

"Which is *why* I should do the research. As the motto goes, a good familiar should always be prepared."

"That's the Scouts."

"Same, same." She wrinkled her nose. "In all honesty, the spirits are uneasy, though they're not saying why."

"Now *there's* a surprise."

Her gaze became somewhat distracted as she listened to the other side. "They don't appreciate your sarcasm."

"They never do."

"And whatever it is they're sensing," she continued, ignoring me, "it has a very old feel."

"Well, that totally clarifies *everything*." I took another drink. "It'd be rather nice if they gave us a heads-up the next time a dark witch stepped onto the reservation."

"They're here to offer advice, not do our work for us." Her tone as filled with an old-fashioned primness—an echo of whatever spirit guide was currently chatting to her. There were several who tended to follow us around, which in itself was rather unusual. They—no doubt through Belle's connection with me—obviously heard that particular thought, because she added, "They also wish to remind you that lower house witches generally *aren't* graced by the presence of spirit guides, and that you should be grateful they deign to help us at all."

"I'm being chastised by spirits? Seriously?"

"They're merely stating a little appreciation every now and again would not go astray."

I smiled. "I do appreciate. Seriously."

"They're unconvinced."

"Then I'll try to curtail my sarcasm for at least a day or so." My phone beeped. I dug it out of my purse and saw a text from Ashworth. I read it quickly and then said, "The new witch arrives at the airport around five."

"Does he know who it is yet?"

"Apparently not." I hesitated as a second message came through. "Oh, great—there's not one witch arriving, but two. The second is a possible candidate for the reservation position. He's to be interviewed by the council."

"Because things weren't already interesting enough," Belle said, voice dry.

"Apparently not." I shoved the phone away then finished my coffee and swung my purse back over my shoulder. "I'll run upstairs and get changed, then come back down and help you."

Belle nodded. I dumped my clothes in the washing basket then changed to jeans and a T-shirt and headed back down. The café was busy all day, with spare tables being snapped up almost before the previous patrons had fully left. Which, with tomorrow night being Christmas Eve, was a good thing. We were closed for three days—the two traditional days of Christmas and Boxing Day, as well as the reservation-wide holiday on the twenty-seventh—but busy days like this gave our bottom line a nice little boost.

And the congratulations we kept getting over being allowed to stay were much-needed moral boosts. Our cake prowess had obviously spread farther than we'd figured.

We closed at three. By the time we'd cleaned up and done the prep for the next day, it was close to five.

Belle gathered the dirty tea towels and kitchen cloths to take up to the washing machine. "I'm surprised you haven't heard from Aiden yet."

I wrinkled my nose. "He said there'd probably be a chunk of paperwork to do and that I shouldn't expect to hear from him until at least seven. You want a drink?"

She nodded and disappeared down the corridor to dump the washing into the machine. I grabbed a couple of glasses and opened a bottle of white wine, then walked across to the table.

As I did, energy whisked into the room, bright and sharp, and filled with an odd sort of cognizance.

Not just wild magic, but the portion controlled by Aiden's sister.

It spun around me, filled with an odd sort of urgency as something clattered to the floor. I glanced down sharply and saw a watch sitting next to my feet. A man's watch.

"What the...?" I bent and picked it up.

Images and emotion hit, so thick and fast that I didn't have a chance to throw my shields up before they dragged me deep into the mind of the other.

They are coming. Still coming. Running isn't losing them, isn't shaking them. I can hear them, laughing, joking. Anticipating. Heat. In my body, in my heart, in my brain. Legs won't obey. I fall. Still they come, still they laugh. Their excitement fills the air, thick in my nostrils. I try to get up. Can't. Try to tear at them with teeth. Can't. Immobilized. Burning. Silver flashes. Skin peels. The pain. Dear God, the pain....

The watch was wrenched from my hand and the images stopped. My legs went from underneath me, and I had to grip the edge of the table to keep upright. For several seconds, I didn't move. *Couldn't* move. My heart was racing so hard it felt like it was about to tear out of my chest, and my throat was thick with horror.

"Here," Belle said. "Drink this."

She shoved a filled glass under my nose. Whiskey, not wine. I gripped it with shaking fingers and drank it all. It burned all the way down and made my head spin, but didn't entirely erase the lingering remnants of utter, utter agony.

"What the fuck was that?" Belle's voice was grim.

"I don't know." I stared at the watch with trepidation. As much as I didn't want to pick it up again, I'd have to if I wanted to understand what was going on. I held my glass out and Belle topped it up.

"Then where did the damn thing come from?"

"The wild magic brought it in."

"Meaning Katie rather than the truly wild stuff, I'm guessing."

I nodded and tossed back the whiskey. Then I put the glass back on the table and reached for the watch. But I didn't pick it up. I didn't need to. Abject suffering pulsed from it in thick waves. I took a deep breath and glanced grimly at Belle.

"I'm obviously meant to help the watch's owner."

"Given the agony I felt—which was only the backwash of what hit you—I'm doubting that's actually possible." She glared at the watch for a second and then picked it up. "I'll get the silk gloves and your kit. You'd better call Aiden."

I took a deep breath then pushed away from the table and walked a little unsteadily—thanks to the fact my legs were still shaky—across to the counter to retrieve my phone.

Aiden answered almost immediately. "I'm hoping this is impatience, but given every other time you've rung me unexpectedly it's been because there's trouble, I'm not holding out hope."

"Wise man." I took another deep breath but it still didn't do a lot to help the inner tension. "You need to get over here ASAP."

"Do we need the truck?"

"Yes."

"Be there in two."

He hung up. I shoved the phone into my pocket and glanced around as Belle came out of the reading room. The watch was now safely incased in a silk bag, but she never-theless gave me a silk glove. The combination should mute the vibes rolling off the watch while still allowing me to track the owner through it.

Once I'd put on the glove, she placed the bagged watch on the counter, then handed me the pack. "I've stuck in your spell stones, a couple of warding potions, and my silver knife."

"Thanks." I slung it over my shoulder and then said, "Could you ring Ashworth? He'll need to know something has happened."

She frowned. "It's not as if he can do anything given he'd be at the airport—"

"I know, but he's still acting reservation witch and what-ever is happening out there involves magic."

"The same magic that our dead witch was creating? Because the timing of the two situations suggests they could be connected."

I hesitated. "I can't say for certain, but I don't think so. It doesn't feel as dark."

"Then I guess that's something."

I swept the watch into my hand and tried to ignore the agony rolling off it.

Belle followed me across to the front door. "Ashworth will want to know how that watch came into our possession."

I shrugged. "I'll tell him the truth—the wild magic gave it to me. He doesn't actually have to know it was the portion infused with Katie's soul."

Belle grunted. "Sooner or later, he *will* find out. Or the new reservation witch will. And that will just up Canber-ra's interest in this place."

"Maybe the new witch will hold the reservation's

interest ahead of Canberra's." Outside, a car horn sounded. "I'll keep you updated."

"Do. And be careful."

"Always. Make sure you lock the door."

A smile touched her lips. "Always."

And she did the second I'd stepped outside. The day seemed colder despite the sunshine and the heat in the air. I had no doubt it was a feeling caused by the vibes rolling from the silk-wrapped watch. Vibes that held the gathering chill of death.

I jumped into Aiden's truck, shoved the backpack onto the floor, and then said, "Go."

He immediately pulled out and hit the accelerator. I dropped the watch into my lap and pulled on the seat belt. "Turn right onto the Midland."

He did so, tires screaming, and then motioned to the watch. "That watch looks vaguely familiar—who does it belong to?"

His nostrils flared as he spoke but if the owner's scent lingered on the watch then he either didn't know him or wasn't about to say.

"I don't know. Your sister gave it me."

"My sister?" Confusion briefly crossed his expression but was quickly replaced by understanding. "Katie."

"Yeah. And wild magic isn't supposed to be able to interact—in any way—with either people or an object without direction from a witch, so it's just more evidence to the fact that Gabe's spell has indeed made her this reservation's protector."

"A protector who only interacts with you," he said, voice grim. "And to think we'd come close to evicting you—"

"I think it's a fairly safe bet Katie would somehow have made her feelings known had that actually happened."

"She never was one for keeping her mouth shut." He paused, and sorrow stirred through his aura. "Except at the end of her life."

I reached out with my free hand and touched his leg. "She's happy, Aiden. She's where she wants to be, doing what she wanted to do."

He gave me a lopsided smile. "I know. I just wish I could talk to her, even if for only a few seconds. Left onto the freeway or onto the overpass?"

I briefly gripped the watch tighter. "Over."

We sped through a roundabout and then took a sweeping curve to the left. This area seemed to be a mix of new and old houses on larger blocks, but the death rolling from the watch still held some distance. Whatever was happening to the watch's owner, it wasn't happening here.

We quickly moved out of the residential area and into scrublands. As we began to climb a long hill, I said, "Right at the road near the top of this."

He did so, the tires once again screaming in protest. "This road skirts the back edge of my pack's territory."

I glanced at him sharply. "Does this watch belong to a pack member?"

"The faint scent emanating from it suggests it does."

"Would you be notified if any pack members were missing or under threat?"

"Normally, yes, but I'm gathering this threat is still eventuating."

I hesitated. "The threat has been and gone. Only death is gathering now."

He swore and pressed the accelerator harder, though the big truck didn't have a whole lot more speed to give. We swept past the raised banks of a reservoir and then around another left turn.

"Right at the next road," I said.

"Which is another of our boundary roads." His voice was grim.

I didn't say anything. There was little point given I had no idea yet where this trail would end or who was involved. We sped down the narrowing road; the sweeping fields of grapevines on one side and thick scrub on the other were both little more than a green blur. We skidded around sharp bends and roared through gullies shadowed by gum trees that arched high overhead. And still the watch pulsed, an agony that went on and on.

"Left or right," Aiden said, as we approached a T-intersection terrifyingly fast.

I hesitated. The watch was finally beginning to lose its life, which meant the owner had finally stopped fighting. But agony was still his to hold. I shuddered and said, "Left. Are we still on the edge of your pack's territory?"

"No."

Which didn't mean anything. I knew it. He knew it.

We continued down another small road. There were open fields on one side, wilderness on the other. The pulse in the watch was fading faster. I ripped off the silk glove and gripped the watch tightly. Horror squeezed through me, making breath catch and my heart ache fiercely. Dear God, the pain....

We swept up a gentle hill and around a slow curve to the right.

"Here," I said abruptly. "Stop here."

He obeyed so fast the truck slewed around sideways and ended up facing the wrong way on the shoulder of the road. I grabbed my backpack and scrambled out, and then paused briefly to get my bearings from the watch. After checking there were no oncoming cars, I raced into the scrub and trees on the other side of the road. Aiden was a step behind me, his tension filling the air, a thick heat that had my nerves jumping and tingling.

The ground began to rise, becoming increasingly rocky. My left foot rolled over a loose stone and I would have fallen had Aiden not grabbed me.

"You okay?"

"Yeah." I ran on, doing my best to ignore the twinge in my ankle. We reached the top of the hill, but all I could see was more scrub, trees, and rocks, sweeping downward. But we were close now. So close.

But so was death.

I swore and plunged down the hill. Aiden remained at my side, grabbing my elbow several times to steady me as I slipped.

"I can smell water." He paused, and then added, voice flat and yet somehow dangerous, "And raw meat."

"Whoever it is, they're just up ahead."

I forced my feet on, despite the instinctive urge to slow, to *not* confront what waited ahead.

But I couldn't let Aiden face it alone. Not if my suspicion was right and there was magic involved.

The trees retreated with startling abruptness, revealing a clearing that was dominated by a half-empty dam.

On the edge of the high bank on the far side was a red form. It took me a moment to realize it was a dog.

A *wolf*.

One that had been totally and utterly skinned.

CHAPTER FOUR

B ile rose and this time there was absolutely no stopping it. I stumbled back to the trees, where I was completely and violently ill.

Aiden followed me over and handed me a handkerchief once I'd finished. "You'd better stay—"

"No." I grimly wiped my mouth then tucked the handkerchief into my pocket. I'd no doubt need it again, even if I had nothing left in my stomach to bring back up. "There's magic involved in this somewhere. You won't see it, but I will."

Which *didn't* mean I'd be able to do anything about it— especially if my hunch was wrong and the magic used here *was* connected to the dark witch.

He hesitated, his gaze sweeping me in concern, and he then stepped to one side and motioned me to lead the way.

I cautiously approached the body. It was a raw and red mess of muscle, but there was surprisingly little blood considering what had been— A leg twitched. Horror crashed through me again and my eyes went wide.

He was *alive*.

Despite losing his pelt from nose to tail. Despite the agony and shock being stripped would have caused. Despite the brightly plumed dart that was sticking out of his right flank, which I suspected might be made of silver. The precious metal was not only poisonous to wolves, but it also kept them locked in whatever form they were in.

Aiden swore rapidly and put an urgent call out for the paramedics.

I swallowed bile yet again and studied the ground around the red form. There was no hint of major magic here —no pentagram, no circle, nothing to indicate any sort of spell had been used in this gruesome deed.

And yet the fading caress of magic remained.

I forced myself to step closer, but kept my gaze down rather than on the dying wolf. The ground was stony, so held no footprints, and there was no evidence of any sort of struggle. This wolf had apparently just quietly lain here while he was skinned.

Unless, of course, the magic was the reason *behind* his lack of action. But to find out one way or another, I'd have to go even closer than I already was, and I couldn't do that just yet. And it wasn't just a natural aversion to getting any nearer, but the simple fact that I needed to find the source of the fading magic first. To do anything else would be fool-hardy, given we had no idea if this foul deed was also some sort of trap.

The heartbeat in the watch died. The wolf was finally free from his ungodly agony.

His soul rose from his remains, sparkling brightly in the evening sunshine. Though it held even less substance than a ghost, it was obvious they'd hunted and killed a young man, not an old one—but why? What had this wolf done to deserve such a fate?

His soul didn't stop, didn't pause, which meant this brutal death had been his destiny. Otherwise, he would have been bound to this place—to this dam—for eternity.

I briefly closed my eyes against the sting of tears that were a combination of both anger and relief, and sent a prayer after him, wishing him a longer life and cleaner death the next time.

"He's dead," I said, the minute Aiden got off the phone.

"Which is not surprising, considering what's been done."

I rubbed my arms. "Has anything like this ever happened before?"

"Not on this reservation."

I glanced at him sharply. "But it *has* happened on other reservations?"

"Not in Victoria, and certainly not for a while." He flicked his phone's camera on and began recording. "About ten years ago there was a series of murders across five reservations—the two in Western Australia, one of the two reservations in Queensland, and those in South Australia and Northern Territory."

"How many deaths in all?"

"Twenty-one. Those behind the atrocity were never caught."

"So we could be dealing with the same people."

"Or a copycat." He moved to the other side. "I'll have to request the reports from that period to see if there are any similarities."

"But why on earth would anyone want to skin a werewolf?"

"For the same reason hunters hunt and skin other animals but don't take the meat—for their pelts."

I stared at him, unable to believe such a thing was even possible. "But werewolves aren't animals. They're *human*."

Or rather, a branch of humanity that had, over time, evolved specific DNA adaptions that allowed them to shift effortlessly from one form or another. No one really understood why it had happened, despite the fact that science had been studying werewolf DNA for decades.

"That wasn't always the case, remember," he replied, tone grim. "For a long time we were considered an unholy evil delivered straight from the gates of hell itself. In fact, throughout most of the Middle Ages and even some of the early modern period, there were just as many specialized werewolf eradicators as there were vampire."

"The witch population didn't exactly have a free and easy time of it throughout that period of history, either, but that hasn't been the case for centuries now."

"No, but the pelt industry still lives. It's just gone unground."

Horror shivered through me. "So you think this could be the first of many more deaths?"

"I hope not. Is it safe to approach the body?"

I hesitated, testing the air with my "other" senses. "There are still faint wisps of magic coming from the victim's body."

His gaze sharpened on mine. "Meaning this could be connected with the shooting victim?"

I hesitated. "Belle asked the same thing, but the two magics feels very different. I think it more likely that this is another example of just how big a draw the unprotected wellspring is to those who follow darker paths."

"If we *are* dealing with pelt hunters, they're likely to be human."

"Which only means they're not here for the magic itself

but doesn't discount the fact that the unprotected well-spring nevertheless drew them here, even if they have no idea why." I swept my gaze across the body again. "I suspect the magic is coming from the silver needle that's stuck in his flank, but I'd need to get closer to be sure."

"Are you able to?" There was sympathy in his voice but also determination. This was the ranger rather than the lover speaking, and the ranger didn't want to wait for Ashworth and the other witches to arrive if he could at all help it.

And considering what had been done here, it was a desire I could totally understand.

I took a deep breath and nodded.

"Thanks, Liz."

I nodded again and forced my feet forward, keeping my gaze more on the ground than the raw mess of sinew and meat that had once been human. When I was close enough, I took another deep breath and then glanced at Aiden. "You ready?"

He nodded and raised his phone. I squatted beside the body and reached out, letting my hand hover just above the end of the needle jutting out of the wolf's flesh. Faint wisps of power teased my skin but they weren't coming from the needle itself. I frowned and skimmed the rest his body. It wasn't until I reached his front leg that the magic grew stronger. I frowned and, after a moment, spotted a light indentation near his wrist. He'd been wearing a bracelet tight enough to leave a mark even after he'd been skinned, which was rather odd. Werewolves had what was generally called a set point—a natural biomarker that slowly changed as they aged. It meant that no matter what happened in *either* form, by shifting their shape their body basically repaired itself *back* to that set point—with the exception of a fatal wound, of course. Which meant that even if the bracelet had been tight enough to mark his human wrist, it shouldn't have in any way left a mark on his wolf form.

I shifted slightly and skimmed my hand down the leg. The nearer I got to the indentation, the stronger the sense of magic became.

"You've found something?" Aiden asked.

"Yes. Can you come around this side?" Once he had, I added, "Pick his leg up."

He pulled two pairs of gloves from the apparently never-ending supply he kept in his pockets, offered me one set, and pulled on the other. Then, very carefully, he lifted the stranger's right leg.

I pressed one gloved hand against the ground to steady myself and peered closely at the limb. After a moment, I saw it—the fading curl of a magical thread; this time, it was attached to an *actual* thread.

I glanced at Aiden. "Can I have your phone?"

He gave it to me instantly. "What have you found?"

"A thread."

"What type of thread?"

"Some sort of cotton, by the look of it. The magic I'm sensing is coming from it."

"How can you attach spells to something as simple as that?"

I took a couple of shots then handed the phone back to him. "You can attach spells to anything at all. All it takes is knowledge and skill."

"How big a thread are we talking about?"

"Tiny. I'd guess it was part of some sort of charm he'd been wearing that has been left behind when the rest of it was removed." I glanced up. "Do you want me to pull it free?"

"If it's not dangerous to do so, yes."

"It doesn't feel dangerous." I carefully touched the tip of the thread with gloved fingers. Magic swirled, whispering its secrets. The tension within me eased. "It's little more than a magical tracker."

"Does that mean we have a second unknown witch on the reservation?"

"Not necessarily, because trackers like this can be bought at most craft markets. They're not difficult to create."

I carefully gripped the thread and tugged on it. The thread came free easily enough, but the faint wisps of magic slowly spinning around the bloody piece of cotton started fading even faster. I doubted Ashworth or the heretic tracker would be able to use it to uncover its origins, but *I* just might.

I held up the small piece of thread so that Aiden could see it. "Do you want me to use my psychometry skills to try and track down either the source of this thing or the rest of it?"

"Will it be dangerous?"

I hesitated. "To be honest, I don't know. I guess it's always possible this thread was left behind deliberately, but given the magic is fading and appears to be nothing more than a simple spell, I doubt it."

"Can you nevertheless employ a protection circle? I don't want to be picking up your bloody pieces as well."

I rose. "It's not something I particularly want either, given the hole it would blow in future seduction plans. Hold this."

I handed him the thread, then walked back down to hill until I reached a flat, relatively stone-free piece of ground. I dug my spell stones out of the backpack and then placed them carefully on the ground until I had a circle large enough to sit cross-legged in.

"Right," I said, and held out my hand.

He came down the hill and carefully handed me the inch-and-a-half-long piece of thread. What little magic remained was leaching away rapidly—something that often happened when small magical items were broken.

I frowned and wondered why instinct seemed to think the charm had been pulled off rather than simply unlatched. The indentations on the wolf's wrist certainly *didn't* indicate the former, given such an action would have forced the charm's threads to dig deeper into the skin on one side of his wrist than the other.

I glanced up at Aiden. "I'm going to have to touch this with my bare hand if I'm to have any hope of dragging information from it. Will that piss Ciara off?"

"I doubt it, as it's not like we'll be able to pull prints from it. It's more about matching that thread to whatever cloth or material it might have come from. Can I film you doing the reading?"

"Once I've fired the circle up, yes."

I sat down and then began to spell, carefully laying the threads of protection across the stones, weaving one upon the other, until the circle was as strong as I could make it under the circumstances.

I told Aiden to start filming then pulled off one glove with my teeth and switched the thread to my bare hand. Even though there was only a tiny amount of blood on the thread, it oddly seemed to burn against my skin, and held within it echoes of the agony the wolf had suffered. My stomach flip-flopped but I narrowed my gaze and tried to concentrate on the remnants of magic rather than the emotions. Whoever had created the bracelet or charm this thread belonged to hadn't, in any way, flirted with the darker side of the art. The spell felt cool and light, free of evil or taint.

I closed my eyes and unleashed my psychometry skills. For several seconds, nothing happened—no real surprise given how tiny the thread was. But just as I was about to give up, images stirred. But they were faint. So faint. I frowned and tried to pin them down, but I might as well have tried ensnaring a fairy.

"You need to tell me what you're seeing and experiencing," Aiden said quietly.

"I'm seeing a teapot." I tried to adjust the mental dial and sharpen the images but it didn't work. "A black one. The air is sharp with incense—a protective mix of violet and angelica. The room is small and dark. There's a woman; she's got dark brown hair shot with grey and silvery eyes...." The image faded and I swore softly. "I'm sorry. That's all I could get."

"Do you think it was a memory of where—or who—he'd gotten the charm from?"

"Possibly." I hesitated and glanced at the body. "I might be able to get more if I tried to read his mind direct, but there's only a six-minute window of brain survival after the heart stops before memory deterioration begins." Even then, some levels of memory could be affected, particularly short-term. "And given the way he died, I really doubt I'd get anything more than his agony."

Not to mention the whole issue of having to touch his skinned body to even make the attempt. My stomach was unstable enough as it was.

"I'm not about to put you through that, Liz."

"Thanks." I carefully wrapped the thread in the rubber glove, then made the circle safe and collected my stones. I rose and handed Aiden the glove. "Sorry I couldn't have been of more help."

He caught my hand and tugged me close. He didn't kiss me; he just wrapped his arms around me and held me silently for several seconds. It was nice.

More than nice.

"Jaz, Tala, and Ciara are on the way," he said eventually. "I've asked Jaz to drive you home."

"I'll head back to the road, then." I somewhat reluctantly stepped back. "I'm gathering it could be a long night?"

He grimaced. "More than likely. But if you'd prefer to spend the night on a more comfortable mattress that has certainly seen far less traffic than that hotel bed, you're more than welcome to go back to my place."

Amusement twitched my lips. "Given the lack of sleep last night, I might well be snoring by the time you arrive back."

"Do you snore?" he asked, somewhat curiously.

My grin broke loose. "I guess you'll discover that one way or another tonight. Is the spare key still in the same spot?"

"Yes."

"Then I'll see you sometime tonight."

He nodded and walked back up the hill. I shouldered my backpack and left, making my way back to the road and his truck. Jaz and Tala arrived at the same time. After pointing Tala in the right direction, I climbed into Jaz's SUV and was whisked quickly home.

Belle was sitting at one of the tables, her feet up on a chair and a red leather book sitting on her lap. There was also a rather large, partially eaten slice of banana cake sitting on the table beside her.

She glanced up as I entered. "Whiskey or wine?"

"Given the unsteady state of my stomach, neither. I'm making tea—you want one?"

"Yeah, thanks." She scooped up another mouthful of cake, and then said, "If this death had nothing to do with the dark witch, then what the hell was the dark witch doing?"

I shrugged. "I guess we'll know more once Ashworth and the heretic hunter deconstruct that protective circle and the spell inside."

"The fact that it's still live bothers me. Magic doesn't generally last past the death of its creator."

"Black magic might be a different, though. It's not like either of us know much about it."

"No. But Gran has a book on it."

"Your gran had a book on everything." I glanced at the one on her knee. "Is that it?"

"Yeah, and it's actually quite fascinating."

I tossed some green and pear tea into a large teapot then poured hot—but not boiling—water on top of it. "In what way?"

"Well, did you know that it's rare for a dark witch to take on an apprentice but, when they do, they're often used as a quick and easy source of blood for certain rituals?"

"Ashworth mentioned something along those lines last night, but I bet the apprentices aren't aware of it going in." I picked up the teapot and mugs and carried them over.

"Except that they are. There's some sort of spiritual contract agreed to and signed by both parties before the apprentice is taken on."

I deposited the pot and mugs, then reached across and snagged some of her cake. My stomach might still be a little dicey, but I wasn't about to ignore cake. "I can't see a dark witch ever honoring such an agreement."

"Except they have to, as it's a binding agreement witnessed in blood and sworn to whatever dark entity the witch is dealing with. If either party breaks it, their soul is basically cactus."

"Their souls are cactus anyway. They're dark witches." I licked the frosting from my fingers then picked up the teapot and filled our mugs.

"Well, true." She wrinkled her nose. "Another interesting fact is that in order to become a master, the apprentice must first defeat *his* master."

I slid the mug over to her and then picked up my own. "Does it say why?"

"Something about it being the only way to fully utilize the onset of power or some such crap."

I snorted. "I bet it doesn't actually say that."

"And you would be wrong." She flicked back a couple of pages and then raised the book. It did indeed say exactly that.

I snagged another piece of her cake. "I wish we'd had the chance to meet your gran."

"Yeah." Belle grimaced. "But for all her knowledge—for all the books she'd studied, collected, and made notes on—she was still caught unawares by a rogue spirit."

"She wasn't the only one, though." That spirit had ended up killing five witches in all before it was taken down. Belle's gran had been the only lower house witch killed, and there'd apparently been a lot of speculation as to why. Belle's mom—Ava—was of the theory that it was going after the strongest witches, and while Nel certainly hadn't been *magically* strong, her historical knowledge about spells and spellcraft had outstripped any in Canberra at the time.

"True." Belle snapped the book closed and then swung her legs off the chair. "Anyway, I haven't yet found anything that relates back to the sort of spell threads you described, but I'll keep looking."

I raised an eyebrow. "I take it from this sudden flurry of action that you're going out tonight?"

"Zak called—"

"Full of apologies for his distance last night and once again willing to bend a knee before your magnificence?"

She slapped my arm. Tea slopped over the rim of the mug and splashed across the table. "Hey, watch the tea, woman."

"He wants to talk."

"Horizontally. After sex."

She grinned. "Possibly."

"Did he say about what?"

"No, but the gossips were in full flight today, and I couldn't help but listen in when I heard the Marin name mentioned. Apparently three women have arrived at the compound from the South Australian pack via the exchange program. According to the gossips, Zak's taken quite a shine to one of them."

The exchange program was a worldwide agreement between all werewolf packs that allowed those in search of a mate to go outside their own pack to do so. It was a means of stopping the packs from becoming too inbred—something witches also had to be wary of.

I raised my eyebrows. "I wouldn't have thought Zak the type to be settling down. Not yet, anyway."

"Love sometimes has a way of clubbing you over the head when you least expect it." She pursed her lips. "Of course, in your case, it's been a wet fish, which would explain your many very bad choices over the years."

"I refute your use of many," I said mildly. "There's only been two. The rest were mere infatuations."

"Losers one and all, and totally undeserving of your heart."

"So I discovered. But we were talking about you, not me, so stop changing the subject."

She grinned. "If it *is* true, then I'll be sad to lose the good times, but we'll still be friends. And hey, let's face it—I won't be single for long unless I wish it."

I raised my mug and tapped it against hers. "Here's to being hotly pursued by even hotter men."

"Indeed." She paused, her gaze narrowing. "Speaking of hot—or rather, its antithesis—Ashworth is marching toward the café, and he has another witch in tow."

"Do we know him?"

Her gaze narrowed. "Can't tell."

"You can't read him?"

"No. There's some sort of magical interference, which is rather frustrating."

But not surprising if said witch was a heretic hunter. The last thing he'd want was a rogue witch reading his thoughts or possibly even controlling his mind. "You'd better skedaddle."

"Do you need the car?" She rose, grabbed her cup, and raced over to the counter.

"I'm going back to Aiden's tonight, but I can catch a cab easily enough."

"Great." She grabbed her handbag from under the counter, then snagged keys off the hook and wiggled her fingers. "Have fun."

"Later tonight, maybe. Right now, unlikely." My voice was dry.

Her grin flashed, then she was gone. I slid her cake closer and tried to ignore the butterflies stirring in my stomach as I grabbed the spoon and started eating.

But even though I'd been forewarned about Ashworth's arrival, I still jumped when the bell above the door chimed merrily. I turned and watched him and a second man come in. The other man was a tall and middle-aged, with hair such a deep crimson it gleamed purple and eyes so light the silver of his irises was almost indistinguishable from the whites. His power rolled before him like a wave, a force so strong and heated it snatched my breath and had sweat breaking out across my skin.

Thankfully, he wasn't someone I knew.

But he certainly was someone I didn't *want* to know.

"Lizzie Grace," Ashworth said, as he closed the door, "I'd like you to meet Chester Ashworth."

"No relation to Ira," the taller man added. He strode toward me and stuck out his hand. "Pleasure to meet you."

I had no choice but to shake his hand. His energy crawled across my skin, an inferno of magic that tested and tasted mine, causing the charms at my neck to flare in response. Ashworth had done exactly the same thing when we'd first met, but this man's magic felt more invasive. More knowing.

I tugged my hand free and resisted the urge to wipe my palm. "I thought there was a third witch coming in? One that was supposed to be interviewed for the position here?"

"The idiot missed the plane," Chester said. "Got caught in traffic or some such rot."

"Which is not likely to make a good impression," Ashworth added. "The council here is hard to please under the best circumstances."

Despite my uneasiness, I couldn't help smiling. "Oh, I don't know about *that*. I heard you impressed them enough to be offered the position."

"And we all know they only did it because I forced

them to confront their stupidity. It was a matter of expediency rather than common sense."

"Have you two been over to the circle yet?"

"No." Ashworth pulled out a chair and sat down. I had to bite my tongue against the urge to tell him not to get too comfortable. "We're actually waiting for Tala to get back here—she's going to take us across."

I frowned. "You can't remember where it is?"

"It's dark, lassie, and my night sight isn't what it once was." A smile briefly twisted his lips. "What's this I hear about another murder?"

"It's a skinning, and I don't think it's got anything to do with our dark witch."

Chester raised an eyebrow as he sat down opposite. It was a position that brought the force of his magic way too close and had sweat breaking out across my body again. "What makes you say that?"

"The magic didn't feel the same." And *his* magic was stirring—probing—again. Not me, but rather the spells that protected this place. Which was why Ashworth had brought him here, I realized. Despite accepting my statement that I was running from abuse, he'd wanted to see this man's reaction to my spellcraft—and *that* meant it was more important than ever Chester *didn't* see Belle and me together. "Would either of you like something to drink?"

"No, but I wouldn't mind a piece of that cake you're eating." Ashworth glanced at the older man. "She and her partner make the best cakes and slices you've ever tasted."

"A claim I'm more than willing to investigate," Chester said, amusement evident. "And a black coffee would be good."

"As long as you don't mind instant—we've cleaned the machine for the night."

"That's fine," he said. "In what way was the magic different?"

I rose, snagged Belle's book from the spare chair, and headed behind the counter. "It was clean, not dark."

"And you sensed it how?"

I tucked the book safely away and then glanced at him. "I didn't. Not initially. I found the body via my psychometry skills."

I made the coffee and plated up two slices of cake, then put everything on a tray and carried it over. As the two men picked up their plates, I grabbed my mug and leaned a shoulder against the nearby wall. I did *not* want to get closer to the wash of Chester's magic. Why the hell he wasn't controlling his output, I had no idea. Had he been in Canberra, he would have been quickly reprimanded, if not fined.

"And the magic?" he asked.

"Came from a cotton thread that was left on the body. I believe it was part of some sort of tracking charm. The rangers have it, if you want to examine it."

He grunted. "If it's not the same magic then there's no need. I'm here to track a heretic, not chase a minor practitioner with blood on his or her hands."

Which meant our paths probably shouldn't cross too often, and I couldn't be sad about that.

I took a sip of tea and wished it were something stronger. "I don't suppose you have any idea who our practitioner might be?"

"Not without seeing the body, no," Chester said. "Even then, we'll have to confirm with blood and DNA tests, as most erase more identifiable marks such as fingerprints."

I frowned and glanced at Ashworth. "I didn't think the council kept fingerprint records of heretics."

"They don't," he said evenly. "But blood and DNA samples are taken from every full-blooded witch at birth. It's the easiest way to keep track of the bloodlines to avoid inbreeding mishaps."

Which meant all anyone unconvinced by my story would have to do was somehow grab a sample of my DNA —even something as simple as a few strands of hair—and they'd uncover the truth of who I was quickly enough. It was a somewhat scary thought—and one that made me want to race upstairs and hide my hairbrush.

I downed the rest of my tea, but it didn't do a whole lot to ease the dryness in my throat. "Even without that sort of confirmation, you must still have some idea as to who it might be. I mean, how many blueblood heretics are there?"

"At last count?" he mused. "Fifteen, I believe."

I blinked. "Seriously?"

"Yes. But given the overall number of blueblood witches in Canberra, that's actually a very low percentage—the lowest it's been for decades, in fact."

Maybe it was, but it was still fourteen too many for my liking—especially when he was *only* talking about the blue-bloods gone rogue. I daresay there were a whole lot more malcontents running loose from the lower witch houses.

"But given the description Ira has given us," Chester continued, "there are three possibilities. All are rather nasty individuals, but there's one we've been hunting for a very long time. I seriously hope he's *not* the person behind the live spell."

I frowned. "Why?"

"Let's worry about that when and if we identify the body."

In other words, it was none of my damn business. Which it wasn't, but that didn't assuage the need to know.

"Which leads me to a question that's been bugging me—spells generally don't last long past their creator's death, so why aren't the protection circle and the spell within it fading?"

"That is a jolly good question, and one I can't answer until I see the circle and the spell." Chester scooped up a big chunk of cake on his spoon and ate it; bliss immediately crossed his features. "Damn, you're right. This *is* good."

"But there *is* a precedence for spells lasting beyond their creator?" I said.

"Under certain circumstances, yes." Chester glanced up at me. "Why don't you know any of this? It's basic study at the university."

I smiled, but it felt thin. False. "As I'm sure you're already aware, I never went to witch university. Underpowered half-breeds rarely do."

"Indeed, but there's nothing underpowered about the spells that protect this place, even if the witch that produced them is less than impressive."

"Almost as impressive as a statement that's both a compliment and an insult, perhaps?"

He waved his spoon. "Which is not what I intended."

I put my mug down on the nearby table and crossed my arms. They'd undoubtedly see it as a defensive gesture, which was perfectly fine given it damn well was.

"As I've already told Ashworth, I have no idea how the wild magic got entangled within the protection spells. But it came to the aid of the head ranger and me out in the cemetery when we were attacked by a magic-bearing vampire, and I think threads of it must have been lingering when I boosted the spells here afterward."

Chester grunted. "A logical explanation, though it is rare for the wild magic to interfere in such a manner."

"It's also rare for a major wellspring to be left unprotected for well over a year," I bit back. "Given that—from everything I've ever read—it's something that's never happened before, maybe it's forced the wild magic to gain some sort of cognizance in order to protect itself."

"Wild magic is an energy that develops deep in the heart of the earth. There is no way it could ever develop the sort of awareness to self-protect—"

"Except this place has," Ashworth said.

"So you said in your earlier memo," Chester said. "I'd have to see proof of such before I—or anyone else in Canberra—could dare to believe."

I glanced sharply at Ashworth. He grimaced and shrugged. The memo had obviously been sent *before* our discussion about why I didn't want Canberra investigating this place—and us—too deeply.

It also suggested that perhaps I'd been wrong earlier—perhaps Ashworth had been given no choice about bringing Chester here. It might, in fact, have been a directive from Canberra—a means of figuratively killing two birds and discovering whether this reservation and the magic within it, be it wild or witch, deserved deeper investigation.

The doorbell chimed again, and I glanced around to see Tala enter. She didn't look impressed, but I guess that was to be expected given they had two dead bodies in as many days to contend with.

She gave me a nod and then said, "Right, gentlemen, let's go. The council doesn't appreciate too much overtime—it does all manner of nasty things to their budgets."

Her voice was as curt as ever, but there was a slight glimmer in her eyes that suggested amusement.

Chester hastily gulped down his coffee and then rose. "I don't suppose you've a bag...?"

"No cake in the car, I'm afraid," Tala said. "Come along, gentlemen."

Hence her amusement, I thought. I pushed away from the wall, followed the two men across to the door, and locked it behind them.

And sighed in relief, even though I knew full well the danger Canberra represented wasn't really over yet.

I listened to the sound of Tala's SUV pulling away then turned and headed back to the table. After clearing the plates, mugs, and teapot and washing them, I headed upstairs to grab toiletries and fresh clothes for tomorrow. Then I called a cab and headed across to Aiden's.

The key was in a magnetic tin under the base of the outside aircon unit. I grabbed it, opened the door, and then tucked it back in position. Once I'd dumped my bag in his bedroom, I headed back downstairs to investigate his fridge. It was very obvious that a bachelor who ate out a lot lived in this place, because there was damn little in the way of food. Thankfully, there was some cheese that wasn't green despite it being past its "best by" date and a loaf of sliced bread in the freezer. After making myself a toasted cheese and Vegemite sandwich and another cup of tea, I headed across to the sofa and settled in to watch TV and wait.

By the time eleven rolled around, I was barely keeping awake. I dumped my dishes in the sink then trundled upstairs, stripped off, and climbed into his crisp, fresh-smelling sheets. Within minutes, I was asleep.

Only to be woken several hours later not by the softly snoring warm body pressed against my spine, but rather an explosive rush of magic.

Blood magic.

CHAPTER FIVE

I swore and scrambled out of bed.

"What's wrong?" Aiden immediately said, even as he threw the covers aside and began pulling on his jeans.

I hauled on panties then grabbed jeans and a T-shirt out of my overnight bag. "There's been some sort of explosion."

"Magical?"

"Yeah."

"Do you need to go back to the café to get any equipment?"

"I don't think we have the time." I grabbed a sweater then shoved my feet into my runners, thanking the stars I'd packed additional clothes and shoes to cater for the weather turn they were predicting for Christmas Eve. I reached mentally for Belle, but there was no response. That meant she was back home, sleeping in her own bedroom rather than the hotel room we'd rented. And while I could probably break through all the shields that surrounded her room—shields that not only protected her from a magic attack, but also from the constant barrage of my thoughts—it wasn't worth either the time or the energy. Not when there was a much easier method. I grabbed my phone out of my purse and followed Aiden down the stairs. He grabbed his keys and ushered me into his truck.

As he drove out of the complex, I called Belle.

"What the fuck?" came her somewhat groggy answer a few rings later. "Why are you using the damn phone?"

"Because you're in your own bed rather than Zak's or the hotel's."

"Oh. Yeah. Sorry. What's the problem?"

"There's been an explosion of blood magic, and I suspect it might have come from that protective circle we found."

"And you need the backpack?" she said, suddenly sounding less sleepy.

"Yeah, and given I have no idea what we might be dealing with, pack everything."

"Will do." Her voice was grim. "It'll take me a good twenty to twenty-five minutes to get there though, given I have to load the pack."

"It'll probably take us that long," Aiden said, voice grim.

I glanced at him. "You know where we're going?"

"I'm guessing it's where Tala took Ashworth and the new witch to deconstruct the active protective circle." He hesitated, his expression becoming even grimier. "Please don't tell me we've a second—and different—wave of dark magic happening."

"I don't think we do, but I can't entirely be sure as yet." I wound down the window and stuck my hand out. The night air ran across my fingers, its force increasing as Aiden accelerated away from the apartment complex. The dark magic ran through it, but its fierceness was fading.

Aiden turned on the siren once we were on the main

road and we screamed through the night, the red and blue lights washing across the darkness.

The waves of magic continued to diminish, but it was definitely coming from the same area where we'd found the protective circle.

Aiden pulled up beside Tala's truck, and then scrambled out. "Tala! You out there?"

There was no response. Aiden swore, ran around to the back of his truck, and grabbed out his gear and a flashlight. As he slammed the back closed, headlights pinned us. Belle.

She stopped on the other side of the road and then got out and ran across. "Here," she said, shoving the pack at me. "I put in everything I can think of, including a small first aid kit. You want me with you?"

I shook my head. "Better if you remain here, and safe, just in case I need to call on your strength."

While the main task of any familiar was to monitor and protect their witch, they were also a lifeline—a last avenue of strength to draw on if all else had failed. Though it was extremely rare, there *had* been cases where familiars were so completely drained by their witch that death had claimed them. And in the case of spirit familiars, that meant becoming a shade and never being able to either operate in —or communicate with—anyone in the spirit or the living realms again for all eternity. Rather weirdly, that didn't seem to apply to cat familiars, who simply moved on. We had no idea if that would also apply in Belle's case, and I had no intention of ever discovering if it did.

She nodded and crossed her arms. "Be careful. The force of the spell has almost faded, but I wouldn't put it past this bastard to have a second line of defense."

I grabbed Belle's silver knife out of the backpack and then slung the pack over my shoulder. Blue fire flickered briefly down the blade, evidence enough that the lingering spell remnants were indeed dark in origin.

Aiden switched on the flashlight. The sudden brightness had me blinking. "Do you want me to lead the way?"

I hesitated and then shook my head. "Just in case there *is* a secondary line of defense."

He nodded and motioned me on. I took a deep breath and then headed for the trees, carefully following the flashlight-lit path that Ashworth and I had created yesterday. Aiden kept close, his tension so fierce I could almost smell it.

Then, from deeper into the trees, a groggy voice said, "Boss, that you?"

Tala. Aiden's relief was so fierce it washed over me in a wave.

"Yeah. You okay?"

"Think so." She paused briefly then grunted. Getting up, I suspected, even though I couldn't yet see her. "I was standing back in the trees, so only copped the backwash. It was still strong enough to throw me back into a tree though, and knock me unconscious."

"What about our two Ashworths?"

A longer pause this time. "In the clearing, unmoving but whole."

"Dead?"

"Can't tell." She paused. "I can't smell death, though, so that's a good sign."

Up ahead, low-hanging tree branches moved, and then Tala appeared, one hand raised against the brightness of the flashlight. Other than a torn left sleeve and a slight trickle of blood rolling down the right side of her face, she appeared okay.

Aiden immediately lowered the flashlight's beam.

"Head back to the truck and treat that wound. I'll update you once we know what happened."

She nodded and moved past us. Aiden's gaze came to mine. "Is it safe to continue?"

I nodded. "I haven't felt a secondary line of magic as yet."

"Good."

We pressed on until we got to the clearing's edge. This time, there were two unmoving bodies rather than one, but at least neither was missing half their head and brain.

Ashworth was the closest. Though his clothes were singed and there was what looked like a scorch mark across his right cheek, he didn't otherwise look hurt. He was also breathing, which meant he was simply knocked unconscious.

Chester had been thrown clear across the other side of the clearing, and was lying in a crumbled mess at the base of an old eucalyptus.

I studied the clearing for a few seconds longer. Though there were some spell remnants drifting lazily on the soft breeze, they weren't even strong enough to make the protective magic on the knife react. Even so, I asked Aiden to remain where he was and carefully stepped into the clearing. The knife remained inert and the spell remnants didn't react in any way.

I walked across to Ashworth and squatted down beside him. The blade flickered but it was only a faint pulse. I suspected it was reacting to the lingering echoes of the spell that lay on his skin and clothes rather than a secondary line of magic. I switched the knife from my right to my left hand and then carefully felt Ashworth's pulse. It was strong and steady.

"Is he alive?" Aiden asked.

"Yeah. Just knocked out. Have you called the paramedics?"

"Yes—though I'm doubting Ashworth will actually appreciate it."

I grinned. Ashworth could be missing a limb and he'd still no doubt tell them he was okay and to stop damn well fussing. I rose and moved around him. The area where the dark witch's protection circle had been was scorched, the black stones in shattered shards that lay in forlorn pieces all around the clearing. While the magic clinging to them was only faint, I carefully avoided stepping on any of the bits that lay between me and Chester; though I doubted they'd hold anything that would harm me, I had no idea what was and wasn't possible when it came to blood magic, and there was no way known I was going to take any sort of chance.

The scorching on Chester's clothes and skin was far worse, and there were bits of stone embedded also, but he was breathing and I couldn't immediately see any sign of deeper injury. I swept the knife over his body; as had been the case with Ashworth, the blade's reaction was weak. If there was magic here, then it was on a much deeper level than either Belle's or my magic was capable of sensing. I touched his neck; his pulse was a little more erratic than Ashworth's but still very strong.

"Chester's also alive." I pushed upright. "And I can't sense much in the way of secondary magic on either of them."

Aiden walked into the clearing. "I'm gathering Chester is the heretic hunter that's been called in?"

"Yes—and this isn't exactly an auspicious start to his investigation."

"No." Aiden stopped a few feet short of the scorched circle and studied it. "But I guess if the body we have in the morgue is confirmed to be our dark witch, no one else is dead, and whatever spell was here has now been counter-manded, we should consider it a win."

"Let's just hope his spell *has* been countermanded."

Aiden glanced at me sharply. "Meaning what?"

"I don't know." I swung the pack off and tucked the knife safely away. "Something about all this just isn't making sense."

"Like what?"

I waved a hand toward the blackened earth. "Like why would a spell live beyond the life of its creator? As far as I'm aware, it shouldn't. And then there's the whole question of why a dark witch would even *leave* his circle in the first place."

"Maybe he trusted whoever he was with."

"Maybe."

"But you don't think so."

"I don't know what to think. I just know we're missing something."

He grunted. "Given how often those instincts of yours have proven to be right of late, I'm not about to discount them." He waved a hand toward the scorched ground. "What actually happened here?"

"Either the deconstruction didn't go well or, for some weird reason, this explosion is exactly what the dark witch intended."

"I'm thinking it's probably both," Ashworth said.

I spun around. He'd pushed into a sitting position and was rubbing a grimy hand across even grimier features. "Damn if it doesn't feel like I've been hit by a truck."

"You shouldn't move too much—"

"I'm fine," he said sharply. "Stop your fussing."

I hid my smile. Aside from the fact he'd reacted exactly

as I'd figured, he sounded *exactly* like my grandfather in that moment.

Aiden walked over and offered the other man a hand. Ashworth gripped it and was easily hauled up. He brushed away the grit and grime from his clothes and then glanced across at Chester. "He alive?"

"Yes. Just knocked unconscious, same as you," Aiden said. "Can you tell me what happened?"

"The bloody protection circle exploded, that's what happened."

"Yes," Aiden said, very obviously containing his annoyance. "But how?"

Ashworth took a deep breath and released it slowly. "I'm not exactly sure. Everything seemed to be going fine and then boom."

"Did Chester say what sort of spell it was?"

"A multilayered one reinforced with blood." He glanced at the burned earth and grimaced. "Whose blood is a question that needed answering, but I'm guessing it won't be easy to get a sample now."

"That depends on how deeply the blood soaked into the ground and how far down the earth was burned," Aiden replied. "Did you uncover anything about the witch behind the magic?"

"Some," Chester said, voice hoarse and edged with pain. He started sitting up but grabbed at the arm he'd been lying on and cursed loudly. The arm wasn't broken. There was a knife-like shard of quartz imbedded in it.

As he reached across, obviously intending to rip it out, I yelled, "Don't!"

I swung my pack off my shoulder and hurried over.

He raised an eyebrow. "Why on earth not?"

I snorted. "Don't they teach you first aid up in Canberra?"

"Yes, but—"

"But nothing." I dug the first aid kit out of the pack and quickly unzipped it. "Until the paramedics get here and can assure you there's been no major blood vessels sliced by that thing, we keep that shard immobilized and in your arm. It might just be the only thing standing between you and bleeding to death."

"And all the other little bits?" His voice was dry. "Surely I can take them out?"

I hesitated, and then nodded. There might have been plenty of those other bits embedded into his clothes but very few of them seemed to be digging into his skin.

As I began to wrap a bandage around the quartz to hold it in place, Aiden said, "Are you able to explain what happened here?"

Chester snorted. "Yeah, the bastard who made the protection circle was cannier than I expected."

"Meaning what?" Aiden asked.

"Meaning that while the protection spell placed on the stones initially seemed simple enough—strong, but simple— there were several sub-layers woven into it that got more and more complicated. I caught three. I saw the last one too late."

"What sorts of spells were layered in?" I finished tying up the bandage and then repacked the kit in the pack.

He shrugged. "They were basically trip-spells of growing complexity, and are usually meant to test rather than hurt."

"Except for the last one," Ashworth said. "If you hadn't

have sensed it at the last moment, both of us might well be dead."

"I'm not so sure on that," Chester said. "If it had truly been meant to kill, I think we'd both now be dead."

I sat back on my heels. "Then what do you think was intended?"

"That is a damn good question, and probably one I won't be able to answer until I see the body of our practitioner in the morgue."

Meaning he did have a theory but wasn't willing to share it just yet.

"Were you able to tell anything at all about the witch from his magic?" Aiden asked.

"His magic is strong and dark, and it's not one I've encountered before. It at least means it's not Frankel Kang, who's the number-one most wanted on our heretic hit list."

"Which sounds like a good thing, but probably isn't," I muttered.

He glanced at me. "And you'd be right. Two and three are also pretty nasty pieces of work."

"They're dark witches," Ashworth commented. "That comes with the territory."

"Indeed it does." Chester held out his hand. "Help me up, young woman."

"I don't really think you should—"

"Hogwash," he said. "Besides, I'm no fool. If I thought for a second there was any internal damage, I'd be waiting for the paramedics as you were no doubt about to suggest."

It wasn't like he'd actually know if there was internal damage, as sometimes these things simply didn't give you any sign. But I didn't bother arguing, just rose and clasped Chester's hand. His magic curled around my fingers as easily as his hand, but it was little more than a faint splutter of energy. Deconstructing the spell really *had* weakened him and that had unease treading lightly through my soul. If this witch was stronger than Chester we were in deep trouble....

I frowned at the thought. The witch was dead, so why the hell were my instincts twitching?

I didn't know.

And to be honest, I really, *really* didn't want to know.

"So how strong was our dead witch?" Aiden asked.

"He was fairly high up on the power scale," Chester said heavily. "Which means it's probably just as well he was betrayed by those who'd employed him. The stronger the witch, the deeper his connection to the dark energies and spirits of this world, and the harder it is to track and kill them."

"Is that why Frankel Kang is still on the loose?" I asked mildly. "Because he escaped your noose?"

Chester glanced at me sharply. "You don't miss much, do you?"

I half smiled. "I'm a psychic who's very good at reading people."

"Oh, I think you're a hell of a lot more than that." He released my hand and walked across to the scorched circle. "Whatever the actual intent of the magic here, it's been fragmented and destroyed. The area is quite safe if you wish to bring people in."

Aiden nodded. "Do you think it possible he's left other such traps around the reservation?"

"Right now, anything is possible, given we have no real idea what his intention was."

The sharp sound of an approaching siren bit across the night—the ambulance and paramedics were arriving. We escorted the two men back through the trees.

Belle was waiting inside our old wagon. Tala leaned against her truck, her arms crossed and weariness evident in both her expression and the way she was standing. There was a fresh Band-Aid across her forehead and yellow smears I suspected were antiseptic across several other scratches on her cheek and her arms.

The ambulance pulled to a halt beside the trucks and two paramedics hopped out. Ashworth was cleared, but Chester—despite his protests—was placed in the back of the ambulance and whisked away so that the shard in his arm could be scanned before it was removed.

"I'll check the hospital for Chester's condition in the morning," Ashworth said. "But it's likely he won't be released until at least midmorning, and that means we won't be able to check and ID the body until the afternoon."

Aiden nodded. "We're running an outside facial recognition check on the off chance we can find a match."

Ashworth snorted and moved toward his truck. Despite his claims to the contrary, he was now limping and his aura swirled with a mustardy color, signaling pain. "I wish you luck, Ranger, but I personally doubt you'll get anything given he's missing half his face *and* he's a dark witch. Concealment is part of the whole game of survival for those bastards, and they're very damn good at it."

"It still doesn't hurt to check," Aiden said mildly.

"I take it from that the witch's fingerprints had indeed been removed?" I asked, as Ashworth climbed into his truck then reversed and left.

"Yeah, and some time ago given the skin had healed over." He glanced past me. "Tala, go home."

"But what about taping off—"

"I'll do it. You go home and get some rest."

She nodded and climbed into her vehicle. Aiden's gaze

returned to mine. "You're welcome to go back to my place—"

"No," I said, before he could finish. "I'll go home. I think we both could use the sleep."

He smiled then stepped forward and kissed me—gently but passionately. "I'll talk to you tomorrow, then."

I nodded and walked across to the wagon. By the time I'd climbed in and buckled up, he'd disappeared into the forest.

"So," Belle said, once we were back on the main road and heading toward Castle Rock. "Do you think this is all over?"

A tired smile touched my lips. "What do you think?"

"I think your trouble antenna is twitching."

"And you'd be right." I wrinkled my nose. "This whole thing is stinking higher than sour milk."

"Did Aiden say anything about the body? Or the motorbike we heard?"

"I really haven't had a chance to question him." I shifted to study her. "So, you and Zak? On or off?"

"Officially off. He does indeed fancy one of the newcomers and wants to be free to pursue her during the Christmas celebrations." She glanced at me. "Apparently, the three packs come together tonight for a two-day celebration that not only involves lots of drinking and sex, but is also a time during which new relationships are started and old ones formalized."

"Meaning I have to hope Aiden *doesn't* find a nice little wolf to play with. Not this Christmas, anyway."

"You've barely even explored that man's goods, and you're already worrying about when he's going to leave?"

I whacked her arm lightly. "You know what I mean. You

are, after all, the one who goes on and on about my habit of picking short-term losers."

"Yeah, but Aiden's not one of them. I think the fates have finally taken pity on your relationship woes and given you a nice break."

"Hopefully a *longish* break given the amount of cobwebs that have gathered."

"You're fully capable of self-service, so don't be whining about no cobwebs." The glance she cast my way was stern, but it was somewhat spoiled by the amusement dancing in her eyes. "Besides, given the fact half the town was betting on when you two would finally get together, it's a pretty safe to say he *didn't* indulge last Christmas."

"Which doesn't mean he can't and won't this year."

"True." She pursed her lips. "I can't see it though."

I hoped she was right, but I wasn't betting my heart on it. It didn't take us long to get back to the café. Belle parked the car around the back and we entered via the rarely used back door. The Christmas lights twinkled brightly, washing color through the dark room, and the air was thick with the scent of apple and cinnamon. Belle had obviously been baking again before she'd gone to bed—a sign that, despite her fortitude, she was going to miss Zak.

We ducked under the plastic and headed upstairs to our separate bedrooms. The builders had worked their butts off and the roof was once again intact. There was still a heap of plastering and painting to do, but at least we were weatherproof and could once again start sleeping here.

I stripped off, climbed into bed, and was pretty much asleep as soon as my head hit the pillow. But it wasn't dreamless; instead, it was filled with portents of doom—of power seeking power, fancy black teapots with legs dancing to the tune of magic, and wolves running through forests, shedding blood and skin as they howled in pain to the moon.

I woke with a start, a soft cry of denial dying on my lips. My heart was racing and my limbs twitched as if trying to run with those wolves. To help them, even though that wasn't possible.

I threw off the sheet and swung my feet out of bed. Magpies were chorusing outside and the hall was filled with light, so dawn had obviously come and gone. I grabbed my phone to check the time: six forty-five. Which, despite the fuzzy need for more sleep, was in reality only fifteen minutes earlier than my usual wake-up time.

I grabbed a T-shirt long enough to cover my butt and hauled it on as I headed down the stairs to make breakfast. Bright sunlight streamed in through the windows, warming the room and holding the promise of another hot day. I flicked on the coffee machine and aircon, and then walked over and lowered all the blinds. The Christmas lights we'd left on last night instantly brightened, sending flashes of color spinning throughout the room. Which was just as well, because I doubted our customers were going to get much in the way brightness out of me today.

Belle stumbled down the stairs just as I was plating up bacon and eggs for our breakfast. "I'd say good morning, but given the bags under your eyes and the unhappy vibes I'm getting, I'm gathering you didn't have a good night."

"No."

I grabbed knives and forks and then carried our plates over to a table. Belle made us each a cappuccino and then joined me.

"Did you dream about anything in particular, or was it just the usual nonsensical mess?"

I gave her a brief rundown as I started in on my food.

"That whole power thing suggests that even if the dark witch is dead, he hasn't finished with this reservation yet."

"Chester did say last night that it was possible he's set other traps." I swished some bacon around in the yolk and added, "Except that really doesn't makes much sense given my dreams suggest it's power *seeking* power."

"But maybe it simply means that power is seeking to *kill* power rather than control it—that explosion almost took out both of them, remember."

I wrinkled my nose. "I guess that's possible."

"But you don't think so?"

I hesitated. "I really can't say."

She snorted softly. "And you bitch about my spirit guides being obtuse."

I grinned. "We'll they are."

"Twenty-four hours," she said mildly. "That's how long you managed without taking a swipe at them."

"If I went any longer they'd keel over in shock."

She paused, obviously listening to the incoming comments from the other side. "They said while that might well be the case, they are more than prepared to risk such an event."

I snorted. "It's good to see they remain in such fine form."

"They like this place. They're hoping we don't have to move."

"They could put in a good word to the fates for us. You know, do a little wrangling and divert any possibility of us having to leave happening."

Belle gave me the look—the one that said, "don't be daft." "That sort of stuff happens in kids' books, not real life."

"It still can't hurt putting it out there. Maybe someone

will actually listen." I finished my breakfast then picked up my coffee and nursed the mug between my hands. "The dancing teapots obviously have something to do with the witch who gave our skinned shifter the charm, given I saw the same sort of thing when I was doing the reading on that bloody thread."

"Have you googled black teapots? It might actually be the name of the shop."

"Of course I haven't—and when has anything been that simple?"

She smiled, grabbed both plates, and then rose. "Never, but that doesn't mean things can't change."

She disappeared into the kitchen to dump the plates then grabbed her phone and came back to the table. After a few minutes, she wrinkled her nose and said, "Well, you were right. It's not that simple."

"Try the dancing teapot instead."

She typed that in and then shook her head. "It's got to be some sort of clue, though, however cryptic. Your dreams might generally be ambiguous, but they usually do hold some grains of truth."

Usually being the telling word there. I drank more coffee. "Ashworth might have more luck finding her. I did get a vague impression of the witch from the thread we found on the first victim—enough to give him a general description, anyway."

"It's certainly worth a shot." She downed her coffee and then rose. "I'll grab first shower."

I followed her upstairs and googled a bit more for any witch shops that related in any vague way to teapots. Again, there was nothing.

Once I'd showered, I headed downstairs to help Belle do the day's prep. We opened at nine and were super busy all day—a good thing given it kept me thinking about Aiden and what he might do over the next couple of days. Or, rather, what I *wouldn't* be doing.

We closed at three, gave our staff a bottle of champagne as a thank you, and let them leave early. It was close to six by the time Belle and I had finished clearing and cleaning. Belle grabbed a couple of glasses and another bottle of champagne while I washed the strawberries then followed her across to a table.

She popped the cork and filled the glasses. I dropped a couple of strawberries in each, and then picked one up. "Merry Christmas, my friend. May the goddess continue to bless our lives—"

"With health and happiness." She touched her glass against mine. "So, are we soloing tonight or going out together? Because I discovered Émigré is open all night despite the fact it's Christmas Eve."

Émigré was an extremely popular, alien-themed night-club that had recently opened within the reservation, and one that was owned and run Maelle Defour—a very old, very powerful vampire. While the council was well aware of her presence, Aiden and his rangers were not. Maelle was currently in our debt thanks to the fact that we'd tracked down the people responsible for murdering several of her "feeders"—the men and women who supplied her with both blood and sex in return for a very luxurious lifestyle.

Those killers were now dead. While Maelle had kept her promise to the council not to cause any harm within the reservation, both Molly Brown and her brother had disappeared while being transported down to Melbourne for trial.

I had no idea how Maelle had arranged that; I only knew Molly's and Jack's deaths would have been agony itself. It was never a good idea to double-cross a vampire, but Maelle Defour wasn't any old vampire. In addition to her age and power, she was also one hell of a scary bitch who walked the edge between remaining human and becoming something else.

None of which would stop us from going to her establishment, if only because there really wasn't anything else like it in Castle Rock. Or, in fact, the entire reservation.

I took a drink and then said, "I'm guessing your vote lies with Émigré?"

"Indeed. I'm feeling the need to rub shoulders with a hot man or two."

"Sounds like a plan to me."

Surprise ran across her expression. "I was expecting at least a moment of hesitation."

"Why?" I asked mildly. "If he's going to enjoy two and a half nights of alcohol and sex, I can't see why I shouldn't have a little fun."

"You say that, and yet your thoughts seethe at the thought of him getting it on with another."

"I figure enough alcohol will more than drown them out." I grinned. "Which is *not* saying I'm about to fall into the arms of the nearest good-looking male and shag him senseless. But I don't want Aiden thinking I'm willing to hang about and wait, either."

"Even though you *did* wait ages for the man to ask you out."

"*That* is beside the point."

She snorted but any reply she might have made was cut off as my phone rang. The tone told me it was Aiden. I jumped up and ran behind the counter to grab it.

Belle filled up her glass then said, "I'll head upstairs to get ready, and leave you to chat to the man in peace."

I nodded then hit the answer button. "Hey, how was your day?"

"Long," he replied. "And about to get longer."

I frowned at the edge in his voice. "Shouldn't you be finished work by now?"

"I'm head ranger—the job technically never finishes. Especially when there's bad news to be delivered."

I hesitated, and then said, "I take it you've identified the skinning victim?"

"Yeah—Jamison O'Connor. He was barely twenty."

"I'm sorry, Aiden." I paused again. "Did you know him well?"

"Not well, given the age gap, but he was a good friend of Michael's."

Michael being one of his younger brothers. "Had anyone reported him missing?"

"No. But we found his car parked in Byrne's Road—one of the many small tracks that run along the edges of our compound. His clothes, wallet, and shoes were all neatly stacked on the front seat."

I frowned. Werewolves didn't actually need to strip off when they changed. While their shape shifting ability was a DNA adaption, there was still magic in their souls—magic that not only hid the shift from one form to another, but somehow also took care of whatever items they might be wearing or carrying. "Why would he do that?"

"We have no idea. And given the fact he took the time to fold his clothes, it's not likely he was under any sort of duress at the time."

No, but he could have been under some sort of spell. Just because I hadn't sensed anything other than tracking magic on that thread didn't mean the bracelet, as a whole, couldn't have been entwined with multiple magics. They were easy enough to do—all you needed was to place each spell on a different piece of twine or ribbon, and then weave them all together.

"It could be worth getting Ashworth to have a look at both his car and his personal items before you hand them back to his parents. There might be enough magical residue left behind for him to get some idea of the witch who made the charm." Or, at the very least, what sort of spell was being used.

"Once we've finished going over the car, we will." He took a deep breath and released it slowly. "Confronting parents with this sort of news would have to be the hardest damn part of my job."

"Especially on Christmas Eve, and the start of a major celebration for all three packs."

"Yes." He paused. "Speaking of which—"

"I shouldn't expect to see you for the next couple of days," I replied. "I know."

"It's a tradition, and, as the firstborn child of one of the packs' alphas, I'm expected—"

"Aiden, you don't have to explain anything to me. We're both free agents, and you certainly *don't* owe me anything." The words came out surprisingly even considering how much my stomach was suddenly twisting.

There was a rather lengthy pause. "Right."

I suddenly wished we were doing this face-to-face rather than over the phone. Wished I could get a feel for what he was thinking and feeling.

"What are you and Belle planning to do over the next couple of days?"

"Probably just rest up after partying tonight. We're heading over to Émigré to dance the night away." I hesitated, waiting once again for a reaction. The silence stretched for several seconds before I added, "Did Chester and Ashworth make it to the morgue this afternoon to identify the witch's body?"

"Yes." His voice once again held the hint of an edge. I wasn't entirely sure whether it was aimed at the two witches or at me, and that was frustrating. "Chester believes our corpse is Jonathan Ashworth, who went rogue when he was nineteen, which was some thirty-five years ago. He's asked Ciara to send DNA and blood samples to Canberra for confirmation."

"I take it Jonathan is on their most wanted list?"

"Yes, but not in the top ten, as far as I can ascertain. Chester is playing his cards pretty close."

Chester, I suspected, didn't want to make any more mistakes. Missing that last spell and almost getting himself and Ashworth killed would have been something of an embarrassment—and blueblood witches didn't do embarrassment at all well. "Did he have any theories as to why our dead witch stepped out of a fully functioning protection circle and allowed himself to be shot?"

"He undoubtedly has them, but he's not as yet sharing those, either."

"So the investigation is on hold until we get confirmation as to who the dead witch is?"

"Basically, yes." He paused. "Enjoy your night out, Liz, and Happy Christmas."

"You too, Aiden. I'll see you in a couple of days."

"Yes, you will."

And with that, he hung up. I blew out a frustrated breath, cursed my errant hormones for setting their sights on a damn wolf, and then headed upstairs to get ready.

Émigré itself was surprisingly packed. The music was

loud, the alcohol cheap, and there were plenty of men and women as intent on having a good time as we were.

To say we spent the remainder of the night partying hard would be something of an understatement. We didn't often get a chance to blow off steam—for a good portion of the last twelve years we'd alternated between working in cafés and running them. With the weekend work and the long hours, it had basically put paid to most of our out-of-hours activities.

Dawn was sending tentative wisps of pink and yellow across the sky by the time we left. We caught a cab back to the café and staggered across to the door, our shoes in our hands and an arm slung around each other as we happily sang a Christmas carol at the tops of our voices. Thankfully, we were in no danger of disturbing anyone, as this area of Castle Rock was basically retail.

It took me three goes to get the key in the lock, despite the fact I'd stopped drinking alcohol several hours ago. But as I pushed the door open, energy stirred around me. Wild magic, filled with anxious urgency.

I swore, a sound swiftly echoed by Belle.

"Seriously, could you not give us Christmas Day?"

She was talking to the wild magic rather than me. The energy stirred again, more urgently this time. I tossed my shoes inside and thrust a hand through my somewhat sweaty hair. Neither of us were in a fit state to drive, and I really didn't want to call Aiden.

"Ashworth," Belle suggested. "He knows about the wild magic and unless he's a solo partier—and I don't believe he is—he should be sober. Plus, he's aware of your link with the wild magic and Chester isn't—beyond what he's sensed in the magic protecting this place, at any rate."

"Unless Ashworth has mentioned it."

"I don't think he would."

I grunted and grabbed my phone out of my purse. The phone rang seven or eight times before a gruff, grumpy voice said, "Do you have any idea what time of the fucking morning it is?"

"Yes, I do. But the wild magic apparently doesn't care about such things."

"What?" Ashworth's tone was suddenly more alert. "What do you mean?"

"I mean it's here and it wants me to follow it, but I can't drive because I've had far too much—"

"I get the picture," he cut in. "Be there in ten."

I hung up. Belle was behind the counter, filling up the kettle we kept under the bench for those times we couldn't be bothered turning on the machine to make ourselves a coffee.

"You go upstairs and change. I'll do a detox brew."

I snorted. "It's going to take more than one brew to get the alcohol out of my system."

"Yes, but I'll add clarity herbs, which will at least help the brain power. Go."

I gripped the handrail and quickly hauled my butt upstairs. Jeans, a T-shirt, and sneakers were quickly thrown on, but the pulsing energy of the wild magic was becoming more desperate.

I stumbled back down the stairs. Belle handed me a cup of coffee that smelled faintly of licorice—a herb often used to boost energy levels—and the backpack. She was carrying a second cup—one that smelled like straight coffee.

The sunrise had gathered strength in our brief time inside, but her golden flags were now tinged with a bloody red and I seriously hoped it wasn't an omen of what we were about to find.

Ashworth's old truck came roaring around the corner and slid to stop in front of our café. Belle opened the passenger door, handing Ashworth his coffee before stepping aside to let me in.

"Keep in contact," she said. "And be careful."

"Always."

She slammed the door shut and then stepped back. I shoved my coffee mug into the center console's cup holder and pulled on the seat belt.

"Where to?" Ashworth's voice was only a little less gruff than before. He'd pulled on old track pants and weather-beaten runners, but he was still wearing what looked to be a pajama top.

I hesitated as the wild magic gathered around me. It was so damn thick I could barely breathe, but while it held a sense of awareness and purpose thanks to the woman whose spirit now controlled it, there was no clear sense direction coming from her. Unless....

I glanced at Ashworth. "The only way I'm going to get a clear sense of direction is if I make direct contact with the wild magic."

He frowned. "I know the magic in this place has an odd sort of cognizance, but I wouldn't have thought it was capable of any sort of communication—"

"Technically, it's not. I'm going to draw it into my body, and let it guide me that way."

His frown deepened. "That's damn dangerous—"

"Yeah, but I've done it before, and it's the only way we're going to get to whatever it is it's trying to show us."

He studied me through narrowed eyes for a second and then nodded. "Do it."

Belle, can you monitor me? If things get dangerous, pull me out. While I'd certainly drawn the wild magic into my body before, I'd never consciously given it any sort of control, even though I'd briefly shared Katie's senses when she was helping me hunt down the man who'd bombed our café. I doubted she, in any way, would want to cause me harm, but there was nevertheless always a risk inviting another into your body.

But no spirit or power, no matter how strong, could ever break the bond between Belle and me. We knew *that* from experience.

Will do.

I took a deep breath in an attempt to ease the gathering tension, and then closed my eyes and reached out for the wild magic that sat thick and heavy all around me. *Come to me.*

She did. Swiftly, and with such force that for a moment it felt as if it would tear me apart. The wild magic was a white-hot energy that thrummed through my muscles and veins, and everything around me suddenly seemed brighter —sharper. I could smell the somewhat stale pine remnants of Ashworth's aftershave, hear the steady pounding of his heart, and feel the caress of the aircon on my skin as sharply as a gale. Katie's natural werewolf capabilities were once again sharpening mine, despite the fact she was little more than a soul within energy.

But that soul gave me a clear path to follow. And then she fled.

It still left me weak and shuddering. I took a deep breath that did little to help, and said, "Head for Luna."

He threw the truck into gear and immediately took off. I picked up my coffee cup and tried to ignore the fact my hands were shaking so badly little waves of dark brown were washing up through the drinking hole. I sipped the waves away; the coffee was strong and tart, tasting of licorice and a multitude of other herbs I couldn't name. But at least it was drinkable, and that was a vast improvement over many of Belle's brews. It didn't immediately ease the ache behind my eyes, but it did at least help calm the somewhat scattered pounding of my pulse.

Once Ashworth was on the highway out of Castle Rock, he gave me a long, somewhat wary look. "What is it between you and the wild magic? Most of us can sense it, but I've never witnessed the sort of interaction you've got with it—not without disastrous consequences, anyway."

I knew all about those consequences—my mother, despite the fact she was one of a handful of the most powerful witches in Canberra, had almost died the one and only time she'd tried to redirect wild magic. Or so I'd been told—I hadn't actually been born at the time.

"I honestly don't know why this connection has formed. It's not like it should, given I'm not even a highly powered witch."

He grunted but didn't say anything, undoubtedly because we'd been over this ground more than once before, and I couldn't in any way provide the answers he was seeking.

Besides, if there *had* been more to my powers, it surely would have been picked up sometime over the sixteen years I'd been in Canberra. It hadn't, simply because there *was* nothing more to me. Nothing other than a merging between my powers and Belle's—and that seemed to have happened after we'd run.

"Did the magic give you any idea what we're going to find at Luna?"

"No. Just that we need to get there quickly."

He grunted. "Luna's a reservation border town—I wonder if that's got anything to do with it?"

"I don't know." I hesitated. "But the body of the skinned wolf we found was right on another border, so it's possible."

He glanced at me again. "How did you find that wolf? Aiden wasn't exactly forthcoming with details."

I snorted. "And this surprises you why?"

He grunted, a sound that weirdly held an edge of amusement. "Our head ranger is a closed-mouth bastard at the best of times, but given he'd wanted us to examine a thread he'd found on the body, I would have expected a little more cooperation."

If he'd thought that, he still hadn't gotten the measure of Aiden and his rangers. "And were you able to sense any remaining spell remnants on that thread?"

"No." He glanced at me. "Did you?"

I shrugged. "If felt like a simple tracker."

"But you don't think it was?"

"That wolf stripped down naked and left all his possessions in his car. That's not normal behavior."

"No," Ashworth agreed. "It's the behavior of someone likely spelled."

I studied the road ahead, trying to match the images I'd received from Katie with the brightening landscape. "Turn right at the next road, and then a sharp left. It's a back road to Luna."

He obeyed. As the truck slewed sideways and dust flew high, he said, "How did you find that wolf, then? Psychometry works with possessions that hold a person's resonance, but his were all neatly stacked in the car—all of which were found *after* his body—so you couldn't have used them track him."

I hesitated. While I had no intention of telling him about Gabe's wellspring or the spell that had infused Katie's spirit into the wild magic and made her the guardian of this place, there was little point in lying about how that watch had come to be in my possession. "The wild magic gave me the watch."

His head snapped around so fast it was a wonder he didn't break something. "Wild magic *can't* physically interact with anything in this world. Not without the direct interaction or command from a witch."

"Until I came to this place, I certainly believed that."

"I'd be calling anyone else a liar, but having witnessed your interaction with the wild magic—" His voice trailed off and he shook his head. "I've never seen or heard of anything like this happening before. And if you think you'll be able keep it a secret for very long, lassie, you're seriously mistaken."

"Have you mentioned it to your superiors?"

"Yes and no." He grimaced. "I mentioned in my report on the soul stealer murders that there appeared to an odd level of awareness in the unguarded magic of this place."

"It's not unguarded now."

"Yeah, but while the mix of my magic and yours magic will protect it for now—"

"I seriously doubt my magic will stop anyone for longer than a second or two," I cut in, amused.

"Perhaps not, but don't put all your hopes in mine holding out too long against a blueblood witch in the full bloom of his or her magical strength."

My pulse rate leapt into a higher gear. "And a dark witch?"

His expression was grim. "Even less likely."

"Meaning it's just as well our dark witch is dead."

"If he *is* dead."

That uneasiness I'd felt earlier sprang back into being full force. "You don't think he is?"

"Oh, there's no doubt the witch on the slab is dead. The question that needs to be asked is, does that body belong to our dark witch or is it someone else?"

"Why would you think it's someone else?"

He shrugged. "It's nothing more than a gut feeling that none of this is what it seems."

I frowned. "What do you know about Jonathan?"

"Very little—we were at the uni the same time but I was a few years ahead of him. I only remember the name because of the hullabaloo that happened when he went bad."

"So he'd be what? Fifty or so?" I knew Ashworth was in his midfifties. "I didn't really spend a whole lot of time looking at his face, but I did get the impression he was far older than that."

"That's because dark magic prematurely ages a body."

"If that *isn't* Jonathan lying in the morgue, who do you think it is?"

"That is the million-dollar question." Ashworth's expression was grim. "But believe me, lassie, it's un-fucking-likely this has all ended."

Amusement ran through me. My grandfather used to say the same damn thing. If not for the fact Ashworth would have been born well before my grandfather had died, I would have suspected a soul rebirth. "Does Chester have the same sort of doubts?"

"Who knows? That bastard is as closed-mouthed as your ranger."

My lips twitched. I'd thought the two men were getting along, but that very obviously was not the case.

I glanced ahead again. At the top of a slow rise in the road, was a car. A parked car.

The wild magic stirred, its message clear.

Whatever I was meant to find, it was in that vehicle.

"Slow down," I said.

Ashworth instantly did. "The vehicle ahead the target?"

"Yes. I'm getting no indication as to why, though."

"I'm guessing it's not going to be something good, lassie."

That was certainly a given. Once he'd parked a little back from the car—an old blue Holden sedan that had certainly seen better days—I climbed out. The wild magic continued to stir around me, but its urgency was once again increasing. This car might have been our first stopping point, but we were here to find far more. Ashworth grabbed his kit out of the car then caught up with me. "There's magic here, but it's not strong."

"I'm not feeling anything other than the wild magic."

"Maybe it's dulling your senses to anything else."

"And maybe my senses aren't strong enough to pick up anything else. Underpowered witch, remember?"

He snorted and ran his hands just above the flanks of the car. I crossed my arms and watched from a safe distance. If he triggered something, I wanted room to run.

"There's no spell attached to the vehicle, and no one inside." He peered in the driver-side window and swore softly. "There is, however, a neat pile of clothes and personal items sitting on the front seat."

"Meaning we've got another possible skinning victim."

"Yes." He opened the door, reached in, and then tossed me what looked to be a gold chain.

It had barely touched my fingers when I felt the heart-beat within the metal and the growing sense of the wolf's confusion and fear. I glanced back to Ashworth. "He's still alive."

"Then let's try and keep it that way—where is he?"

I carefully unlocked my psychometry skill and was almost overwhelmed at the rush of information. *Why is this happening? Why can I not stop? Why am I running, just running, while they hunt? Sweat, heat, oh God, pain in my chest. The burn of silver, thick, languidly in my limbs, falling, falling... the scent of anticipation as the hunters draw close....*

I hastily threw up a mental wall to block his emotions while still getting some sense of place, and glanced across the road. The paddock to our right rose sharply, and I couldn't see if anyone or anything lay on the crest of the hill thanks to fact the sun was just rising over the top of it. To the left, the ground swept gently down before rising again in the distance. Our wolf had gone right, not left.

"He's up there somewhere." I pointed to the hill.

"Right," Ashworth said. "Get back into the truck. I saw a farm gate just down the road—we can get into the paddock from there."

Ashworth spun his truck around, raced back down the hill, and then wrenched the wheel sideways. Tires squealed as the big vehicle skidded and then surged through the already open gate. The long, yellowed grass had been freshly mowed down; we weren't the first vehicle to come crashing through this paddock.

The chain's heartbeat was becoming more erratic; the wolf was in a world of pain and fading fast. "Drive to the left shoulder of the hill," I said, "and hurry."

Ashworth didn't reply and the big truck didn't go any faster. We were already at full speed.

Then the heartbeat in the chain came to a stuttering stop.

"Damn it, no!"

The truck became airborne as we all but launched over

the top of the hill. Below us, at the base of a long slope, was a truck. Two men stood in the back; one was holding what I presumed was a rifle, though I couldn't actually be sure from this distance.

Twenty or so yards in front of them was the prone, unmoving figure of our wolf.

The two men standing in the back swung around as we crashed back to the ground on the other side of the hill. One punched the top of the truck; the other raised the rifle.

In between one heartbeat and the next, three things happened.

Ashworth wrenched the wheel sideways, the windshield shattered into a myriad of pieces, and the big truck slewed sideways.

Then, in what almost seemed like slow motion, it toppled and began to roll down the hill.

CHAPTER SIX

"Lizzie, wake up."

The voice was filled with gruff urgency. I groaned, but couldn't immediately do anything more. Nor could I force my eyes open—something appeared to be gluing them together.

Lizzie, wake up.

This time, the voice whispered through my brain, but it was no less urgent.

What happened?

I had no idea if I said that out loud, but it was Belle who answered, not Ashworth.

From the few bits I got before you were knocked out, the damn truck rolled. Now open your eyes and assess the damage.

I raised a hand and rubbed at the stickiness gluing my eyelids shut. It was blood, I realized. I quickly felt the rest of my face for injuries, and discovered a long but somewhat shallow cut on my chin—undoubtedly a result of the truck's windscreen exploding. But aside from a sore neck, a bruised chest, and a myriad of other minor glass cuts, I seemed to have escaped relatively intact.

But my seat belt was pressed so tightly against my neck and chest that I could barely breathe, and I was the wrong way up in the truck—my head was hanging in midair, and the blood from the cut on my chin was trickling toward my hairline rather than down my neck.

The truck's engine had been silenced and, considering the amount of damage it must have sustained in the rollover, there were very few creaks and groans.

What I *could* smell was gas....

While it was unlikely the tank had ruptured, if a gas line had split and was now leaking, there was a chance—a very small chance, granted—that the hot exhaust could start a fire. Not so much a vehicle fire but rather a grass one. We were in the middle of summer, in a field that was filled with long, dry grass; major bush fires had certainly been started by far less over the years.

Energy surged into my system, its source external. Belle, refueling me from afar. *Now,* she said, her mental tone sharp, *stop fucking about and get the hell out of that truck.*

On it. I looked across at Ashworth. His face was a mess of small cuts and smears of blood, and his expression was pinched with pain. Then I saw why—his right arm was so badly broken that I could see a bloody shard of bone.

How in the hell was I going to get him out without causing more damage?

He obviously guessed my thoughts, because he said, "Lass, let me worry about the arm."

"But—"

"Ignore it," he growled. "My seat belt is jammed so you'll need to cut me out. And you'll need to do so before that gas catches or the bastards gather their courage and come back to finish us off."

It was a thought that had adrenaline surging. I stretched a hand over my head, shoved my backpack out of the way, and spread my fingers against the roof to brace myself. I hit the seat belt release and crumbled down, then shoved the door open, grabbed my pack, and scrambled out. The truck had come to rest upside down at the base of the hill; a quick look up revealed a trail of truck bits, flattened grass, and barely missed rock outcrops, all of which told the story of just how lucky we'd actually been. The surrounding area was still and quiet—there was no sound of approaching vehicles, either on the road or in our field. The hunters, it seemed, had fled.

But we weren't alone. Lying on a flat stretch of ground not far away from Ashworth's truck was the wolf.

Why would the hunter leave their prey behind when it would have only taken minutes—if that—to throw the body into the back of their truck?

It didn't make any sense.

How about you take care of the living before you start worrying about the idiots behind these kills? Belle commented. *I've already called the ambulance—you want me to call the rangers?*

I'll do it. I ran around to the driver side of the vehicle and, after a number of tugs, forced the crumpled door open. Sweat mingled with blood on Ashworth's face now, and his eyes were little more than narrow slits of bright silver. But his lips were moving and magic stirred, briefly caressing my skin even as it tightened around Ashworth's body. Or, more specifically, his arm. He was immobilizing it magically.

He tied off the spell and then glanced at me. "Right—cut the damn belt."

I swung my pack around, grabbed the knife, and quickly sawed through the belt's webbing. He fell awkwardly and jarred his arm. His curses flowed thick and fast, but he nevertheless twisted around and pushed his way out. I helped him up and then, with his good arm wrapped around my shoulders for support, we walked away from the truck.

Once we were a safe distance away, I lowered him onto the ground and then grabbed my phone out of the pack and called the ranger station. I had no idea who was on call over the next few days, but the stubborn—Belle might have said unreasonable—part of my soul didn't want to call Aiden direct.

Several clicks ran down the line and then an all-too-familiar voice said, "Ranger Aiden O'Connor speaking—what's your emergency?"

"Ashworth's truck rolled, and our hunters have claimed another prize."

"*Lizzie?* Are you okay?"

My heart warmed a little at the urgency in his tone. "Bruised and a little bloody, but otherwise, yes, I am. Ashworth has a broken arm."

"Where are you?"

I told him the road we'd been on, described the area and the gate, and then said, "You'd better get Ciara here, too."

"Is this victim skinned?"

"No. We got here in time to at least stop that."

"And I'll be wanting a full explanation as to why neither of you called me first." His voice was tight. Angry. "It'll take us forty minutes to get out there—are you both going to be okay?"

"Ashworth might be a screaming mess of pain by then, but otherwise, yes."

"The ambulance will have to come from Creswyn, so it'll be no more than fifteen minutes."

"I'll head up the road and flag them down, then."

"*Don't* touch anything around the body until I get there."

He hung up. I put the phone away and glanced at Ashworth. "I've Panadol in my first aid kit if you think that would help."

He snorted. "That'd be like trying to hold back a flood with a feather. Help me up."

"The less you move—"

"Yeah, yeah, but I want to check the body of that wolf before the rangers get here."

"I can do—"

"Except you *can't*," he cut in. "Underpowered witch, remember?"

My lips twitched. Nothing like having your own words flung back at you.

"It would have been a hell of a lot easier if you'd mentioned this need before you'd actually sat down."

"Except I had to sit because my strength was about to give. The legs are less shaky now."

I didn't bother commenting—he'd undoubtedly just tell me he was perfectly able to judge his own fitness and strength.

I rose and held out a hand. Once he'd grasped it, I shifted my weight and pulled him upright. His curses flowed again and pink-stained sweat now dripped onto the shoulder of his pajama top. But the cuts on his face were minor, like mine. He pulled his hand free and slowly made his way down the slope. I kept close, just in case, but we reached the body without him needing further assistance.

The wolf's pelt was black—suggesting he'd been lured

from the nearby Sinclair reservation—and there was no obvious reason for his death. Despite the fact both men in the back of the truck had been holding guns, there was no immediate sign of a gunshot wound. They'd had no time to skin him, either, which—given that was how the first wolf had died—suggested there was another reason behind the death of this one. But the brightly plumed silver dart was here once again—though it was in his shoulder rather than his flank—and magic was also present. It rolled from him in waves that were far stronger than the remnants that had clung to the thread I'd pulled from the flesh of the first victim.

Ashworth squatted, a faint hiss of pain escaping his lips. "See that?" he said, pointing to the wolf's front leg.

I bent and studied the area. After a moment, I spotted the charm bracelet. It was barely visible against the wolf's dark coat, and appeared to be little more than a weave of five black cotton threads. Though it looked quite fragile in design, the magic rolling from it was anything but.

I raised my gaze to Ashworth's. "That's more than a simple tracking charm."

He nodded. "At a guess, I'd say it was both a tracker *and* a controller."

I frowned. "For a control spell to work properly, doesn't the witch have to be present?"

"When it comes to basic control spells, yes. This is more complex."

"Meaning what?"

"That we're not dealing with a simple street witch." He glanced at me. "Whoever created this charm has had proper training."

Again that sense of dread began to trip lightly through

my veins. "Do you think this charm is in any way linked to our dark witch?"

He hesitated, and then shook his head. "While the witch behind this is strong, I'm not sensing any darkness."

Which didn't necessarily mean anything given how easily evil could be concealed in the deeper layers of any spell.

"There *is* darkness in intent, though, given what's happening to the recipients of the charms."

"Which suggests, at worse, he or she simply doesn't care how their magic is employed. I've come across more than a few of them over my years with the RWA, and there's one thing they all have in common—they'll turn a blind eye to anything as long as you pay them well enough."

I grunted. "When I touched the thread I found on the first wolf, I got a vague impression of black teapots. I don't suppose you know of any registered witch stores with a name revolving around either tea or teapots?"

He raised an eyebrow. "I work for the RWA, not the business register."

"Yeah, but aren't witches supposed to notify the RWA if they're setting up shop in your area?"

"Yes, but that doesn't mean squat, and you and Belle are perfect examples of that."

I smiled. "That's because we're unregistered and under-powered."

"So you keep saying."

"And maybe one of these days you'll actually believe it." I glanced around at the sound of a distant siren. "I'll head up and flag that thing down."

He nodded. "I'll see if I can unravel the charm's magic and pin down its intent."

"Aiden said we weren't to touch anything-"

"I don't need to touch it to unravel it, as you well know. Besides, it's never a wise move to leave unknown magic active—especially in a case like this, when the hunters unexpectedly leave their prize behind."

All of which was certainly true. "Just try not to blow yourself up this time."

He snorted. "I'm not as arrogantly confident as our heretic hunter, so you can rest assured I'll unpick the magic *very* carefully indeed."

I raised my eyebrows. "I thought Chester's caution was the only thing that saved you both?"

He snorted again. "I had to give that impression, didn't I? The rangers don't need another reason to distrust a witch right now."

Which was fair enough. I swung my pack off my shoulders and handed it to him. "There's an assortment of potions and blessed items in there if you need any additional magical help."

"I wouldn't have thought it'd be in your best interests to give me free access to such items," he said, amusement evident but with an odd sort of seriousness. "How do you know I won't pick apart your magic rather than the charm's?"

"Aside from the fact I have nothing to hide when it comes to my magic," I replied evenly, "you're not the type to go behind my back to do something like that. You'd tell me flat out what you were doing, why you were doing it, and then curse me when the results weren't exactly what you were expecting."

He laughed, a sharp sound that ended in a wince. "That is all certainly true. You'd best head up before than damn ambulance drives past us."

By the time I'd scrambled up the hill, my breathing was

little more than short wheezes. While the hill was certainly steep, it was more to do with the fact I was damned unfit. I somehow made it across to the fence and leaned against it heavily. As I sucked in air to ease the fire in my lungs, I decided—not for the first time in my life—that I really needed to do something about my fitness levels.

Two ambulances soon came into sight. I waved them down and was almost immediately escorted into the back of one to be checked and treated while the crew of the second ambulance went into the paddock to help Ashworth. Despite the fact I had little more than a cut on the chin, the medics insisted I go back to the hospital for observation. Apparently, abrasions and bruising like mine were classic signs of "seat belt syndrome" and it was possible there was deeper internal damage even if I was feeling perfectly fine right now.

While the last thing I wanted or needed was to be in hospital over Christmas, I didn't particularly want to drop dead, either.

The tow truck and Aiden arrived at the same time. Ciara wasn't with him, which meant she was either still on the way or he'd called in an off-reservation substitute. He climbed out of his vehicle, his gaze sweeping the area and the two ambulances before coming to rest on me. Relief briefly surged across his expression before it settled into one of annoyance.

He strode over, talked for a couple of seconds to the paramedic who'd treated me, and then climbed into the back of the ambulance and sat down on the attendant's seat opposite me. His nostrils flared as he did so, and something flickered across his expression—something that looked a whole lot like relief.

It said a lot about the current state of my brain that it

took me several seconds to realize why—he'd been searching for the scent of sex and hadn't found it.

Annoyance, anger, and all manner of other unreasonable emotions surged, and I couldn't help snapping, "So are you going to return the favor?"

Confusion crossed his expression. "What favor?"

I touched my nose. "You now know I didn't have sex last night—so did you?"

Amusement twitched his lips. "What happened to the two of us being free agents and not owing each other anything?"

"Nothing happened to it. I'm just asking you what you were apparently afraid to ask me."

He laughed and caught my hands in his. "Liz, I've already told you more than once that until you came along, there was no one currently within this reservation I was sexually interested in. Why would you think that has changed?"

"Because I'm not a wolf," I said bluntly, "and I have no idea what really goes on in these two-day celebrations of yours."

"Lots of things go on, but the ones you've no doubt heard about—the drinking and sexual hookups—are *not* mandatory nor, for the most part, even encouraged. Especially when you're the head ranger and on call twenty-four seven over that period."

"Well, that's good to know." I took a deep breath and released it slowly. "But just so *you* know, I don't like sharing. If you *do* ever become attracted to another wolf, tell me first."

"How about you stop worrying about the future and just concentrate on enjoying the present?"

"I've spent a good portion of my life worrying about the future, Aiden. It's a damn hard habit to break."

"Then I guess it's something we'll have to work on together." He kissed my fingers then released me and leaned back in the chair. The warmth in his expression faded. I was again facing the ranger rather than the lover. "Why didn't you call me before you went chasing after the hunters?"

"Because I didn't know what the wild magic was trying to show me. It could have been nothing."

"Since when has its involvement led to nothing?"

"She didn't want us to wait, Aiden, and I didn't want to call—"

"Because you were pissed off at me."

"A statement that might or might not be true."

He smiled. "I suspect there might be a mighty fine temper hidden beneath those well-controlled layers of yours."

"Another thing that might or might not be true." My answering smile didn't last all that long. "But it doesn't alter the fact I wanted to find out what we were dealing with *before* I pulled either you or whoever else was on call out of the celebrations. I *was* trying to do the right thing."

"I appreciate that, but next time—"

"I'll probably do exactly the same thing."

"You," he said heavily, "can be very bloody annoying at times."

"So Belle keeps telling me." I reached into my pocket and drew out the gold chain. "This was the wolf's. I used it to track his location once we'd found his car."

I dropped the chain into his palm. He studied it for a moment and then said softly, "I know three wolves who wear chains like this. It may sound horrible, but I hope our victim isn't one of them."

"For your sake, I hope so too."

"It's more for my father's sake than mine." His mouth twisted. "Death is never easy to accept, even at the best of times, but it's always that much harder when it's someone you knew or loved."

Something I knew from experience. But at least Aiden wasn't responsible for this death—and wouldn't ever be held accountable for it.

I swallowed back the bitter sadness that accompanied that thought, and glanced past him as a paramedic appeared.

"Ranger, I'm afraid I'll have to ask you to leave. We need to get Ms. Grace to the hospital."

Aiden nodded and rose. "I'll get your full statement once you're cleared by the hospital. Until then, try to behave."

"It's not me you have to worry about," I grumbled. "But rather the bad guys intent on havoc."

"Them I can cope with. It's you getting caught in the middle that worries me." He kissed me tenderly but all too briefly. "So please stay out of trouble, and we'll talk again soon."

He left. Once the paramedic climbed in, the doors were closed and I was quickly whisked over to the hospital. They did a CT scan, ran all manner of other tests, and then decided they'd better keep me for the next forty-eight hours just to be on the safe side. But as Belle reminded me a number of times over the long days that followed, better *that* than discovering way too late that I was bleeding internally.

The day after Boxing Day—and after another full battery of tests to ensure nothing untoward was happening to my insides—they finally declared me fit enough to leave. Belle came to collect me and, after checking on Ashworth— who was rather hopeful of also being released, despite the fact the orthopedic surgeon had only operated on his arm yesterday—we headed home.

The first thing I did was take an extremely long, extremely hot shower. It helped ease the lingering aches and made me feel a lot better. While I'd been able to shower in the hospital, it was never the same as your own. A quick look in the mirror revealed a rainbow assortment of bruises blooming over my right shoulder and a good portion of my breast, but for the most part that was the worst of it. The cut on my chin wasn't deep or sore, and the multitude of scratches I'd gotten from the flying glass were barely visible. Once again, lady luck had been on my side.

It was nearing midday by the time I finally clattered down to the café. Belle had busy in the kitchen while I'd been upstairs, and there was a huge spread of ham, turkey, salad, thickly cut buttered bread, gravy, and cranberry sauce laid out on one of the tables. There was also the traditional large jug of very potent eggnog, and one of Michael Bublé's many Christmas CDs playing softly in the background.

"This," I said happily, "all looks fabulous."

"A late celebration is better than none." She held out a brightly colored Christmas cracker. "And I have news to celebrate."

"What news?"

"Traditions before explanations." She waved the cracker at me.

I grinned. We'd long ago decided to not to give each other Christmas—or even birthday—presents, but silly things like cracker hats, Christmas carols, and eggnog—like our singing and dancing on Christmas Eve—had become something of a ritual. I grabbed the other end of the cracker and pulled. There was a faint *pop* as the cracker split, leaving Belle with the main portion of it. She pulled out the purple paper hat and shoved it on her head while I picked up the other cracker so we could repeat the process. My hat was a vivid pink. I shoved it on and ignored her snort of amusement. "Give with the news, woman."

"The council has rejected the witch who was coming here to be interviewed on the grounds that if he couldn't manage to make a damn plane, he wasn't likely to be a good match for this reservation."

I picked up the eggnog and poured us both a glass. "And how did you discover this when all three packs are coming off a two-day celebration and are likely to be hunkered down in their compounds sleeping it all off?"

"Well, an elderly wolf might just have been brought to the hospital as I was leaving last night, and I might just have skimmed his mind to see what was happening."

Amusement twitched my lips. "I take it this wolf might just have been from the Marin pack?"

"Indeed he might have. And he might also have turned out to be a pack alpha who'd been part of the emergency meeting convened after the witch's no-show."

"Is said wolf okay?"

"Suspected heart attack, according the duty nurse."

I frowned. "I'd have thought wolves immune to those sort of problems, given their bodies have natural set points for health."

"Yeah, but they still do age, regardless, and with that comes problems." She paused and wrinkled her nose. "And this one was rather on the tubby side—too much wine and hamburgers."

"Did you steal *that* from his mind, as well?"

"Didn't have to. His wife was berating him long and loud." She picked up a plate and began filling it. "Anyway, they rather surprisingly haven't gone back to their stand of not having an official witch on the reservation, and have instead asked to interview their second choice."

"Canberra's aware of the true size of the wellspring here now, so that's really not surprising. It was either they choose a witch, or Canberra was going to do it for them."

She took a sip of eggnog. "Whoa, I think I overdid the rum this time."

I tried mine, felt burn all the way down, and then grinned. "Neither of us need to drive anywhere, so it doesn't really matter."

"Yeah, but we open again tomorrow and we do need to be mobile."

"Given a good portion of the reservation has been partying for two and a half days, I'm thinking no one will actually notice if we're carrying a little alcohol hangover." I pulled out a chair and sat down. "Don't suppose you managed to get a name while you were digging around?"

"He's apparently younger than they would have preferred." Belle wrinkled her nose. "He's an Ashworth—Frederick Ashworth, I think."

"Which is not a name I'm immediately familiar with."

"No, but it *is* a rather old-fashioned one, which suggests he's from one of the older Ashworth lines."

"There are plenty of branches in the Ashworth family tree," I said. "All that really matters to *us* is the fact he's not from my particular family branch."

"Yes." She paused. "Aiden's heading this way. You'd better pour the man a drink, because his thoughts are full-on grumpy."

I hastily grabbed and filled another glass then walked

across to the front door, opening it just as he'd raised his hand to knock. He was wearing a black T-shirt that emphasized his muscular body and—rather sadly—baggy jeans that didn't. His hair looked to have been roughly finger-combed and dark honey-colored whiskers shadowed his chin and jawline.

Scruffy or not, he looked damn fine.

"Morning," I said, and offered him the eggnog. "I'm informed you need this rather badly."

His nostrils flared. "There's a hell of a lot of alcohol in that thing, and I start work in precisely one hour."

"No wonder you're all sorts of grumpy this morning," came Belle's comment.

Aiden kissed me briefly and then stepped inside. "Seriously, can you just stay out of my brain?"

"I wasn't in your brain, Ranger. Didn't have to be when you're radiating unhappy vibes all over the place. You had lunch?"

"No. I haven't even had breakfast. I thought I'd come see Lizzie, and take her statement while I'm here."

"And they say romance is dead." Belle came back out of the kitchen and handed him a plate.

He pulled a chair out and sat down. "Hey, I'm here, and that took a heroic amount of effort considering the lack of sleep over the last few days, let me tell you."

"So was the lack of sleep work related or party?" I asked mildly.

"Mainly work related, although there were a few official things I was expected to be at given I'm the oldest, and will become pack leader once either of my parents die."

Belle frowned and waved her fork at him. "How does that actually work? In actual wolf packs, the alpha cubs are sent packing once they're old enough to start their own family."

"Yes, but werewolves are an offshoot branch of humanity rather than wolves." He picked up his plate and began loading it up. High. The man was *hungry*. "Our pack consists of five different branches of the O'Connor bloodline, and each one is ruled by one alpha pairing."

"That's a rather small gene pool, isn't it?" I said.

He nodded. "Which is why we have the exchange system running. All three packs here have the same problem."

"Which is undoubtedly why Zak went a-running when a new piece of tail came into his pack."

"Zak is an idiot."

Belle grinned. "That is *exactly* my thought, but why would you think it?"

"Because I've met the wolf in question. She's pretty, but not in your league."

"Ranger, I think that's the nicest thing you've ever said to me."

"Stop raiding my thoughts every other minute, and I'd be nice more often."

She leaned over and patted his arm. "I promise I've never done anything more than a surface raid—and only then because I'm a good familiar who wants to protect the emotional well-being of her witch."

"That's not exactly comforting, you know."

"So just treat her well, and we won't have a problem." She picked up her eggnog and took a drink. "The latest target of Zak's affections does have one advantage over me, though—the fact that she *is* a wolf."

"Yes, but it's pretty evident she's after something more than a bartending handyman. Zak's a good bloke, but he'll never be pack alpha." He glanced at her, his expression curious. "Would you accept him back?"

"Hell no. He made a choice, now he has to live with it."

Aiden's gaze came to me and I smiled and raised my glass. "Ditto, in case you're wondering."

"Then I sure as hell won't be as foolish as Zak."

Which didn't at *all* comfort me.

It should, Belle said. *Unless and until a new wolf comes into this reservation and catches his heart, he's all yours.*

I know, I know. But it still didn't stop the deep down niggle—the one that already knew I was going to be a mess when he finally did leave.

He finished demolishing the rest of his food and then leaned back with a happy sigh.

"There's plenty more if you want it," I said, amused.

"Maybe once I've taken your statement." He took out his phone, hit record, and started asking me questions as I tucked into my meal.

Once he'd finally stopped recording, I said, "How are the investigations going?"

"You do know I technically shouldn't be talking to either of you about them now that we have a reservation witch."

"He's temporary. And I'm prettier."

"And you also happen to have a friend who would has absolutely no qualms about dragging the information out of my brain."

Belle grinned and raised her glass in acknowledgement.

He snorted. "The blood we found in that burned-out protection circle doesn't match the blood group of our dead witch."

"Meaning he's used something or someone else to create his spell," I said.

"The blood was human, not animal."

"Then I guess the question needing to be answered," Belle said, "is, was that person a willing apprentice or unwilling random stranger snatched off the street?"

"And if the latter," I added, "why haven't we got a body?"

"He might not have killed the source," Belle said.

"Maybe, but the blood stain in the middle of that circle was a large one. He's at least lost a lot of blood even if he isn't dead, and that probably means he'd need a transfusion." I glanced at Aiden. "I'm guessing you've already checked the hospitals?"

"Yes. No one with a serious knife wound has fronted up at the emergency departments in either of the reservation hospitals."

"What about the nearest one outside the reservation?"

"Them neither." Aiden picked up a slab of bread and threw some turkey on it. "And Chester is not being overly helpful—his answer to just about any question ranges between vague and noncommittal."

Which didn't surprise me if he was, as I suspected, protecting his own butt. "Has Ciara received a reply on the DNA and bloods she sent up to Canberra?"

He nodded. "The body in the morgue is indeed Jonathan Ashworth."

I frowned. "If my math is correct, Jonathan was only fifty-four. The body we found looked at *least* thirty years older than that."

"He did. Chester said it's due to the use of blood magic —the more you use it, the greater the speed of aging."

"Meaning our witch has used it a hell of a lot," Belle commented. "Maybe that explains how he ended up having half his head blown off. Maybe his thinking and reactions had come down to the level of an eighty-year-old."

"I know plenty of eighty-year-olds who could beat the crap out of me when it comes to strength and brain power," Aiden commented, amused.

"Okay, a *decrepit* eighty-year-old then."

"It still doesn't explain what happened to the second person, though." I followed Aiden's lead and made myself a turkey, cranberry, and gravy sandwich. "If he was an unwilling blood source, why wouldn't he have fronted up to report the crime? Or gone to a hospital?"

"Maybe he just went to a doctor's surgery," Belle said.

"Which is why Maggie is currently contacting all medical providers both within the reservation or on our boundaries." Aiden said.

"That could take *ages*," Belle said. "Maybe we should take her over some eggnog to help her get through the task."

Aiden smiled. "She *is* our ranger in training. All the shitty jobs are hers, just as they were mine when I was in the same position."

I raised my eyebrows. "Were you in diapers when you started training?"

He laughed. "I was eighteen."

"Which means you zoomed up the ladder in—how long have you been head ranger?"

"Going on two years, and I was lucky. Jenny Wright—the previous head—was heading interstate in an exchange program, and we had two other retirements in the same year. I was the most senior ranger left; Tala, who was one year behind me, became my second."

"Tala's older than you though," I commented.

He nodded. "She joined our ranks when she was

twenty-five. She worked as a customer service rep at the local bank before that, but it didn't pan out."

"Having witnessed her warm, caring, and extremely helpful attitude," Belle murmured, "color me shocked."

"She *is* all that once you get to know her. It just takes a while." He finished his sandwich and made another, this time with ham.

I finished my eggnog and then grabbed his. There was no point in wasting a perfectly good alcoholic beverage. "What about the skinning case—any movement on that?"

He grimaced. "We found the truck you mentioned. It'd been abandoned and burned out up on Adam's Track in the Dundoogal Nature Conservation reserve. We're pretty damn lucky the fire brigade got there as quickly as they did, because it could have resulted in the whole area going up."

"I guess it's too early to tell yet whether it was stolen or not."

"The number plates were charred but we were able to grab an impression from them—the truck was stolen."

"And the murdered wolf?" Belle asked softly.

He grimaced. "It was Angus Sinclair. He was fifty, and a good friend of my father's."

I briefly touched his arm. "I'm sorry."

"Dad took the news pretty hard." He scrubbed a hand across his jaw, the sound like sandpaper. "First indications are that he died of a heart attack, even though there were no indications of heart problems beforehand."

I hesitated, and then said, "That necklace I used to track him—he was very fearful, Aiden, and I could feel the tightness in his chest."

"Fear doesn't match the nature of the man I knew."

"Yes, but he was being forced into actions against his will," I said, "and he had no idea why."

"Did you see anything else? A hint of the hunters, perhaps?"

"No." I hesitated again. "But when I touched that chain, I got the impression that he wasn't only being forced to run, but also that he'd been brought down by something *other* than a gunshot. We certainly didn't hear a shot and, given how close we were by then, we would have unless they were using a silencer."

"They weren't. That dart in his shoulder was tipped with some sort of poison—"

"Why would they do that," I cut in, "when silver itself is poisonous to werewolves?"

He shrugged. "When Ciara pins down the type of poison they used, we might have a clearer idea. But it's possible it attributed to his heart attack."

"Don't discount the power of fear," Belle said quietly. "While fear might power the flight or fight response, it *is* possible for someone to be so afraid—so terrified for their life—that it causes a heart attack."

"I guess I just find it hard to believe that such a big, powerful wolf in the prime of his life could be so easily taken." He grimaced. "But I guess he'd at least lived a good portion of his life. Jamison had only just started."

Just as my sister had only just started hers. I blinked back the sudden sting of tears and thrust upright. "Anyone for tea or coffee?"

"Yeah, thanks," Aiden said. His gaze followed me as I walked behind the counter, and I very much suspected he'd caught that brief glimmer. "I actually came here to ask if you were busy this afternoon."

I glanced over my shoulder as I filled up the kettle. "Why?"

"Ashworth said you'd asked him about witch stores

whose name had something to do with either black or dancing teapots."

"Yeah—I've seen them twice now. Once when I was reading that thread on the first victim, and once in my dreams the other night." I leaned back against the counter as I waited for the kettle to boil. "Did he find some?"

Aiden nodded. "He got bored when he was waiting for them to operate on his arm, so he nabbed a computer from who knows where and logged into the witch business register to see what he could find."

"And he found something?" Belle asked.

"Four somethings—all of them outside the reservation."

"Then why isn't Ashworth accompanying you?" I said. "I can't imagine he'd want to be left behind, especially after being cooped up in the hospital for the last couple of days."

"You mean aside from the fact I'd rather be with you than him?"

I smiled. "Yes, aside from that."

"He only had the surgery yesterday. He's going to be in for a few more days yet, no matter how loud he protests."

"Remind me to stay out of his way when he does get out," Belle muttered. "I can just imagine the mood he's going to be in."

"What about Chester?" I asked. "What's he doing?"

"I actually don't know. As I said, he's rather closed-mouthed." Aiden glanced at Belle. "Maybe you should try invading *his* mind for a change."

"I did. He's protected."

"Can you get past it?"

"Possibly."

"Will you try?"

"Possibly."

Amusement twitched his lips. "Please?"

"Well, seeing you asked so nicely, I'll give it a go next time he's here. But I make no promises."

I made his coffee and our tea, then placed them all on a tray and carried them over. Our conversation rolled on to other topics, and by the time our hot drinks and a good portion of the remaining food had been consumed, it was time for him to go.

He rose and kissed my cheek. "I'll be back at one to pick you up."

"I'll be waiting out front."

"Good." He gave Belle a nod and left.

I poured the remaining eggnog into our two glasses then leaned back and said, "Don't expect me back tonight. I intend to have my wicked way with that man."

She grinned. "I think you'll find that intention mutual."

"I would hope so." I twirled the eggnog around in my glass for a second. "Chester worries me. He's obviously hiding something and I think it's going to cause us problems."

"Is that a personal 'us' or a more general one?"

"More general." I frowned. "Jonathan Ashworth may be dead, but I don't think we've seen the end of whatever it is he was up to. That circle he created was huge—it was meant to contain extremely powerful and dangerous magic."

Belle frowned. "What were Ashworth's thoughts about it?"

"Ashworth thinks Chester is an arrogant idiot who almost got them both killed."

Belle laughed. "I'm liking that old man more and more."

"Yeah. I'm going to be sorry to see him go."

"We may be the only ones. I'm betting the council will throw a party once he steps off the reservation."

"Possibly, although there's no saying the new witch will be any better."

"He's much younger—"

"Which only means he could be all that much more full of himself."

"All too true." Her quick smile faded. "Did you ever make that full protection charm for Aiden?"

"I did indeed." It was, in fact, his Christmas present.

"Good."

I raised my eyebrows. "Don't tell me the spirits are whispering sweet nothings in your ear again."

She hesitated and then shrugged. "They remain uneasy. There's evil afoot, but they can't track it down. And yes, before you say it, they know that's not helpful."

I grinned. "I'll have to do better with my replies if they're now guessing what I'm about to say."

"They have been hanging about the pair of us for a very long time now." Her gaze narrowed slightly, then a grin split her lips. "They said it only sometimes feels like a very long time."

There was nothing much I could say to that, so I got up, retrieved the two small Christmas puds Belle had put on earlier, smothered them in custard and cream, and served them up.

By the time one had rolled around, I was filled to the brim and ready for a nap. I headed upstairs to change, and then grabbed another bag—the one I'd used last time was still sitting in Aiden's bedroom—shoved in fresh clothes and his present, and then said goodbye to Belle and headed outside to wait.

His truck pulled up a few minutes later, and his look was appreciative as I climbed in. "I'm rather liking all these short dresses you're wearing of late."

"Not that I'm doing it specifically for your pleasure, but it's nice you've noticed." I pulled the small, gift-wrapped box from my bag and handed it to him. "Merry Christmas."

"Thanks." He leaned across and kissed me, his lips warm and passionate against mine. "I'm afraid you'll have to wait until we get back to my place for yours. In my rush to leave enough time to see you this morning, I left it sitting on the kitchen counter."

"Oh, very smooth, Ranger."

"But true."

He unwrapped the present and then picked up the plaited leather charm inside. It had been made of three different colored leathers and copper, and basically looked no different to the leather neck-cords I'd seen many of the younger wolves wearing.

"Do you like it?" I asked.

"I do, but I'm gathering it's no ordinary neck-cord."

"No, it has every protection spell I know woven into it. It'll protect you from ill-intent, evil spirits, and most curses except for those created by blood witches. And you can shower in it."

He quickly slipped it on and then kissed me again, this time taking his time. By the time we'd come up for air, my pulse was racing and desire pounding through my veins. This evening suddenly seemed a *very* long way away.

"I need to stop kissing you like that—"

"No," I quickly cut in, "you don't."

He grinned. "When I'm working and can't rush you off somewhere to complete what we just started."

"There, there." I leaned across to pat his thigh comfortingly. His muscles twitched at the contact, and I couldn't help noticing his baggy jeans suddenly weren't—at least around the crotch area. "As the saying goes, anything worth having is worth waiting for."

"I've more apt saying for you—waiting is the rust of the soul. Or, in this case, the loins."

I laughed. "If you waited over a damn year, you can wait six hours."

He shoved the car into gear and pulled out of the parking spot. "To be precise, five hours, twenty-three minutes, and fifteen seconds. Not that I'm counting or anything."

I *was*, but I wasn't about to admit that. "So, where are we going?"

He shifted slightly and pulled a piece of paper out of the back pocket of his jeans. "Here's the list Ashworth gave me."

I did my best to ignore the warmth lingering on the paper as I unfolded it. "Tea and Tinctures, A Pot of Magic, The Tea Cauldron, and The Black Samovar." I frowned. "What the hell is a samovar?"

"It's a traditional metal container—basically, an urn—that's used in Russia to heat water."

"And how do you know this random fact?"

His grin flashed. "I googled. Some of them were quite fancy—and more than a few actually had a traditional-looking teapot sitting on the top of them."

I was tempted to ask why, but I rather suspected it was simply a decoration thing. "Where are we heading first?"

"I thought we'd start distant and work our way back in."

Which meant A Pot of Magic was our first stop while the last one would be The Black Samovar, as it was in Ballan and was the closest to his place in Argyle.

We made our way across to Woodend. A Pot of Magic was situated between a florist and a real estate agent, and was rich with all the usual paraphernalia low-powered witches used to lure in unsuspecting clients. This particular witch had gray hair, blue eyes, a happy smile, and an aura that glowed with a vivid mix of pink and green, the two colors most associated with healing—which in many respects was the more valuable gift for a witch running a shop that sold healing potions and magic. She certainly wasn't the creator of either of the charms being used on the wolves.

We moved on to the next one—Tea and Tinctures. Although the witch running this shop was far stronger—and was certainly wary about my presence in her establishment —the feel of her magic also didn't match the stuff emanating from the charms.

We got exactly the same result in The Tea Cauldron.

"This is very much looking like a dead end," Aiden said, as he opened the truck door and ushered me inside.

"But it's still a nice way to waste a couple of hours."

His smile flashed. "It's certainly better than sitting in the office catching up on paperwork."

He climbed into the driver side and we headed across to Ballan. It was a pretty typical small country town, with a small main shopping strip filled with a mix of century-old buildings and quite ugly newer ones. The Black Samovar was near the end of the strip, right next to the old Mechanics Hall. It was a tiny place with a wide wooden veranda that was painted silver but decorated with an assortment of black tea pots—some of which had legs and looked to be dancing.

"This is it," I said, as Aiden parked a couple of spaces up from the shop.

He glanced at me sharply. "How do you know?"

I pointed to the images painted onto the beam. "They're

the images I saw in my dream. It'll also mean she'll know I'm a witch the moment I step into her premises."

"Will that be a problem?"

"That depends on whether she has anything to hide or not."

He studied the building for a second, and then said, "I might make a call to the RWA and get them to send someone out. If this witch is responsible for the bracelets that we found on our two victims then she is, at the very least, an accessory to murder. That makes her their responsibility, not ours."

"They may not be able to get someone out here straight away, which means we'll have to transport her back to Castle Rock."

Amusement shone in his blue eyes. "Worried about a delay to seduction time?"

"No, I'm worried about a delay to present time. Get your priorities right, Ranger."

He laughed and got his phone out, quickly making the call to the RWA. I studied the shop, feeling the faint brush of magic even from the truck. Whoever ran this shop might not be a blueblood but he or she was certainly far stronger than the trinket and potion makers who'd run the other shops.

"We're in luck," he said, as he hung up. "They have someone who's just finished dealing with a situation in Bacchus Marsh. They can be here in twenty minutes. They'll contact Ashworth on the way through to get his input on the situation."

"I hope they're ready to get their ears burned off. He's not going to be happy about missing out on the action."

"To say the least." Aiden glanced at the shop again. "It's probably best to let me enter first. That way I've a second or two to spot her before she reacts to your presence."

If she wasn't already aware of it, that was. It just depended on how the spells that protected her premises were designed and layered—and whether she'd included a thread to warn her if another witch was approaching.

I climbed out of the car and followed him across to the shop. A beautifully ornate black metal urn with a teapot perched precariously on its top dominated the small front window. The teapot was obviously soldered on, but that didn't spoil the effect, or the urge to reach out and catch it.

A bell chimed merrily as Aiden entered, and the air was rich with a mix of cinnamon, ginger, and rose—all scents that were generally associated with sex, lust, and desire. The charms and potions that lined the nearby shelves were certainly all aimed at that market.

Her magic swirled around me, its feel very feminine. There was no recognition in it, no sense that it had been designed to warn, only ward.

But it very definitely had the same feel as the tracking bracelet we'd found on the second wolf. Although the RWA would legally have to confirm it, I had no doubt that this was the witch who'd created them.

The curtain at the far end of the shop was twitched aside and a woman stepped through. She had a thick mane of dark brown hair that was shot with silver, pale skin, and eyes the purest silver—all of which said she was from the Waverley line of witches.

"Good afternoon," she said, her voice as warm and sultry as the air in her shop. "How can I help you young lovebirds—"

Her voice died as her gaze swept past Aiden and came to rest on mine. Recognition stirred through her expression, which was surprising given I had absolutely no memory of ever meeting her. Not even during our time in Canberra—although she was a couple years younger than me, and therefore would have been in very different classes.

"We're not here to purchase anything." Aiden flicked open his badge and showed it to her. "We need to ask—"

He got no further.

The witch made a sharp motion with her hands and the contents of the shelves on either side became mini missiles flying directly at us.

Even as the bitch turned and ran.

CHAPTER SEVEN

A iden swore and shoved me down, covering my body with his as all manner of vials and charms crashed above us, showering us with glass, stones, and a stinking, sticky mess of liquid.

Once it was over, Aiden shifted and said, "You okay?"

"Yes."

"Then let's go get that bitch."

He grabbed my hand, helped me up, then released me and ran after the witch. I bolted after him. He wrenched the curtain aside, all but pulling it off its tracks and revealing a small, well-fitted-out reading room. The magic within the room swirled around us again, but it didn't attack because we didn't actually intend its creator any harm. We went through a wooden door, raced down a long corridor, and then out into a yard. The witch was just clambering over the wooden fence at the rear of the property. Aiden lunged for her, catching one foot just as threw herself down the other side. She yelped, and her magic surged.

"I wouldn't finish that spell, young lady," I said sharply.

"Not unless you want to get yourself into a lot more trouble."

I stopped beside Aiden. He was still gripping her ankle but the lower part of leg was the only portion of her body on *this* side of the fence. The rest was hanging over the other side, with her weight being carried by the back of her knee, which was bent over the top of the fence. She had to be in a whole lot of pain.

Her magic continued to rise, so I called to mine, letting it run around me, a storm of power that was sharper and stronger than anything she could produce. I might be an underpowered witch, but I was still from the Marlowe line.

"We only want to talk," I continued evenly, "but if you really want to see whose magic is stronger, I'm more than happy to comply."

Her magic stalled, and then died. I nodded at Aiden. He reached over the fence with his free hand, grabbed a fistful of shirt, and hauled her back onto our side. He placed her on the ground then forced her on her butt and knelt beside her. "Is your knee okay?"

She frowned but nodded.

"Good, we can get straight down to business then. Why did you run the minute you spotted us?"

She pointed with her chin at me. "I recognized her."

"How?" I asked bluntly. "We've never met."

"No, but I saw you in a dream," she said. "I always get warnings of trouble headed my way."

"It's a damn shame you didn't get such a warning when you agreed to make those tracking and control bracelets for a couple of murderous hunters," I said. "I hope you were well paid, because you're going to need the money when the RWA shuts you down."

Her gaze went wide. "I have no idea what you're talking about—and I thought you were only here to talk?"

"We lied," Aiden said.

"But I've done *nothing*."

Her magic began to stir again. I quickly but silently created a restraint spell and flicked it toward her. It fell over her, an invisible cloud that would, until I released her, contain any and all spells she might try.

Her gaze jumped to mine and she cursed me, long and loud.

Amusement creased the corners of Aiden's eyes. "I'm gathering you just magically restrained her?"

"Yes. But you might want to physically restrain her as well. This one's definitely a runner."

"There's very little chance of her overpowering you let alone me, but I do see your point."

As Aiden reached into a pocket to grab the ever-present cable ties, she lashed out, kicking him in the shins and then trying to scramble up. He grunted, caught her foot, and yanked her backwards so that her spine hit the ground. Then he grabbed her hands and quickly cabled her wrists. I knew from experience they were damn uncomfortable—my very first meeting with Aiden had ended with me being similarly restrained. I hadn't been stupid enough to kick him, of course, and I'd therefore remained upright.

"Right, that's one charge of assaulting an officer added to your other crimes," he said. "Keep going and you're going to end up in prison for years."

"Other than kicking you—which is not a prison-worthy crime, and we both know it—I haven't fucking done anything."

"We have one of the tracking and control bracelets you

made for the hunters," I said. "It'll be very easy for the RWA to confirm that those bracelets were made by you."

"So? There's no crime in providing trackers—"

"Except," Aiden replied, with just the faintest trace of anger in his voice, "when those trackers also contain a control element that forces the wearer into actions *against* their will."

For the first time, a hint of fear flared in her eyes. "Look, there's been some kind of mistake here—"

"Yes, and it was yours when you agreed to make those bracelets for a couple of hunters," Aiden said.

"Hunting is *not* illegal—not even in that reservation of yours." Her tone held an edge of contempt. "And we both know you actually have *no* authority outside said reservation. Expect to be hearing from my lawyers, Ranger, and get your purse strings ready to pay out big."

"For the most part, you're right." Aiden's voice was cool and mild—the wolf at his most dangerous. "I don't have any authority beyond the reservation *except* in cases of murder when I'm on the trail of a killer or accomplice. If that murder involves magic, then I'm legally obliged to contact the RWA before I confront and restrain said killer. Which I have."

Fear gleamed brighter in her eyes. "I didn't murder anyone. I didn't *help* anyone murder anyone. I have no idea—"

"Enough," Aiden said. "The bracelets you made were used in the murders of two werewolves—and one of those werewolves was skinned while he was still alive. You had better tell me about the men you sold those things to, and fast, or I'll make damn sure you and your magic never see the light of day again."

Her eyes went wide and she swallowed heavily. "I swear, I didn't know—"

"The men," he cut in savagely. "Descriptions and names if you have them."

She licked her lips. "I don't know their names. But there were three of them, and they paid in cash. "

"When?"

"Five days ago."

"How often do your security cameras loop?"

"Every seven days. It's a simple home system rather than a full-on business one."

"So you should still have their purchase on tape?" When she nodded, he grabbed her hands and hauled her upright. "Lead the way then."

"Shouldn't you be waiting for the RWA?" she said. "Suspect or not, I do have rights."

"Do I look as if I care about rights right now?" Aiden bit back, and pushed her forward. It said a lot about his control that he did so gently. I certainly wouldn't have. "If I were you, I'd be praying to every god you believe in that we catch these bastards before they make another kill."

Her gaze cut to his, but she didn't say anything. Maybe she'd finalized realized there was nothing she could say to make any of this any better. She led us into a small office that sat behind her reading room. In it was a desk, a filing cabinet, a computer, printer, and what looked to be a DVD player with a number of wires sticking out of it—one of which ran down to the computer. She moved the mouse to reactivate the monitor, clicked through a number of programs and screens until the playback started, and then hit the fast-forward.

After a few minutes, she clicked the play button and said, "That's them."

Aiden reached past her and froze the image on the screen. The three men were in jeans and bulky coats—which should have set all sorts of alarms off for a witch with any sort of integrity—and two of them had peaked hats pulled down over their faces. One of those two had a colorful werewolf tattoo stretching up his left arm. The third man had long brown hair loosely tied at the back of his head and a beard that all but dominated his face. He appeared to have no qualms about looking directly at the camera, which suggested he very much believed his image couldn't be used to track him down.

The three of them talked to our witch for several minutes and then left.

"I take it they came back?" Aiden asked.

She nodded. "The next day."

Aiden fast-forwarded until the three men appeared again. Our witch showed them a bracelet, obviously giving them advice and instructions. Once they'd handed over a paper bag that looked to be at least half full—and no doubt contained cash—she handed them a rather prettily gift-wrapped box. I had to wonder why she'd even bothered.

"How many bracelets did you make for them?" I asked.

She glanced at me. "Ten."

"And a control device?"

"A control and tracking charm, yes."

"Basic or multiple?"

"Basic," she said. "They weren't willing to pay for additional training."

Either that, or they already knew how to use such a charm.

"How do these things work?" Aiden asked.

She returned her gaze to him. "Via a type of binding spell. It lightly links the mind of the user with the charm, and allows them to give basic instructions to the wearer as well as location details. Helps greatly if the user has some kind of telepathic ability—the fellow with the long hair said he did."

"How much did you charge them?" When she hesitated, Aiden added more forcibly, "Tell us now or tell us in court. It's up to you, but I can guarantee the second option will not sit well with the judge."

She studied him for several seconds, and then somewhat mutinously, "Ten thousand."

"A thousand per life," I said. "That's pretty damn cheap."

"Especially given the going rate for a werewolf pelt is at *least* ten thousand," Aiden said.

"They said they were hunting kangaroos, I swear."

There was desperation in her voice, but something within me just didn't believe her.

"I guess that's for RWA to find out, isn't it?"

A small bell chimed in the next room and I glanced at Aiden. "I'll go see who it is."

As I walked out, he asked, "Did you bother getting any sort of ID from the three men? Notice what type of car or truck they were driving?"

The witch answered with a short, sharp, "No."

I shook my head at her stupidity and stepped into the main shop. There was mess everywhere, and with so many potions having been spilled, the air was so thickly scented it was barely even breathable. Aiden and I might be covered in the stuff, but this.... I shuddered. This would permeate the floorboards and make the place unusable for months.

"Oh dear," the older woman who'd come through the door said. She hastily grabbed a handkerchief from her handbag and covered her nose. "This is a mess."

"Yes, and I'm sorry, but we're currently closed."

She glanced at me. "Francesca not here then?"

"Yes, but she's busy clearing up at the moment." I waved a hand at the mess. "I've been tasked with cleaning this, and it could take a while, I'm afraid."

"Indeed." The woman looked around, her expression one of disappointment. "I guess it'll just have to wait."

I hesitated, and then said, "What were you after?"

"Oh," she said. "Just my usual—a small damiana and ginseng cordial."

Both of those herbs were used to help overcome impotence, low libido, and enhance sexual vitality. No wonder she'd looked a little disappointed at leaving empty-handed.

I looked around, spotted a bottle on one of the few shelves that hadn't jettisoned its contents at us, and walked over to grab it.

"Here," I said. "Have this, on the house."

"Oh, are you sure?"

"Yes. Take it, and have a good time."

A grin split her lips. "Oh, I will now."

She happily tucked the small bottle into her handbag and left. But as I made my way toward the back of the store and Francesca's small office, the doorbell chimed again and I turned to see a familiar figure walk in.

"Anna," I said, a surprised smile splitting my lips, "I didn't think you'd be back on duty so soon."

Anna was the RWA witch who'd been sent to the reservation to help the rangers hunt down the magic-capable vampire, but she'd been caught—and severely burned—in a magical explosion that had been aimed at me. She had the classic looks of a witch from the Kang line—an oval face, high cheekbones and a prominent nose, and mono-lidded eyes. Her hair was as vivid as mine, but cut extremely short.

She let the door close and walked toward me, moving with surprising ease. Given her torso and chest had copped the worst of the burns, I'd have expected at least at little tightness of movement. "I probably wouldn't have been working so soon if it hadn't been for your quick thinking."

"All I did was pour water over your wounds—I hardly think—"

"It wasn't ordinary water," she cut in, "it was holy water. It killed the spell remnants that were burned into my skin and majorly helped with the healing process."

"I had no idea it could do any of that." And—considering the continuing invasion of evil into the reservation—maybe I needed to keep a bottle or two tucked safely away in my handbag.

Anna stopped beside me and looked around the room. "What happened here?"

"The witch emptied her shelves in our direction in an attempt to escape."

"It's a rather stomach-turning stench, isn't it? And all aimed at sexy times, if I'm reading it right." She glanced at me, merriment evident in her eyes—which were slate-gray rather than the usual silver, the only hint that her heritage wasn't pure Kang. "I hope you and the ranger are prepared for the possible fallout."

"Totally looking forward to it, actually."

She laughed, the sound warm. "You've got the witch restrained, I take it?"

"In the rear office. Did Ashworth update you on what's been happening on the way over?"

She nodded and fell in step beside me as I headed for the rear of the building again. "Yes. If she *is* the witch behind those bracelets then she's in serious trouble." Her gaze came to mine. "Your opinion?"

"That it's her." I pushed the remnants of the curtain aside and motioned her toward the small office.

"Evening, Ranger," she said, as she stopped just inside the door. "Have you got all you need from her?"

"For the moment, yes."

"Good." Anna eyed the other woman for a moment then glanced back at me. "That's a very nice net you have around her."

I smiled. Anna, like Ashworth, didn't entirely believe that I was a low-powered witch, but unlike him, she hadn't —as far as I knew—taken it any further.

"Thanks. You want me to remove it?"

She nodded. I immediately did so, and a heartbeat later her magic surged, wrapping a far stronger web around the other woman. Francesca didn't say anything; her body was slumped, her expression grim. The reality of her sins was well and truly kicking in, I suspected.

"Right," Anna said. "I'll take this one back to headquarters. Do you want to secure the premises? We'll need to send a team back to do a more thorough examination of both her workrooms and her records. It's very likely this is not the first time she's provided gray magic to those willing to pay enough."

"You'll let us know if you find out anything more about the three men she sold the charms to?" Aiden asked.

Anna nodded and roughly hauled Francesca to her feet. Anna might be the smaller of the two, but what she lacked in height was more than made up for in muscle. "As long as you return the favor, Ranger."

"I will."

She nodded again and then, with a twinkle in her eye and a quick, "Have fun you two," she left.

Aiden glanced at me. "Is there something I'm missing?"

I grinned. "You know all those potions that cascaded over us earlier?"

"It's kind of hard to ignore them given the wretched stuff is all I can smell."

"Yeah, well, they were mostly lust and sexual empowerment potions." I glanced at my watch. "And we probably have another half hour or so before they truly start working."

He looked amused. "I don't actually need lust potions when I'm around you. Besides, do those things actually work?"

"Done properly, yes. And, given the sheer amount that tipped over us, let's just say things could get very hard and heated *very* fast."

"Seriously?"

"Seriously."

"Then we'd better hurry up and get out of here."

He grabbed the tape out of the recorder and the photos he'd printed off. Once the rest of the building was secure, we headed back to the truck.

"It's just over half hour to Argyle from here," he said, as he reversed out. "And you've still got your overnight bag at my place, haven't you?"

"Yes, but we really could be pushing your self control."

"I think we've already established I have none where you're concerned. Besides, it's not just me that was hit by that muck."

"No, but you shielded me from the worst if it."

"And in payment for being chivalrous, I'm going to be hit by a gigantic wave of uncontrollable lust? How wonderful." He paused, his expression thoughtful. "Will it help the situation if we wash it off quickly enough?"

"Yes, as most love and lust potions are designed to drink.

It's only thanks to the volume that fell on us—or you—that it'll have any effect." I studied him for a moment. "Why?"

"Because there's an old swimming hole not far from here. It used to be quite popular before the farmer got shitty about the sheer number of people using it and fenced off the entire area." His glanced at me, his eyes twinkling and his desire becoming more evident. "But we can climb over the fence easily enough and it's a warm enough night for a swim."

"Are they any critters in this water?"

He raised his eyebrows. "That depends on what sort of critters we're talking about."

"You know—fish, yabbies, snakes, eels—slimy things that bite, basically."

He laughed. "I daresay there'll be yabbies, but they generally don't make a habit of feeding on toes."

"That's not comforting."

"It'll be fine, I promise."

I harrumphed. He laughed again and hit the accelerator. Ten minutes later, we were pulling off the road into a well-treed area. The fence was a six-foot wire mesh thing that was certainly designed to keep people out.

"Isn't what we're about to do basically breaking and entering?"

He walked around to the back of the truck. "The farmer's a friend. He'll understand."

"I hope so." I studied the fence for a moment then added, "I am not going to get my butt over that very easily."

"I'll boost you."

He slammed the back of his truck down and locked it up. He had a picnic blanket, a towel, and what looked to be a fresh shirt and a pair of tracksuit pants all slung over his shoulder.

"Do you carry half your wardrobe around with you or something?"

"A good ranger is prepared for any eventuality."

"Even seduction on the banks of an old watering hole?"

"Indeed." He touched my spine and lightly pressed me forward. "I used to come here a lot when I was a teenager."

"Oh, yeah? And how many seductions happened here?"

"A few." He grinned and cupped his hands. "I'm a ranger, not a Boy Scout."

I snorted and placed my foot into his hands. He boosted me up easily, waited patiently while I rather awkwardly clambered over the top and dropped down onto the other side, and then followed me over. He was decidedly more graceful than me.

He caught my hand and then led me forward. We were soon deep within a forest of beautiful old gums, but the area wasn't silent. The hum of cicadas filled the air, and magpies sang melodiously in the distance. We walked up a slight incline and came out of the trees. The swimming hole was oval shaped, fed by a spring on one edge and draining into another on the opposite side. The water was dark, which indicated depth, and the bank a mix of green grass, wild-flowers, and dirt.

"This is very pretty," I said.

"Which is why it was once such a popular seduction spot."

We walked down to a thick patch of grass, where he dropped the towel, blanket, and the clothes he was carrying. "Do you need help stripping off?"

I ignored the wicked twinkle in his eyes and began pulling off my clothes. "You're the one that majorly stinks right now. How about you just get into that water ASAP, before the full force of the potions hit and you get the mother of all boners?"

"Not a bad thing—"

"It is if it lasts days."

"And could it?"

"Yes."

"Moving as ordered, then."

He hastily undressed, then ran for the water and dived in. I stopped close to the water's edge and warily dipped a toe in. "It's damn cold!"

He grinned. "I'll warm you up quickly enough."

I snorted and went as deep as my ankles. A shiver ran through the rest of me. "I'm not a fan of cold—" The rest of my sentence ended in a splutter as he swept an arm across the water and sent a huge wave over me. "Damn you, Ranger—"

He laughed. "I'll do it again if you don't get in."

I dived in and swam over to him. "You still smell. Dunk under a few more times."

He did so. Once the stench was all but gone, I wrapped my arms around his neck and kissed him. He caught my waist, drew me even closer, and deepened the kiss, his mouth hungry against mine.

"Condom impossibility is the one problem with seductions in water," he said eventually, his words little more than a harsh rasp. "Are you protected?"

"Yes." I raised an eyebrow. "Are you clean?"

He grinned. "As a whistle. I'm a very careful werewolf."

"Good, because I'm a very careful witch who doesn't want anything nasty."

"You'll get nothing more than a good time from me," he said. "A promise I make in the full knowledge that you could probably send a curse my way that would totally end my sex life if I was stupid enough to lie."

"You'd better believe it, Ranger."

He laughed again. I wrapped my legs around his waist and felt him slide deep inside.

"This is getting to be something of a habit," I murmured, as I began to move ever so slowly.

"What is?" His voice and expression were as distracted as any woman could want.

"Me having my legs wrapped around your waist." Pleasure grew as his thick heat slid deeper and his movements became more demanding.

"And this is a problem why?"

"It's not, it's just that maybe we should aim for a bit more variety."

"Why do you think I brought the picnic blanket? I intend to make a full evening of it."

"The bugs will be out and biting later."

"They won't be the only things," he muttered. "Now will you just shut up and concentrate, woman?"

I laughed and did so—both then, and the multiple times that followed on the picnic blanket. We might have washed the potions off, but they'd still had enough time to work some of their magic on us both. Not that I was complaining any—not when I had three years of abstinence to make up for.

As dusk began to settle in and the bugs started to bite, he propped up on one arm and said, "I'm hungry—for food this time, you'll be relieved to hear."

"Good, because I think I've worn off all the energy from my Christmas lunch, and I need a refuel."

"I've stocked my fridge, so I can make good on my promise to cook for you."

"Can you actually cook?"

"As long as you want nothing fancier than steak, eggs, and chips, yes."

"Sounds perfect."

His phone rang, the sound sharp and loud in the serenity that surrounded us. "Sorry," he said, and reached for it.

I walked back into the water and quickly washed off. I had a vague feeling I wasn't going to get that steak. Not in the immediate future, anyway.

He listened for several minutes, then said, "Be there in thirty. Keep the area secure until then."

My heart was beating a whole lot faster. Even though part of me really didn't want to know, I said, "Another murder?"

"Another skinning." He climbed to his feet. "These bastards certainly aren't wasting any time."

And obviously it had happened in an area that the wild magic—and Katie—wasn't patrolling. I had no doubt she would have come for us otherwise.

I grabbed the towel and quickly dried off. "Isn't this your night off?"

He nodded. "Byron's on call tonight, and that's not why I was called. With Ashworth still in hospital and Chester not picking up his phone, I'm afraid you're it." He hesitated. "That sounds bad, but you know what I mean."

"I do." I picked up my clothes, but the scent wafting from them was so strong my eyes started watering. "I'm not going to be able to wear these."

"Which is why I brought extras." He tossed me the checked shirt and pulled on the track pants. "We'll have to stop at my place on the way through—I can't go to a crime scene half-dressed."

I pulled on the shirt. It fell to my knees and surrounded me with his smoky, woody scent—which was far more pleasant than the toxic mix of love potions. I gathered my clothes and his in the towel while he folded the picnic blanket, then we headed back to his truck.

The trip back to his house in Argyle was done in silence —with the siren screaming, there was little point in conversation. We quickly changed then continued on through the spa town of Rayburn Springs but took the road that led to Newstead and Maldoon rather than Castle Rock.

We made a right turn miles out of Newstead, and the road quickly changed from bitumen to stone. Aiden didn't slow down, even as the road began narrowing and the farmsteads gave way to true bush.

Eventually the flash of lights broke the deepening darkness of the night. Dust was settling around the nearest one, suggesting it hadn't been here long.

Aiden parked near the two ranger vehicles and then climbed out. I did the same and followed him across. Ciara was just grabbing her gear out of the back.

"Bryon down at the site?" Aiden asked.

"Yeah, keeping it secure," she said. "There's a few foxes about in this area."

Aiden grunted and continued on. I fell in step beside Ciara. "I wouldn't have thought foxes dumb enough to enter a werewolf reservation."

"They generally do keep out of pack compounds, but the reservation as a whole is fairly large, and there's certainly plenty of them in the areas that ring the reservation's boundaries."

"Has Byron said anything about the kill?"

"Just that they've grabbed the pelt." Her gaze came to mine. "Are you going to be okay with this kill?"

I nodded. "I know what to expect this time."

"Good."

We continued on in silence. Up ahead, light glowed, throwing the man who stood within its circle into shadow.

The wolf's skinless form lay in the middle of that bright circle. A silver dart was embedded in his shoulder, the metal gleaming in the harsh light. I swallowed heavily, keeping my eyes on his front leg rather than the rest of him. The bracelet stood out starkly against the bloody muscles of his leg. Very obviously, it had been deliberately left behind. Maybe they simply figured that now that we had one of them, there was little point in them retrieving any.

It also meant they were totally sure we couldn't identify them through either the witch or the security cameras. And that, in turn, meant the man who'd so confidently stared into the camera had to have been wearing some form of disguise, whether it was magic or not.

I took a deep breath and forced myself closer. This wolf looked smaller than the other two and, when I got around to the leg side, I saw why—it was female rather than male. Which, for some weird reason, just made me angrier.

I took another deep breath and then squatted next to her body and studied the charm bracelet. The twin spells woven through the entwined threads were strong, but certainly nothing I couldn't undo. And though I doubted the witch had, in any way, layered in any sort of trap, caution nevertheless stirred through me. I wasn't about to do a Chester and arrogantly assume everything was as it seemed.

The Ballan witch had received some training, because the patterns here were textbook spells and obvious even to me. There were three spells in all, one thicker than the other two. That was the control vein—and it meant one of the hunters had to be wearing the command bracelet. Given the spell on such a bracelet had to be powerful enough to compel, Ashworth should be able to sense its presence if the hunters ever came near him. Hell, even Belle and I should feel it.

I reached out and, without actually touching the woven leather itself, carefully untwined the first thread from its brethren. Once I'd deactivated it, I repeated the process with the other two. As the magic died, I pushed to my feet and said, "It's safe."

"Thanks." He tossed me his keys. "Do you want to head back home? I'll get Ciara to drop me off when we finish here."

I hesitated, and then nodded. "I'll park your truck around the back of the café. If we head to bed, I'll drop the keys in the power box at the back."

His smile was almost wistful. "It's sure not the way I'd hoped to be spending the evening."

"Definitely not." I nodded at Bryon and Ciara and got out of there. Reversing his truck was a five-point maneuver as the road was narrow and lined with trees, and I didn't want to hit either them or the two SUVs.

"Why are you home?" Belle said, the minute I walked in the back door. "What's happened?"

"Our hunters happened." I dumped Aiden's and my clothes in the washing machine, filled it with powder, and turned it on. I couldn't let them sit in the basket because they'd stink the entire café out in a matter of hours. "Aiden's at the scene now."

"That man's work ethic is commendable, but there are other rangers in this place. He should try leaving them to it more often. You want a coffee?"

I nodded and followed her behind the counter to make

myself a couple of ham and cheese toasted sandwiches. It certainly wasn't steak, eggs, and chips, but it was better than nothing—and all I could be bothered cooking at this hour.

"We did at least find the witch," I commented. "She's currently in RWA hands, being interrogated."

"Did you get much out of her beforehand?"

"Only that she charged a thousand a bracelet, and that she made ten of them."

"Which proves she's not part of an underground gray magic ring, because she would have known that the going rate for death—which is what those bracelets actually provide—is a whole lot higher."

I shoved my sandwiches into the press. "And how, pray tell, do you know that?"

She grinned. "Been doing a little covert research via Google and fell down the rabbit hole of links. There's some sick fuckers out there, let me tell you."

"That doesn't surprise me." The sandwich press began to sizzle as the cheese started to ooze. I grabbed a plate, slid the two sandwiches onto it, and then turned off the press. "The one thing I do want to know is, how are the hunters getting these bracelets into the hands of their victims? I wouldn't have thought they'd randomly accept one from any old stranger off the street."

"No." Belle followed me across to the table, placed the two coffees down, then snagged half a sandwich and sat on the other side. "There's plenty of weekend markets around. Maybe they're selling them there?"

"But they've only ten—"

"Unless they've hit up more than one witch."

"That's possible. The ones I visited today might not have had the skill or power to create command bracelets, but I daresay there are plenty of others who could."

"And there's no saying that they've bought them all in Victoria, either." She picked up her cappuccino and took a sip. "If you're going to hunt werewolves, I suspect you'd better get in and get out quick."

"That's possibly why our hunters weren't afraid of being seen on the cameras. Aside from the fact they were disguised, they're not actually intending to be around long."

"More than likely." Belle reached for another sandwich but I slapped her hand away. "Damn it, woman, I haven't had dinner and I'm *starved*."

She chuckled. "I won't ask what caused this starvation factor, because it's very evident in the contented swirl of your aura."

I grinned and didn't deny it. "I might go talk to Ashworth tomorrow and see what he knows about control bracelets. There might be a way we can track them—aside from sensing the magic when it comes within range."

"You'd think there would be," Belle said. "University is a five-year commitment for any witch, after all. I bet they learn all sorts of interesting shit we don't know about."

"We do have one advantage over them, though." I licked the last bit of melted cheese from my fingers and then picked up my coffee and leaned back in my chair. "We have all your grandmother's books."

"We do indeed. I might go check the index and see if there's anything on locating specific spell elements we might be able to use."

"It's worth a shot." I paused as a phone began to ring. "Is that mine?"

Belle snorted and thrust to her feet. "You know damn well it is."

I grinned as she dug it out of my bag, tossed it across, and asked, "You want a bit of cake?"

"I'll have some pud and custard if there's any left."

"Shall I reheat it in the microwave?"

"No, thanks." I glanced at the phone's screen, saw it was Ashworth, and hit the answer button. "If you're calling to bitch at still being in hospital, I will hang up."

"I'm not in hospital nor am I ringing to bitch."

I frowned at the edge in his voice. "What's happened?"

"I just got a very strange call from Chester."

"He's a strange man," I said, amused, "so that's not unexpected."

"True, but this was something else. It had my trouble radar stirring."

My amusement died. I wasn't about to discount Ashworth's trouble radar any more than I would mine. "What did he say?"

"That he's not dead. That he's still fucking alive," Ashworth replied. "I can only think he's talking about our dead witch."

I frowned. "But our dead witch *is* dead—we have his body in the morgue to prove it. Unless he's risen as a zombie, that's impossible."

And even if he had become a zombie, he still couldn't be called alive because zombies were merely reanimated flesh. They had no soul, no willpower, and no capacity to think or act. Their "life" was totally dependent on the strength and skill of the witch who'd raised them.

"I know, and I've tried ringing the morgue—"

"It's close to ten. There's not going to be anyone there at this hour—this isn't Melbourne, you know."

"I'm not a damn fool," he snapped. "There's been another skinning, has there not? I thought there was a chance someone was there to receive the body."

"You're right—sorry."

171

He grunted. "Anyway, working on the presumption that he's not a zombie, we have something else going on. I need to get over to Chester's, and I need you to drive me there."

"Me?" I asked, surprised. "Why?"

"Because I've a shattered right arm and can't drive."

"No, I meant why me specifically? Why not just grab a cab?"

"Because instinct is saying I may need a second set of eyes and ears familiar with magic, which means you're it, I'm afraid," he said. "And yes, before you say it, I'm well aware you're underpowered, but you have a link with the wild magic of this place, and that may yet come in handy."

My pulse rate leapt several notches. "You don't think whatever is happening has something to do with the wild magic, do you?"

"Anything is possible at this stage," he growled. "Especially when we're dealing with a powerful wellspring that's been left unprotected for far too long. How soon can you get here?"

"Ten minutes?"

"I'll be waiting out the front."

He hung up. I downed the rest of my coffee in several gulps that nigh burned my throat and thrust to my feet. Belle came out of the reading room with the backpack. "It's still stocked and ready to go."

"Thanks." I grabbed my purse, dug out the keys to Aiden's truck, and tossed them to her. "Do you want to move the truck so I can get the wagon out?"

She nodded. Five minutes later, I was pulling to a halt outside the short-term rental Ashworth was using while he waited for the council to make a decision on a full-time reservation witch. It was a basic two up, two down building, with both ground floor apartments having big picture windows and their own front doors. The top floor apartments were reached by stairs at rear of the premises, and had the additional benefit of wide balconies that enjoyed good views over Castle Rock—a fact I knew because Belle and I had inspected one of them before we'd decided to buy the café and live there.

"Chester's staying in a boutique hotel over in Rayburn Springs," he said, as he climbed in. "I think it's called The Randley—it's just up from the Motor Inn there."

"Why there? Castle Rock has more than one upmarket boutique hotel if that's his style."

"He's a heretic hunter and they tend to take lots of precautions, lassie. He's not even staying there under his own name."

I took off while he battled to get his seat belt on. I would have offered to help but he'd undoubtedly tell me he wasn't an invalid and to concentrate on the goddamn road.

It took us just on thirty minutes to get down to Rayburn Springs. As the Motor Inn came into sight, I slowed down and said, "Which side is it on, left or right?"

"It's just up ahead, on the left. You have to park in the side street."

I caught sight of a sign three quarters hidden by graceful old willow tree and turned into the street just beyond it. Ashworth was clambering out of the car before I'd turned the engine off. I cursed, grabbed the backpack, and hurried after him.

The Randley was a sprawling—and very beautiful—old Victorian building surrounded on two sides by a cream picket fence over which a vivid red-leafed hedge hung. The wrought-iron gate situated on the corner of the two streets creaked as Ashworth thrust it open, and a light came on, highlighting the path up to the front door.

As Ashworth strode toward it, energy stirred through the night. His, not Chester's or anyone else's. I had no idea what type of spell he was creating, but it gathered in a tight ball around the fingers of his left hand. I studied the pulsing patterns, seeing some familiarities in the structure of the threads. It was a glamor of some kind of—but not one designed to conceal. It was, I suspected, instead meant to deceive.

"Press the doorbell," he ordered.

I did so. Inside, the strains of "Knockin' On Heaven's Door" rang out and I couldn't help but smile. As musical doorbells went, it was certainly better than some of the ones I'd heard over the years. For several seconds, nothing happened, and then the sound of footsteps could be heard. The door eventually opened, revealing a man who was short and thin, with a long gray ponytail and round, hippy-style reading glasses perched at the end of his large nose. "I'm sorry, but we're—"

The rest of his words died as Ashworth's spell settled around his shoulders. Ashworth raised his hand, palm up, and then said in a rather stern voice, "Is Raymond Chester staying here?"

"Yes, he is." The thin man's gaze darted between the two of us. "What is this about, officers? Has there been some kind of trouble?"

It was interesting that he saw us as police, not rangers, if only because it suggested he hadn't been living in the reservation long. A deceiving spell generally worked with whatever vision the recipient was most likely to accept.

"No," Ashworth said, "we just need to speak to him as a matter of urgency."

"Of course." The thin man unlocked the screen door

and then stepped aside. "He's in 3B—take a left at the end of the hall, and it's the second on your right."

"Thank you."

Ashworth strode down the hall. I hurried after him, the sound of my steps lost under the clomp of his. We found the room easily enough but the door was locked and Chester wasn't answering. There was no sound coming from within the room and nothing to suggest there was anything out of place or wrong.

But trepidation crept through me anyway, though whether that was due in part to the tension gathering in Ashworth I couldn't say.

He glanced past me and said, "Have you got a key?"

"Yes, of course." The short man disappeared briefly into another room and then hurried down to hand Ashworth the rather old-fashioned brass key.

Ashworth shoved it into the lock, turned the key, and pushed the door open.

The room was a mess. Chester's bag had been upended, his bedding torn apart, all the drawers in the dark-stained TV cabinet pulled out and lying in an untidy pile on the floor,

As was Chester.

His hair was wet, and he was naked except for the white towel wrapped around his waist. There was no surprise in his expression, no shock, and if not for the puckered red wound on his chest, right above his heart, it would have been easy to think he'd simply fallen asleep.

But he wasn't asleep. He'd been shot.

Murdered.

CHAPTER EIGHT

"**O**h my *God*," the short man whispered. "Is he—?"

"I don't know," Ashworth said, even though Chester very obviously *was*. "You'd better call an ambulance, though."

"Of course, of course."

As the short man hurried away, I said, "Is it not a rather odd coincidence that first our heretic is shot, and now his hunter has been?"

Ashworth snorted. "I'm thinking coincidence has nothing to do with it. In fact, I bet when the rangers run their tests, they'll find both bullets were fired out of the same gun."

"If that's the case, then maybe we're dealing with nothing more than someone out to kill witches."

"I doubt whatever is happening here is that simple."

A statement I agreed with, if only because none of the killings in the reservation of late could be described as simple. "How could he have been shot without anyone here knowing about it, though? You'd think someone would have heard something."

"Not if a silencer was used." He knelt beside Chester and felt his neck.

"But silencers don't suppress all sound, do they?"

"No, but they reduce it down to what you might hear if you were wearing ear protection. In this case, that was obviously enough."

"Obviously, but it's still rather odd, given the place is so damn quiet."

"The owner might be the only other person here, and he did take a while to get to the door." He looked up at me. "There's no pulse."

"Which is no surprise given where he was shot." I scanned the room, looking not at the mess but for something far more ethereal. "I've no sense of a soul or ghost in the room."

"No. This is obviously another death that was meant to be." He pushed to his feet with a grunt of effort. "You'd better call in the rangers."

I did so. To say Aiden was less than impressed with the news we had another body would be something of an understatement. I tossed my phone back into my handbag and then said, "They'll be here soon."

Footsteps once again echoed out in the hall. The short man stopped beside me, his expression anxious. "The ambulance is on their way."

"Thank you, Mr.—"

"Joseph. Joseph Hardcourt." His gaze went to Chester. "Is he okay?"

"I'm afraid not, Mr. Hardcourt," Ashworth said. "Tell me, did Chester have any other visitors this evening?"

"Not that I'm aware of, but I can check the security cameras if you'd like."

"The front desk isn't manned at night?" I asked, surprised.

He looked up at me. "Until seven, yes. After that, guests use their own key to get in. Late arrivals must buzz, as you did."

"Is there a separate guest entrance, or is the front door the only one?" Ashworth asked.

"There legally has to be at least a separate fire exit—it's around the side of the hotel—and there's also a rear entrance for guests using the parking area."

Meaning our killer more than likely had come and gone through one of them—and done so without setting off alarms or alerting Hardcourt.

"I'm afraid we've had to call in the rangers," Ashworth said, "so if you could go out front and wait for them, that would be appreciated."

Hardcourt nodded and hurried away. I met Ashworth's gaze. "Chester would have felt the approach of another witch, so whoever did this was either human or wolf."

"Yes, but I still think we're looking at a professional hit. It's not easy to get silencers in this day and age."

"No." Not with the strict gun laws we had in Australia. "It appears he wasn't expecting to be attacked, given he answered the door in a towel."

"Which makes me wonder if this hit has anything to do with our dead witch, or perhaps a past case. Heretic hunters aren't the most popular folk around."

"He's the first one I've met, but if he's a good example, I'm not surprised."

"He's actually one of the better ones." Ashworth studied the room for a moment. "I know your ranger would prefer us not to touch anything but I want to check if Chester has hidden any information."

I frowned. "Why would he have done that when he wasn't expecting to be attacked?"

"It's nothing more than a gut feeling, and the fact he sounded unusually anxious and out of sorts on the phone. He mightn't have been expecting a visit from a hit man, but he *was* expecting something."

"And yet I'm not feeling anything in the way of wards or protections in the room."

"No, and that makes this situation a whole lot stranger."

I hesitated, and then said, "You know, there's one way we can find out for sure—ask the man himself."

Ashworth glanced at me. "Newer souls are notoriously difficult to contact."

"Belle specializes in difficult."

He raised an eyebrow. "She must be a pretty damn strong spirit talker then."

"She is." One of the strongest in recent history, if my mother was to be believed—and I certainly did. It wasn't like compliments to either of us had ever dripped easily off her tongue.

"It's certainly something we can try, then, but I'd still like to see what we can find here first."

I glanced around the room again. "I guess given the state of the place, Aiden's not really going to know if we've interfered with anything. Just be sure not to leave finger-prints everywhere, because that will both tip him off *and* piss him off."

"I've been doing this job and working with rangers and the law for more years than you've been alive, lass, so don't be telling me how to do things," he growled. "I'll check in here—do you want to take the bathroom?"

I restrained my smile and headed across the room. The bathroom styling could be described as both over the top and "manly." The slate wall tiles were a mix of heavy browns and gold, the floor tiles were black, and so were bathroom cabinet, the washbasin, and the toilet. All the taps were a gleaming gold and had to be hell to keep clean. There was no window—there wasn't even a skylight—so the only thing that saved the room from looking like a cave was the white-painted ceiling.

There were wet footprint puddles coming out of the shower, and a white towel lying on the floor near the washbasin. But the whirlwind of destruction that had hit the main room had also ventured in here—Ashworth's health bag had been emptied out and the bathroom cabinet's drawers and cupboards were open. Even his shampoo and conditioner hadn't escaped—they'd been slashed open with a knife and were currently sitting in a broken pile in the screened-off shower area.

I ran my hand across all the bits and bobs scattered across the washbasin. None of them held any sort of magic, which again spoke to the fact he wasn't expecting trouble. Not even the most blindly arrogant blueblood witch would risk confronting an unknown—untested—witch without taking steps to protect themselves. Not even if said witch was thought to be friendly.

And we were certainly weren't dealing with friendly here.

I kept checking, looking in the open drawers and cupboards, and even shaking out the towels still sitting in the rack. Nothing.

I went back out. Ashworth was peering under the bed. "Did you find something?"

"There's a very faint wisp of magic coming from under

the bed." He glanced over his shoulder. "I can't see anything and it's too awkward for me to climb under."

"Which is the polite way of saying, lassie, get your butt under and check it out for me."

He chuckled softly. "I think you've gotten more of my measure than I've got of yours."

"I had a grandfather very much like you."

"I didn't think there was anyone as grumpy and as frank as me."

"You obviously didn't live in Canberra long enough."

"Only for as long as it took to get through university."

"I take it you weren't born there, then?" I hitched up my jeans to give my knees more bending room and then peered under the bed. I had no immediate sense of magic, so it was indeed faint. "Whereabouts did you feel the spell?"

"Middle of the bed, around the butt zone," he said. "And no, I was born in Brisbane. Lived there until I was seventeen, then got a scholarship to the uni."

I swiveled around and then edged under the bed on my back. "Did you join the RWA straight after you'd finished?"

"Again, no. I travelled a bit, as you do, until I met my partner and decided I wanted to settle here in Victoria. He got me into the RWA."

"Is he still working with them?"

"No, he retired a few years ago. Have you found it?"

"There's not exactly a lot of moving room under this bed," I muttered.

"Another reason why I didn't go under—I've got a bulkier frame."

"Yeah, but I have boobs." Magic whispered past my nose. I narrowed my gaze and studied the bed's metal struts. Finally, I saw it—the spell was little more than a spark of violet-black hidden in between two of the cross-struts. "Got it."

"What sort of magic is it?"

I studied it for several seconds until the nature of the threads began to reveal themselves. It was a simple but low-powered spell, which was why it was so hard to see—a choice that had no doubt been deliberate. "I think it's a very basic concealment spell."

"Can you unravel it?"

"I think so."

I wiggled a bit closer and then, very carefully, began the deactivation process. The threads didn't put up any fight, withering away with barely a touch. A small piece of rolled-up paper fell onto the carpet. I grabbed it and shuffled out from under the bed, handing it to Ashworth before sitting up.

He carefully unrolled it. It was only a small piece of paper, and the writing appeared to be little more than black scratchings. Witch script, though not the general form I'd learned when I'd been in school.

Ashworth swore and scrubbed a hand across his chin. "This isn't good."

"Is it about our dead witch?"

"Yeah, and according to Chester, his body might be dead, but his soul likely isn't. He suspects it has simply transferred to another body."

"*What?* How is something like that even possible?" I peered over his arm at the note in the vague hope the writing would make more sense than his words. It didn't.

"There's a long history of strong spirits taking control of a body and ousting the soul, lass—"

"Yes, but that's spirits or ghosts, not a *living* soul leaping from his own body into someone else's." I shook my head.

"But it would at least explain the size and power of the protection circle. It'd take some pretty dark and powerful magic to perform a stunt like that."

"Yes. And it's also probably why that circle remained active after we found the witch's body." Ashworth's expression was grim. "The bastard's flesh might be dead, but *he's* very much alive."

If that were true, then this reservation could be in very deep trouble. Neither Ashworth nor I were capable of dealing with such a strong witch. Not without help. "Does he say why he suspects this?"

"Briefly. The note appears to be written in a hurry."

Suggesting maybe he *did* suspect trouble was approaching. But then, why sit down to write a note rather than protect the damn place? It was really strange behavior from a man who'd obviously spent a good portion of his life hunting heretic witches.

"He was researching the spell thread sequences via the university's database," Ashworth continued, "and came across a vague mention of large black quartz being the perfect containment stone for darker spells such as soul transference."

"Which is what our heretic witch used."

"Yes, and there are only a few areas within Australia in which that quartz can be found."

"Let me guess," I said, voice dry, "this reservation is one of them."

"This region, not specifically the reservation."

"Which suggests he might have come here to collect some of those stones for the spell transference, and stayed because he sensed the wild magic."

"Either that, or he was drawn here because he was

aware there was a large wellspring that had only recently been protected, and decided to combine needs."

That was probably the more likely scenario. "It still doesn't explain how the witch found Chester, though, or why this place has been torn apart, or why he sent a shooter rather than finishing the job himself."

"It's more than likely he's not yet physically able to do anything himself," Ashworth replied.

Because all magic had a cost, and the stronger the spell, the higher that cost. It wasn't hard to imagine that magic strong enough to rip a soul from one body to another would deplete reserves so completely that if death didn't come calling, you'd be incapacitated for days—if not longer. "If he *is* incapacitated, then someone has to be looking after him."

Ashworth shrugged. "That task more than likely falls to his familiar."

I frowned. "But not all witches get them, and if his familiar is a *cat*—"

"If that's the case, he'll have someone else running after him. He's a very powerful dark practitioner, lass. He won't go without."

"Then I feel sorry for whatever that is."

"Indeed." Ashworth studied Chester for a moment. "It's possible the still active magic within that circle was also a means of tagging the reservation witch."

"Why go to the trouble of tagging someone and then sending a shooter after them when he could have easily taken you both out with that explosion?" I said. "It was certainly powerful enough to kill—I felt it from miles away."

"I agree, and it's a fact that lends support to the idea that death hadn't been the intention. If Chester is right about the soul transference—and I don't doubt for a second that he is—then it's possible the dark witch needed to reserve most of his strength for that spell." Ashworth paused. "It's a theory that is supported by the fact that, while most of the warding stones became little more than dust in that explosion, the one closest to him instead shattered. It's possible he's still got a few small fragments embedded into his skin."

My gaze immediately went to Chester. Aside from the waterproof bandage over the penetrative wound on his arm, there were plenty of smaller ones scattered over his torso and arms. Most were little more than scratches, but a few were raised and angry looking, suggesting the shards had dug deeper. "So you think the heretic witch used the shards as some sort of tracker?"

"It wouldn't be the first time something like that had happened."

"Wouldn't Chester have sensed something like that, though? He was stronger than either of us, and must have encountered similar tricks in his years of hunting the bastards."

"He should have, but he very obviously didn't." Ashworth's voice was grim. "It's possible the explosion rattled him more than he let on."

"I guess." I motioned to the note. "Does it say anything else?"

"Only that he's requested additional information from the HIC."

My mouth twitched. "That is such a weird acronym for such a serious organization."

"Indeed." He folded the note up and tucked it into his pocket. "I'll contact them and see if they'll send us the information."

"And another hunter." I hesitated. "Aiden will want to see that note, you know."

"He can—after I've translated the rest of it."

I frowned. "I thought you had?"

"No. As I said, for whatever reason, it was written in a hurry. There's an end passage I can't quite make out."

Which was fair enough, but I suspected Aiden would be far from happy about him keeping the note.

Out in the hall, footsteps began to echo. It said plenty about my awareness of Aiden that I knew he was approaching from just the sound of his steps. I rose, as did Ashworth.

Aiden stepped into the room and then stopped. His gaze quickly swept the area, pausing briefly on Chester's body before coming to rest on us. "You both okay?"

"Yeah, there's no magic involved in this kill," Ashworth said. "We've checked the entire place out and it's safe."

"Meaning you've also had a look around for clues, no doubt." Aiden's expression gave little away, but I nevertheless caught the brief flare of annoyance in his eyes.

"I'll remind you that this *is* technically a RWA investigation, even if I'm also acting as reservation witch," Ashworth replied evenly. "And I have every right to investigate any crime scene that involves a witch—whether or not a ranger or an officer of the law is also present."

That spark of annoyance got stronger in Aiden's eyes. "Did you find anything?"

"Nothing you can use or read, Ranger."

"Ashworth—"

"It's a note, in witch script," I said, before the conversation could escalate any further. "It suggests that the heretic witch isn't dead, that he has instead transferred his soul into another body and is currently recovering strength somewhere unknown."

Aiden's gaze went from me to Ashworth and back again.

"Not kidding, then."

"No, unfortunately," Ashworth said. "There's a passage at the end of the note I can't read properly—either because it was hastily written or because something else was going on. Once I decode it, I'll give you the note and the transcribed information."

"Does that mean you've finished here?"

"Yes," Ashworth said. "When the autopsy is being performed, could you ask Ciara or whoever else does it to look for small slivers of black rock embedded in his skin?"

"Anything embedded into flesh would be noted in the results as a matter of course, but why?"

"Because this was obviously a deliberate hit, but the question is, how was Chester found? He paid cash upfront, wasn't staying here under his own name, and would have noticed if a location spell had been activated in the area."

"If we do find something embedded, will it be safe to handle, or should we notify you before it's removed?"

"I doubt it would be anything more than a low-grade tracking spell, but it's always better to be safe than sorry. Come along, lassie, I need to get home."

With that, he strode past Aiden and left the room.

Aiden glanced at me. Frustration and regret briefly swirled through his blue eyes, their force echoing through me. "I'll see you tomorrow."

I grabbed my backpack and walked toward the door. "And hopefully for a good reason rather than a bad."

"*That* would be a nice change."

He touched my arm lightly, his fingers sliding down to mine and briefly squeezing them. The warmth of his touch lingered well after I'd left the hotel.

It was a much slower journey back to Castle Rock. Ashworth threw the door open almost before I'd fully stopped outside his apartment, but I caught his arm before he could get out. "If that explosion was meant to do nothing more than throw out trackers, you might want to take extra precautions for the next few days."

"I didn't get hit—"

"You can't be absolutely sure of that, so just do me a favor—throw up extra protection spells, shield the doors and windows against intruders, and if someone unexpectedly knocks on your door, don't answer the damn thing."

He snorted. "I may be an old witch but I'm—"

"Yeah, yeah, I know, but this young witch is concerned, so just humor me and do as I ask."

A smile twitched his lips. "It's nice to know I'm not totally hated in this reservation."

"No one here hates you."

"No, they mostly just can't tolerate my attitude." He chuckled softly and patted my hand. "I'll be careful, you can be sure."

"Good. Ring me when you transcribe the rest of that note. I want to know what it says."

"Will do."

He climbed out. I watched until he was indoors and then headed home. Belle was already asleep, so I went into the reading room, emptied the backpack and put everything safely away, and then headed for my own bed.

Only to be hit by dreams that shifted between skinned wolves howling to the moon and blood that seeped through the forests and the fields, killing all that it touched until nothing was left but a landscape that was barren and black.

I was on my third cup of coffee and in the kitchen cooking breakfast by the time Belle clattered down the stairs the next morning.

She took one look at my face—which undoubtedly looked as haggard as I felt—and said, "Another shitty night?"

"Yes." I plated up our breakfast then slid one across to her. "Dreams of doom and death, all of which were, of course, ambiguous."

"Do you ever do anything other than ambiguous?"

"Apparently not."

I picked up my coffee and plate and followed her out into the café. In between eating my bacon and eggs, I updated her on Chester and the possibility that our heretic witch was still alive.

"Hence the reason for the incomprehensible dreams," Belle said.

"More than likely." I licked the last bit of egg off my knife, then picked up my coffee and leaned back in the chair. "If he *is*, then it's very possible he'll make a play for the wellspring once he's mobile."

"More than possible," Belle said. "I can't see any other reason for a dark witch to come here. I mean, it's a great place to live and work, but it's too staid for the bad boys."

"You say that with such authority, and yet I believe this is the first time we've come across a blood witch since we left Canberra."

"No—we did cross paths with one in Wollongong, remember?"

"Crossing paths being the key words there." We'd done nothing more than walk in front of the woman. "And *she* was so unthreatened by our presence she didn't even notice us."

"Probably because it was obvious to anyone within a half mile radius just how scared shitless we were." She wrinkled her nose slightly. "You know, a tracking spell can sometimes work two ways—if Chester *has* got small shards left in his body, it might be possible to reverse the spell and use it to track the heretic witch down."

I raised my eyebrows. "You've obviously been reading your gran's book, because they certainly didn't teach us that when we were at school."

"We're lucky they taught us anything at all given how much they hated a Sarr witch being in their presence." She paused to drink some coffee. "I actually thought we might be able to do the same with those bracelets the hunters are using to control the werewolves."

I frowned. "This whole thing has the feel of an operation that's been run before, though. They were obviously very certain that any photos taken of them at the Ballan witch's shop wouldn't lead to them being identified, and I suspect they know enough about the bracelets and magic to store them separately until they're needed."

"Finding those bracelets will at least stop any more kills within the reservation."

"True, but Aiden's after justice, not just a cessation of kills." I grimaced. "And while I don't know a lot about tracking magic, I suspect the control bracelet would have to be active and in use for us to be able to track them down."

"It's still worth a shot."

I took a sip of coffee and then nodded. "I'll talk to Aiden about it."

Belle picked up a piece of bacon and munched on it. "I wonder how they got these bracelets to their victims in the first place? It's not like they could walk up to any old person in the street and hand it to them. Given the large numbers of humans now living, working, and visiting the reservation, they couldn't be positive they were handing it to a werewolf."

"I daresay that's a question Aiden has already asked the victims' families."

"Speak of the devil, he's just approaching the door. I suspect he wants breakfast, and I'm not talking about food." She rose and gathered the plates. "I'll leave you to 'discuss' matters while I go get dressed."

I picked up a peppershaker and tossed it at her. She dodged and ran up the stairs, laughing.

I walked over to the open the door and then leaned out. He'd parked farther down the street and was striding toward me; the tiredness so evident in his expression fled when he spotted me. "Morning, gorgeous."

I smiled. "You look utterly beat."

"And you look good enough to eat."

I stepped back so he could enter. "Eating is always appreciated, but I'm afraid the time and location are totally wrong."

He made a low sound in the back of his throat that was part laugh, part growl, and then wrapped an arm around my waist, pulled me close, and kissed me. It stole my breath and made me dizzy with desire.

"Damn," he muttered eventually, his breath a short, sharp blast of heat against my lips. "We really need to work on our timing."

"Yeah." I leaned my forehead against his for a moment and dragged in air in a vague effort to calm the inner firestorm. "Are you going home or back to work?"

"Home."

"You've been working all night?"

"There's only seven of us in all," he said. "We need to

keep an operational team going during the day."

"And being the boss, you feel obligated to do the lion's share of the out-of-hours work."

His quick smile was somewhat wry. "That too."

I raised a hand and ran it lightly down his stubbled cheek. His eyes were bloodshot and the shadows under them deep. "Are you coming in for breakfast? Or are you going straight home?"

"I'd love breakfast, and I'd love to spend more time with you, but I think I need sleep more."

"Then I appreciate you dropping by for a quick kiss."

"A man cannot survive on food alone—or so I've recently rediscovered." He smiled. "Right along with the fact I simply cannot get enough of you."

As if to prove it, he kissed me again, with such intensity that if it hadn't been for his grip around my waist I would have been little more than a puddle around his feet.

"However," he eventually added, voice husky, "that's not entirely the reason why I stopped."

"You shatter my heart, Ranger."

It was dryly said and he chuckled softly. "That's certainly *not* on my agenda. Not now, not ever."

Which was good to hear but rather meaningless given I could never be what he really wanted or needed. Sooner or later, heartbreak would come. Unless, of course, I could control my stupid heart, and history had already proven that was impossible. "So why else did you come here?"

"To ask a favor." He brushed the back of his hand down my cheek, his touch so light and yet so heated.

A tremor ran through me and I drew in a deeper breath in an effort to control the surging desire. But I might as well have tried to stop the sun from rising.

"I gather it's a magical sort of favor?"

He nodded. "And from Belle, more than you."

I raised my eyebrows. "If you decide to kiss her like you just kissed me, there will be words said. Unpleasant words."

He laughed. "I have no intentions of ever kissing Belle—"

"And why not, Ranger?" she asked as she clattered down the stairs. "I'm a stunning piece of womanhood."

"Indeed," he agreed sagely. "And one who scares the crap out of me."

She grinned. "Yeah, I can see those boots of yours shaking. What favor do you want?"

"I was wondering if it be possible to contact the spirits of either Kenny Sinclair, Jamison O'Connor, or Jeni Marin."

"The werewolf victims?" Belle asked. When Aiden nodded, she added, "I can certainly try, but those who have only recently crossed over are sometimes the most difficult to converse with. I'm guessing you want to know where they got those bracelets from?"

Surprise ran through his expression. "Yes—how did you know? Or shouldn't I bother asking?"

She smiled. "Never fear, Ranger, your lascivious thoughts are safe from me. Liz and I were discussing those bracelets this morning."

He glanced down at me. "And?"

"There's a possibility we could use one to at least track down the other seven recipients."

"That would be—"

"Difficult," I cut in, "so don't get your hopes up. In fact, it might be better if you ask Ashworth to do it. He's the stronger witch."

"I'll talk to him this afternoon, after I grab some sleep." His gaze went back to Belle. "I'd still like to

contact the victims and see if we can find out where they
got those bracelets. I can understand the two younger
victims wearing them, but I just can't see why Kenny
would. The only jewelry he ever wore was that
gold chain."

"Have you asked their families?"

"Yes, and they can't remember seeing the bracelets or
any mention of buying them."

"I can try to spirit talk tonight, if you'd like," Belle said.
"If you can get something personal from at least one of
them, it'll help the contact process."

"I see what I can do." He kissed my forehead, his lips so
warm against my skin. "I'll see you both tonight."

"You will." I crossed my arms to curb the instinctive
desire to reach for him and watched as he strode down to
his truck.

"Oh dear," Belle said. "You've got it bad, haven't you?"

"Lust? Hell yeah." I closed the door and met her gaze
evenly. "I might go add some additional layers around the
café and the reading room before you attempt to contact
any spirits, either today or tonight."

She frowned. "Why? I can't see any of the three being a
threat, but even if they were, there's little hope of them
getting through the multiple levels of protections we've
layered around both areas."

"I'm not worried about something getting in, but rather,
something leaking *out*."

Her frown deepened. "Magic? But spirit talking—"

"Doesn't involve magic, I know." I pulled a hairband out
of my pocket and swept my hair into a ponytail. "But the
various layers will react, if only faintly, when a spirit
answers. Given it's very possible the dark witch is not only

alive, but actively taking out all the competition, I'd rather we not come to his attention."

"But a muting spell is still a spell—"

"Yes, but it's a very low-level one—at least externally. He'd have to be driving past to even sense it, and even then —given the unconventional nature of our magic—he'll hopefully think it's nothing more than a very minor barrier spell from a couple of fairground witches."

And *that* was certainly something we'd been called more than once growing up in Canberra, even if it was obvious that—while I might not live up to the family name and expectations—I did at least have a greater capacity of magic than the fortune tellers and tricksters who usually worked at such places.

"And remember," I continued, "both Ashworth and Anna commented on not only the unusual construction of our network of spells, but also the fact there's wild magic woven through it. If this witch *is* after control of the main wellspring then—"

"Any indication there's already a witch on the reservation capable of using the wild magic is dangerous," she finished. "But there's still one major flaw in your thinking— anything you and I might create isn't going to fool him for long."

"We don't need long. We just need to keep him from sensing our magic from either a distance or even as he's driving past, and coming to investigate."

"Good point. You go do that, and I'll do the prep."

It took me a couple of hours to weave the muting spell through all the threads we'd placed not only around the reading room, but the café itself. I wrapped the strongest dampening around the layers that contained the wild magic —because there was, rather surprisingly, more than one, even if Ashworth and Anna hadn't been aware of it. While the wild magic might have only recently "outed" its attachment to Belle and me, it had very obviously been with us since the beginning. There was no other reasonable explanation for the very base layer spells—the ones we'd created when we'd first moved into this place—to be touched and strengthened by its presence.

Belle handed me a vitality-boosting potion the minute I came out of the room, and for a change it didn't smell like a swamp—consideration for the customers who were eating their breakfasts rather than my stomach, I suspected.

We were surprisingly busy that day. Belle and I alternated between helping Mike and Frank—our chef and kitchen hand—out in the kitchen, and Penny—our waitress —in the café. It made the day pass a whole lot quicker, although things were never boring when a good portion of the gossip brigade descended. Mrs. Potts wasn't there, but she was the topic of much conversation. I was rather pleased to hear that she and her husband had talked things out, and that Henry's possessions had not only escaped rain damage but had in fact been accepted back into the house. But not, Gina had noted in a rather superior voice, into the main bedroom, as was proper considering the secrets he'd kept.

Once we'd closed and done the next day's prep, Belle made us both a hot chocolate while I made ham and salad sandwiches.

But just as I pulled out a chair to sit down, wild magic whisked in, its touch urgent as it pulled at my clothes, my hands, my fingers.

A heartbeat later, I heard the sirens. Whether they were ambulance or ranger, I couldn't say, but fear nevertheless stepped into my heart.

Something had happened. Something bad.

"Go," Belle said. "Don't worry about the pack—the wild magic is with you so use it if you have to."

I grabbed my purse and keys and bolted for the rear of the café. The car lights flashed as I pressed the remote but as I climbed in, the wild magic wrapped around me, its energy so thick and heated that sweat immediately broke out across my skin and fear struck my heart.

That fear wasn't mine. It was Katie's.

Her force rolled through me—a swift but intense moment that left my whole body feeling stretched and shaky. But it also left me with the impression of where I had to go.

Ashworth's apartment.

I swore, threw the car into gear, and roared out of the parking lot, barely missing one of our customers as I did a quick left onto the main road. Five minutes later, I was pulling into the road where Ashworth lived.

To be greeted by sea of ambulances and ranger trucks.

And, in Ashworth's driveway, Aiden's truck.

CHAPTER NINE

W hich explained Katie's urgency. This wasn't about any old werewolf—it was about her *brother*.

I parked in the first available spot then ran toward the apartment. Jaz swung around and held up her hands. "Whoa, Liz, this is a crime scene. You can't go in there."

"Are they... is he?" I somehow managed to get out as I slid to a stop.

"No one's dead except the shooter, so you can relax."

I didn't. Not immediately. "Then why are there so many ambulances here?"

"Because Aiden made a code nine call—"

"And that is?" I cut in.

"Officer requiring urgent assistance," she replied. "We had no idea what we were facing, so we called up the entire team and sent two ambulances. Better to be safe than sorry, especially with all the shit that's been going down lately."

"Are either of them hurt?"

"I think Aiden might have broke Ashworth's other arm when he pushed him down, but aside from a few cuts and bruises, they're both okay."

The tension that had been twisting my guts into knots slithered away, and my legs suddenly felt like water. I groped for the nearby fence and took several deep breaths.

"What about the shooter?" I said eventually. "Where is he?"

"Behind the screens. There's three other apartments in the building, including one with kiddies."

Anger touched her tone and I could understand why. All it would have taken was one or more rounds to go astray, and they would have been dealing with something far worse.

"Aiden and Ashworth weren't caught unawares then?"

"No, thankfully. Apparently the shooter tripped some sort of magical alarm Ashworth had set up last night, and it gave them just enough time to get under cover."

I shifted my gaze to the apartment and, for the first time, noticed the shattered windows and the holes blasted into the door.

"What kind of gun did he use?" It obviously *wasn't* the same type that had been used on Chester.

"He had both a handgun and a semi-auto shotgun on him. He wasn't pussyfooting around this time."

"No." I crossed my arms and tried not to imagine what a shotgun blast would have done to either man—not a difficult task when the apartment door provided ample enough evidence. "I wonder why he was ultra-careful killing Chester, and the opposite here?"

"I guess that's something we'll never know given he's dead."

"Maybe," I muttered, "and maybe not."

Jaz raised an eyebrow. "I can assure you—"

"That's not what I meant. Belle's a spirit talker, so she

can have a chat with his ghost if it lingers here, or his soul if it doesn't."

Whether it would be worth it or not was another matter entirely—not all ghosts were fully sentient. For some, the confusion over their sudden death lingered in their afterlife, and it made dealing with them very difficult. Aside from that, he might not actually know all that much about the heretic witch.

If he was working for him, then he must have had some means of contacting him, Belle said, *even if it's something as simple as a phone number.*

The rangers will undoubtedly track down anyone he's been in contact with as a matter of course, I replied. *But I rather suspect our witch will be too canny to leave such an easy trail.*

Meaning maybe the shooter was being contacted face-to-face, she said. *After all, someone has to be looking after this heretic bastard if the ceremony drained him as badly as Chester suggested. Maybe that same someone has been contacting the hit man and giving him directions*

Maybe.

Jaz's gaze had widened at the mention of ghosts. "*Is* he lingering here? Can you sense it?"

My gaze swept the front yard and the screens hiding the body. "Not immediately, and certainly not from here. Belle's the stronger witch when it comes to sensing the otherworld elements."

Depends on the element, Belle said, amused. *You're far more attuned to the nasty ones.*

Which makes me wonder what I did in a past life to deserve it.

I glanced back to the door as it opened. Aiden stepped

out and scanned the area, and didn't look surprised when he spotted me.

"Jaz, you can let her in."

Jaz immediately raised the crime scene tape and waved me on. I ducked under the tape and hurried toward the door, making no attempt to look past the screens to see the hit man's body but nevertheless feeling a wisp of energy. It wasn't the wild magic, but rather a ghost.

And one that was very pissed off.

Obviously our hit man didn't expect to encounter any resistance, Belle said. *Makes you wonder just what he'd been told about Ashworth. You want me to wander over?*

I hesitated. *I'll clear it with Aiden first, but get the pack ready. I can't see him refusing given we have no real information about the heretic as yet.*

I stopped one step below Aiden and studied him critically. There was a bloody tear in his shirt just above his right elbow, a couple of minor scratches across his face, and several glittery spots in his dark blond hair I suspected were glass shards rather than silver strands.

"I'm very happy to see you're okay."

"And I'm happy to be okay."

"Do you know who the shooter was as yet?"

"No—he wasn't carrying a wallet or anything else that would have provided an ID." He paused. "Don't take this the wrong way, but why are you here?"

I smiled. "Do you really think your sister was going to sit by and let her big brother be attacked?"

"Ah." His gaze went past me, seeking the magic he couldn't see but was nevertheless nearby. "Thanks, Katie."

The wild magic stirred and warmth pulsed briefly through me. "She says you're welcome."

A bittersweet smile touched his lips, but he didn't say

anything. He just stepped to one side and motioned me inside. The place was a mess. Glass was everywhere, holes had been blasted into the walls, and the sofa was oozing stuffing and springs. Ashworth was sitting on the floor with his back against the fridge and his left arm being tended by one of the paramedics. He glanced around as I entered, his expression a mix of amusement and annoyance.

"It seems you were right, lass."

I raised an eyebrow. "And this annoys you?"

"I'm honest enough to admit it does." He grimaced. "I'm also honest enough to admit that if you hadn't nagged last night, I might not have set that trap and we both might now be dead."

"Then I'm extremely glad I nagged. How's the arm?"

"Not broken," the paramedic said, before Ashworth could answer. "He's just sprained the elbow. I don't think he's done too much damage to the ligaments, but we'll take him to the hospital for a scan—"

"No, you fucking won't," Ashworth cut in.

The medic gave him the look; the sort of look medics the world over used when their patient was being daft. "We need to ensure—"

"I can move my arm without undue pain. I'll keep it in a sling when and where possible to help it heal, but I'm *not* going back to the hospital."

The paramedic didn't look happy, but all he said was, "Avoid using it, then, and if the pain gets too bad, get to the hospital."

Ashworth grunted. I was well enough acquainted with the man now to know *that* was as far from an agreement as you could get.

Once the paramedic had finished up and walked out, I

said, "The shooter's ghost is hovering outside. Do you want Belle—"

"Yes," Aiden said, before I could finish. "We have no answers and no clues as to who this bastard is, so if there's a chance the shooter can tell us something, it's worth a shot."

"It would be better, however," Ashworth said, "if I created the protection circle."

I quickly passed the news to Belle that she was wanted, then said, "That's hardly practical given you've two arms—"

"Arms," he cut in irritably, "have nothing to do with my ability to raise magic. You can place the spell stones for me, lass, but beyond that, I don't need my limbs."

My smile was echoed in Aiden's bright eyes. "Given I don't know a whole lot about magic, can I asked why you'd rather do it than Liz?"

"Because of what's going on," Ashworth said. "Because the heretic witch seems intent on erasing the competition. If he *is* here for the wellspring, then it's not going to take him too long to figure out I'm alive given my magic still protects it. I'd rather he not figure out Chester and I aren't the only witches he has to worry about."

"Except my magic lies underneath yours at the wellspring," I stated. "He'll sense it the minute he starts to unravel your spells."

Ashworth glanced at me. "No, he won't. The first thing I did was weave a concealment spell around yours. He won't sense it until he gets through both my protection and concealment spells, and even then—given the amount of wild magic you either intentionally or unintentionally wove into that spell—he may not suspect the originator is another witch, but rather a last line of defense spell from me that has been warped by the presence of the wellspring."

I hadn't actually intended to weave the wild magic

203

through my spell, but given what I'd discovered at the café this morning, I guess it also wasn't surprising.

"If he's as powerful as Chester suggested, then he's surely not going to be fooled long-term by anything you or I could produce. I mean, no offense, but you're an RWA investigator for a reason."

"That reason being underpowered." Ashworth smiled as he echoed my usual claim. "And by the standards of some in Canberra, I most certainly am. But I'm also a canny bastard who knows a thing or two about concealment—just ask some of the bluebloods who were in my year at uni."

"I sense a story in that statement."

"One that is better told over alcohol once this mess is tidied up *and* I can actually lift a pint or two," Ashworth said. "For the moment, just believe me when I say he's not going to know anything about your magic until he breaks through all mine."

Aiden glanced at me, his expression concerned. "That still doesn't put you out of danger, though, does it? Not when you've all sorts of protection spells around that café of yours."

"Yes, but I wove a dampening spell around them this morning. Unless he actually walks into the place, he's not going to sense anything other than what might normally be expected from a couple of fairground charlatans."

"Good." He returned his gaze to Ashworth. "Did you manage to translate the rest of that note Chester left?"

Ashworth nodded. "It was a name—George Sarr. He found some evidence that the young witch had taken up with our heretic some ten years ago."

"Which means George Sarr has paid a very heavy price for deciding to become a heretic's apprentice."

"And I, for one, will afford him no sympathy," Ashworth

said. "I've contacted headquarters and the HIC to see if they've any information, but I haven't had a reply back yet."

Which seemed to be a developing theme. Marking something as urgent didn't really seem to make all that much difference to the powers that be.

Aiden's phone beeped. He pulled it out of his pocket, read the message, and made a quick reply. "Belle's just arrived," he said, as he put the phone away again.

"Then help me up, laddie, and we'll get this show on the road."

Aiden immediately hooked one hand under the older man's armpit and half hauled, half steadied him as he climbed awkwardly to his feet.

"Right," Ashworth said, his face a little paler than it had been only a few seconds earlier, "my spell stones are in the pack near the door."

I blinked. "You don't keep the securely tucked away?"

"They're stones, lass, and are of no use to anyone who isn't a witch."

"I know, but—" I shook my head. "I guess therein lies the difference between a witch with a steady income and one who has had to scrimp far too often in her life to be anything less than careful with *any* magical implement."

"Never actually thought of it like that." He shook off Aiden's hand and walked over to the living area. "We'd better try the spirit-talking inside, just in case the heretic, his spirit guide, or whoever else is helping him is watching. It shouldn't make any difference to Belle's ability to contact the shooter's ghost."

"It won't."

I picked up the pack, rested it on the nearby phone table, and reached inside for his spell stones. They were easy enough to find—even though they were wrapped in silk, the resonance of his power eddied around them, an inert force that tingled warmly across my fingers.

I pulled them out and then glanced around as Aiden opened the door and Belle stepped through.

"Well, there's definitely a ghost here and he's seriously pissed, as you said."

"Did you have any sense of his state of mind?"

"He's sentient." She glanced across at Ashworth and added, sympathy in her voice, "I hope like hell your partner is the caring and sharing kind, because you're going to need a hand with some of life's basics."

"I'm well aware of that. I don't need you to be reminding me."

Belle grinned, not in the least perturbed by the annoyance in his tone. "So, what's the plan?"

"Ashworth will create the protection circle," I said, "and we'll contact the ghost."

"We might want to vacuum the floor a bit first," Belle commented. "Otherwise we're going to end up with glass in unpleasant places."

"You could always sit at a table like normal people," Aiden said. "Or doesn't spirit talking work like that?"

"Ranger, you should be aware by now that we don't do normal." Her voice was cool but her silver eyes gleamed with mirth. "But it'll also be less of a drain on Ashworth's strength if we use as small a protection circle as possible."

"I'm totally—"

"No, you're not," she cut in. "But like most men, you hate to admit any sort of weakness even if you are swaying like a drunken fool about ready to collapse."

Ashworth snorted, but all he said was, "You'll find the vac in the laundry down the hall."

I handed Belle his spell stones then walked down to

grab it. Once Aiden had shifted the coffee table, I quickly vacuumed both the small floor rug and the floorboards immediately around it. Belle then placed the stones around the rug while I put the vac away.

"Right," Ashworth said, once Belle and I were sitting within the circle of his spell stones. "You ready?"

"Protect away," Belle said.

It took several minutes before his magic began to layer around us, but the sheer strength of it had me sucking in a breath.

There's no need for a circle this strong, Belle commented. *We're only dealing with a pissed-off ghost, not a demonic spirit.*

I suspect it might be something of a magical one-finger salute aimed at our heretic witch.

Belle's chuckle ran warmly through my thoughts. *Are you sure your great-grandfather didn't share his DNA with the Ashworths? Because he really could be your grandfather's much younger brother.*

Given everything I ever heard about my great-grandfather suggested he was something of a Casanova, that's more than possible.

Ashworth's magic reached a peak and then fell away. I could see the multitude of layers surrounding us—it was a thick net that nothing other than the most determined dark spirit would get through—but the power of it had fallen silent. Given my suspicion he was sending a message to the heretic witch, maybe we simply couldn't sense the magic because he was amplifying it *outward*, away from us.

"Righto, ladies," Ashworth said. "The stage is all yours."

"I'll be recording," Aiden said, "so if you can follow usual practice, Liz, and repeat whatever Belle is seeing or hearing, I'd appreciate it."

I nodded and inched a little closer to Belle so that our knees touched. She took a deep breath to center herself and clear her thoughts, then placed her fingers in mine and closed her eyes. While some spirit talkers used personal items to make contact, or objects such an Ouija board or even a spirit pendulum, Belle had no need.

Though our hands were only lightly touching, I nevertheless felt the moment she silently summoned the killer.

He answered somewhat reluctantly. His anger burned through her and echoed through me—anger that was wrapped in a thick sense of betrayal.

What is it you wish? His question was curt.

Your name.

Why?

Because I'd rather call you by name than mark your ghostly existence with the moniker of killer.

It was a weight he'd be wearing anyway, given he'd lived and died in violence. In many respects, becoming a ghost—even one fated to forever linger over the spot of his death—was far better than the life that probably would have been his on rebirth. Fate did not take kindly to those who killed others for their own gain, and she seriously believed in retribution and lesson learning. Not just in one life, but many. Do unto others was a witch creed for a very good reason.

I have many names, the ghost muttered eventually, *but you may call me Trent.*

Full name, please, Trent.

He hesitated. Belle frowned, and the force of her magic crept into the connection, pressing down on him, compelling him. It was something very few spirit talkers could do.

It's Price. Trent Price.

I repeated his answer for Aiden's benefit, but kept my attention on Belle and the ghost. While it was very rare for ghosts such as he to be dangerous, he'd been working for a powerful witch. I wasn't about to risk this being in any way another trap. It was unlikely, but still....

Why are you so angry, Trent? Belle said.

Because I was deceived.

How were you deceived?

Because the charm he gave me to protect me from magic somehow instead allowed him to get into my brain and make me do as he wished.

A compliance spell usually had severe distance restrictions, which meant the witch had to have been nearby watching. Unless, of course, he had an intermediary— someone he controlled, and who he could use as his eyes and mouthpiece.

Is that why you shot the shit out of this place, Trent?

Yes. Given the choice, I would have retreated the minute it became obvious Ashworth wasn't alone. The witch had other ideas.

Belle frowned. *And the name of this witch?*

Don't know, and don't want to know.

So how did this unknown witch contact you?

All communications was done through an intermediary.

And there it was. Our dark witch was no fool, but then, he'd outmaneuvered the HIC for years, so that was no surprise. *His or yours?*

His. He paused. *Why do you want to know?*

We want to track down the witch and stop him.

Kill him?

That isn't our task, but rather that of the heretic hunters we work for.

But he will be killed?

I haven't been told otherwise.

Good. Trent paused. *My contact was Abby Jones—she's blonde, with brown eyes and a raised mole on the left side of her face, near her lips. Probably around thirty. We met in roadside rest areas, where there was little chance of us being seen or recorded.*

What sort of car did she drive?

She didn't. She had a motorbike.

Undoubtedly the same motorbike we'd heard pulling away the afternoon we'd discovered Jonathan's body.

Number plate?

What makes you think I got that?

Because you're a contract killer, Trent, and I daresay that's a job that involves a good deal of caution. In fact, I'd bet that you even know where she's staying.

His amusement spun through the link between the three of us. *IB 6T4 was the plate, and she's staying in a house in Argyle.* He gave us the address and then added, *There was a car in the driveway, so it might have been the witch or it might not.*

You didn't check?

I'm not a fool. It was risky enough following the intermediary.

Did you get the plate number of the car?

No, because I didn't want to make it obvious I was checking out the joint. But it was a dark blue Mercedes, and the plates weren't Victorian.

Which would hopefully make it easier for Aiden to track down—after all, how many blue Mercs with interstate plates could there be in the reservation?

Were you contracted to kill only the two witches? Belle asked.

Yes. What happens to me here? Is this the afterlife?

I'm afraid there is no afterlife for the likes of you. Not the type you'd appreciate, anyway.

So what am I?

A ghost. One destined to haunt the location of your death for eternity.

His anger surged. *What? That's fucking unfair, isn't it? Can you help me? Move me on or something?*

I could, but I won't. You killed people for a living, Trent, and you deserve exactly what you've gotten. She paused, and a warning note crept into her mental tones as she added, *If, however, you make life difficult or in any way interfere with the residents of this building but especially the children, I'll send your soul to purgatory. And trust me, you wouldn't want that.*

His anger boiled over, sweeping over the two of us like a tidal wave. Belle pulled briefly on my strength to resist the wash of it then bid him never to enter this building and dismissed him. He was forced out, howling in fury.

She took a deep breath to re-center, then squeezed my hands and released them. "Right," she said. "He's gone."

"Brilliant job, Belle," Aiden said. "At least now we've got an address—"

"Which you won't be going to alone," I cut in, as Ashworth began dismantling his protection circle. "If our heretic *is* there, then you could all be in deep shit."

He frowned. "Won't the charm you gave me offer some form of protection?"

"Against all manner of ghouls, spirits, and vampires, yes. Against a heretic or blueblood witch—no."

"Ah." He glanced over to Ashworth. "You up to it?"

"Yes, but Liz will have to come with us, as backup."

Because he knew he wasn't strong enough to counter such a powerful witch alone, I thought. And because I could summon the wild magic, and *that* might just be our last line of defense if we did encounter the other witch.

Aiden grunted. Whether it was acceptance or annoyance I really couldn't say. "It'll probably take us a few days to process the apartment, which means you won't be able to stay here—do you want me to book you a room somewhere else?"

Ashworth shook his head. "I'll contact Eli and get him to book us another place. He'll have to come up here anyway, thanks to my arm situation."

Aiden nodded and returned his gaze to me. "Do you need to stop at the café to grab anything?"

I shook my head. "Belle came here fully prepared."

"Good—then let's go before these people escape us again."

I scrambled to my feet, exchanged the backpack for the car keys, and followed the two men out the door.

Be careful, Belle said. *The spirits aren't liking the way things are developing.*

Oh fab, something else to worry about. I helped Ashworth with his seat belt—much to his chagrin—then jumped into the front passenger seat of Aiden's truck while he continued on toward the rest of his rangers. *I don't suppose they care to elucidate on what's causing them concern?*

No, but whatever they're sensing is coming from the Argyle area. Wouldn't be hard to guess it's got something to do with our heretic witch.

No, it wouldn't. *Make sure you lock the doors when you go home, Belle, just in case.*

Always do. She paused. *Well, aside from that one occasion, anyway.*

I half smiled but didn't reply as Aiden jumped into the

driver seat, reversed out, and then headed for Argyle. Evening was settling in by the time we got there. Abby Jones's house was situated along a narrow gravel road that ran along one side of the old skate park. Aiden slowed as we neared the address we'd been given, but there wasn't a whole lot to see. It was a single-story weatherboard house with a tin roof. A metal carport was attached to the far end of the house, and a solitary motorbike sat underneath it.

"Number plate matches the one the ghost gave us," Aiden said.

He cruised past and pulled onto the grass verge several houses farther along, where the road became wider and merged into another. He undid his belt then twisted around to look at Ashworth. "What's the best way to play this?"

"I'll go for a stroll and see if I can sense any perimeter magic." He glanced at me. "And before you say it, it's more than safe for me to do so. But I do need you to help me out of the damn car."

My lips twitched, but I didn't say anything as I climbed out, opened his door, and then helped him out of the truck. As he strolled down the hill, I moved around to the front of the truck and leaned against the hood, letting the warmth radiating from the engine bay chase the gathering chill from my spine.

Aiden propped next to me, his shoulder brushing mine and his arms crossed. "Can I just put this out there? I'm not a fan of putting you into the path of danger."

"I think it's safe to say that I'm not a fan of it, either." My voice was dry. "But it's not like we've any real choice."

"Maybe not right now, in *this* situation, but perhaps when the reservation gets a full-time witch, it might change."

I glanced at him. "A full-time witch isn't going to

communicate with your sister, Aiden. For whatever reason, both she and the wild magic have chosen to communicate—and move—through me. And they were doing so even before you and I got involved. I have no idea why that might be so, but I doubt it'll change when the reservation witch arrives."

"Perhaps, but at least with a full-time witch, you're not going to be at the pointy end of investigations as much."

"I'm not at the pointy end right now. For example—" I motioned toward Ashworth, who was just passing the single-story house.

He snorted and lightly nudged my shoulder. "You know what I mean."

"I do, and I appreciate the concern, but I've just got this feeling that my involvement will continue regardless of how powerful the reservation witch turns out to be."

Aiden grunted. It wasn't a happy sound. He watched Ashworth for a few minutes and then said, "I don't suppose you know anything about Frederick Ashworth—the witch who's coming to be interviewed for the position?"

"Frederick's a rather old-fashioned name, which suggests it's a family name rather than the name he actually uses." I shrugged. "And given he's younger than the council apparently wanted, it's likely he was either in a lower-class level in school than us, or came in after we'd left to attend uni."

"And how," he asked mildly, "would you know something like that? Or is it another of those stupid questions?"

I grinned. "Apparently a rather loud and feisty wolf came into the hospital the night I was admitted, and Belle might or might not have caught some thoughts of his."

He shook his head but didn't reply as Ashworth motioned for us to come down. Aiden touched a hand to my spine, replacing one type of heat with another as he lightly guided me down the gravelly road.

"There's not a skerrick of magic." His expression was grim. "Our heretic witch might have been here, but he isn't any longer."

"Is it possible he's done exactly what we've been doing —raised a concealment barrier?"

Ashworth hesitated, looking back at the house with slightly narrowed eyes. "I can't feel anything, but I guess it's possible he's inverted the flow of his magic so that nothing leaks beyond the walls. Ranger, are you smelling anything odd or out of place?"

Aiden's nostrils flared as he drew in a deep breath. His expression darkened. "I can smell blood and death."

"But no life?" Ashworth asked.

Aiden tasted the air once again. "No."

Ashworth immediately headed down the long gravel driveway. I followed, my gaze sweeping across the house and the small carport in which the trail bike sat. The thing was muddy, so if it was the bike we'd heard when we'd found Jonathan Ashworth's body, it should be easy enough to match the dirt to that of the clearing we'd found the first body in. Or, at least, place the bike in the same general area.

But there was nothing else here, and no sense of power or magic of any kind. There *were* a couple of remnants floating along the breeze, but they were little more than echoes of the energy that had once protected this place, and held no life or threat.

Our heretic had definitely fled.

I guess the next question was, what had he left behind?

Ashworth paused on the veranda steps and his power surged, searching and testing. There was no response and there would have been if this place was in any way protected by magic.

"Open her up, laddie, and we'll see what happens."

Aiden stopped to one side of the door then carefully grabbed the door handle. It turned. After a glance at Ashworth, he thrust it open.

Nothing stirred. Nothing jumped out at us. There was no flash or surge of magic. The house was as inert on the inside as it was on the outside.

"I'm smelling a lot of blood—and it's fresh." Aiden drew his gun and glanced at Ashworth. "Is it safe to go in?"

When the older man nodded, Aiden edged around the doorway. He paused again, and then swore.

I quickly followed him inside.

Lying on the floor between the old sofa and the TV stand was a blonde-haired woman who looked to be no more than thirty or so, and who had a dark mole near the left corner of her lip. Trent's contact, Abby Jones.

She was dead.

Murdered.

CHAPTER TEN

I f the rawness of the gaping wound across her throat and the blood still dripping from the nearby coffee table was any indication, her death had happened *very* recently.

We might have missed the heretic, but we hadn't done so by much.

Her blood was a dark halo that surrounded her head. I wasn't a wolf and my sense of smell was pretty ordinary, but even I couldn't help but notice the sickly sweet, metallic odor that rode the air. I swallowed heavily, dragged my gaze away from the gruesome sight, and quickly scanned the rest of the room. There was no soul or ghost lingering either near her body or in the room itself, which meant this brutal death had been destined. I briefly closed my eyes and said a silent prayer to the gods that her next life was a longer, happier one.

Aiden shoved his gun away and then moved across to Abby, dragging my gaze back to her. Her hands were up near her neck, as if she'd tried to stem the flow of blood. But even from where I was standing, it was pretty obvious her windpipe and her two main arteries had been cut. Unconsciousness or even death might have hit within a minute, but that minute would have been utter hell.

Aiden grabbed a pair of gloves from his pocket and then knelt beside the woman. "Judging from the positioning of the body and the knife used to kill her, I'd say she was attacked from behind."

Ashworth walked across. "There's some residue on that knife."

Aiden glanced up at him sharply. "Magical residue?"

Ashworth nodded. "It's fading, though, and has the feel of a mobility spell."

Aiden frowned. "Meaning magic was the force behind this deed rather than a human hand?"

Ashworth nodded again. "Our witch wouldn't have had the strength to cut her throat so deeply or precisely with a kitchen knife. Few people would, let alone a man who'd still be recovering from a soul transfer."

"How long ago was she killed?" I asked.

"Five minutes, if that." Aiden glanced up at me. "Do you think you can grab information from her mind?"

I hesitated and rubbed my arms. There was something about this house that just didn't feel right, something *other* than the brutal death. "To be honest, I don't know, because I have no idea if her bleeding out so quickly would make a difference to what she might or might not remember. But it's worth a try if it helps us track this bastard down."

But my stomach was already churning at the thought of not only getting any closer, but the risk of being overrun by the emotions and horror she must have experienced in the brief minute between life and death.

"Do you want me to construct a protection circle?" Ashworth asked.

I hesitated again and then shook my head. "I have no

sense of evil lingering near this place, and you've already said there's no spell work here."

"That doesn't mean her body can't be spelled," he said.

My gaze unwillingly jumped back to Abby's prone form, but this time I studied her with my "other" senses. "I can't see anything suggesting that's the case."

Which might not mean anything given I wasn't even sensing the lingering magic on the knife still lying under her head.

"Neither am I, lass, but it's more than possible he's left some other kind of trap—like a nasty little dream imp that'll cause all manner of nighttime craziness."

"Dream imps?" Aiden said. "Seriously?"

"Yeah, and vicious little buggers they are, too," Ashworth said. "Had one attach itself to me a few years back. I thought the job was doing my head in before Eli finally figured out what was happening."

"The more I learn about the spirit world, the less I like it," Aiden growled.

"A dream imp couldn't possibly cause me any more hassle than my prophetic dreams already do," I said bluntly, "and I've enough charms on me to protect against all but the strongest spirits anyway. But I need a decision and quickly, because her memories will be degrading pretty rapidly by now."

"Then go," Ashworth said. "I'll keep a magical eye out for you."

I moved around the two men, squatted behind Abby, and then placed a hand on either side of her head. I tried to ignore the wetness under my fingertips, the too-close wound, and the look of utter horror forever frozen onto her face. After another of those breaths that didn't do a whole lot to ease the tension surging through me, I closed my eyes and reached for my psychometry abilities.

For several seconds, nothing happened. All I felt was the lingering remnants of her disbelief, horror, and pain. The emotions crawled across my senses and dragged tears from my eyes, but there was no immediate memory of anything else. No indication of who'd she'd been with before her death.

I pushed past the barrier of shock. Images began to flicker through the deeper recesses of her mind, but they were extremely fragile things. The minute I reached for them, they fragmented and spun away into the gathering darkness in her head.

The deeper I went, the darker it became. And yet, gradually, memories rose. They remained little more than fragments, mostly resembling either torn photographs or movie reels that only ran for seconds, no doubt thanks to the death that had come too fast. But they still gave me some clues.

"I see two men," I said. "One is the witch who now lies in the morgue, the other is a Sarr."

I paused as the images flitted away, dove even deeper, and this time caught the tail end of memories that were far more personal in nature. *A touch, a caress, kisses that burned, passion that was fierce and urgent, a shaft that was thick and long and felt so good as he thrust inside....*

The heat of the encounter echoed through me. I quickly released those memories and caught other fragments. "She and the Sarr witch were lovers. It's how the two men came to stay here."

I hesitated, seeing fleeting glimpses of the wounds on George Sarr's wrists—long cuts that sliced up both arms, and which still dripped blood as he came out of the forest and staggered toward Abby. Felt her horror at his refusal to explain what had happened or go to the hospital, and the speed with which the wounds healed. Was almost smothered by the tide of her hatred at being suddenly unable to refuse him, at being forced to do whatever he wanted, be it act as his cook, nurse, messenger, or simply someone for him to fuck whenever he felt the need. Gone was the tenderness, the caring. In its place was fear and brutality.

Then, finally, I caught an image of the witch Jonathan Ashworth had become. "George is tall, with silver eyes, a large nose, two thick scars running the length of his left cheek, and many more running up the insides of both arms."

"Another other identifying marks?" Aiden asked.

"Other than a gigantic dong, apparently not."

As Ashworth snorted, I pulled my hands away from Abby's head and pushed back, landing on my butt well away from the body and the blood splatter. For several seconds, I didn't move. Couldn't move. I just sucked in air in an effort to ease the trembling in my body. Psychometry was draining at the best of times, but using it like this—to connect with the mind of someone who'd crossed over—was nigh on incapacitating. I wouldn't be much good—physically or psychically—for the next few hours, at least.

Aiden squatted down beside me and handed me a handkerchief. "You've lost all color—do you need to go home?"

I nodded and quickly wiped my hands. "I'll get Belle to come and collect me. You can't leave here and I won't risk driving your truck. Not in this state."

"I've some jerky and muesli bars in the backpack—eating one or both might help boost the reserves."

"Is the muesli bar the type with chocolate? Or is it one of those useless healthy kinds?"

He smiled. "The latter, I'm afraid. The only chocolate I

like is in the form of cakes and brownies. I find anything else too sweet."

I gasped in mock horror. "Just as well I lust after you, Ranger, because that, right there, is a relationship-ending statement."

He laughed. "I'll make a mental note to stock both the pack and the fridge at home with a suitable variety of chocolate bars and blocks for you."

"*That* would certainly be appreciated," I said primly, and then let my smile break loose. "You can keep the jerky, but a muesli bar might help."

Probably not as much as one of Belle's rotten-smelling potions, but it was better than nothing.

I'm on my way now with one of said rotten potions in hand, she commented cheerfully. *Be there in twenty.*

Thanks.

"Do you want help getting up? Or walking back to the truck?" Aiden said.

I shook my head and climbed slowly to my feet. Pain flickered through my brain, the first stab of the tsunami yet to come.

Aiden rose with me, one hand hovering near my elbow, ready to catch me should I tumble. I gave him a quick smile. "I'm fine, Aiden. Really. I just need to sleep."

"Is Belle on the way?"

I nodded. "I'll wait for her near your truck. Ashworth, do you want a lift anywhere?"

He hesitated, and then shook his head. "I'd better stay here, just in case."

I nodded, lightly touched Aiden's arm, and then walked out of there as quickly as I was able. Once outside, I sucked in several deep breaths to wash the scent of death and blood from my lungs. The smell lingered on my clothes and filled my nostrils at every breath, but there was little I could do about that right now except ignore it.

Once I'd trudged up the hill, I grabbed a muesli bar then sat on the hood of his truck and munched on it as I waited for Belle.

She arrived twenty minutes later. Once I'd climbed in and buckled up, she handed me a two-cup-sized drink container that smelled a little less like a swamp than her usual concoctions.

"Thought your stomach might be dodgy, so added extra cinnamon and ginger to override the less pleasant aromas."

"Thanks." I still sipped it warily, but it was, in fact, quite drinkable—at least as far as potions went, anyway.

It was dark by the time we arrived back home, and the deep headache that came with reading the dead had well and truly settled in. I trudged up the stairs, stripped off, and all but fell into bed.

And didn't stir until the next morning.

The rattle of china and the bright chatter of many voices told me it was late enough for the café to be open. I glanced across at the clock and saw it was nearly ten. I had a quick, hot shower to wash the lingering scents from my skin then got dressed and headed down to help out in the café. We were flat out serving for the next couple of hours, but once it started to ease off, I went into the kitchen to help Frank—who was both our kitchen hand and dishwasher— get through the mountain of dishes.

It was close to five by the time Belle and I finally got a chance to sit down and relax. I took a sip of my hot choco-late—which, as usual, had lashings of cream and marshmal-lows—and then said, "I wonder if your gran's books have anything about soul transferring?"

"As it happens, I wondered the same thing, and was looking it up last night while you slumbered rather noisily."

I raised my eyebrows. "I snored?"

"Loudly. I hope Aiden has earplugs."

I snorted—not a bright move given I was also in the process of taking another sip of my chocolate. As cream went flying, I swiped a hand across my nose and then licked it off my fingers. "The way things are going, it won't matter. I'll be over the weariness by the time we get another chance to hit the sheets."

She raised an eyebrow, her silvery eyes gleaming with amusement. "I was under the impression that the good times were happening everywhere *but* between the sheets."

I tried to slap her arm in mock outrage but she quickly leaned away from the blow and laughed. "I found what amounts to little more than a side note in a book about witches who are turned by darker magics."

"Just one book?" I said, surprised. "I would have thought—given how detailed her knowledge was about dark spirits and dark forces—that she'd have more than one on dark witches."

"Except that the HIC don't really share information about heretics, even amongst the bluebloods," Belle said. "So it's not really surprising that someone like Gran—a lower-class Sarr witch—would only be able to glean snippets. She was a first-rate compiler but even she had limits."

"Have you had much of a chance to read through it?"

She nodded. "It says that those who are powerful enough—and who have a strong enough connection with whatever dark spirits they've entered into a pact with—can extend their lives by transferring their soul into the body of another. The cost of this is paid by the soul of the body's original owner, which is taken by the dark spirits.

And *that* makes me wonder if George Sarr knew what exactly was involved in becoming a dark master's apprentice."

"Why?" I grabbed a teaspoon and scooped up a semi-melted blob of marshmallow.

"Firstly," she said, "apprentices apparently have to swear in blood to their master, which binds them to their dark witch's command. They are subsequently marked, with each dark master having their own brand. It's a means of warning other powerful dark witches not to encroach."

I raised my eyebrows. "Why would *that* be a problem?"

Belle shrugged. "Maybe suitable dark witch apprentices are few and far between."

"Maybe." I scooped up the rest of the marshmallow and then said, "I'm guessing the two knife cuts on George's cheek was Jonathan's brand?"

"I'd presume so. Gran said it was usually in a very visible spot such as the face." She leaned forward and crossed her arms on the table. "The second thing is the fact is that a soul transfer can *only* happen between a master and his apprentice. It's apparently the one reason so few masters have an apprentice."

"I'm betting it's a condition of employment that's *not* mentioned in whatever contract is signed between the two."

"Either that, or the apprentice is willing to take the risk that his master will teach him enough that he'll be able to resist or even defeat his master."

"I wouldn't think that would happen too often."

"No, but maybe they think the promise of ultimate power is worth the gamble."

"I guess their life is one big gamble anyway given the forces they use on a daily basis."

Behind me, the door opened, and I turned to see Aiden

walk in. He looked a whole lot fresher than he had yesterday and there was no sign of the deep shadows that had been ringing his eyes.

"Evening, ladies." He kissed me warmly and then pulled out a chair and sat down.

"Would you like a coffee, Ranger?" Belle asked.

He nodded. "That would be great, though I *am* here on official business."

I raised my eyebrow. "That being?"

He pulled a plastic bag out of his pocket, inside of which was a tracking bracelet—the one taken from the female wolf, I suspected, given I could feel the vague wisp of magic emanating from it. The spell would probably have faded from the other bracelet by now.

"I know it's a long shot," he said, "but could you try tracking down a location of the rest of the bracelets?"

I plucked the bag from his grip and shook the bracelet out into my hand. After carefully pulling apart the three strands, I ran my finger across the strip onto which the control and tracking spell had been woven. It was still present, and still reasonably strong, even if it was no longer dangerous.

I met Aiden's gaze again. "I might be able to, but if I fail, there's always Ashworth and his—"

The corners of his bright eyes crinkled. "Eli arrived in Castle Rock this morning and has read the riot act to Ashworth. I don't believe he'll be doing much in the way of helping us for the next couple of days."

"Is Eli aware that Ashworth might have been tagged in some way by our dark witch?"

Aiden nodded. "He did a thorough check and found a sliver of black stone in Ashworth's thigh. The magic was only faint, but it obviously was enough for the heretic witch to track him."

But not enough for Ashworth to sense. Trepidation shivered down my spine. If the heretic could fool Ashworth's senses, what hope did I have against the bastard?

And why would you be thinking that you're going to face this creep? Belle asked, mental tones sharp.

I don't know. Maybe it was nothing more than pessimism. Maybe it was the knowledge that Belle and I were currently the only witches left standing.

And maybe it was the fact that this reservation seemed to have picked me as its defender, and that this problem would somehow in the end be mine to solve.

I raised my gaze to Aiden's. "I could possibly reverse the magic in this thing, but whether that will lead us to either the other bracelets or the hunters themselves is another matter entirely."

"Right now, I just want to track down everyone who has been given one of those things. I'll worry about finding the bastards behind the killings later."

Later might well be too late given the first thing any logical person would do on discovering the game was up was run. But he knew that as much as I did.

"If we're lucky, they might not have handed all the bracelets out yet."

He frowned. "Why would you think that?"

I glanced down at the bracelet in my hand and again let the muted but not erased energy run briefly across my senses.

"Because any sensible witch creating spells such as this would ensure that, once activated, they had a limited lifespan." My mouth twisted. "It's one way of getting repeat customers."

"And the magic on those things has that feel?"

"Yes. But even so, I can't imagine the hunters would hand them out wholesale, if only because she said the control charm was basic. Receiving multiple signals is generally beyond the capability of such a device."

"Then we need to find the rest of the bracelets before they get the chance to release any more."

I nodded. "It'll take about half an hour to do the groundwork and create the spell, so if you've anything else to do, you might as well go do that."

"That sounds like you're trying to get rid of me."

"Well, no, but you said you were working and I wasn't sure if you wanted to hang around here doing nothing."

"I'm not doing nothing—I'm sitting here talking to two lovely ladies about a current case."

"A comment that suggests he's angling for a brownie as well as a free coffee," Belle said, as she placed a basic white mug down in front of him.

While we had all manner of cups and mugs in the place—many of which held resonances of those who had owned and used them in the past, and which could often be used to brighten someone's day by bringing back memories of happier times or events—we'd learned very early on that most werewolves, Aiden included, had no sensitivity when it came to such things. We now gave them the cheap white ones and reserved the others for those who needed them.

Aiden's smile broke loose. "Well, if you're going to insist, I'd love one."

Belle shook her head and headed back to the counter. I

picked up my hot chocolate and rose. "I'll go do the spell. I'm sure Belle can keep you entertained while I'm gone."

"No, she can't, because she's heading across to Émigré tonight to do some dancing." Belle placed the brownie in front of him. "But I'll bring down the book on dark witches —that will keep you out of trouble, I'm sure."

"More than happy to read it," he replied. "But I'm not likely to pick up much given my knowledge about magic and witches in general is pretty basic."

"I'll just get you to tag anything you think is crucial," Belle said. "We can check it out later."

"Sure," he said, but his gaze was on me as I walked toward the reading room rather than Belle—something I knew by the heat burning into my spine.

My awareness of the man seemed to be developing into an almost psychic-like link.

No, it's just your sex-starved hormones kicking into a higher gear, Belle said, amusement evident. *I daresay it'll all die down once you've spent a few more weeks in the man's bed.*

I've three years to make up for, I replied blandly. *That's going to take more than a few weeks given we both have jobs and do need to sleep.*

Stamina, she said, a sorrowful note in her mental tones. *My witch has none of it.*

I snorted mentally and felt her wince down through the line.

Tart. She paused. *Do you want me to stay behind tonight, just in case something goes wrong yet again?*

Hell no. We can't remain in this reservation if we're going to start putting our lives on hold on the off chance something goes wrong.

I know, but—

No buts. Well, not that kind, at any rate. I'm sure you'll find more than a few of the other kind ready to share a little caress or two while dancing.

Amen to that, sister.

I grinned but didn't reply as I stepped into the reading room and closed the door. The energy here was warm and calming, and the tension that had been riding me since the first skinning once again fled. It would undoubtedly settle on my shoulders anew once I walked out, but for the moment it was nice to be without burden.

I pushed the table and chairs to one side and then rolled up the carpet square. The spell work we'd painted onto the floor gleamed softly in the pale glow of the single globe that lit this room, and the intricacy of the patterns was something I was very proud of. Neither of us was university trained, but we did have two advantages over those who were—the books from Belle's gran, and a willingness to explore and experiment. At the very least, *not* following conventions when it came to spell work gave us time to either react to an attack or flee.

And that would save us. Save *me*.

I frowned at the thought and the trepidation that came with it. But as usual when it came to those sorts of premonitions, there was little in the way of explanation or follow-up.

I gathered all the things I needed and then, once I'd created my protection circle—an extra layer that I didn't really need in this room but did out of habit—I sat cross-legged on the floor and studied the bracelet with my "other" senses. After several minutes, I began to see the pattern with the magic. While the spell wasn't one I'd ever come across before, it wasn't all that complicated.

I took a deep breath to center my energy, and then slowly began my counter spell, weaving the threads of it through and around the other witch's spell until it was securely wrapped. Then, carefully, I began the reversal procedure. It wouldn't prevent the bracelets still in the hands of the hunters from being used, but we would at least be able to use this bracelet to track the other seven—or maybe even eight, depending on whether the thread we'd found from that first tracker had disabled it—down.

I completed the spell and activated it. The magic now wrapped around the bracelet pulsed across my fingertips and whispered secrets to my mind.

It had worked.

I took another deep breath, deactivated my protection circle, and then slipped the bracelet into a small silk bag to protect it in my pocket. I finished the final dregs of my hot chocolate and then climbed to my feet. Once I'd replaced the carpet, chairs, and table, I picked up my mug and headed out. Aiden was reading an old, red, leather-bound book, his feet resting on the chair Belle had vacated and a half-eaten brownie slice sitting on the plate next to him. Either we'd finally managed to fill the man or the book had killed his appetite.

His expression, when he glanced up at me, was less than impressed.

"Seriously, why are these bastards allowed to run about?" He snapped the book closed and waved it slightly. "Surely the high witch council must have some idea who will turn and who won't—why don't they just kill them before they can?"

"Maybe they believe in intervention before death." I walked around the counter to drop my empty mug into the small sink and then grabbed four slices from the cake fridge. While the toll on my strength from spell work wasn't anywhere near that of reading the minds of the dead, it was close to dinnertime and I needed something to stop my stomach grumbling.

"They're obviously not too successful at it if you have a whole division dedicated to tracking the bastards down."

"Maybe, but when you consider how many witches there are in the world, the fail rate isn't really that bad." I shoved the slices into a bag and then walked back around.

Aiden rose. "Were you able to reverse the spell on the bracelet?"

"Yes." I exchanged the paper bag for the book. "I'll just go put this away."

"I'll be out in the truck."

I nodded and raced up the stairs, carefully tucking the book—complete with the Post-it Notes stuck to pages Aiden had thought interesting—back into its well-protected spot on the bookshelf.

Belle came out of the shower, her long hair wrapped in a towel. "All good?"

I nodded. "The reversal spell seems to have worked, so we're heading straight out. Have fun tonight."

She grinned. "Hoping you have the chance for the same."

"Amen to *that*."

I clattered back down the stairs, grabbed my purse and my keys, and then headed out, making sure I locked up on the way out.

Aiden had parked several spaces up from our café, and handed me the paper bag once I'd climbed into his truck and buckled up. Once he'd driven out of the parking spot, he said, "Where to?"

I pulled the silk bag out of my pocket and gripped it tightly for several seconds. "Right into Barker Street."

He made the turn and then accelerated away. I handed

him one of the slices and munched on the others in between giving directions. All too quickly we were on the Calder Freeway and speeding away from the reservation's boundaries.

He immediately made a call to notify the Bendigo Police that he was seeking suspects in their area. He must have sensed my surprise, because once he'd hung up, he said, "We haven't the authority to investigate outside the reservation."

"But didn't you tell Francesca Waverley you *could*?"

A smile touched his lips. "That was something of a white lie."

"Then you're a damn good liar, because I had no idea."

"The best lies are always the ones wrapped in partial truths." His gaze met mine. "We actually *can* investigate beyond our boundaries, but only in the company of a cop from whatever area we're in. We've a good relationship with the Bendigo boys, and I'm not about to do anything to jeopardize that."

I glanced down at the silk bag as the magic within whispered its secrets. "Keep to the right up ahead, and then slow down. We're close."

He didn't reply, but the tension emanating from him jumped several notches.

The connection between the bracelet I held and the others had strengthened to the point where the invisible leash that was my spell was practically burning my hand. I scanned the area ahead and then said, "Turn left into that holiday park."

He slowed down and did so. The park entrance was pretty, filled with an assortment of native flowering trees and shrubs. The manager's cottage and reception area was a three-story A-line house surrounded by graceful old willows, with parking to the right and a concrete driveway that swept around to the left. "Keep left."

He dropped the speed to the park's limit and continued on. We crawled past several more A-line houses, then a row of on-site caravans. At the far end of the park was a row of old-fashioned log cabins that had a porch and a carport at one end, and three windows along the rest of the building. As we neared the cabin at the very end of the row, the bracelet grew so hot that I had to grip the silk bag by its ties.

"They're here," I said. "How we going to play this?"

"By the book."

"Meaning, I'm gathering, we're not going to break and enter?"

A smile touched his lips. "Definitely not, if only because we don't know if the place is empty or not. The last thing I need or want is to get into a shooting match with these bastards."

"You getting shot would certainly put a dent in future seduction plans."

"Which is one hell of a reason not to get shot." He directed the truck around a rather tight curve and headed back to the park's entrance. "Of course, I would advise against making any plans for tonight. If our hunters aren't here, we'll have to stake the place out."

He obviously *wasn't* including me in that "we." "I wish the bad guys would give us a break. Surely a month or two without their sort of drama wouldn't be too much to ask?"

His grin flashed. "Maybe when we get a proper reservation witch and the wellspring is shored up tight, that'll happen."

"Maybe." But more than likely not. "I gather the stakeout will be a joint operation?"

He nodded. "I'll send the address to the Bendigo crew

once we park, and then we'll go talk to the manager and see if he or she can tell us anything about the three men."

He pulled into one of the parking spots near the manager's house and, once he'd sent the text, climbed out and walked across to reception. I followed. I might not be a ranger, but I *was* nosy.

A small bell chimed as the door opened, and a few seconds later a middle-aged woman with a bright smile and merry blue eyes stepped into the room and walked behind the desk.

"What can I do for you folks?"

"We're after some help." Aiden got his ID out and showed it to her. "We've had a couple of men illegally hunting within the reservation, and we believe they might be staying here in Cabin 10C. Do you know if they're currently in the park, Mrs.—?"

"Allan. Lucy Allan." The cheerfulness left her expression. "I'm afraid the men in that cabin left fairly early this morning, and I haven't seen them return as yet." She hesitated. "Don't you need permission from the local cops to be active outside the reservation?"

"Yes," Aiden replied evenly, "and they're on their way as we speak. I just thought I'd do the prelim investigation while we're waiting."

Relief ran through her expression. Maybe she had images of getting into trouble with the local force for helping us out. "What do you wish to know?"

"Would we be able to get a copy of their registration paperwork?"

"I'm not sure I can legally—"

"The Bendigo boys will have a search warrant with them, so you'll be in the clear."

"Ah, good. Just a minute, then." She disappeared into

the small office behind the desk; after a few minutes, she reappeared with several sheets of papers.

"I've photocopied their papers for you and the cops," she said, "but you can check them against the originals. Hope that's all right."

She placed the three sheets down on the counter. Aiden checked them both and then slid the original back across to her. "Thanks."

As she disappeared into the office again, I murmured, "Charles Randall? Are we taking bets on whether that's his real name or not?"

"The odds would be far too short to bet on, but I can check the car registration, as it's a reservation plate."

I raised my eyebrows. "I didn't realize the reservation had its own number plates."

"It's basically only officialdom that does—rangers and council vehicles, mainly."

"Does that mean this Charles Randall lives and works within the reservation? Or that the plates are stolen?"

"Possibly the latter, but at this stage, I'm not discounting anything." He glanced up as the woman returned. "What can you tell me about the three men who've been staying in the cabin?"

"Nothing much," she replied. "They've been keeping to themselves, don't make any noise, leave in the morning and come back at night."

"Would you able to give us a description of them?"

"None of them are remarkable," she said. "They're all around six foot, with long brown hair and dark eyes. They could be brothers, they look so alike."

"Did any of them have a beard?" I asked.

She shook her head. "Not unless you consider a five o'clock shadow a beard. One did have an ear stud, though, and the one who looked the youngest had a tat of a wolf up his arm."

"What sort of car were they driving?" Aiden said.

She hesitated. "A dark blue pickup until a day or so ago, but I noticed there was a red vehicle parked in the carport this morning."

"Same number plate or different?"

"Well, it wouldn't be the same, would it?" she said. "But if I'm honest, I didn't really take much notice. Thought it might have belonged to one of the other two."

"Thanks for your help, Mrs. Allan," Aiden said. "We'll just head out and wait for the Bendigo division to arrive."

She nodded, and watched us walk out the door. Aiden climbed into his truck and punched the number plate into truck's computer. After a few seconds, the result flashed up onto the screen.

"Not unexpectedly, the plate was stolen two weeks ago."

I frowned. "Isn't it rather dangerous to be driving around with stolen plates—especially one as rare as I presume a reservation plate would be?"

"Depends," he replied. "If they're only using them outside the reservation, then probably not given how big an area the Bendigo cops have to look after."

"Why steal reservation plates at all then? Why not pick a regular Victorian number plate that's less likely to stand out?"

He shrugged. "You're asking the wrong person that question."

"So you share that sort of information with the regional forces?"

"Yes, but in the case of reservation plates, most are taken to sell rather than use. Believe it or not, they're something of a collector's item." He glanced around as a blue Commodore pulled into the park. "And that will be Jack."

He climbed out and went over to the other vehicle. I walked around the back of the truck then stopped, watching the two men greet each other. Jack was perhaps five or so years older than Aiden, several inches shorter, and built like the proverbial brick wall. Even his muscles appeared to have muscles.

"Liz, meet Jack Byrnes, senior detective from the Bendigo station," Aiden said, as the two walked toward me. "Lizzie's one of our acting reservation witches."

Jack held out his hand, his smile warm. "If Aiden had mentioned the new witch was so pretty, I might have visited more often."

I smiled and placed my hand in his. His grip was firm and friendly. "Pleasure to meet you, Jack."

He nodded and returned his gaze to Aiden. "So, are our culprits here?"

"No, but the bracelets they're using to track and kill werewolves are. If nothing else, we need to get into their accommodation and find them. Did you get the warrant?"

"Yes, though I used a few favors in the process. You owe me a beer." He paused and glanced toward reception. "I gather you've already talked to the manager?"

"Her name is Mrs. Allan, and she won't release the keys without seeing the warrant."

"Good on her."

He disappeared inside, but came out a few seconds later with the keys in hand. Once we'd neared the cabin before it, Aiden motioned us to stop and then continued on alone, his footsteps barely audible as he approached the nearest window. After carefully checking all three, he motioned us forward.

"I can't see or scent anyone," he said softly, "and they're certainly not keeping the pelts in the cabin."

"They'd be stupid if they did," Jack commented. "This close to the reservation there's always the risk of a random wolf happening by and smelling the blood, even if it's not fresh."

He stepped up to the door and quickly unlocked it. Aiden pressed his fingers against the door and pushed it open, his nostrils flaring as he drew in the scents of the room.

"Definitely empty," he said, and stepped inside.

Jack and I followed. The room was a basic all-in-one kitchen and living area, and not that large. At the far end was a small hallway, off which were four doors.

Aiden glanced at me. "Any idea where the bracelets might be?"

I tightened my grip around the silk bag. The magic burned into my skin, whispering its secrets. "In the end bedroom."

"Stay behind me, both of you."

He led us across to the hall. The floorboards creaked under our steps and the air was filled with a weird mix of lavender and sweaty man. At least one of the three living here wasn't a fan of deodorant.

Aiden opened every door down the hallway, revealing two bedrooms and a combined bathroom and toilet. The last door led into the final bedroom, and it was both the biggest and the tidiest.

I paused in the doorway, my gaze scanning the room. The magic was now so damn hot that even holding the silk bag by the ties made little difference to the heat I was feeling, and I really had no idea why.

Probably something to do with the combination of

239

magics, Belle commented. *It's possible that by encasing and then reversing her spell, you've created some sort of "spell friction."*

That makes sense, I said. *But what in the hell are you doing following my thoughts? Aren't you at the club?*

Indeedy, but there's nothing much happening as yet and I was bored.

Then you're not trying hard enough.

I will when there's someone more interesting to dance with than married men, she said. *It seems I've stumbled onto couples' night, although Maelle assures me it'll change as the night wears on.*

Maelle came out of her den to greet you?

I headed across the room and unzipped a canvas travel bag. Inside was an assortment of clothes; some of them were clean, some not.

Yes. And I had to tell her I don't swing that way.

I swallowed my laugh. *I hope you let her down gently.*

Oh yeah. I have no intention of ever getting on the wrong side of an old and scary vampire.

I picked through them but couldn't feel anything resembling either magic or bracelets. But they had to be here somewhere—if the one in the silk bag got any hotter, it'd erupt into flame.

They're not likely to be in an easy to find place, Belle said. *These hunters are too cautious to do that.*

"Any luck?" Aiden asked.

"They're here somewhere, but my counter spell seems to be rubbing the Ballan witch's magic the wrong way, and I can't pinpoint them."

"What exactly are we looking for?" Jack asked.

I undid the silk bag, tipped the bracelet into my hand,

and held it up. A faint wisp of smoke was now emanating from it. "Seven or eight bracelets identical to this."

"Complete with that smoke trail?" he asked, obviously amused.

"No." I glanced at Aiden. "I'd better go deactivate this one otherwise your evidence might get destroyed."

He nodded, his attention already on searching a corner of the room. I walked back down to the living room, sat down at the small table, and careful unpicked my spell, until nothing—not even the muted remains of the Ballan witch's magic—remained.

The sound of approaching footsteps had me looking toward the half-closed front door. It was pushed fully open and a man appeared.

He was tall, with dark hair, dark eyes, and a colorful werewolf tat stretching up his left arm.

It was one of our hunters.

CHAPTER ELEVEN

"What the fuck—?" His gaze jumped from my face to the bracelet in my hand. Realization dawned, and without another word he turned and ran.

"Aiden!"

I dropped the bracelet on the table and bolted after the hunter. I jumped down the steps and began threading an immobilizing spell around my fingertips, but before I could finish, silver flashed past me—Aiden in wolf form.

The hunter must have sensed his presence because he suddenly stopped, spun around, and raised his hand.

In it was a gun.

Before I could react, I was hit side-on and sent flying. I fell with a grunt, skinning my knees on the concrete as my hands slipped forward on the grass.

Saw Jack run past.

Heard gunshots. Two of them. One from the killer, and one from Jack.

Saw Aiden's form shimmer as he shifted from wolf to human; there was no blood on him. No sign of a wound.

The same could not be said of the hunter. Or, in fact,

Jack. In shoving me to one side, he'd been clipped by the bullet meant for me. It had torn through his left arm in what looked to be a straight in-and-out wound.

My gaze went back to the hunter. He was dead. Shot through the heart, from the look of it.

Aiden swung around, his gaze sweeping me before moving on to Jack. "Thanks for the save, mate."

Jack grimaced. "I wasn't quite fast enough to stop the bastard pulling the trigger—and I certainly didn't mean to kill him."

"Better him than any of us." I climbed to my feet then bent to study my knees. Thankfully, my jeans had taken the brunt of my fall, which meant my knees had escaped with only a minor amount of lost skin.

"You need to stop that bleeding, Jack," Aiden said. "Do you want me to bring down the medical kit from the truck?"

"No," Jack said. "I have to go call this in anyway, so I'll rough bandage it while I'm up there. Just make sure you keep a record of anything you do."

"As ever." He waited until Jack had moved away and glanced at me. "What are the chances of you reading the hunter's memories? I know you haven't got your spell stones with you but—"

"I actually don't need the stones. They're more a precautionary measure when there's some form of magic involved in the death."

"So you'll try?" When I nodded, he added, "Good, because if we can get some idea where the other two are, we might be able to stop this madness today."

I walked over, wincing a little as my knees protested. "One of these days I'll get through an investigation without being injured in some way."

"But today is *not* that day," he mused.

I grinned. "I wasn't aware you're a Lord of the Rings fan."

"I marathon the movies at least once a year."

"What about the books?" My gaze went to the younger man, but I had no sense of his ghost and, thanks to the light connection Belle was maintaining, could see that his soul had already risen. I just hoped fate and reincarnation made him pay for his crimes the next time around.

"I've never read the books," Aiden said.

"Ranger, *that* is another outrageous statement which needs to be fixed immediately."

"Not going to happen. I *have* tried, but the language is too ponderous and old-fashioned."

I did a wider loop than necessary around the body and stopped at the top of his head. "Trust me, you get used to it after the first hundred pages or so."

"I'd rather just watch the movies." He got out his phone and hit the record button. "Ready when you are."

I took a deep breath to center my energy and then sat cross-legged behind the hunter and placed my hands either side of his head. Almost immediately, information and images stirred. "His name is Bryan Browning and he's been at the pub," I said. "His brothers weren't there. He met a woman and left with her."

"Address? Description?" Aiden asked.

I paused and chased down the appropriate memory reel. "She's working out of a small house just outside Kangaroo Flat." I gave him the address and then added, "She's white, has dyed blonde hair, and brown eyes."

"A prostitute?"

"Yes." I reached deeper. "Hale—the middle brother— has gone back into the reservation to snare their next target. The other brother—" I paused as the information slipped from my grasp. I chased after it, but it kept frag-menting and I had an odd sense of uncertainty. "Either he isn't sure what the oldest—Shaun—is doing or, for what-ever reason, that particular memory is fading faster than the others."

"How many trackers do they have in total? Is it only the ten they bought from the witch or is there more? And can you grab any idea where in the reservation Hale has gone?"

I frowned as I continued to sort through the various memories in an effort to find the right information. It was rather like searching through a library catalog—a very random, ill-organized, and rapidly fading catalog. Bryan obviously *wasn't* the one who'd been sleeping in the tidiest of the three bedrooms. After a moment, I found a breakfast memory.

"They have seven viable trackers left, and one inert. The thread we found on the first victim rendered that one useless."

"We found seven in the cabin, so that means Hale has one tracker with him."

I dove deeper into the breakfast memory. "Kingstone was discussed, but I can't be sure whether that's the next target area."

"Do they have more than one vehicle?" Aiden commented. "Because the red one is now in the carport."

I tried to find some sort of answer but there were simply too many conflicting images to be sure which was the right one. Bryan, it seemed, was something of a car nut and had a sideline in modding cars for resale.

"I can't find that information, sorry." I removed my fingers and took another deep breath. Weariness pulsed through my brain, but it wasn't as fierce as it normally was—I guessed because this death, and his memories, were both far fresher than any of the previous times. "That's really all I can get."

"It's still far more than we had a few minutes ago." Aiden put his phone away and then squatted beside me. "Are you okay?"

"Surprisingly, yes." I'd need food and Panadol, but at least I could still function.

He studied me through slightly narrowed eyes. "I'm still thinking you shouldn't drain—"

"Aiden, as you've already said, we need to stop these people before they kill someone else."

"Yes, but—"

"I'm fine." I reached out and placed my hand over his. "I appreciate your concern but spelling doesn't take it out of me anywhere near as fiercely as reading the dead."

"As long as you're sure—"

"And I am."

"Then do what you need to do, and I'll go talk to Jack." He hooked his hand under my elbow, helped me rise, and then kissed me tenderly. "The minute you start feeling like shit let me know. Kingstone isn't huge and given we have access to Hale's clothing, we can hunt him down the old-fashioned way, using scent and sight."

My way would be quicker and we both knew it. But I nodded and walked back into the cabin. Once I'd retrieved the bracelets, I sat back down at the table and tipped them out of their evidence bags, carefully sorting through them until I found the strongest resonance. Then, with only the slightest tremor of unease at the thought of performing this sort of magic without the benefit of a protection spell, I unpicked the bracelet's layers to reveal the controlling thread and wound my reversal spell around it. I also attempted to ease the friction between the two, but only time would tell if I was successful or not.

My head was pounding by the time I'd finished tying off the spell threads. I pushed to my feet and walked down to the bathroom to see if the men had painkillers stored there. Luck was with me. Once I'd washed down a couple with water, I placed the new tracking bracelet into the silk bag, tucked the tracker Aiden had given me into one evidence bag, shoved all the others back into another, and headed out.

A screen had been placed around the hunter's body, and while there were now a few curious onlookers from the other cabins, they were all keeping their distance. Jack was talking to Mrs. Allan and there were two uniformed officers taping off the area.

"Aiden's waiting in his truck," Jack said, as I approached. "Good luck catching the other two."

I nodded and held out the evidence bag holding the other bracelets. "Do you want these?"

He hesitated. "Yes, but don't you need—"

"I have what I need."

"Good." He plucked the bag from my fingers. "I'll need to take a statement from you, but we can do that at later time, after you've gotten the other hunters."

I nodded and walked back up the parking area. Aiden glanced at me as I climbed into the truck and held up a finger to indicate silence.

"Duke and Mac are on their way to Kingstone," Tala was saying. "Do you want me to pull Byron in?"

"Yes," Aiden replied. "We won't be able to block all exits out of Kingstone, but if we get the main four, our chances of catching this bastard is pretty good."

"It's going to piss the locals off, boss."

"Better that than one of them becoming the next

victim." His voice was grim. "It'll take us just under thirty minutes to get there."

"We should have everything in place by then."

"Thanks, Tala." He signed off then started up the truck and reversed out. Once we were back on the main road, he said, "Did you manage to rejig another bracelet?"

I pulled the silk bag from my pocket and held it up. Energy crawled across my fingertips, but it was nowhere near as sharp or as fiery as my first tracking spell. "I also kept the one you gave me, but handed the rest to Jack."

He nodded. "It's his jurisdiction, so the evidence at the park is his to collect."

"How long have you two known each other?"

He shrugged. "Ten years? Maybe more? We meet at least once a month to discuss cases and problems over a beer or two."

I frowned. "I wouldn't have thought there'd be many problems shared by both forces."

"Criminals—be they wolf or human—tend not to restrict themselves to one particular area, and that means a good working relationship between us all is vital. In fact, ever since we instigated the meetings, the crime rate has gone down in both the reservation *and* the surrounding towns." He motioned to the rear seat. "My backpack and a bottle of water are sitting behind us. Take whatever you need."

I immediately twisted around and grabbed both—and was pleased to discover several chocolate bars.

"You've restocked," I said, with a delighted grin.

"I figured that since I appear to be stuck with you being our unofficial eighth ranger, I might as well fully cater to your needs."

"Stuck. Such a lovely term for all the assistance I give you."

His grin flashed, belying the seriousness in his eyes. "You know I appreciate your help, but I really wish we didn't need it."

"That's a wish I share." I sorted through the various snack bars to see what there was, and finally settled on a couple of Picnics, reasoning that the inclusion of nuts made them a healthier choice than plain chocolate. "So is the crime problem more wolves going out of the reservation, or humans coming in?"

"It tends to be weighted toward humans. While wolves *do* cause problems out of the res, if they're caught, they're held and tried in that region's court system, not in the reservation."

"But major crimes committed inside the reservation are tried in Melbourne anyway, aren't they?" I said. "And would regular police cells even be able to hold a werewolf?"

"Not all major crimes are dealt with in Melbourne—it really depends on who the victim or indeed the perpetrator is," he said. "And most stations close to the reservation's boundaries now cater for werewolf prisoners."

Which was totally sensible—though I rather suspected getting a pissed-off werewolf into said cell in the first place could be rather difficult. But I daresay the authorities had means and methods to do that—and calming spells were certainly easy enough to get and apply.

Aiden switched on the siren as we swung onto the freeway, the lights sending flashes of color through the gathering darkness. The noise didn't do a whole lot for my headache, but at least the painkillers I'd taken were keeping it at bay.

It didn't take us long to get across to Kingstone. Up

ahead, a ranger SUV was parked in the middle of the road, and two figures were visible in the glow of its flashing light.

Aiden flicked off the lights and siren, and then stopped and wound down the window. "Any luck, Mac?"

The other wolf leaned in and gave me a polite nod. "Nothing more than locals here so far."

Aiden glanced at me. "Is he still here?"

I wrapped my fingers around the silk bag and listened to the secrets being whispered. "Yes."

"Good." Aiden returned his gaze to Mac. "Keep sharp. Let me know if anyone tries to run the barrier."

"Will do." He tapped the edge of the windowsill and stepped back.

Aiden drove on. Kingstone's layout wasn't that of a typical small country town. Rather than having one main road that ran straight through the center, Kingstone's main street was T-shaped, which meant there'd been more room to spread out as the town grew. As a consequence of that, many of the grand old buildings had survived rather than being torn down to build bigger and better.

I gripped the bag tighter as we neared the intersection of the main shopping precinct, my gaze sweeping the surrounding area as the pull of magic grew stronger.

As we crawled past the showgrounds, Aiden said, "Are we going right or straight through at the junction?"

I hesitated. "Right, and then slow down. We're close."

He turned, then pulled to one side, allowing several cars to go past before he continued on. This part of Main Street was a mix of weatherboard, brick, and stone buildings, some of them no doubt heritage listed given they looked to have been built in the gold rush days. But as the burn of magic against my skin grew stronger, my gaze was drawn to a beautiful double-story bluestone building with a cream-painted balustrade and brown tin roof.

"He's in the Royal Hotel," I said. "How do you want to play this?"

"What I'd really like to do is simply go in there and bust the bastard." He continued on until he found a parking spot farther up the road. "But I've no doubt they've researched who the rangers are in the reservation and—given the youngest brother has already shown a willingness to shoot— I don't want to risk either you or the public getting hurt. And the last thing we need is a hostage situation."

"Then I'll go in, see what's happening and where he is."

He hesitated, his expression decidedly unhappy. "It's probably our best—"

"It's your *only* option if they have researched."

He didn't bother denying that. "I haven't got any bugs on me—"

"You'd be in trouble if you did," I cut in, voice bland.

A smile tugged his lips as he continued on, "So call me and then leave the line open. That way, if shit hits the proverbial fan, I'll know."

"Once I've located him, I'll lock him in an immobilizing spell so fast he won't know what hit him."

"Good." He hesitated. "Be careful."

"Always."

He raised an eyebrow but didn't say anything as I climbed out of the truck. I swung my purse over my shoulder, then got out my phone and dialed him. Once he'd answered, I tucked it into my back pocket. I wasn't sure if the closeness to my butt would mute the sound in any way, but it either that or my full-of-crap purse.

I waited until several cars had passed and then ran across the road to the hotel. The lights both within the

251

building and without gave it a warm amber glow and added to feeling of old-world charm—one that continued once I'd stepped inside. The ceilings were pressed silver tin and the paper on the walls an old-fashioned flower print. The dark wood bar ran the length of one side, and was lined with old stools and patrons. There were a number of tables scattered around the rest of this room, most of which were occupied. The man we were hunting wasn't here, but he was close. The pulse coming from the silk-wrapped bracelet told me that. I continued on into the dining area. Again, the room was filled with warmth and noise, and most of the tables were taken.

A young woman approached and said, "Welcome to the Royal—are you after a table?"

I hesitated, and then said, "I'm supposed to be meeting a friend here, but I'm not sure whether he's booked a table or not."

"I can check our bookings, if you'd like." She stepped behind the nearby desk. "His name?"

"Hale. Hale Browning."

She ran her finger down the book and then shook her head. "He's not listed, I'm afraid. Do you want to grab a table and wait?"

I shook my head. "I might look around first, just in case I missed him coming in."

"You could try the beer garden—we do serve food out there."

"How do I get there?"

"Just go back out through these doors, take the set immediately to your right, and head on down the corridor."

"Thanks for your help."

Her smile flashed. "No problems."

I followed her directions, the silk bag gripped tightly in

one hand and its whispers confirming I was headed in the right way. I silently began weaving a containment spell around the other hand.

The beer garden was a long, rectangular pergola lined on two sides by thick ferns. A number of very old wisteria plants climbed over the wooden slat roof, providing a lush green cover for the rows of tables underneath. The fairy lights woven through the wisteria twinkled brightly and gave the place an almost magical feel.

Once again, most of the tables were occupied and a number of people were standing. At the far end of the pergola there were a couple of tables on which there appeared to be a mix of craft items and cakes for sale. A sign in the middle said "All monies raised go to Kingstone's Country Fire Association." There were two people manning the table—one was a woman wearing the local brigade's uniform, and the second was a man who could have been an older version of the man Jack had shot.

Our second hunter, Hale Browning.

He was talking on the phone and looked very agitated. Though I couldn't hear what he was saying, it was obvious even from this distance that whatever news he was receiving wasn't good.

I dragged my phone out of my pocket then stepped to one side and leaned against the hotel's old bluestone wall, keeping out of Hale's direct line of sight.

"He's on the phone, in the beer garden," I said, "and manning a fundraising table for the CFA."

"Which is a damn clever way of getting the bracelets to people," Aiden said. "And explains why Angus was wearing it—he was a serving CFA member."

"What do you want me to do?"

"Have you got that immobilizing spell at the ready?"

"Yes."

"Then let it loose, and give me a shout when it's done."

"Okay."

I shoved the phone away, tucked the silk bag into my other pocket, and then flexed my fingers. Energy stirred around my fingertips, a brief sparkle that spoke of readiness.

With a deep breath that did little to ease the tension gathering in the pit of my stomach, I pushed away from the wall and walked toward the aisle that ran down the center of the pergola.

Hale chose that moment to turn around. He spotted me and, just for an instant, froze. Then he spoke animatedly into the phone, hung up, and ran.

He'd recognized me. How and why, I couldn't say, nor was it important right now.

I bolted after him, but didn't release the spell. Even though it was ready, immobilizing spells were somewhat limited in what they could and couldn't do. The worst restriction was the fact the whole spell had to hit the target directly—and preferably on their torso. If they moved at the wrong moment or were caught only by the edge of the spell, it wouldn't work.

I grabbed my phone, quickly said, "He's running. Rear fence," and then shoved it back into my pocket.

The woman in the CFA uniform said, eyes wide, "What on earth—"

"Explain later." I caught a glimpse of the bracelet on the table. "And under no circumstances sell that bracelet. It's evidence."

"Of course, Officer—"

I didn't waste time or energy refuting her statement. Hale was weaving his way through the old trees and run-down sheds that dominated the rear of the hotel's back garden, suggesting he'd not only recognized me, but knew what I was and what I might be capable of doing. And the bastard had long legs and was putting them to good use, pulling away from me with every step.

He leapt for the rear fence. I swore and flung my spell at him. The air sparkled briefly and, at that precise moment, he twisted around, saw it, and threw himself over the top of fence. The spell clipped his right leg and spun off sideways, splattering instead into a nearby tree. A shimmering net instantly wound around the truck, pinning the already immobile tree to the ground.

I swore again and ran for the fence, grabbing the top of the old palings and clambering up.

To find Hale face-first on the ground with his arms behind is back and Aiden cable-tying his wrists.

"Oh, good." I shifted my grip on the fence to a more comfortable position and shoved both feet onto the cross brace to support my weight. "I missed with the spell and I was afraid he might have gotten away."

"It'd be a cold day in hell before a human is faster than a werewolf." He hauled Hale up and added, "Who were you talking to on the phone?"

"That's none of your fucking business, Ranger."

Blood dribbled from his nose and there was a deep gash over his forehead. Aiden hadn't been gentle when he'd tackled our felon, and the mean part of me wished he'd caused more damage.

"It's very *much* my business when you and your brothers come into this reservation to gather wolf pelts to sell." Aiden's voice was deceptively mild given the anger vibrating through his aura. "I suggest you cooperate—"

"Or what?" Hale cut in. "I have no idea what you think

I've done, but you'll be hearing from my attorney sooner rather than later."

Aiden's mouth twisted. "A song every felon sings when they're first caught. Thing is, the rule of law is somewhat different within a reservation. And the IIT will, in this case, be on our side given we've three dead wolves, and the means by which all three were tracked down and killed found in the cabin you were staying in the A-Line Accommodation Park."

Hale glanced at me, his expression one of both fury and hatred. He obviously knew about the events in the park that had led to the death of his brother, but how? Shaun—the oldest of them, and who was obviously the man who'd so blatantly looked at the security camera at the witch's place given neither of his brothers were—couldn't have been there. We would have spotted him if he had been. At the very least, Aiden would have noticed his scent given he'd been into all three bedrooms and would surely have caught it on the breeze.

"Ranger, you speak in riddles. I've nothing to do with any of that. I was simply here to help raise money for the CFA."

His gaze was on mine as he said that, and his dark eyes were promising retribution. I shivered but in truth, the threat was one without substance; he'd soon be in jail and out of circulation.

Of course, there was *one* brother still out there.

Aiden shook him, drawing Hale's gaze away from me. "Why were you hunting werewolves?"

Hale snorted. "Like I'm going to incriminate myself by answering a question like *that*."

The sound of an approaching siren had me looking around. A ranger vehicle pulled up, lights sending blue and red flashes through the night. Tala and Jaz climbed out and walked across.

"You got him, then," Tala said, her expression pleased.

"Yes. Mac and Byron can take him back to the station and start processing him. I want you two to take statements here—he was working with a woman to raise money for the CFA, and they have a table here tonight. We need to know whether she's involved or simply being used by them."

The two of them nodded and headed around to the front of the hotel rather than hauling themselves over the fence. As a second ranger SUV pulled up, Aiden grabbed Hale's arm and marched him across. Once the hunter was secured, Aiden slammed the door and walked back to me. "Thanks for your help tonight."

I smiled. "Other than immobilizing a poor old tree, I really didn't do much."

He laughed, caught one hand, and kissed it. "I need to go interview our prisoner and inform the IIT we have him. I'll drop you home on the way through."

"Cool," I said. "I might go join Belle at the club."

"Is that a not so subtle reminder that you're a free agent and might just get tired of hanging around for me?"

"Possibly," I said, keeping my voice light. "As Belle keeps reminding me, there are plenty of fish in the sea. Or, in this case, werewolves in the kennel."

"I'll have to keep on my best behavior then, won't I?"

"Keeping the backpack stocked with chocolate is a mighty fine start, trust me."

"Good. I'll meet you at the truck."

I nodded and jumped down from the fence, but didn't immediately leave the hotel. Instead, I walked back to the tree I'd "immobilized" and undid the spell. While the tree was in no danger from it, it was never a good idea to leave

257

active spells hanging around. An immobilizing spell might be less dangerous than many other spells thanks to the restrictions that came with it, but all it would take was someone to lean against it, and they'd be ensnared.

Tala was interviewing the woman from the CFA as I went through, but I couldn't see Jaz anywhere. I continued on through the hotel and headed across to Aiden's truck. The taillights flashed as I approached it and, a few seconds later, he came running up beside me. Once he'd opened the door and ushered me in, he climbed in to the driver side.

It didn't take us all that long to get back to Castle Rock. I undid my belt then leaned across and kissed him. It turned out to be one of those long, heated kisses that stirred the blood and made me ache for things that just weren't possible right here and now.

"I hate my job sometimes," he murmured, cupping my cheek with one hand.

I smiled, turned to drop a kiss on his palm, and then pulled back. "No, you don't. I'll see you tomorrow sometime."

"You will."

I climbed out, watched him drive away, and then headed into the café, making sure I locked the front door before I headed upstairs. After making myself a cup of tea, I pulled the book on dark sorcerers out of the bookcase and sat down to read the pages Aiden had marked. They really didn't offer up any more information about our dark witch, although there was one small side note that rather interestingly said that for the first week or so after a soul transference, the older soul often had to contend with a thick need for sex dark in tone, thanks to the nature of the spirits who help them through the ceremony. Which was *exactly* what I'd seen in Abby's mind.

It might be a way to find him—with Abby now dead, he'd have to find someone else to satisfy his darker urges. Unless, of course, he'd gone off the reservation to both deal with those needs and to regain his full strength.

I snapped the book closed then pushed to my feet and walked over to the glass sliding door, opening it up and stepping out onto the balcony. Despite the heat of the day, the night air was quite cool. I shivered and crossed my arms, but didn't retreat back inside. An odd sort of restlessness was stirring through me, and I wasn't entirely sure why. It wasn't a premonition—not exactly—and there was no sense of evil slipping through the darkness. I walked across to the railing and leaned my forearms against it, studying the nearby buildings and then the darkness beyond them. The whole area was quiet aside from the occasional roar of an engine as a car sped along the street. The gathering clouds hid the moon's brightness, but her power nevertheless shivered through me, and oddly seemed to fuel the restlessness.

I frowned, pushed away from the railing, and walked back inside. After locking the door, I grabbed my cup and finished my tea in one long gulp. As I did, the pages of the book fluttered and flipped over, and an underlined paragraph caught my attention. *No matter how strong the dark forces employed to help steal the body of another are,* it said, *there will be a period of adjustment in which the body tries to reject the soul that has taken it over. This leads to an aura that appears to be at war with itself as well as a very tumultuous energy flow. Such energy infests the air, and can be used to track the dark witch, but it must be done in that first week of the old soul's rebirth into its new body.*

Infests the air.... *That's* what I'd been sensing in Abby Jones's place—the twisting, tumultuous energy of the man who'd killed her.

And if I went back there.... I stopped the thought cold. I wasn't going to do *anything*. Not alone. I took a deep breath to calm the instinct to get my keys and go, and walked down to my bedroom to grab my phone out of my purse.

Ashworth answered after the sixth ring. "Do you know what fucking time it is, lass?"

I glanced over to the clock and grimaced. "Sorry, I didn't realize it was nearly eleven."

He grunted. "Well, it is but I'm awake now, so you might as well tell me what you're ringing for."

In the background, a voice muttered something and bedsprings squeaked as someone moved. Eli, no doubt.

"I've been doing some research on dark witches," I said, "and I found a rather interesting passage in a book—"

"What book?" he cut in. "Because there's not much information on those bastards that can be found outside the halls of the HIC, let me tell you."

I hesitated. "It's something of a family heirloom that's been handed down to Belle. It has all manner of unusual information in it."

"Is that where you've learned some of your spelling from?"

"Yes," I said. "But that's not important right now."

I told him what the paragraph had said and then added, "It's possible that if we go back to Abby's house, we might be able to catch a sense of his energy and use it to track his current location. But we'd have to do it before it fades."

"No," a deep voice said in the background. "You're not going out there—not in your current state."

"Eli," Ashworth said. "Be reasonable. This bastard has to be caught and Lizzie can't—"

"Aside from the fact you can hardly move without wincing in damn pain at the moment," came Eli's retort, "you've chugged down a bucketload of painkillers that *will* slow your reactions. You'd be a liability out in the field more than anything else."

"It's okay," I said hastily, "I can—"

"No, you damn well can't," Eli said. "And you know it, otherwise you wouldn't have rung Ira in the first place."

Eli, it seemed, was as blunt as Ashworth. "I know, and I'm sorry, but I just thought he could provide some backup and advice—"

"Well, you were wrong," Eli said. "However, I can."

I blinked. "You can't leave Ashworth alone—he has no hands to manage the basics."

"I'm not a damn invalid," Ashworth grouched. "And I'm quite capable of going to the toilet by myself. Besides, even if it *does* turn out that you can track the heretic through his energy, I'd suggest no one actually attempts to do so until the new HIC witch gets here tomorrow afternoon."

"What time is he coming in?"

"About four, I think. I believe a councilor is heading down to the airport to pick him up, and they'll drop him off here so we can update him. If you and Eli are successful tonight, we can head out tomorrow evening."

"Will it be safe to hunt him at night?" I asked. "Don't their powers increase with darkness?"

Ashworth snorted. "I'm betting you didn't get that nonsense from a book."

"Well, no—"

"Dark witches are no better served by night than the rest of us," he continued. "They simply use the moon's power, the same as we do."

And the moon was once again moving to full, and that meant her power—and *his* access to it—was rising. I tried to ignore the trepidation that rose with that thought and said, "Eli, do you want me to come pick you up?"

"Sure." He gave me their new address then said, "It'll take me twenty minutes to get everything ready."

"I'll meet you out the front, then." I hung up and then silently said, *Belle, were you listening in?*

No, I was too busy dancing. What's up?

Nothing. I'm just letting you know that I found a possible means of tracking down the dark witch, and I'm about to accompany Eli back to Abby Jones's place so we can see if it'll work.

Who the hell is Eli?

Ashworth's partner and a recently retired RWA witch. Ashworth's taken a shitload of painkillers and isn't up to it.

You want me there with you?

No. I just didn't want you to be concerned if you came home and I'm not here. Especially given you wouldn't be getting any contentment signals suggesting I was with Aiden.

Her mental chuckle rolled down the line. *Already knew that wasn't going to happen. The frustrated vibes, they are strong in you.*

With good reason.

Indeed. She paused. *Shout if you need anything*

I'm with Eli so I should be all right.

Let's hope they're not famous last words.

Amen to that.

I headed down to the reading room, threw on every charm and ward against darker magics that we currently had, and then stocked the backpack. Eli would undoubtedly bring everything he'd need for whatever spell he created to follow the dark witch's energy, but I wasn't about to follow him into that house without some means of creating my own spells should it be necessary.

Once I'd grabbed my purse and the car keys, I headed out the back and jumped into the wagon. It didn't take long to drive across to the other side of Castle Rock; Eli walked down the front steps just as I pulled up. He was a tall, well-built, and very handsome man who looked to be in his late sixties. His thick salt-and-pepper hair was neatly cut and his eyes were bright blue.

He opened the door and leaned down. "Lizzie, I take it?"

"There's no other red-haired, green-eyed witch in this reservation," I replied cheerfully, and held out my hand once he'd climbed in. "Pleased to meet you, Eli. How's Ashworth?"

"Sleeping the sleep of the drugged to the eyeballs."

"I'm sorry to drag you away—"

"Forget about it." His smile flashed. "Ira would have had my nuts if I'd let you do this alone. He rather likes you, I'm afraid."

I grinned. "And that's a bad thing because?"

"Because he has this habit of getting involved in the lives of those he truly likes—and there's not many of them, let me tell you."

I raised an eyebrow as I pulled back onto the road and drove toward Argyle. "How involved are we talking about?"

"As in, he's very free with advice and likes to keep in regular contact."

I chuckled softly. "*That* I can handle. I used to get the same thing from my granddad when he was alive—and Ashworth very much reminds me of him."

"And here I was thinking they broke the mold when they made Ira," Eli said, amused.

"They might have—my granddad was much older. He died when I was fourteen."

I could feel Eli's gaze on me but I kept mine on the road.

"Sounds like you miss him," he said, "and yet from the little Ira has told me, I was under the impression you didn't get along with your family."

"I don't. Granddad was the one exception." And while he wasn't exactly my champion, had he been around when Cat had been murdered, I suspected events would not have escalated as far and as fast as they had. He certainly would have prevented Clayton from getting involved.

Dread slipped through me, and I had to deliberately unclench my grip on the steering wheel.

If Eli noticed, he didn't say anything.

It took us just over half an hour to get to Abby Jones's place in Argyle. The gravel road that led to her house was dark, and there was little in the way of lights coming from the other houses along the street. Which, considering the late hour, wasn't really that surprising.

I pulled up in the driveway just short of the blue-and-white tape that had been strung up between the fence and the front door, then stopped the engine and killed the headlights. The night seemed to close in, thick and heavy.

"I'm gathering," Eli said, tone dry, "that since there's no ranger here to meet us that you haven't actually told them about this little venture."

"No." I climbed out of the car. The chill air raced around me, holding just the slightest hint of power. The wild magic was here, but I sensed no warning in her presence. "They're busy dealing with the death of one of the men behind the skinning murders and interviewing the second. But if the notes are right and we can track the heretic down through his energy, I'll let them know straight away. They'll want to be involved when you make the attempt tomorrow."

He raised an eyebrow as we walked toward the front door. "And I'm sure they're going to be *totally* all right with us invading a crime scene like this."

I grinned as I ducked under the tape. "Aiden sort of expects this behavior from me."

Eli grunted and tested the front door. Unsurprisingly, it was locked. Energy stirred and the handle sparkled briefly. He gripped the handle again and pushed it open.

"That's a very handy spell." I followed him through the door. "I might need you to teach me that one."

He glanced around, eyebrow raised. "How can you have a book on dark witches but not one on a spell as basic as opening a door?"

I shrugged. "Belle inherited the books, so it's a case of making do with what's there."

His magic stirred, a brief but warm swirl of power. He immediately swung left and headed through the living room toward the hallway. I followed, but my gaze went unerringly to the spot where Abby had found her death. Though her body was no longer there, the bloody stains remained, as did the lingering sense of desperation and agony. This house would need a thorough cleansing if the next occupants were to live here in any sort of happiness.

I rubbed my arms as the deeper darkness of the hallway closed around us. The odd sense of uneasiness I'd felt the first time I was here intensified, crawling across my senses like a swarm of bees. I had no doubt it was that foulness Eli was following, given he'd never been here and had as little idea of the layout of the place as me.

He walked into a bedroom at the far end of the house. I

stopped in the doorway, my skin jumping and tingling. I swore softly and flexed my fingers; sparks swarmed around them, thick and angry.

Eli's glance was sharp. "You can feel that?"

"You say that like I shouldn't be able to."

"Only because it's very faint and I wouldn't have thought—"

"It's not faint to me," I cut in. "It feels like I'm being stung by a thousand bees."

His gaze narrowed as he studied me for a few minutes. "There is an odd energy around you—it's not the remnants of the heretic's output, however, but rather something far more intangible."

I hesitated and said, "I did feel the wild magic outside. Maybe it's still hanging around."

"It would appear so," he said. "It would also appear that it's enhancing your ability to sense the emotions in this room."

"Well, I'm sure the wild magic would rather *not* have a heretic witch get hold of its wellspring."

"The problem with *that* statement is the fact that the wild magic has no sentience."

"Except that, for whatever reason, it apparently *does* in this reservation."

He grunted, his expression unconvinced. "I can see why Ira suddenly wants to move here. This reservation is something of a conundrum."

I blinked. "He what?"

Eli grinned. "Yeah, just imagine, he could come in and chat to you about the wild magic and your relationship with it every single day."

"Neither of us are *that* interesting," I muttered, and shoved a hand through my hair. "Does the fact you're not getting much of a feel for the heretic's energy mean you won't be able to create a spell to track him down?"

"Perhaps." He hesitated. "I suspect that my chances of success would increase greatly if I have your assistance."

I frowned. "While I can trace people through psychometry—and I really don't want to try that with this bastard—I have no idea how to do it through magic—"

"You don't have to. You just have to be inside the protection circle with me," he said. "I'll form a light connection with you, and use that to contain the heretic's energy."

"You're telepathic?" I asked, suddenly uneasy. While I doubted he'd in any way raid my thoughts, a strong enough telepath could pick up things I'd rather keep hidden.

Although he *would* have to get past Belle first. Thanks to the light connection that was always active between us—the only time she was truly shut off from my thoughts was when she was in her bedroom—she'd feel any such intrusion and retaliate in an instant. And I'd back *her* against almost any other telepath out there.

He waved a hand dismissively. "Only marginally—"

"Define marginally."

He smiled. "I can catch the occasional unguarded surface thought but little more than that. But you have nothing to fear, my dear, because I doubt even the Royal Australian Mint is as secure as your mind."

I grinned. "There are benefits to having a friend who is a strong telepath."

"Apparently so, but it does make me wonder just what you're afraid of revealing."

"Certainly nothing you should be worried about."

He raised an eyebrow, but all he said was, "At any rate, I won't be connecting with your mind, but rather drawing on the force of your energy—"

"Like a psychic vampire does? I'm not sure that's a much better option."

"I won't be consuming your energy as they do, but simply connecting with it so that I can see the remnants of the heretic's output as clearly as you do. It'll enable me to gather it and then use it to form the basis of a tracking spell." His smile flashed. "It's more a brief meshing, nothing else."

"Any side effects? Possible problems?"

He hesitated. "If the wild magic *is* responsible for the depth of your awareness of the heretic's output here, then it might well interfere with my ability to perform the spell."

I frowned. "Why?"

"Because there are few witches who walk away from contact with the wild magic unscathed. How you're inter-acting with it without any sort of blowback is one of the many things that has intrigued Ira."

"I wouldn't call what I do interacting." Not for the most part, anyway. "And in this case, I certainly *haven't* made a deliberate attempt to connect with it. It's just here."

And given the fact I couldn't feel Katie's presence within it, that perhaps meant the energy here came from the main wellspring rather than the one Katie and Gabe were now protecting.

"It's not only here, but clinging to you like a second skin and enhancing your senses," he said, and then held up a hand to cut off any reply I might have made. "But right now, the 'why' doesn't matter. Let's just get this spell done so I can get back to my man."

"Sounds good to me—what do you want me to do?"

"Help me clear some floor space."

I stepped into the room and helped shove the bed and the dressing table to one side. He ordered me to sit down in the middle of the cleared area then grabbed his spell stones —which were green amber, a favorite amongst those witches who could actually afford to buy the hard to find, larger stones—and began placing them on the carpet.

Once a large enough circle had been completed, he sat cross-legged in front of me and opened his backpack. "I'll construct a protection circle and then begin the spell that'll draw in and contain a portion of the dark energy within this room."

He pulled out what looked to be one of those plastic pods small kids' toys often came in.

"What's that for?" I asked.

"Said energy containment—we don't need that much for the spell to work." He paused. "*If* it works, that is. I've never tried anything like this before."

"What do you need me to do?"

"For the moment, nothing."

He handed me a garland of assorted herbs, placed a similar one around his neck, and then began raising the protection circle. The rhythm of his magic flowed around me, a powerful force that burned across my skin in a very different way to the heretic's energy. I narrowed my eyes, watching the way he constructed the protective layers, fascinated with how he wove the various deterrents and inhibitors through each thread to make every level that much stronger. It oddly felt like I was back at school, watching my spell master at work, trying to remember everything I was seeing, everything he was doing. Both Belle and I had been in the system long enough to learn the basics, and we'd certainly honed our skills in the years since we'd left Canberra, but watching Eli construct this protective circle made me realize just how far we still had to go.

The air shimmered briefly as he tied off the spell and then activated it.

"Okay, now I just need you to touch my hands, and we'll get the gathering spell underway."

He held his hands out, palms up. After I lightly placed mine on his, he uttered another incantation—yet another spell that was unfamiliar to me. Magic once again stirred around me, a force that briefly touched the outer level of my aura, making a bridge between my energy output and his at the point where our hands touched. The wild magic immediately ran down my arms and flowed around our joined hands, a brief swirl of power that glimmered brightly in the darkness of the room.

He sucked in a deep breath. "Fuck, that's *strong*."

My gaze jumped to his. "Are you okay?"

He nodded and licked his lips. "The wild magic itself is not flowing into me; it's simply meshing with my energy at our connection point."

"In the same way as our auras are connected?"

He nodded. "Which in itself suggests the wild magic is very much a part of your DNA, though how that can be possible I have no idea."

"That's not possible, and we both know it." I might have drawn the wild magic into me to fight a vampire and survived the experience with little more than silver-ringed eyes, but it hadn't lingered. Hadn't become a part of me—of that, I was sure. "Will its presence affect your ability to spell?"

"No. I can feel its force but it's not impacting me."

"Which is no different to how it's affecting me." I could see the disbelief in his eyes, but he didn't give it voice. "Can you also feel the dark witch's energy?"

He nodded. "The spell shouldn't take too long, but I'll

need you to ensure the connection between us doesn't break."

"That, I can do."

He nodded and then took a deep breath, centering his energy before he began the spell. Again, his magic stirred around me but this time, I concentrated on keeping our connection, on the bright flow of energy that was once again encircled across our hands, and the thin slivers of darkness that were being pulled from it. Then the plastic pod rose from the floor and hovered several inches above our hands. The thin filaments of darkness twisted and heaved, as if fighting the commands being placed on them. They were nevertheless forced together until they were little more than a small sphere of churning evil, and then thrust into one half of the pod. The other half snapped closed over it, and the threads of Eli's magic wove around it, quickly sealing it.

As the pod dropped into his lap, he tied the ends of the spell around it and then severed the connection between us. As the wild magic retreated up my arm, he took a deep breath and pulled his fingers from mine. His aura was dark with weariness and his eyes bloodshot.

"Damn, that took more out of me than I thought."

Because of the wild magic, I suspected. "But it was at least successful."

He nodded, pulled a silk glove out of his backpack, and then carefully picked up the pod. The dark filaments locked inside roiled and heaved, still fighting the magic that now contained them.

"Will it be hard to create a spell using that energy?" I asked.

He shook his head. "While the energy in this room will probably fade within the next twelve hours—unless, of course, he comes back—this compacted mass should last for another twenty-four to forty-eight beyond that."

"Which at least gives you some recovery time before you have to activate the next part of the spell."

He nodded again and then took another deep breath before deactivating his protection circle. He wrapped the pod in a silk bag, placed it carefully into his pack, and pushed to his feet. I rose with him, one hand lightly cupping his elbow to steady him.

His smile flashed, but its wattage was far below what it should have been. Once he'd gathered his spell stones, we headed out.

"There's some protein bars in the glove compartment, if you want them." I climbed into the driver side of my car. "They always help me when a spell has left me so drained."

He immediately opened the compartment and then chuckled. "There're not only protein bars here, but a veritable candy store."

I grinned. "One has to cater for all emergency situations."

He snorted softly and sorted through the various bars, eventually deciding on a good-for-you protein bar as well as a more regular chocolate and nut bar.

It was well past one by the time we pulled up in front of his and Ira's new place. I bid him goodbye, watched to ensure he didn't collapse in weariness before he got inside, and then headed home.

Belle wasn't home, so I had a quick shower to wash the lingering smell of death and darkness from my skin and then climbed into bed. I was asleep almost before my head hit the pillow.

I woke at seven the following morning but it took a good three cups of coffee before I was really able to get into the day's prep. I was drinking my fourth and eating a toasted cheese and Vegemite sandwich when Belle finally clattered down the stairs.

"Morning," she said, sounding altogether too cheerful for someone who'd had less sleep than me.

I raised an eyebrow and propped my feet up on the nearby chair. "And don't we look like the cat who's eaten all the cream."

Which was an echo of exactly what she'd said to me only a few days ago and had her smiling.

"Sadly, no cream has been consumed as yet, but I did meet a rather divine wolf last night and we have a dinner date this evening." She walked behind the counter and began making herself a cappuccino. "He is, in fact, picking me up at three and taking me to see the *Rocky Horror Show* in Melbourne. One of his mates had a couple of spare tickets."

"Meaning you'll need the afternoon off to make yourself gorgeous."

"I don't need *all* afternoon." She waved a hand airily. "You forget I already *am* gorgeous."

I snorted but didn't disagree, as it was nothing but the truth. "And does this divine piece of manhood have a name?"

"Raphael Beaumont. He's here to visit his only sibling for Christmas, as she's married into the Marin pack."

The Beaumonts owned one of the two reservations in Queensland, and while it was even smaller than this one, they were the sole occupants. How they'd managed that when so many of the other reservations—including the other reservation in Queensland—hadn't was something of a mystery. At least to those of us who were human. I daresay the wolves all knew—and, given witches had been involved in the peace pact that had finally settled all three wolf packs into this reservation, the high witch council was more than likely in on the secret as well.

I grinned. "How fortunate that you met a wolf from the very same pack as the one who'd recently dumped you."

"Said wolf was there last night. I even danced with him." She leaned her butt against the counter and took a sip of her coffee. "We remain friends but he made his decision and now he has to live with it."

"Sounds as if he's already regretting it."

"He is." She wrinkled her nose. "But in truth, I understand his decision and why he took the risk. Love is something we all want to find eventually."

"But until we do, here's to fine times and finer men."

She laughed. "Says the woman who took *ages* to get back into the hunt."

"But the wait was worth it." I lowered my feet from the chair and pushed upright. "I'd better go open the back door so the gang can get in."

"Good idea. I'm not in the mood to cook today."

We opened an hour later, and the day moved on quickly from there. I didn't hear from Aiden but that wasn't surprising given everything that was going on. Belle headed upstairs at two and was picked up at three by Raphael, who was every bit as gorgeous as she'd said.

By four, most the staff had gone and I was just tying up the last bag of rubbish to take out to the bin when someone knocked on the side window. I looked around and saw that it was Frank.

"Forgot me keys," he said.

I grinned, motioned him to the front door, and walked over to open it.

"Sorry," he added.

"No problems. Just make sure the door is locked on your way out."

He nodded and headed into the rear storage area, where the staff lockers were. I picked up the bag and headed out the back.

Only to open the door and find a double-barrel shotgun suddenly stuck in my face.

CHAPTER TWELVE

My heart stuttered and for several seconds I couldn't breathe. All I could see was the two metal cylinders that, at any moment, could blow my brains to smithereens.

"Don't scream." The voice was flat. Deadly. "And don't try any of your funny stuff. This thing has a hair trigger—the minute I even suspect you're trying to spell me, I'll spread your brains far and wide. Is that clear?"

I swallowed heavily and nodded. I couldn't do anything else. I could barely even think.

All I could see was the goddamn gun.

What the fuck? came Belle's mental scream. *What gun? What the hell is happening back there?*

No time now. Explain later.

"Right then," the stranger continued, "give me that bag."

I promptly released it. The gun shifted slightly as he tossed the bag behind him, and my pulse jumped several notches. My heart was now racing so hard it felt like it was going to rip through my chest at any moment.

The rubbish bag hit the ground with a clatter, and I couldn't help but hope the noise would drag someone outside to see what was happening. It didn't. The area remained empty, and the plastic bag—which had split on impact—was now leaking its contents onto the concrete. It was a somewhat visual reminder of what would happen to my brains if I wasn't very careful.

"Raise your hands, step back into the hallway, and then stop," the stranger ordered.

I obeyed. He followed me inside and kicked the door shut. The sound echoed through the empty silence.

Only it *wasn't* empty, I realized.

Frank was still here.

I mentally crossed fingers, toes, and everything else I could think of that he didn't come out of the storeroom unexpectedly, that he'd heard what was going on and was now plotting some means of help. Whether that was texting the rangers or doing something himself, I didn't really know or care.

I just knew that, while I didn't want him to get hurt, I desperately needed some help. And Belle was too far away.

But I can call in help via the damn phone.

Do it. And tell them to hurry.

"What do you want?" I raised my voice a little so that Frank would hear me. "If you're hoping to grab the cash from the till, you're out of luck—it's already been banked."

"I don't want your stinking cash," the gunman growled. "I want my goddamn brother out of jail. And I want revenge on the bastard who shot my youngest brother."

His words had my gaze moving beyond the end of the shotgun, and for the first time I actually looked at *him*. Though he had neither long brown hair nor a thick bushy beard, this was very definitely Shaun Browning, the man who'd looked without concern into the security camera, and who was the oldest of the three brothers. He'd obviously been using some sort of basic glamor at the witch's place, though why he'd been so confident the spell would fully protect his identity when it hadn't actually altered his facial structure or eyes, I couldn't say.

I swallowed heavily. "The rangers aren't likely to release your brother. Not after three kills."

"Oh, I think you're very wrong," he replied. "Especially given I now have the head ranger's girlfriend as a hostage."

"I'm not his girlfriend. We're merely—"

"I don't care if your situation is deep and meaningful or you're simply fuck buddies," he growled. "I've learned enough about Aiden O'Connor to know he won't risk your life."

"A prisoner exchange *won't* get you out of this reservation, though." My voice remained loud. There was no movement, no sound, coming from the storeroom, and I had no idea if that meant Frank had left without me hearing him or if he was simply waiting for the right opportunity to help.

I hoped it was the latter. I now feared it was the former.

But I couldn't check. Couldn't do anything that would make Shaun suspect there might be someone else here.

"We'll get free if we take you with us." He made a motion with his chin. "Turn around—slowly—and move into the main café area. And remember, one wrong move and you're dead."

"You kill me, and any chance your brother had of being released is gone."

"Then I guess I'll just have to shoot your boyfriend, won't I?"

He didn't shoot Bryan, I wanted to say, but that would only add another name to Shaun's kill list.

I slowly turned, and keeping my hands up, . As I neared the storeroom, it took every ounce of control I had to maintain my pace and resist the urge to check if Frank was there. And I seriously wished my olfactory senses were as keen as a wolf's; at least then, I might have had confirmation one way or another.

I walked past the storeroom door; still no sound or movement from within. The beating of my heart was now so fierce it felt like one long scream, and sweat was dribbling down my spine.

Please be there, please be there, I found myself mentally chanting.

Air stirred the hair at the back of my head, and was quickly followed by a sharp grunt, and then a gunshot.

I yelped and dropped, but nothing more than a spray of plaster hit me.

I twisted around. Saw Frank with a wine bottle in one hand, the gun in the other. Saw him kick Shaun—whose face was bloody and broken, and who looked more than a little out of it—in the nuts. The hunter went down with a gurgle of pain and didn't move.

Oh my fucking God, came Belle's mental shout, *what the hell has happened? Are you okay?*

I took a deep, shuddering breath, and felt the sting of tears. *I'm fine. As to what just happened—I just got a visit from the last brother. But don't worry—everything's good now, thanks to Frank.*

Frank?

Later, as I said. Relax and enjoy your night.

Her confusion and uncertainty washed down the line. *Do you want me to come back?*

Hell no. I'm fine. Really.

Are you sure?

Yes. Now stop listening to my thoughts and start talking to that luscious man beside you.

Expect to be woken for details when I get home.

Expect grumpiness and swearing if you so dare.

Her amusement swam around me then her thoughts faded from mine.

Frank made the gun safe and then looked at me. "You okay?"

"Yes," I repeated out loud, but reaction chose that moment to fully set in and the tears that had been threatening started falling and my whole body began shaking. I hugged my arms across my chest and tried to stop the tears but they just wouldn't be controlled.

"Ah, come now, it's okay." Frank knelt down beside me and gave me a rough hug. "The bastard's out to it and you're safe."

"I know, I know, and it's all thanks to you." The words came out quickly and were interspersed with hiccups. "I just keep thinking of what might have happened if you hadn't forgotten your damn keys."

"But I did, so it's no use fretting about things that could have been." He pulled a clean handkerchief out of his pocket and offered it to me. "Now dry those tears. I need to roll the shooter onto his side so he doesn't choke on his own blood."

I accepted the handkerchief with a quick, if somewhat diluted, smile. "As much as the bastard *deserves* to choke, I guess you'd better."

"I gather from the bits I heard that this is one of the boys responsible for the skinning murders?"

I nodded. "The rangers have the middle brother, and the last one was shot—killed—outside the reservation."

Frank rolled Shaun onto his side and then opened his mouth and cleared his throat.

"You've had first aid training?" I asked.

"Some, when I was in the military. Long time ago now, but you never really forget the basics."

I smiled. "The spirits said the omens were good for your employment. I'm glad we listened."

He glanced at me, his eyebrows raised. "You checked with the spirit world before employing me?"

"Not just you, but everyone. It never pays to ignore their thoughts, even if they can be annoying at times."

He chuckled softly. "I'm glad they approved, then. If you're okay, you might want to call the rangers. I'll keep an eye on our prisoner."

I pushed to my feet and went to grab my phone. The tears had at least stopped by the time the call went through, and though my heart was still bounding at an altogether too fast a rate, it was at least slower than it had been.

"Liz," Aiden said, "I was just about to ring you. Everything okay?"

"Nope. You know that third brother? Well, he's here, on the floor, unconscious."

"Are you okay?"

I smiled at the sharp concern in his voice. "Yes, but only thanks to Frank. He knocked the bastard out with a bottle of wine, and then disarmed him."

Aiden swore. "I'll grab Jaz and be right over."

"Thanks." I hung up, and then leaned over the counter. "Frank, I'm about to pour myself a drink—you want one?"

"Thanks, but no. I've got to drive home."

I grabbed the bottle of Glenfiddich whiskey from its hiding spot under the counter, poured myself a full glass, and then gulped down most of it. The alcohol burned all the way down and took with it a good portion of the fear that had held my heart in its fist. Something approaching calm descended.

The rangers arrived a few minutes later. Aiden's gaze swept the entire café and then returned to me. He motioned Jaz and Byron toward Frank then walked over to me. He didn't say anything; he just took me in his arms and held me close for several minutes. And damn if the tears didn't start again.

As the siren of an approaching ambulance grew near, I pulled away. "Soaking your shirt with tears is becoming something of a habit."

He smiled and gently thumbed some moisture from my cheek. "I'm just happy you're still here to soak my shirt."

"He wasn't here to kill me—at least, not straight away. He wanted to use me as hostage, both to get his brother released *and* to escape the reservation."

"Neither of which would have happened," he replied. "I would have asked either Ashworth or Eli to spell the man."

"I told him he wouldn't succeed, but he was apparently convinced by everything he'd heard about you that you wouldn't let anything happen to me."

"And he was right, but not just because we're going out."

Going out, not in a relationship. I wondered if that was a deliberate choice of words or just the way all wolves categorized their time with a human.

I pulled completely out of his grip then picked up the whiskey glass and downed the rest of the alcohol. A very pleasant buzz began to run through my system.

I poured some more whiskey, well aware that he was watching me. "I'd offer you a glass, but you're still on duty."

"Actually, I clocked off about five minutes before you rang."

I raised an eyebrow. "Then you'd like one?"

"No—I still have to drive home, and as head ranger I do have to set an example."

I nodded and glanced around as the bell above the front door chimed and two medics walked in. Aiden pointed them toward the rear of the building and then said, "I was going to ask if you wanted to go out to dinner, but I'm thinking you need some cosseting."

I couldn't help smiling. "A little cosseting never goes astray, but I'm not about to break, Aiden."

Not once I'd consumed the second lot of whiskey, anyway. I knew from experience this stuff was very good at keeping all manner of fears at bay—and, at least in *this* particular case, it only had to bat away imagination and "what-could-have-been."

"I'd still like to cosset."

I waved a hand to where Frank, the paramedics, and the other rangers were all now standing. "Don't you have to look after that mess? Take statements and stuff?"

"I was on late last night. It's someone else's turn tonight." He hesitated and then added softly, "Will you come home with me?"

"Yes—as long as the cossetting involves chocolate. A girl can't recover properly from such a scare without it, you know."

"The fridge is now well stocked, let me assure you."

"Good. But I'll need to shower first. I've been working all day and I stink—"

"You smell just fine," he said, voice bland, "and you can shower at my place."

I raised an eyebrow. "Alone?"

"If that's what you want, yes."

I grinned, even as anticipation stirred. "I'll just go grab some things then."

I leaned forward, dropped a kiss on his lips, and then headed up the stairs. It didn't take long to pack—I still had some stuff sitting in a bag in his bedroom so I didn't need all that much more.

I grabbed the spare set of keys then clattered back down the stairs. "Jaz, would you mind locking the place up once you've finished?"

"Sure." She accepted the keys with a grin. "Least I could do after all the brownies you feed us."

"Thanks." I spun around, grabbed my handbag from under the counter, and then walked toward Aiden, who was now standing midway between the counter and the door.

He grabbed the bag from me, slung it over his shoulder, and then waved me on. I paused outside, looking right and left. "Where's your truck?"

"Still in the parking lot behind the station."

I glanced at him. "You *ran* here?"

"Yes. I would have wasted too many minutes getting the truck out. It was much faster to run, given how close you are to the station."

I smiled and tucked my arm through his. "Anyone would think you were worried about me."

"I don't think I've been that scared about anyone since we found Katie's note and realized what was about to happen."

It was a statement that warmed me deep inside—and *that* was very dangerous. "You sure it wasn't the possibility of losing your brownie supplier that you were actually worried about?"

He glanced down at me, amusement creasing the

corners of his bright eyes even if the rest of his expression was serious. "Anyone with any brains can see I much prefer you over the brownies. For a start, it's impossible to seduce a brownie in the shower—they just fall to pieces."

"It's very possible *I'll* fall to pieces if the seduction is done right."

"Is that a challenge? Because I'm very up for such things."

I let my gaze slide down his length. "So I can see."

He laughed. "Challenge accepted then."

It didn't take us long to get to the ranger station and collect his truck. Once he was on the A300 and heading toward Argyle, he said, "Got a call from Eli this afternoon."

Oh shit, I thought, suddenly remembering I hadn't told him of our adventure last night.

"What did he want?"

"To know if the new witch from the HIC was going to arrive on time this evening. Said he was anxious to try out the improvised tracking system he'd created last night." He glanced at me. "I don't suppose you know anything about that, do you?"

I grimaced. "If I say yes, are you going to be mad?"

"Probably."

"Will shower sex make it better?"

A smile twitched his lips. "Probably."

"Then yes, I do. I was there last night when he created it." I hesitated. "In fact, the whole thing was actually my idea even though I didn't have the knowledge or power to pull it off."

"So this tracker is what, exactly?"

I hesitated again. "It's basically the lingering threads of the heretic's energy that have been forced into a container—or in this case, a small plastic toy pod—which can then be used with the appropriate spell to track down the owner of said energy."

"I'm guessing that all means you broke into Abby Jones's place?" His voice was an odd mix of annoyance and resignation.

"I'm afraid we did."

He shook his head. "You should have called me. One of these days, your side ventures are going to get you into deep trouble."

"I can get into deep trouble without them—this afternoon was proof of that." I shifted in the seat to study him. "What time is the HIC witch is coming in?"

"Should be here somewhere between five thirty and six, depending on the evening traffic," he said. "Why?"

I glanced at my watch and saw that it was already close to five-thirty. Trepidation stirred once again, although as usual, I had no real idea why.

"Eli said last night that they might try and hunt the heretic down as soon as the other witch got here."

"I gather from your tone that you don't think that's a good idea."

"No." I glanced across the fields of endless gold and noticed dark clouds were now gathering on the horizon. I hoped it wasn't an omen. "Tonight's moon is waxing gibbous and, aside from the full moon, it's one of the most powerful."

"If the heretic intended to use the moon's power to enhance his spell, why wouldn't he wait one more day for the full moon?"

"Because if he *is* after control of the wellspring, then he wouldn't risk the full moon. Not when a gibbous will supply him close to the same amount of power." I met Aiden's gaze. "Besides, it's the night the wolves run free, isn't it? Given the wellspring is within the O'Connor compound, the chances of discovery would be far greater."

"That's true," he said. "I might contact my dad when we get home, and ask him to set up extra patrols tonight."

"Solo patrols could be dangerous given who we're dealing with. It might be better if there's two wolves in each patrol unit—it'll give one of them a chance to get a warning off before the heretic spells or kills them."

"Wouldn't he be able to spell two people as easily as one?"

"Yes, but the greater the number you have to deal with, the longer the spell takes." It might only be a matter of seconds, but when those being attacked were werewolves, that could be all the time needed.

Unless, of course, the heretic set whatever dark spirit he was in league with onto them.

Another shiver ran through me. I fervently hoped a dark spirit *wasn't* that indefinable something the bit of me that suffered prophetic dreams was worried about.

"I'll warn my father." He glanced at me again, eyes narrowed slightly. "That's not all that you're worried about though, is it?"

I shrugged. "It may be nothing more than an overly active worry gene."

He snorted softly. "Given everything that has happened over the last month or so, I'm thinking you've a right to worry."

I smiled. "*That* is an undeniable fact. And I am probably worrying for no reason—the HIC wouldn't have sent anyone inexperienced. Not after Chester's death."

"That's probably the only certainty in this entire situation." He reached across and squeezed my thigh. "How

287

about you stop worrying about other people's problems, and just relax for a change?"

If the heretic escaped the hunt tonight and somehow got to the wellspring, it was going to be everyone's problem. But I kept that comment inside and placed my hand on top of his. "So what does this cossetting you speak of entail? Aside from shower sex?"

He grinned. "How does a home-cooked meal of steak and chips, followed by a store-bought chocolate and honeycomb cheesecake—which isn't as amazing as the ones you and Belle make, but comes close—sound?"

"Anything I don't have to cook sounds amazing."

"Good."

We continued on in comfortable silence, but the closer we got to Argyle, the more I kept looking at the clock, and the deeper the sense that something was about to go wrong became.

But we reached his house without incident. The clouds I'd noticed earlier were now skittering across the sky and the threat of rain hung heavily in the air. The wind had sharpened dramatically, and the nearby lake was choppy and uneasy. Which matched my mood.

Aiden opened the door and ushered me inside. After tossing his coat and my overnight bag onto the nearby sofa, he said, "So, what would you prefer first? Food or shower?"

"Would you be terribly upset if I said food?"

"Anticipation will only heighten the end experience," he said cheerfully.

Only if the end experience wasn't interrupted by whatever it was I feared. I followed him down to the kitchen, slung my handbag over the back of a bar chair, and then sat down.

"Drink?" He pulled out a couple of glasses. "I have wine, bubbly, whiskey, scotch—"

"I'd better stick with whiskey. Mixing drinks is never a good idea for me."

He moved across to the alcohol rack and pulled a bottle of Sullivan's Cove—a Tasmanian whiskey that had recently been voted one of Australia's top ten whiskeys by a number of wine merchants. I had a bottle tucked away for when the Glenfiddich ran out.

He poured two generous glasses and then got onto the business of cooking. There, I discovered, something very sexy about a man in the kitchen.

He served up the meal and then sat beside me. Conversation flowed easily and ranged from music we loved to books and then on to movies. The cheesecake was served with coffee and both were absolutely divine.

I sighed in contentment as I scooped up the last chunk of honeycomb. "Thank you. I feel so much better now."

"No more portents of doom happening, then?"

I wrinkled my nose. "They're being held back by the weight of cheesecake."

He laughed softly but any reply was halted as his phone rang sharply.

"If that's work, there will be words said." He stalked down to the other end of the room and retrieved his phone from his coat pocket, glancing at it before he answered it. "Tala? What in the hell has happened now?"

He listened for several minutes, his expression getting darker. My heart sank and the trepidation I'd felt earlier broke free from the cheesecake and began pounding through my system.

"We'll be there in thirty," Aiden said eventually. "Secure the scene but don't go inside until we get there."

"What's happened?" I grabbed my handbag and hurried toward him.

"It seems those instincts of yours were right." He opened the front door and then hit the truck's remote. The lights flashed brightly as the door slammed shut behind us. "There's been an almighty battle at Ashworth's place. Half the house has apparently fallen down. There's strange puffs of purple smoke swirling above the remains of the building and what appears to be lightning intermittently erupting from it."

"What about Ashworth, Eli, and the new HIC witch?"

"No sign of any of them as yet, and no one is going inside that building until we know it's both magically *and* structurally safe to do so."

"But they might be inside and in need of urgent medical attention—"

"They probably are, but *I* won't risk the lives of any of my people until it's declared safe."

"If the heretic witch is responsible for that magic, it may well be beyond my capacity to contain it."

"Then let's hope for the sake of the three men that's not the case."

He opened the door, ushered me inside, and then ran around to the driver side. Once he'd reversed out of the driveway, he hit the lights and sirens and then accelerated along the quiet street and out onto the main road. This time, he wasn't being thoughtful when it came to the neighbors.

The journey back to Castle Rock was a tense one. I really, *really* hoped Ashworth and Eli were both okay, but Aiden had been getting constant updates from his crew and there'd been no mention of either of them. Hope, it seemed, might be futile.

Aiden swung into Ashworth's street then hit the brakes

hard, forcing the truck into a sideways sliding stop. The street had been blocked off by a number of ranger SUVs as well as blue-and-white tape, and the nearby houses had obviously been evacuated, because people milled on the pavement on either side of the road.

I climbed out of the truck and followed Aiden across to the tape. Mac gave me a nod and then said, "Nothing has changed, boss, though the stabs of lightning appeared to have stopped."

"No sign of movement from inside?"

"Nothing we can see. They could be buried, though."

"Anyone get close enough to scent anything?"

"Tala tried but the lightning lashed out at her."

"That sounds like a spell more than magic gone wild," I commented.

"We'll need to find out one way or another before we risk going in there," Mac said.

Aiden glanced at me. "Will you need any equipment from the café?"

"I won't know until I see what's actually happened and what sort of magic we're dealing with."

"Then let's do that first."

He ducked under the tape and strode down the street. I hurried after him, my gaze on the purplish glow emanating from up ahead. I couldn't see the actual building as yet because there were vehicles, rangers, and paramedics all clustered around the house this side of it.

We wove our way through them and approached Tala, who was standing, arms crossed in front of the glowing building.

"What the fuck is that light?" she asked, without looking at us.

"Magic. Or the remains of it," I said.

I stopped beside Aiden and studied the building. It had once been a modern replica of a Victorian-style two-story house, but most of the roof and a good portion of the first floor had collapsed into the ground floor. The purplish glow seeping from the building was the magical equivalent to a radiation cloud, and suggested there'd been an almighty battle. Even from where I was standing, that cloud felt fierce and dirty.

I rubbed my arms and wondered two things—where the fuck had our heretic witch gotten the strength to conjure up such a spell, and how the fuck was I going to deal with it. I had to—there was really no other choice *but* me if the men inside were to have any hope.

If they were still inside, that is.

Though there was no sense of a dark spirit being involved in this calamity, that didn't mean anything. For all I knew, the purple glow was a barrier hiding all manner of things, including dark spirits.

Aiden's phone rang, the sharp sound making me jump. He tugged it out of his pocket then answered it with a quick, "What's up, Mac?"

He listened for a few seconds and then said, "Let her in."

"Problem?" I asked.

"Indeed." His voice was dry. "And I'd appreciate you informing Belle to stop threatening to turn my people into toads when they're simply doing their jobs and following orders."

"And you can kindly inform your people *not* to get in my way when my witch is in need of help," she said, as she strode toward us.

She'd obviously stopped at the café to change, because

she was now wearing jeans, a singlet top, and runners. She also had our backpack slung over one shoulder.

"Belle, what the fuck are you doing here?" My voice was a mix of annoyance and relief. "You're supposed to be in Melbourne."

"And I was. But I could hardly stay there given the vague premonitions of doom that kept rolling down the line. I grabbed a cab and hightailed it back here as soon as I could —and it cost a goddamn fortune, let me tell you." She grimaced. "Raphael, I'm afraid, may never forgive me."

I rubbed my eyes. "I'm sorry—I thought I had my thoughts locked down."

"That's always going to be a hard task given the strength of our connection and the force of your fears." She stopped beside me and studied the building. "That feels *really* nasty."

"Yes, and I'd like to know how he found the strength given he'd still be recovering from the soul transference."

"You're talking about someone who uses the blood of *others* to strengthen his spells. He wouldn't have to use his own damn strength." She paused. "Have we located the three witches yet?"

I did not want to even *think* about whose blood might have gone into that spell. "No, and we probably won't be able to until we deal with that barrier."

"I'm not sure that if even we did combine strength we'd be able to do that."

"No." I hesitated as energy stirred around me. Not the dark energy, but wild. And once again the source was the old wellspring rather than the new. "We could try a simple containment spell—if it succeeds, we might be able to push it far enough away from the building to get inside and see if the men are alive."

Belle's expression was dubious. "Aside from the fact that stuff feels volatile, the building itself doesn't look safe."

"We've people at the rear of the building," Tala said. "There's a small portion of the house unaffected, and it's the one spot the purple glow isn't emanating from."

"Can we get around there?" Aiden asked, before I could.

Tala nodded. "It's safe to go through the yards of the neighbors on either side—the purple glow isn't reaching that far."

Aiden glanced at the two of us. "Follow me."

We moved swiftly down the sideway of the old single-story weatherboard house to the right of Ashworth's place, clambered over the fence, and then walked across to where Byron was standing.

"Still no sign or sound of movement," he commented.

I studied the intact portion of the building; magic that wasn't purple or foul in feel encircled that entire area and relief surged.

"At least one of them is definitely alive and conscious," I commented, "because that section of the building is being protected by magic that *doesn't* belong to the heretic. He's also left an entry point into the magically protected area around the rear door."

"Meaning it'd be safe to go in?" Bryon asked.

"Not without us dealing with the other stuff first."

The wild magic stirred around me again. I frowned, reached out, and felt it settle on my fingers. Felt the surge of power both within it and me. For whatever damn reason, it appeared my connection to the force of this land was growing.

Belle sucked in a breath, and I glanced at her sharply. "What?"

"I can feel it—feel the wild magic. It's a distant storm surge, but more powerful."

"Is it affecting you in any way?"

"No." Her gaze moved to the building. "You know, while neither of us has the power to contain whatever that haze is, if you enhanced our spell with the wild magic, it might be a different story."

"I'm not sure that's safe or possible—"

"Ladies," Aiden cut in. "Whatever you're going to do, it needs to be done quickly, before the strength of whoever is protecting that end of the building gives out and the whole lot comes down on top of them."

My gaze went to the purple haze pulsating above the ruined section. Even though we weren't standing within attacking range, I could nevertheless feel the feel the force—the strength—behind the spell. Belle was right—even if we combined our magic, we more than likely didn't have the strength to contain or destroy whatever that spell was. And *that* left us with very little choice in the matter. But using the wild magic in any capacity was still damned dangerous.

I glanced up at her. "Did you throw your spell stones into the pack as well as mine?" When she nodded, I added, "Let's do a weave protection circle around the entire building. I'll go clockwise, you go anti. If anything goes wrong it should at least contain the magic."

Which won't help us, given we'll be inside said circle, Belle commented.

Nothing will help us if that glow is some sort of trap and our attempts to contain it either trigger it or go ass up. But we have to try.

Yes.

She tugged the silk bag containing my spell stones out of the pack then walked away. As she began placing her stones, I returned my gaze to Aiden. "Once we've contained the heretic's magic, we'll create a doorway in our protection circle so you can get through. You'll only have a finite time to get into that building and get the men out, though, so don't stuff around."

His expression was grim. "Then let's just hope no one has any serious injuries."

"Even if they have, you'll have to move them. Neither Belle nor I will have the strength to contain the heretic's spell for long."

He nodded. "How will we know when it's safe to enter?"

"The doorway will be visible. Until you see it, tell everyone to keep well away from the building and our spell stones, no matter what happens."

He frowned. "What if something goes wrong?"

"If something goes wrong, none of you are going to be able to help us. Only another witch will be able to deconstruct our protection circle and get in to help."

"Not good news given you're the only witches currently left on the reservation," he growled.

"And for that, you can thank your damn council." I rose on my toes and dropped a kiss on his lips. "We'll be okay. We have a hot date with a shower, remember?"

A smile tugged his lips but didn't erase the concern from his eyes. "Be careful in there."

I didn't say anything. There was little point given we'd be as careful as we could. But we were about to play with forces we didn't entirely understand and more than likely couldn't control.

I went in the opposite direction to Belle and carefully placed my stones in spots where they'd be easy enough to find again—although that shouldn't be a problem given the white quartz glinted softly in the dusky light of the oncoming evening. I passed Belle out the front of the building, and started placing my stones about a foot away from hers, the first one on the outside, the next on the inside, and so on. Once we'd both finished, we stepped into the circle and warily approaching the building. The purple barrier flared brighter at our approach and flickers of bright light stabbed toward us. We immediately stopped. The flickers didn't abate, but they didn't stab any closer, either.

"I'm not liking the look of that," Belle muttered.

"No."

I sat cross-legged on the ground and took a deep breath to center my energy. She sat opposite, inched forward until our knees were touching, and then dug into the pack and handed me a fistful of charms. "Just in case."

I didn't comment. I just put them on. Whether they'd help or not was anyone's guess, but I still felt safer with them.

Once she was similarly protected, she breathed deep to center her own energy. Then, as one, we psychically opened ourselves up to one another. Our energy and auras pulsed and merged at the point we were touched and once again she sucked in a breath.

"That distant thunder is a *whole* lot closer right now," she said. "And it's not just around us or on your skin. It feels like a part of you—a part of your DNA."

"That's a conundrum we can worry about later. Right now, we need it to contain whatever the spell over that building is." I took another deep breath to still the gathering nerves and then added, "Right, let's do this."

I began raising my protection circle, weaving multilayered threads across each of the stones, making them as strong as I possibly could and ensuring there were no entry exceptions in this initial spell, not even for Belle and me. We had no idea what the heretic's spell actually was, so until we'd either contained or destroyed it, we had to make sure it couldn't in any way use us. If it wanted the circle destroyed, it would have to take over both of us, and I doubted the heretic had catered for that possibility, as it was highly likely he didn't even know about us.

Belle's magic rose around me, a familiar touch of energy almost as strong as my own. Both her magic and the uninvited but ever-present wild magic wove in and out of mine, until we'd formed a circle that was more a tapestry, and the strongest thing we'd ever created.

Hopefully it would be enough.

I held my hands out. Belle gripped them tight and, as one, we began the containment incantation. I didn't look at Belle or the building—I could see them both in my mind, as vivid and as clear as the stirring wild magic. It wove in and out of the spell we were now weaving around the building—and around the darker magic—bolstering the weight of our words, strengthening the threads of our magic.

The dark magic reacted. *Violently.*

It began to churn and twist and shake. Pieces of the building were thrust into the air, deadly missiles that never made it past the tapestry of our protective circle. We continued to spell and the tremors got worse. Lightning struck at us, vicious forks of energy that came close but never hit. The purple haze began to pulsate and the wind surged, tearing at hair and clothes, until it felt like we were sitting on the edge of a cyclone. But our words rose above the noise and our spell began to draw its net around the haze.

Sweat trickled down my spine and my grip on Belle's fingers started to slip. Her fingers clenched mine tighter, her nails digging into my skin as she fought to hang on. I drew the wild magic inside, using its strength and power to bolster my own. Heard her gasp. Felt her tremor. It wasn't in pain, though, and right now, that was all that mattered.

Our magic surged—silver against purple—flowing up from the ground to fully encapsulate the heretic's spell. His magic pulsed and writhed and fought, but it couldn't escape.

But our task was not over yet and every movement of the heretic's magic took its toll on our strength.

Belle, we need to create the gateway so Aiden and the paramedics can get in.

Okay. It was little more than a whisper.

We needed this done, and quickly.

My focus went to the cluster of men standing behind our circle, and I began whispering the incantation that would open a gateway in our magic. After a few seconds, a silver line rose up from the ground and swept around in an arch, creating a safe space through which to walk.

"Go," I croaked.

Aiden, Byron, and three paramedics immediately entered the safe space. They raced toward the back door, kicked it in, and then disappeared inside. I returned my attention to the building; the heretic magic was becoming increasingly violent. I wasn't sure how much longer we could hold on to it.

"Hurry," I whispered, hoping the keen ears of the wolves would hear it.

The gentler magic protecting that one pocket of the building started to ripple, and a massive crack appeared in the brickwork, spreading like a canker sideways from the broken edge of the top floor to the one remaining solid corner of the building.

Two men reappeared, carrying a third between them. I didn't recognize him, meaning it had to be the HIC witch.

More cracks joined the first and dust was now drifting like dark snow through the door. The building was beginning to collapse from the inside out.

Byron and another paramedic appeared, this time with Eli between them. He was battered and bloody, but he was conscious and walking.

Which left Aiden still inside. As the plumes of dust got stronger and the entire building began to shake, I yelled, "Aiden, get out."

He didn't. Not immediately. But as the building began to collapse, he leapt out of a cloud of dust and debris and ran for our gate.

Alone.

Denial screamed up my throat but I clamped down hard on it. Once he was through, we shut the gate and made the protection circle complete again. But before we could do anything else, the house collapsed and the heretic's magic exploded. The force of it blew a hole through our containment net and hit us both like a ton of bricks. It tore our hands apart and sent us rolling, end on end, until we stopped by the barrier of our still intact protective circle.

For several seconds, I couldn't move. Pain swept through every inch of me, and my head was pounding like a bitch.

The buzz of Belle's energy through my brain told me she was okay—aching like me, but okay—and the wild magic was once again stirring around me rather than through.

"Liz!" Aiden, his voice edged with fear.

"I'm okay." I rolled onto my stomach. The building in front of me was little more than a mound of bricks and wood, and the purple glow had disappeared. The only thing staining the sky now was dust.

But we hadn't been able to save everyone. Ashworth was still in there. I closed my eyes briefly against the sadness and wished his soul peace and a speedy journey on to his new life.

"Fuck," Belle muttered. "I have never felt so shitty in my entire life."

Despite the sadness, amusement rose. "Yeah, you have —that time we were on the Gold Coast and you got into a drinking contest with Mr. Beefcake."

She laughed, then winced and raised her hands to her head. "It appears I have the hangover without the satisfaction of alcohol."

"And it'll get worse because we still have to take the circle down."

She groaned, but pushed upright and sat back on her heels. I didn't bother moving—I just stayed on the ground, on my stomach. As her magic rose around me, I silently followed her around the circle, unthreading my magic from hers and then letting it dissipate, until the circle was completely gone and the stones were just stones again.

"Okay," I said, "all magic has now gone. The area's safe."

A heartbeat later, feet appeared in my vision, then knees, as Aiden squatted in front of me.

"You okay?"

I looked up at him. "I'm feeling weaker than a newborn, I'm in need of chocolate and coffee, but yeah, I'm okay."

He glanced at Belle. "And you?"

"What she said." She drew in a deep breath and released it slowly. "I gather you couldn't find Ashworth inside?"

"His scent was vague and hard to track. He wasn't in the protected area, but whether he was in another part of the building I couldn't say. That purple stuff attacked me the minute I stepped out of the protected zone." He hesitated. "There were a couple of other bodies in there though. From the brief glimpse I got, it looked like their throats had been cut."

Meaning I'd been right—the heretic witch had fueled his spell with the blood of others. And it also meant that Ashworth hadn't been a third fuel source; he'd probably lost his life when the building first fell. I hoped it was quick. Hoped he hadn't suffered. "What about Eli and the HIC witch? How are they?"

"The HIC witch was out cold. Eli is now floating in and out of consciousness."

"The net that protected them both must have been his, because that sort of magic generally needs consciousness to hold steady."

"Given the utter destruction, it's a goddamn wonder anyone was alive."

"Which is odd," I said. "The heretic witch was obviously stronger than all three, so why did he leave two of them alive—one of them being the man who was sent here to kill him? It makes no sense."

"Unless," Belle said, "that purple haze was intended to finish what he'd started. It did attack anyone who got too close to the building, and Eli's strength would have given out sooner rather than later."

"I guess."

She raised an eyebrow. "In other words, you don't agree."

I waved a hand. "Something just feels off. Why

wouldn't he just kill them when he had the chance? Why leave it to fate to decide?"

"Maybe the HIC witch will be able to answer that question once he comes to," Aiden said. "Are you two ready to go home?"

A somewhat wry smile twisted my lips. "So much for it being someone else's turn to do the late shift tonight."

His phone beeped before he could reply. He pulled it out of his pocket, glanced at the screen, and then grunted. "Eli is refusing to go anywhere until he talks to you."

I frowned and pushed onto hands and knees. My head swam with dizziness but overall, I felt better than I had in the past when the wild magic had swept through me.

Maybe you're acclimatizing, Belle said.

I'm not sure it's something you can acclimatize to.

Aiden jumped upright, grabbed my elbow to steady me as I rose, and then offered Belle his hand and hauled her upright easily.

She hissed softly and a sliver of her pain ran through the connection between us. She'd pushed herself—pushed her magic—well past what either of us had thought she was capable of, and she was now paying for it.

"Looks like I'll be making you a potion tonight rather than the other way around," I said.

She groaned again. "You don't have to say that with such glee. Really, you don't."

Belle—with Byron close by her side to make sure she was okay—went one way to collect our spell stones, while I went the other. I handed her my pile at the front of the destroyed building and then, with Aiden at my side, made my way to the remaining ambulance. Its rear door was open, and Eli was sitting up on the bed inside. His head had been bandaged, as had his left leg, and he was as pale as a ghost, but he certainly didn't look as if he was about to fade into unconsciousness. In fact, he looked rather frantic.

One of the paramedics stepped forward, grabbed my hand, and helped me up into the ambulance.

I touched Eli's good leg lightly and said, "I'm so sorry—"

"No, you don't understand," he cut in. "He's not dead."

"But the building—"

"He wasn't *in* the building," he cut in again. "He was taken. He's alive, but in the hands of the heretic witch."

CHAPTER THIRTEEN

B ecause of the wellspring, I realized. Because Ashworth's magic now protected it.

But why? Belle asked. *Surely a heretic with decades of dealing with the darker forces of this world could have easily gotten past Ashworth's spells?*

I would have thought so. After all, while Ashworth was a far more powerful witch than me, he was here rather than in Canberra for a reason. The high council very rarely let those of exceptional abilities or power leave the confines of that place.

Eli reached forward and grabbed my hand. His grip was tight, as desperate as his expression. "He's still alive, Lizzie. I can feel it. We have to help him."

"Hang on, there," the paramedic said. "You've more than likely got a concussion. You need to go to the hosp—"

Eli flicked his fingers and the paramedic's words stopped. Just like that—there'd been no surge of power, no telltale sign of magic, and yet magic had just been applied. The paramedic's eyes went wide and his nostrils flared as he sucked in a deep breath.

"My partner is out there in the hands of a madman. I *will* go after them, and you *will* do nothing to stop me. Got that?"

The paramedic raised his hands and nodded frantically. Eli made another motion and the paramedic sucked in air. "Fucking witches," he muttered, and sat back on the nearby chair.

I swallowed my uneasiness and said, "Eli, if the three of you couldn't defeat the heretic witch, what hope have you and I got?"

"Probably very little," he said. "But we do have *one* advantage he doesn't know about."

I briefly closed my eyes as the uneasiness got stronger. "Using the slivers of wild magic that randomly float around this area is very different to calling the stuff that surrounds the wellspring. I'm not sure—"

"If he's heading toward the wellspring, he's not going to get far," Aiden said. "We've set up patrols—"

"Which will mean jack shit to a witch capable of hiding both scent and sight," Eli cut in. "Your people will never know he's there until it's too fucking late."

"None of which," I said, "negates the fact that the two of us will never be enough—"

"If he gains control of that wellspring, you can kiss this entire region goodbye. He will be undefeatable—even the most powerful witches in Canberra might not be enough."

"No single witch, no matter how strong, has ever been undefeatable," I said. "Especially when the high council has gotten involved."

"That's because no single witch—light or dark—has ever gotten full control over a very large wellspring," he bit back. "But thanks to the fact the fucking idiots in *this* reservation allowed a major spring to go unprotected for over a year *and* gain at least some sentience, that's the situation we now face."

"There was reason enough for their actions," Aiden growled. "Don't start playing the blame game, because if the council's fucking witch—"

"Don't," I said, touching his arm in warning. The last thing we needed was anyone knowing there was a second wellspring here. Gabe and Katie might be all protection it would ever need, but who was going to protect them from the high council if they ever found out what had been done there?

Aiden's gaze shot to mine. After a minute, he nodded and then said, "I no more want Ashworth to die or the heretic to get hold of the wellspring than you, but the fact of the matter is, unless we attack on multiple fronts, you two aren't going to be enough to defeat him."

"But the wild magic—"

"Can't be relied on, Eli," I said. "I used it tonight to save your ass, and my reserves are damn low. It's doubtful I'll have the strength to even control it."

It's doubtful any of us will have the strength to do any sort of magical damage, Belle commented. *And he has to be aware of that.*

I'm sure he is, but you can't blame him for needing to try, Belle. You'd do exactly the same for the man you loved. Or, in fact, me. And we both knew I'd do the same thing for her.

Good point.

Eli hesitated, his gaze sweeping from me to Aiden and back again. Then he blew out a breath and said, "How good are you with a rifle, Ranger?"

Aiden's smile had little in the way of humor. "Good enough."

"He'll more than likely wait until the moon has fully

risen before he makes any attempt on the wellspring, and that gives us time."

I frowned. "But why would he even go to the bother of taking Ashworth? Killing him would have been far easier, given his spells around the wellspring would fall the minute he died."

"I can't explain his actions, but I'm eternally grateful for them. Ira still has a chance and, right now, that's all I care about."

"I'm surprised he gave the three of you the opportunity to even counter his attack," Aiden commented. "From everything I've been led to believe about heretics, that's unusual."

Eli snorted. "He didn't give us *anything*. We put a number of physical and magical warnings in place after the hit man was sent after Ira. The heretic disarmed all the magical warnings easily enough, but he missed the physical. *That* saved us."

"Even if he *is* intending—for whatever reason—to force Ashworth to dismantle his magic," I said, "it won't gain him access to the wellspring. Not entirely."

Eli frowned. "Why not?"

"Because the final line of defense is mine," I said. "Mine and the wild magic's."

His eyes widened. "Ira didn't mention *that*. And maybe that's why he's taken him. Maybe our heretic sensed the wild magic's presence within the overall protection spell and thinks Ira is responsible."

"But Ashworth's magic has a different feel to mine—surely a heretic witch with decades of experience behind him would be able to tell the difference."

"Not when there's wild magic involved. It has a tendency to alter a spell's form, which is why spelling is so dangerous around the stuff." He paused. "Even if he does become aware of the second spell layer, it's very possible he'll think you've beaten him to the wellspring."

"I don't see how that actually helps us," Aiden commented.

Eli's gaze switched to him, his growing excitement evident. "It provides a distraction. If Lizzie goes in there buzzing with wild magic, he'll be concentrating on her rather than what else might be going on. If you can get within shooting range without him spotting you—"

"He's not likely to have gone into the wellspring's clearing without setting up his own perimeter defense," I said.

"But that's where I come in," Eli said. "I'll dismantle enough of his spell to get you through."

"Are you sure you can do that?" I couldn't keep the doubt and fear from my voice. "After what you did here—"

"It's far easier to create a wormhole past a shield than it is to bring them down. Remember when I said this wasn't my first encounter with a heretic?" When I nodded, he added, "Well, that time, a wormhole and a gun was what brought the bastard down rather than the magic of the HIC witch."

"And what happens if, for some damn reason, Aiden can't shoot him?"

"Then I'll be there to fry his goddamn mind," Belle said. *You're not doing this alone. No way on God's green earth.*

"Liz, it's up to you," Aiden said. "You're the one that's going to be in the biggest danger."

I glanced at him. Knew that he'd back me, no matter the decision. "We have to try."

"But before we do," Belle commented from behind Aiden. "We go back to the café. You'll both need a revival and strengthening potion if you're to have any hope of this succeeding."

"That," Eli said, "sounds like a good idea."

"You obviously haven't tasted her potions," Aiden muttered, and got clipped on the arm for his trouble.

He led both Eli and me from the ambulance, then—after handing control of the area over to Tara—we walked back to his truck and drove over to the café.

An hour, two potions each, and a few phone calls later, we were driving toward the O'Connor reservation. We didn't take the main entrance—which I'd never actually seen, and likely never would—but rather a side road that was barely wider than a goat track. The truck chugged up a steep incline and, once we reached the top, Aiden pulled off the road then turned off the engine and the headlights.

As darkness closed in, a figure emerged from the nearby trees. He was tall, with gray hair, blue eyes, and features that were an older version of Aiden's. His father, I suspected.

"Stay here." Aiden climbed out of the car and clasped the older man's hand. As the two spoke softly, my phone rang, sharp in the hush surrounding us. I dug it out of my bag, looked at the screen, and swore softly.

"What?" Eli said quickly.

"It's Ashworth's number."

"It has to be the heretic," Belle commented. "It's unlikely Ashworth has the scope to actually sneak in a phone call."

"Yes, and it probably means he's discovered your spell and has gotten the details from Ira," Eli said. "Answer it, and feign ignorance."

I hit the button and said, "Ashworth? What the hell are you doing ringing at this—"

"Ashworth is unable to come to the phone right now," a deep, somewhat gravelly voice said. "Is this the witch who is responsible for the pathetic protection strand around the old wellspring?"

"That depends on who's talking."

"I'm the man who hold Ashworth's life in his hands," he said, "so kindly answer the question."

My gaze shot to Eli's. *Make him prove it*, he mouthed.

"Yes, I am," I said. "Is Ashworth okay?"

"That is neither here nor there," the heretic said. "I want you up here within thirty minutes or he will pay the price and then I will come and get you. Trust me, you won't want that."

No, I didn't. I swallowed against a suddenly dry throat and said, "I'm not going anywhere until I have proof of life."

"My dear, I wouldn't advise—"

"Let's cut the bullshit," I said. "We both know you want the wellspring. You obviously can't get past a spell that has wild magic woven through it, so you want me up there to do that for you. So, we do this my way, or no way at all."

He was silent for altogether too many seconds. My heart was pounding so hard it was becoming painful and all I could think was that I'd overplayed my hand, that he was going to call my bluff and Ashworth would pay the ultimate price.

Then, finally, a voice croaked, "Lizzie? You can't do—"

"There," the heretic cut in. "Proof of life."

"Keep him alive, witch; he's your one ace right now."

"Perhaps," he all but drawled, "and perhaps not."

He doesn't realize we know what he is, Belle said. *That is a big tick in our favor.*

My gaze shot to hers. *You can read his thoughts?*

Her nose wrinkled. *Only vaguely. There's too much distance between us.*

"Such impertinence deserves a penalty, however," the heretic continued. "You now have twenty minutes to get here."

"Fine." I hung up. "Belle, I think you need to come with me."

Eli frowned. "I don't think that would be—"

"He'll sense our connection," I said. "He'll think the spell has been done by the two of us and it'll force him to take that into account in any spell he tries. It gives us time to make sure Ashworth is okay, and time for Belle to seize his mind and stop him."

"And once she has, I'll finish the damn job," Aiden said. He was standing beside the open door and had obviously heard a good portion of our conversation. His father had disappeared again. "This bastard is too damn dangerous, and needs to be taken out here and now."

"But not until we know Ira is okay," Eli said.

Aiden nodded and glanced at Belle. "You'll let me know?"

"An invitation to play in your mind?" Belle said. "Hell yes."

He snorted and shook his head. "We've been given the clearance to traverse the compound. No other trespassers have been sighted, not even near the wellspring, but those wolves who do go near it are rather curiously finding themselves turned away without knowing why."

"He's probably incorporated a repelling spell into his protective circle," Eli said. "It should be easy enough to counter."

"Will it affect me, though?" Aiden asked.

Eli hesitated. "The charm around your neck should be

enough to counter it, but I guess we'll find out soon enough."

Aiden moved to the back of his truck, unlocked the weapons safe, and then pulled out a rifle and an ammo clip. He slung the rifle over his shoulder, clipped the ammo to his belt, and walked back around to us. "Let's go."

We followed him across the hill for five minutes and then began to descend. This time the path really *was* a goat track—or rather, a wolf track—and there was lots of rubble to slip on. Luckily, no one's butt actually hit the ground, although there were a few close calls.

As the path flattened out again, the thrum of magic began to stain the air. Not wild magic, but dark. It crawled across my skin, stinging and biting, and it had my heart doing its speed thing again. The heretic might have been weakened by his battle with our three witches, but he was still far stronger than Belle or me.

After another five minutes, Eli said, "Stop."

All of us immediately did so. Aiden swung around, eyebrow raised in query. Eli waved a hand. "The barrier starts ten feet from where you're standing, Ranger."

Aiden took a couple of steps forward and then stopped. "Okay, I'm feeling a light impulse to turn. It's ignorable but I wouldn't want to get any closer. Eli, you might have to accompany me to higher ground so that I don't risk getting caught."

He nodded. "Let me create the wormhole first."

"Wormhole?" I asked.

"Otherwise known as a trench under the protective circle."

I raised my eyebrows. "Why not simply create a doorway through it? He knows we're coming?"

"Yes, but it'll take more power, and might well warn

him there's a third witch out here. I'd rather avoid that if we can."

"But wouldn't he have guarded against the wormhole possibility? If you're aware of it, he must be."

"That's true, but for whatever reason, he hasn't."

I grunted and motioned him to continue. He stepped closer to the unseen barrier and then, without first raising any sort of protection circle, began to spell. The ground around us trembled in response; as Eli's spell strengthened, earth began to throw itself sideways, forming a trench that was barely two foot wide and one deep.

I crossed my arms, trying to ward off the gathering chill with very little success. The open tunnel raced toward the unseen barrier, dipped slightly as it went under it, and then stopped about three feet inside.

The trembling stopped, the magic subsided, and Eli staggered back and would have fallen had not Aiden quickly grabbed him.

"I'm okay," he said. "It's just been a trying day."

"Another understatement of the century," I muttered.

He glanced at me, his smile wan but at least there. "I couldn't dig the trench any deeper, I'm afraid, so I hope you can squeeze under without touching the barrier."

"I take it he'll sense our presence the minute we do?"

"Yes." He paused. "I have some sense of the heretic— he's standing close to the wellspring. I believe Ira is either with or near him, but I can't be certain."

"What sort of distance are we talking about?" Aiden asked.

Eli hesitated again and then said, "Maybe half a mile."

"So if he's that far away, why can't you two come through this trench with us?"

"Because his magic will alert him to the presence of anyone inside the protective circle. Our only chance is to go around it and get above him. We can then create a second small hole in the barrier while you've got him distracted, and shoot him."

A good plan in theory but I really wasn't sure it would work in practice.

Aiden glanced at us. "Give us ten minutes to get in place before you go in."

"Be careful," I said.

A smile twisted his lips but didn't ease the concern in his eyes. "I'm not the one about to step into a viper's nest. Eli, let's go."

Once the two men had disappeared into the bush, I took a deep breath in an attempt to calm the inner quivering and then said, "I'll need to call the wild magic to me before we get into the protected area."

"That's a damn dangerous step given the toll it takes on your strength—especially when I'm nowhere near my peak."

"I'm not about to call on your strength—not when you'll probably need every drop to freeze that bastard's thoughts." I hesitated. "I'll have to let the wild magic roll around you, though, just to fortify the illusion it's attached to the two of us. It'll hopefully stop any sudden attacks."

"Until he figures out it's all a ruse," Belle muttered.

"By that time, Ashworth will hopefully be safe and you'll have frozen the bastard's thoughts."

Of course, hope was something that hadn't always been our friend in the past. I just had to keep my fingers crossed it was different this time.

I glanced at my watch. Eight minutes had passed. Time to get a move on. I drew in another of those useless breaths then closed my eyes, threw out my hands, and said, *Come to me.*

This time, there was absolutely no hesitation.

The wild magic came, and with such force that my knees buckled under the sheer weight of it. All I could feel, all I could see, was the energy that poured into me. It was bright, fierce, and powerful; it was the wildest storm ever created, a volcano on the verge of eruption, a force as ageless and as endless as the earth under our feet. And while it stretched the very fibers of my being to the point of breaking, this time—unlike that very first time I'd welcomed it into my soul—there was an odd sort of rightness to it. It was almost as if this force and I were in fact one being, separated only by flesh that was far too weak to hold such energy for too long.

No human ever born should be able to contain this sort of power. No human was ever meant to control it. But Belle was right—this ancient force was in me. Somehow, it was part of me—part of my very makeup.

I drew in a breath, pushed all the questions and doubts away, and then looked at Belle.

"Your eyes are full silver again," she said.

"Good—he'll think he's dealing with a proper royal witch." I motioned to the trench. "I'll go in first, just in case the heretic does have some sort of ground protection in place."

I dropped down and belly-crawled down the trench's length, sucking in my stomach and pressing deeper against the ground at the point where the tunnel dipped to get under the barrier. Its foul magic caressed my spine and sent my pulse into orbit again. There really *was* nothing weak about the spell that now guarded the wellspring's outskirts, no matter what Eli said.

I rose from the trench and turned to face the well-spring. Even though I'd only been here once—and we'd approached it from a totally different direction—I innately knew where it was. It was a pulse—a heartbeat—that echoed through me.

"Lizzie?" Belle said softly, as she rose from the ground and dusted off the grit. "You okay?"

"Yes." I held out my hand. "Let's go."

Her fingers twined through mine. The force that was in me swirled around our hands, and she gasped softly. The wild magic immediately pulled back, and instead rolled around her entire length, surrounding her in its power but not actually touching her.

She didn't say anything, but her concern slipped through me. I gripped it as tightly as I did her hand, needing both psychical *and* mental contact to counter the fierce, bright pull of the wild magic.

It would be very easy to get lost in that brightness. So very easy.

I led the way through the scrub. With the wild magic infused in my soul, the night was as bright as day. The air was sharper, and filled with so many amazing scents it was beyond my capacity to interpret them all. But it at least gave me some insight as to what werewolves saw and smelled on an everyday basis.

The wellspring's heartbeat grew stronger, a pulse that matched my own. That oneness was increasing, even though it should have been impossible.

I shivered but ignored the growing fear and tried to concentrate on the here and now. On getting close to the heretic, on seeing if Ashworth was okay, and on making sure the three of us somehow survived. While Aiden might be out there, and might well be able take the heretic out without us ever really being in danger, I wasn't about to rely on that.

The trees began to thin out. Ahead, standing within a clearing that was washed in moonlight, were two figures. One of them was Ashworth. The other was little more than an ominous shadow—a shadow whose power stained the air with darkness.

If he ever got hold of the wellspring, it really would be the end of light and happiness in this reservation.

We came out of the trees and then stopped. The wellspring was a fierce white light that was almost blinding, and my spell the sole remaining thread around it. Only it wasn't just my magic—it was the wild magic. Eli had been right—the heretic hadn't dared touch it.

His gaze swept from me to Belle and back again, and a slight frown marred his scarred features. "Well, well, two witches for the price of one."

I didn't immediately say anything, instead studying Ashworth through narrowed eyes. His face was bloody and bruised—evidence that he had not gone quietly—and the plaster on his arm had been smashed and had no doubt caused further damage to his broken arm. His pain and fear was so sharp his aura sang with it.

Then I saw what I was looking for—magic in the form of a leash around his neck. I'd seen its like before—it was a rebound spell, which meant any attack we made on the heretic would hit Ashworth twofold.

But even so, I had a feeling that *wasn't* the reason for the fear and concern I could see in him.

And you'd be right, Belle said. *The heretic's familiar is also here—it's a demon.*

Oh, fuck.

It'll attack us the minute we attack him.

Which won't matter if you can reach his thoughts and freeze him.

I can't. There's a barrier between us.

Magic?

Electronic. It has the same feel as the barrier I felt around Hart and Blume when they came to investigate the vampire kills.

Can you get past it?

Probably, but it'll take a little time. She paused. *The demon might just attack the minute I try.*

I doubt he'd set the demon onto either of us until he has control of the wellspring. I'll distract him—you start pulling that barrier down.

Her mental energy surged as I stepped in front of her. If he did attack, then at least I'd be in the immediate firing line rather than Belle. "You're wasting your time here, George. Or should that be Jonathan? The wellspring has already been claimed."

"What has been done can be undone." His voice held little in the way of concern. "Now, remove that spell of yours."

"Not until you release Ashworth from that nasty little rebound spell."

Jonathan raised an eyebrow, amusement evident in his scarred features. "And why would I do that when we both know you don't have the power to in any way hurt me?"

"If you truly believed that, I'd have been attacked by now," I replied. "At the very least, you would have set your pet demon onto me. That neither has happened suggests you're uncertain about my magic and control of this place. So, release Ashworth, let him walk free, and we'll talk."

Magic stirred around me, a distant thunder that sent a tremor racing across my skin and my heart into overdrive.

He didn't release the gathering energy, however, and after a moment, said, "Deal."

The leash around Ashworth's neck snapped free and he dropped to his knees with a pain-filled grunt.

"Are there any other leashes or spells on you, Ashworth?" I asked, my gaze not moving from the heretic's.

"No." It was little more than a hiss.

"Then get up and get out of this clearing."

"But I can't leave—"

"You can and you will. Trust me, we've got this covered."

The heretic snorted but didn't otherwise comment.

Ashworth studied me for a moment then nodded once and pushed to his feet. After a huge intake of air, he gripped his broken arm with his battered left hand and staggered away.

"Let him through the barrier," I said.

The heretic's mouth twitched. Energy surged again and, after a moment, Belle said, *He's on the other side and safe.*

At least one of us was. *Are you making any progress past that electronic barrier?*

I'm partially through. I'll need another few minutes, at least.

A sharp sound echoed across the night. The barrier encasing this wellspring's clearing rippled, and flashes of blue, purple, and black were briefly visible.

The heretic chuckled. "So you truly thought it would be that easy to take me out?"

"I have no idea what you're talking about," I said, even though I knew what that sound had been—and what it meant.

The barrier had been spelled to divert *any* kind of

attack. Unless Eli could figure out a way to create a small gap in the magic, Aiden wouldn't be able to shoot the heretic. Belle and I were—for the moment—on our own.

I flexed my fingers. Energy surged and sparks danced around my fingertips.

"Release your spell," the heretic said.

"No."

He shook his head, and then flicked his fingers—a very simple motion that unleashed hell.

The distant thunder surged and a storm of darkness hit. It pummeled me, tore at me; it was thousands of tiny claws ripping at my flesh, drawing blood, seeking access to my soul, seeking to control.

Belle screamed. I flung an arm out; wild magic surged from me and around her, protecting her. The storm continued to batter me, a force unlike anything I'd ever felt before.

Reach, something within me said. *Call.*

I closed my eyes. Reached. Not to the power of this place, because to do so this close to such a large wellspring would have indeed torn me apart. Instead, I reached for the other—for the one protected by a soul and a witch.

Both answered.

Strength poured into my limbs even as my senses sharpened—not so much my physical senses, but rather my magical.

I opened my eyes. Saw the haze of purple surrounding the heretic. Saw the slight haziness around the lower part of his torso suggesting he was protecting his head and his heart over the rest of his body.

Saw the demon standing behind him, a twisted, scaly creature with yellow eyes and razor-sharp teeth and talons.

The storm continued on unabated. Blood was now

running down my face, my arms, my torso. But the claws were getting no deeper; there was a barrier inside me now, and it was as fierce as the magic that was keeping Belle safe.

"You will not defeat me." My voice was remote, mine and yet not. "Cease your attack, heretic, or I will consign your soul to the hell you deserve."

"You do not have that power," he growled.

And unleashed his demon.

The creature flew at me. I raised a hand; the wild magic immediately responded, capturing it, containing it even as a spell rose unbidden through my mind. The demon screamed, writhed, and fought within the confines of its prison but there was no escape. With a howl of desperation, it was sent back to fires from which it had come.

A glint of movement caught my eye and reflexes cut in —reflexes that came from the wolf who was, for the moment, a part of me. I flung myself sideways, rolled to my feet, and then lashed out with a booted foot. Caught the heretic side-on and sent him staggering—away from me, away from Belle.

Raised a hand, caught the threads of wild magic that were flickering like angry snakes all around me, and flung them at him. They wrapped around him, cocooned him, and then raised him high above the ground. He screamed in frustration and the intensity of his dark storm increased. It felt like I was being shredded, felt like I was becoming nothing more than bloody muscle and bone.

Belle?

Through the electronic barrier. He's mine.

A heartbeat later, the heretic's storm stopped and then *he* stopped. Not because of anything Belle had done, but because a bullet tore through his head and ended his life.

I dropped to my knees and sucked in deep breaths even

as I thanked the forces that had saved our lives and helped end the threat. Katie's energy kissed my skin, then she, Gabe, and the wild magic itself left, leaving me weak, disorientated, and bloody.

Belle dropped to her knees in front of me, her expression filled with fear. "Lizzie? Hang on—don't you dare leave me. Not now."

A smile touched my lips even as the siren call of unconsciousness got stronger. "Won't. I have a date with a hot shower."

And with that, the darkness claimed me and I knew no more.

They kept me in hospital for a week this time, which meant I not only missed New Year's Eve celebrations, but also forced us to hire in a temp, as the café remained flat out.

The heretic's magic had ripped multiple wounds into my skin, and while the hospital staff had no idea of their true cause, they were nevertheless worried about the extent of blood loss and the possibility of infection.

At least there'd been a constant flow of visitors to keep me company—not just Belle and Aiden, but Eli and Ashworth, who'd been plastered up yet again, Jaz and her husband Levi, *and* a good portion of the gossip brigade. Mrs. Potts, I was pleased to learn, was now a regular visitor to Millie's house alongside the not-so-errant Henry, and she was currently in the process of spoiling rotten the grandchildren she'd never thought she'd have.

When I was finally given the all clear, Belle came to pick me up. Thankfully, it coincided with the one day the café was closed and at least meant I didn't have to get straight back into the hustle and bustle of things.

The plastic sheet that had been protecting the café from all the dust was finally down, and all the repair work was finished. I scooted up the stairs to drop my bag off then headed into the bathroom. Hospital showers, I'd learned, had truly shitty water pressure.

Once clean, I stood in front of the mirror and studied my reflection. In all truth, I'd been lucky. There were very few scars left despite the multitude of wounds I'd had over my body. Of the five that were evident, the most visible was the inch-long scar that ran along my hairline. It would fade with time, but right now it was a pink reminder of just how close the heretic had come to taking me out.

The other visible reminder was the fact that my eyes were no long green. They weren't even green ringed with silver. They were pure silver.

I now looked like the blueblood witch I was supposed to be.

Which was a lie, of course. Magically I was no different now than I had been before—except for the wild magic. It was in me now, a presence—a pulse—that was as steady as my heartbeat.

I was a part of this place, and it me. How and why that could happen, and what it meant for the future, I had no idea.

But one way or another, I needed to find out—though how I was going to do that without alerting my family to my presence, I had no idea.

"You want coffee and cake?" Belle shouted from downstairs.

"Is the sky blue?" I shouted back, and hurriedly got dressed.

I bounced down the stairs to find both waiting for me. I grinned, kissed Belle's cheek, and sat down to happily consume the overly large portion of chocolate mousse cake she'd cut me.

I was just contemplating a second piece—I had a week of bad hospital food to recover from, after all—when the small bell over the front door chimed and Aiden stepped in.

"Hey, lovely ladies, how are you both feeling this morning?" He strode toward us, one hand tucked behind his back.

"I'm good," Belle said cheerfully. "But I'm guessing you'd like me to disappear?"

"Not at all." He bent, kissed me soundly, and then, with something of a flourish, produced what he'd been hiding—a box wrapped in Christmas paper. "I figured I'd better present it to you here in case fate intervened again and prevented you coming back to my place."

"Or you got sidetracked by hormones and forgot again," Belle murmured.

His grin flashed. "That too."

I quickly and ruthlessly tore open the wrapping.

"So much for all the care I took," he murmured, amused.

"Word to the wise—don't bother." I picked off the tape holding the lid down and then opened the box. Inside was something wrapped in tissue paper.

I picked it up and, with a whole lot more care this time, opened it. It was a cup. A shell-ribbed teacup with a pretty blue-and-white pattern and a gold rim. Even as I carefully gripped the handle, I knew it was old. Old and valuable. But it wasn't *that* that had tears stinging my eyes—it was the vibes rolling off it. They spoke of life and happiness. Of contentment and love. Of commitment. Those who'd used

325

this cup—and the matching saucer that no doubt still lay wrapped in the box—in the past had all been involved in long and happy relationships.

"I saw it, and thought of you," he said softly.

I swallowed heavily and blinked back tears. This was a gift, not a commitment. "It's beautiful. Thank you."

I carefully wrapped it back in the tissue paper and then rose, wrapped my arms around him, and kissed him more thoroughly.

"Oh, for heaven's sake, go get a room," Belle said, voice dry.

Aiden laughed and pulled away. "That's sounds like a damn good idea. Want to come home with me, Liz?"

"You're not working?"

"Arranged to have the day off the minute Belle said they were releasing you."

"Excellent work there, Ranger."

He grinned. "There is the outstanding matter of shower sex to be dealt with, remember."

I grinned. "So there is. Give me five minutes—I need to tuck this somewhere safe and grab some clothes."

I was down in four, anticipation beating heavily through my veins and other regions.

And it has to be said—the man did good work in a shower.

ABOUT THE AUTHOR

Keri Arthur, author of the New York Times bestselling Riley Jenson Guardian series, has now written more than thirty-nine novels. She's received several nominations in the Best Contemporary Paranormal category of the Romantic Times Reviewers Choice Awards and has won RT's Career Achievement Award for urban fantasy. She lives with her daughter and very old Sheltie in Melbourne, Australia.

for more information:
www.keriarthur.com
kez@keriarthur.com

Darkness Unbound (Sept 27th 2011)

Darkness Rising (Oct 26th 2011)

Darkness Devours (July 5th 2012)

Darkness Hunts (Nov 6th 2012)

Darkness Unmasked (June 4 2013)

Darkness Splintered (Nov 2013)

Darkness Falls (Dec 2014)

Riley Jenson Guardian Series

Full Moon Rising (Dec 2006)

Kissing Sin (Jan 2007)

Tempting Evil (Feb 2007)

Dangerous Games (March 2007)

Embraced by Darkness (July 2007)

The Darkest Kiss (April 2008)

Deadly Desire (March 2009)

Bound to Shadows (Oct 2009)

Moon Sworn (May 2010)

Myth and Magic series

Destiny Kills (Oct 2008)

Mercy Burns (March 2011)

Nikki & Micheal series

Dancing with the Devil (March 2001 / Aug 2013)

Hearts in Darkness Dec (2001/ Sept 2013)

Chasing the Shadows Nov (2002/Oct 2013)

Kiss the Night Goodbye (March 2004/Nov 2013)

Damask Circle series

Circle of Fire (Aug 2010 / Feb 2014)

Circle of Death (July 2002/March 2014)

Circle of Desire (July 2003/April 2014)

Ripple Creek series

Beneath a Rising Moon (June 2003/July 2012)

Beneath a Darkening Moon (Dec 2004/Oct 2012)

Spook Squad series

Memory Zero (June 2004/26 Aug 2014)

Generation 18 (Sept 2004/30 Sept 2014)

Penumbra (Nov 2005/29 Oct 2014)

Stand Alone Novels

Who Needs Enemies (E-book only, Sept 1 2013)

Novella

Lifemate Connections (March 2007)

Anthology Short Stories

The Mammoth Book of Vampire Romance (2008)

Wolfbane and Mistletoe--2008

Hotter than Hell--2008